Barely Retired

By

Adam Lawler

Barely Retired

By Adam Lawler
Copyright 2014 Adam Lawler
Published by Adam Lawler
West Jefferson, North Carolina

Acknowledgements

I began writing the story of Carter and Connie Sykes without knowing who they were or where their story would lead. Therefore, I first want to thank Carter and Connie for taking the time to come to life in my head and sharing their adventures with me. Carter and Connie, whatever dimension you may be in, thank you.

I want to thank those early pre-completion readers of *Barely Retired* for providing their feedback on this novel. Georgie Rhein, Judy Harris, Karen Lawler, Rick Harris, Cyndi Lawler and Wayne Lawler played a big part in this story's final form. For those of you who said you would read the original manuscript but didn't, well, you missed your chance to make the acknowledgement page.

I want to thank Nancy Reeves for taking the time to edit this novel for me. Nancy, I appreciate the hours you spent providing your comments and correcting all my mistakes. Your suggestions have been most valuable. You provided the critical eyes I needed to make *Barely Retired* the story it is.

Derek Goodman and Bryan Sheets of the West Jefferson Chevrolet service department and Mike DeMoss of Forward Motion provided technical data for the automobiles in this story. Thanks, guys, for your help.

I also thank Carol Skroch for helping with the dress of my characters.

Most of all, I thank my wife, Karen, for putting up with me while I wrote Carter and Connie's story. Karen had to deal with my endless hours behind the computer screen, my mind locked in another universe. She lived with my endless talk about the characters and plot. She didn't even complain as the story became an obsession. And she encouraged me to keep going, even on those days and weeks I didn't feel like writing anymore. I'm not sure I could have finished this crazy story without Karen's support.

A special thanks to Paula Knorr, of Wilmington, NC, for the cover design.

Part One

The Camping Trip

ONE

Carter Sykes walked into the interrogation room and looked at the twenty-year-old man leaned back in the folding chair across the table. With his shoulder length black hair, scraggly goatee, black Judas Priest T-shirt, and blue jeans with holes in the knees and butt, Carter would simply describe him as a punk. He knew the young man would put up a tough front, but also knew that front would fade. Carter had seen his type before, he knew it wouldn't take long to get the information he wanted. Especially not this afternoon.

"So, Dave, breaking into that drug store didn't quite turn out as you expected, huh? Took me a couple of days, but I tracked you down. And now, you'll be spending some time in the big house, son. The only question is, how long do you want to stay there?" Carter started the conversation, still standing.

"Go to hell, old man." David Michael Sturgill looked up at Carter, showing his two missing teeth.

"Nah, I think I'll stay here and talk to you awhile." Carter pulled out the empty chair, sat down, and opened the case folder he brought in with him. "I do want some information from you."

"Fuck you, man." Sturgill stared back at Carter, proud of the way he was standing up to the older cop.

"I wouldn't say that too loud if I were you. Where you're going, they'll take you up on that offer real quick. But it'll be ok. They tell me, after a few times, you learn to enjoy it. Things start to stretch out, if you know what I mean?" Carter paused and smiled at his prisoner. This one had broken out the F-bomb early. Interrogation 101 taught him the quicker they vocalized their toughness, the quicker they would drop the facade when it didn't provide the results they intended. It was usually the ones who said nothing, who sat there stoically, who were the toughest to crack. They were the hardest to read. "Now, I want some information from you, and I plan on getting it."

9

"I ain't telling you shit." The prisoner leaned forward, his elbows on the table, staring Carter in the eye, seemingly not phased by the thought of prison sex.

"I ain't going to sit here all day, wasting my time with you, son. Let me tell you, you ain't the toughest son of a bitch I've had in that chair. I've put a lot of men behind bars over the years. Murderers, rapists, men who'd make you look like Princess Kate. Maybe that'll be your name today, Kate. The boys at Central will love that. 'Kate,' they'll moan, as they pull your hair, making you scream." Carter laughed. "Tell me what I want to know and I'll put a good word in for you with the DA. Or don't say anything and I'll leave you to his mercy. The DA, he don't want to know anything. He just wants to send your ass up the creek; makes his record look good. So, what's it going to be, Kate?"

Sturgill sat in his chair silently. He wasn't being stoic, he was trying to sort thorough his options.

"Who did you sell those drugs to?" Carter asked him.

The man said nothing, still pondering his next move.

"I told you, I ain't wasting all day with you, son. My patience is very thin today. I'll ask you one more time, who did you sell those drugs you stole to?"

The man squirmed in his seat, but remained quiet.

"Well, Kate, if you ain't going to talk, I'm going on home. Let me put a note in your little file here. Uncooperative." Carter wrote in the file. "That sums your ass up, uncooperative. The DA really doesn't like to see that, you know. Makes him push for longer sentences and rougher prisons. But, hey, if that's the way you like it, who the hell am I to complain, right, Kate? At least your sorry ass won't be bothering me anymore. I'll just have the guy taking your place in here next month. Maybe he'll talk and I can get him a deal." Carter closed the file, stood up, pushed his chair back under the table, and took two steps toward the door.

"Hey, wait a minute, man. I can give you names."

"Well, let's get at it, son. And they better be worth my time. I've got a retirement to get to."

****

A half hour later, Carter Sykes leaned back in the chair at his desk and looked around the police station. It was thirty years ago when a skinny, young man from Haysi, Virginia, fresh from four years at Clinch Valley College, a small branch of the University of Virginia serving the coalfields, had walked through the front door of the Kingsport Police Department to apply for a job. His interview with the police chief went well enough that he received a job offer. Young Carter Sykes was quick to snatch that opportunity.

Much had changed since that day. Carter was no longer skinny, nor young. None of the people who were in the office that day remained. The color of the walls had changed a couple of times. The carpet and furniture were different, now only a decade behind the times. New office space had been shoehorned in to accommodate a growing police force. Computer monitors now sat on every desk, replace the typewriters that once occupied those spaces. New technologies invaded every aspect of the department. But even with all these additions, what at the time had been a state of the art police station, at least by Upper East Tennessee standards, was now seriously outdated. But the station would have to do for now. Post recession budget cuts assured that.

During reflective moments, Carter's mind always drifted to the cases he had worked during his years on the force. Unlike the big city homicide detectives that are written about in crime novels, as a small city investigator in a working class city, Carter had worked on cases from burglary to drugs, to, yes, homicides. It always seemed to be the murder cases that came to his mind. After all, murder had the gravest implications of any type of crime, for both the one killed and the killer. His first murder case, the Eastman Kodak worker gunned down by a coworker who was having a not so secret affair with his wife, always seemed to creep into his thoughts. Then there was the case of the city councilman who was skimming from the county's books until his secretary discovered his scheme. The councilman poisoned her while she was making up her mind whether to blackmail him for a cut or to spill the beans. Other cases Carter remembered included people killing their relatives to speed up the inheritance process. Carter came across this scenario more often than one would think.

11

Unfortunately, there were always the few unsolved cases. The case of the coal miner found dead beside the road always bothered him. The death was eventually declared a hit and run, but all evidence led Carter to believe it was a choreographed murder. Other unsolved cases involved a factory worker shot down while mowing his back yard and the kidnapped girl who was never located. It was these cases that haunted Carter Sykes' sleep. What had he done wrong? What evidence had he missed or, worse yet, misinterpreted? What had he simply failed to do or consider? It bothered him because he knew the answers were out there, somewhere; for some reason he was unable to find them. Furthermore, Carter didn't like to lose, and failing to solve a case put one in the win column of the bad guys.

Today, Carter was retiring. He knew deep down he would miss the excitement of closing in on a criminal. But he also knew he had earned the right to relax. The long, uncompensated hours, the sleepless nights as a case replayed in his head, the time away from his wife, Connie, had taken a toll on him. It was time to try to recapture the lost moments of his personal life, while, in his early fifties, he was still young enough to do so.

Sometimes, Carter would wonder why he stayed with a small city force. After all, he had received offers from big city departments and seriously contemplated a couple of them. He also had offers from the Tennessee Bureaus of Investigation, and saw men with lesser tract records ultimately get the positions he turned down. In the end, Carter knew it was his love of the small city atmosphere Kingsport provided that kept him there. He literally knew everyone in town. The fact that he was trusted by those with nothing to hide gave him a distinct advantage in solving cases. Many of those in the criminal element respected him as a fair cop. He spent more time waving at people through the windshield of his police sedan than he did doing paperwork behind his desk. In addition, he was just a couple of hours from his mother, who still lived in the family home in Haysi. Yes, Carter loved Kingsport, Tennessee, and was never willing to give it up for more money or prestige. And many in Kingsport slept better because he never did.

Today, he put his professional career to rest. His wife, Connie, had put up with the twelve hour days, seven day weeks, vacations being cancelled at the last minute, and calls in the middle of the night for way too long. How many family functions had he missed? How many times had he been disturbed from cuddling after making love with her because some scumbag decided to rob a liquor store? Now, after thirty years, it was time for him to devote time to Connie. She had been there for him, and she deserved it.

He knew this afternoon would be difficult. The kidding between police officers, telling him how much better Kingsport's law enforcement would be with him gone, had begun a couple of weeks ago. As the afternoon slipped away, the humor became slaps on the back, hugs, and yes, even a few tears as he loaded the remainder of his personal belongings from his office into his midnight blue and silver two tone Ram 2500 Mega Cab 4x4. While it didn't make leaving any easier, he knew it was the right time for him to retire.. He was ready for new challenges and new adventures. Still young, he didn't see his retirement as the end of the book, but as the opening of a new chapter in his and Connie's lives. It was a chapter he was anxious to begin writing.

"What'cha gona do with all your free time, man?" Tony Ward, his fellow detective and partner for the past ten years, asked him. "I bet the fish off the Carolina coast are having a meeting about your retirement right now. I bet one of them is standing up in front of the Fish Congress saying, 'that son of a bitch Sykes will be here trying to catch our asses soon. Watch out for anything that remotely looks like hillbilly bait.'"

Carter laughed. "They sure as hell better be. I'd say they just raised their security alert to at least bright orange."

"Where are you going first?" asked Fred Bush, a late 20's uniformed officer who had been on the squad a couple of years.

Carter, sensing the time was right, removed his black tie and unbuttoned the top button on his light blue shirt. "If I told you, I'd have to kill you. But let me assure you, you guys will never, ever, not in a million years, find us."

"Oh, you're taking Cons to one of those sex clubs I've read about down in Miami, huh?" Bush asked with a shit-eating grin on his face.

"I'll never acknowledge nor deny anything. But Fred, you know if YOU found us there it would quickly become a comedy club." Carter chuckled and the whole group around them got a good laugh at Fred's expense.

As 5:00 pm rolled around, the joking, goodbyes, and tears subsided and the group began to head home. Carter said his goodbyes to those remaining in the station and walked out the door of the KPD for the final time as a police officer. He walked across the parking lot to his Ram, opened the driver's door, stepped on the running board, and pulled himself into the cab. After one last, quick, visual survey of the building and parking lot, Carter took a deep breath, turned the key and fired up the Ram's 5.7 liter HEMI engine. Of course, Carter's Ram didn't quite sound like most Rams. He had mildly altered the performance of the truck with a performance programmer, a K&N cold air intake and filter, and CAT-back Magna flow exhaust. Even after owning the truck for a year, he loved to hear that engine come to life. He put the truck in reverse, backed it out of the parking place that still had the sign "Reserved for Detective Sykes" behind the parking block, and headed home.

Now it was time to think about the adventure he and Connie had planned for next week.

****

The fifteen minute drive home brought Carter to his modest, single story, brick house in a suburban neighborhood. He and Connie had lived there for the last twenty years. While the house wasn't big or fancy, to Carter it was a mansion. Compared to the houses he called home as a child in Virginia's rural coal mining country, it most definitely was. As he sat in the Ram, he recalled the first home he could remember, a 12x44 house trailer on a hillside in northern Dickenson County. When he was twelve years old his father was murdered; Carter, his mother, brother and sister moved in with his grandmother and uncle. It was a real house, much bigger that the trailer, but Carter did miss the indoor bathroom and hot water of the trailer. It was the summer before his junior year in high school that he and his uncle added the bathroom and hot water heater to the house. Carter remembered the feeling of sitting on that toilet and taking a shit inside that house for the first time, he felt like he was in the lap of luxury.

He looked at the mowed and trimmed lawn Connie had kept up so well since her own retirement a few months earlier. He noted the landscaping she had done, the trees and flowers she had planted. He even laughed at the statues and yard gnomes she insisted on; yeah, she was right, they did look pretty good. As he looked again at his and Connie's home, he nodded as he thought, 'Yes sir, Carter, this is definitely a mansion'.

As he looked at the front of the house, on the right side of its one acre lot stood his 80 foot tall freestanding ham radio tower. Three rather large antennas stood proudly at the top. He laughed as he recalled the "My god, what are you trying to do, talk to Mars," comments the tower and antennas often received from guests. Carter earned his ham radio license while at Clinch Valley College. In the late 70's, long before cell phones and Skype were available. An exchange student at Clinch Valley was talking daily to his family in Brazil via radio, with only a wire strung in the trees behind the dorm for an antenna. Carter was frustrated because he couldn't even talk to his cousin across the county on his CB. It wasn't long before he had learned Morse code well enough to pass the entry level novice ham exam. He caught the radio bug, and it never left him. The exchange student returned to Brazil, and Carter continued to keep a weekly sked with him all these years. He and Connie had even visited his friend and family in Brazil one vacation, and his friend had visited them a couple of times as well.

On the left side of the house was Carter and Connie's prize possession, their thirty-four foot Coachmen fifth wheel with three slideouts. Carter and Connie bought the Coachmen on a whim after his twenty-fifth anniversary with the KPD. The Sykes' used it four or five times each year, usually around the long weekends: Memorial Day, July 4th and Labor Day. Each year they took a trip to Morehead City, NC, where Carter could get in some fishing and Connie could work on the tan she always wanted, but her nursing profession never allowed her the time to obtain. She always got aggravated because Carter returned from these trips with a better tan from fishing than she did from the beach. A smile crossed Carter's face as he realized now was the time he and Connie had dreamed about for the last few years; time to enjoy themselves

15

traveling with their camper. In fact, their first adventure began Monday morning with the Coachmen in tow behind the Ram.

Moving his gaze, Carter's attention turned to the living room window, where he saw Connie looking out, staring at him, no doubt wondering why he was still sitting in his truck. Carter was sure she didn't realize he was locking the moment into his memory, taking in the scene of his last evening returning home from work. He waved at her and she waved back, then, realizing everything was ok, turned and walked away from the window. Carter tried to return to the moment, but it was gone. Carter Sykes was now a retired cop. It was time to move on. He opened the Ram's door and hopped out of the truck.

Carter walked into the house through the side door he and Connie used; they tracked less dirt into the house that way. As he walked into the living room, he saw Connie sitting on the couch with a book in her hands and Thor in her lap. Thor was an eighty pound black lab mix they adopted from the pound when he was just a ten pound puppy, five years ago. Carter always felt a tinge of jealousy at the way Thor clung to Connie; after all, he was supposed to be his dog. Connie was the one who wanted a little Yorkie as her lap dog, but the first time she held Thor in her arms she fell in love with him. She just couldn't believe he would become the big dog he had definitely grown to be. Carter often kidded her, telling her she wanted a lap dog and boy did she get more than she bargained for. He had to admit he loved to see Thor lying across her lap, like he was both loving her and protecting her at the same time.

"How's it feel to be retired, sweetie?" she asked him as her head rose from the book.

"A little surreal, I guess. I don't guess it will really hit me until I don't have to go anywhere Monday morning."

"But you do have to go somewhere Monday morning, or are you trying to chicken out?"

"Oh yes, I know I've got somewhere to go, as do you my dear. I ain't chickening out, are you?"

"Hey, I'm ready. I've been retired a couple of months now. I've got the camper packed; well I guess you call it packed, and it's ready to roll. You got the Ram ready for the road?" Carter had referred to the truck simply as 'the Ram' right after they got her, and it had stuck with both of them.

That's on tomorrow's agenda. Got to run her down to the Dodge Place and get the oil changed, tires rotated, and get her checked out. Then I'll give her a bath. She'll be ready sometime tomorrow afternoon".

"That's good, sweetie, I don't want you to have any reason to back out on me now."

"Why, Cons, you don't even sound the least bit nervous about this trip."

"I'm nervous as hell, sweetie. We've never done anything like this before. But hey, we're retarded, I mean retired now, right?" she chuckled a little. "If we get down there and decide it's just not for us, we can always head on over to Morehead, it's only about three hours away."

"Yeah, and I can catch those fish by surprise," Carter mumbled, remembering the earlier conversation at the police station.

"What? Did I miss something?"

"Oh, just a comment from work today. I'm going to grab a drink, I'll be back."

Carter walked into the kitchen and grabbed the two liter bottle of Diet Dr. Pepper from the fridge. After a quick thought, he put it back and grabbed the bottle of Strawberry-Kiwi soda beside it. He filled his glass with ice, reached into the cabinet underneath the marble countertop and grabbed a nearly full bottle of Southern Comfort. Carter didn't drink a lot, but every now and then it was good to have something to take the edge off and relax him. Thinking about the upcoming trip, he needed a drink. He mixed the Southern Comfort and the Strawberry-Kiwi soda and walked back into the living room with Connie.

Connie had gone back into her book and Carter just leaned back in his recliner, his feet propped up, and watched her and Thor. Sometimes, Carter was amazed at how young she still looked. She was, after all, now in her mid-fifties, a year older than he was. Her medium length auburn hair showed a touch of gray, or maybe it was white, but you had to really look close to notice it. Her face really didn't have any wrinkles and while she had gained a few pounds over the years, and some parts sagged a little bit, she still was a pretty hot chick. She could easily pass for forty. Carter often compared her looks to his own; his thinning and slightly receding hairline, the roundness that had developed in his midsection, which he jokingly attributed to too many donuts, and his lack of muscle tone from too many years behind a desk and the wheel of a Crown Vic. Quite honestly, while he was nervous about how he would handle their upcoming adventure, most of his nervousness dealt with whether he would be able to handle Connie being there. But this trip had been her idea, so he was going through with it, come hell or high water.

****

The weekend seemed to go by in a blur for Carter Sykes. He got the Ram serviced without a glitch. The sales guys at the Dodge dealership always admired his truck when he brought it in. One of them tried to tell him how he needed to move up to a new Cummins diesel, since he was going to be pulling his camper on a long trip. This was annoying to Carter, he had been very careful to buy a camper that wouldn't need a diesel to pull it. He didn't like the rattle of a diesel engine, the smell of the exhaust, or of the fuel for that matter. When the Cummins began requiring the use of diesel emissions fluid to deal with ultra low sulfur fuel and emissions requirements, Carter was even happier with his choice of the HEMI. The guys in service liked his accessorized truck and one of them even made a comment about his small, three inch by two inch police shield he had airbrushed on the tailgate. The silver police shield just seemed to accent the midnight blue and silver truck perfectly. Of course somebody always made a comment about his Tarheel antenna; mounted in the bed of the truck, right up against the driver's side of the cab, for his mobile ham radio. Painted the same blue as his truck, it didn't stand out as bad as it would have if it had been left the standard black. Except, that is, for the capacitance hat on the top of the antenna.

That evening, he and Connie drove her red Dodge Avenger to get dinner. It was a warm early evening in mid June in East Tennessee, and it was evenings like this when Carter regretted getting rid of the Chrysler PT Cruiser GT convertible they owned before the Avenger. If that new RN at the hospital hadn't kept

18

asking Connie to sell it to her, they would still have it. After a couple of months of her asking Connie for a price, Carter told Connie to price it so high she wouldn't buy it. Connie did, and the woman took her up on it. The Avenger was a nice car, and they still had their classic convertible when they really wanted to go out on the town, Carter just didn't want to spend his Sunday washing it before putting it back in the garage and leaving on their trip. So they drove the Avenger to dinner.

Sunday was a day for Carter and Connie to finalize things for the trip. They spent time double checking the Coachmen, making sure everything was packed, checking tire pressure, doing the little things that need done before hitting the road. For Carter, this was done mostly on breaks from watching the NASCAR Sprint Cup race at Dover. Connie had taken care of most of the preparations over the previous month or so, there really wasn't a lot left to do. After the race ended Carter proceeded with hitching up the fifth wheel and raising all the camper's stabilizer jacks. Come morning, all he and Connie would need to do was pack the cooler for the cab, unplug the camper from the electricity, and get Thor in the back seat of the truck; which wasn't a very hard job at all, since Thor loved to go on trips.

Tomorrow morning, Carter and Connie Sykes would set off on their new adventure as a retired couple. It had been almost a year in the making. Ever since her friend, Laurie, had told her about her adventure at this place, Connie had been intrigued. Tomorrow, they would drive to a campground in the middle of a cotton field in eastern South Carolina for the experience of their lives. In planning the trip Connie often wondered how a small town girl from Big Stone Gap, Virginia ended up doing something crazy like this.

TWO

Monday morning, both Carter and Connie were up early with the anticipation of their trip. Neither of them slept much the previous night, which was normal for them the night before leaving on a long anticipated trip in the Coachmen. Thoughts of the upcoming trip usually filled their dreams. But last night, the anticipation was even stronger than normal. It was, after all, the first trip of their new, retired lives, and to a place that, until a few months ago, neither of them ever imagined visiting.

By 9:00 am, they had locked the house, unplugged the camper from the house, and put Thor and a small, 6-pack cooler full of soft drinks and ice, in the back seat of the Ram. Carter hopped in the driver's seat, took a long, deep breath, looked over at Connie, and said "Here goes nothing, babe," as he pulled the shift lever into gear. Within minutes they were in Tri-Cities traffic, which had thinned considerably since the early morning rush hour. About a half hour later, they reached Interstate 26. MapQuest estimated their drive time at just over six hours. They knew they would drive slower with the Coachmen in tow, and figured stops for lunch and to walk Thor would slow them down as well. As such, Carter calculated it would take a little over seven hours for the trip to the coastal plain of South Carolina.

As usual when traveling with the Coachmen, they planned to eat a quick, simple lunch in the camper, hoping somehow their frugality might make up for the nearly four dollar per gallon gas that would only get them nine miles further down the road. Frugality was part of the reason Carter set the cruise at sixty miles per hour while driving on the interstate; reasoning that this speed allowed the best compromise between fuel economy and making good time on the Interstate, with posted speed limits of seventy miles per hour. Carter didn't like getting passed, but it was a fact of life when towing a fifth wheel.

Carter had tuned the radio to the Tri-Cities local classic rock station, and as it faded, found a local rock station in Asheville that called itself "The Mountain". Both Carter and Connie enjoyed listening to music that was on the cutting edge of rock when they were younger; music from groups such as AC/DC, Bad Company,

21

Heart, Molly Hatchet, and Guns-N-Roses. They both found it funny how their parents worried this music was going to lead them down degenerate paths; and yet they ended up with careers as a police officer and a nurse. They would probably eventually switch to Hair Nation on SirriusXM, but Carter liked listening to local broadcast stations better than satellite radio. The challenge of picking them up and the local flair brought back memories of their younger days, days filled with the excitement of uncertainty and adventure.

After their lunch stop at a rest area between Spartanburg and Columbia, the anticipation of reaching their destination began to grow. The tension in the cab could be cut with a knife. Their conversation grew quiet, and Carter and Connie would sneak quick glances at each other, as if trying to read each other's thoughts. If one caught the other in a glace, a quick "You ok?" with a quick reply of "Yeah, I'm fine" would be exchanged. By mid afternoon they came to the signs that indicated the intersection of Interstates 20 and 95 was two miles ahead.

"We can always go north on 95 if you want to," Carter said, looking over at Connie. "It's only a couple hours to Morehead. I could surprise those fish this evening."

"I'm fine, Carter," Connie replied. "Of course if you're having second, or one hundredth, thoughts…"

"Hey, this was you're idea, Cons. There ain't no way in hell I'm going to back out of it now. I just want to make sure you're ok, this is like our point of no return, you know."

"Yeah, I know, sweetie. But ever since Laurie told me about her and Bill doing this, I've wanted to at least give it a try. If we get down there and don't like it, we can always move on. But after months of planning this thing, I'm ready to see what it's all about."

"Ok then, babe, here we go," said Carter, as he turned the Ram and Coachmen onto the ramp leading to Interstate 95 south. "I guess those fish have just been granted a stay of execution."

****

A little over an hour later, the Ram and Coachmen had made their way through some South Carolina back roads that looked like they came from the lyrics of a country song. It was only 3:30; they had made good time. The lunch stop was a quick one and Thor hadn't needed any extra stops. Once they left the rest stop, Carter had reset the cruise to sixty-five, rationalizing that the flat roads would not hurt fuel mileage that much, although he knew it was his anticipation that led him to increase their speed. Driving down the final dirt road, Carter saw the gate guarding the campground's entrance and carefully made the wide right turn to the club's drive, just like so many people making their first visit to a nudist club had done before them. Within seconds, he had the Ram stopped beside the box containing a phone in front of the gate. He moved the shift lever into Park and looked over at his wife.

"Last chance, Cons," Carter said, the nervous apprehension apparent in his voice.

"We're here now, sweetie. Too late to back out now."

"All right, then," he said, in his best Karl Childers imitation.

Carter hit the power window button on the Ram and the opening window let in the hot, sticky, South Carolina heat. Instinctively he looked at the thermometer in the Ram's dash and saw it read 96 degrees. This was hot for mid June, even by eastern South Carolina standards, and even hotter for a couple from Upper East Tennessee. Carter couldn't help but think "global warming" as he reached out the window for the phone in the little box. He pushed the button and heard a female voice say, "Welcome to Utopia".

"H...ello, this is C...arter Sykes," Carter stuttered, something he hadn't done since his college days. "My wife and I have reservations for this week."

After a five second pause, which Carter assumed was to check the reservation book, the lady replied, "Yes, Mr. Sykes, I see you here on our guest list. When the gate opens, just follow the road on in. In about a quarter mile, you'll see the office on the right. Just stop there and come on in. I'll be waiting for you."

"So, sweetie, you've got a naked woman waiting for you," Connie teased.

"She'd have to be something to beat what I've got right here, babe," Carter patted Connie on the thigh and tried to give both of them some assurance as the gate opened. Carter once again put the Ram in gear and slowly moved forward.

As they rolled down the sandy road toward the office, Carter asked, "I wonder if we are supposed to go into the office naked? Or clothed?"

"I don't know," said Connie, a bit defensively." It's not like I've ever done this before."

"There's the office, babe," Carter announced, pointing at the building on the right.

"I guess this is it, then."

"Guess so. I'm going in with my clothes on to start with."

Carter pulled the Ram and Coachmen long-ways, behind a golf cart that was pulled into a parking space, making sure to leave room so it could back out. About that time, Carter noticed a man who appeared to be in his mid fifties, with salt and pepper hair down to his neck, walking across a dirt parking area toward them. All he was wearing was his flip-flops, a Tampa Bay Rays baseball cap, and a smile. Carter looked over at Connie and said, "Looks like you've got a naked man walking over to see you," as he rolled down her window.

"Hello," the man yelled as he quickened his pace to a fast walk toward them.

"Howdy," Carter yelled back. "I assume this is the office?"

"Sure is. Is this your first time here?" the man queried.

"Yes, sir, first time at any place like this," Connie said, for some reason trying to make sure he was fully aware they didn't regularly visit places like this.

"Well, welcome to Utopia. My name's Jim." The man stuck his hand in the window and Connie shook it. "It's always good to have newbies join us. Come on in the office and we'll get you signed in. Then we'll get you set up and give you a tour of the grounds, ok?"

"Sounds good, Jim. I'm Carter, and this is my wife Connie. We'll be in just a second."

"Sounds good to me. Grace will take care of you inside," said Jim, as he turned and walked into the office.

"You ready, Cons?"

"Yep, I'm ready," she chuckled.

"What's so funny?"

"I bet Jim's nickname around here is 'Big Jim'."

"I sure as hell hope so," Carter chucked back. "Cause if he's known as 'Little Joe' I'm in serious trouble."

****

A couple of minutes later, Carter and Connie were standing inside the office, fully clothed, having left a content Thor in the back seat of the Ram. From a small office behind the counter came a small lady in her early 40s, with short, dirty blonde hair. The lady didn't have on a stitch of clothing above her sandals, and her lack of a tan line made it obvious she stayed like this a lot.

"Hello, welcome to Utopia. I'm Grace," she introduced herself. "Y'all must be Carter and Connie."

"That would be us," Connie chimed in first this time. "We're the newbies," she added, trying to use some of the lingo she had picked up from Jim, in an effort to fit in better.

"Well, great," Grace said. "We love getting new people in here. It helps us relive the excitement of our first nudist experience. Sometimes being nude just becomes old hat around here".

"I can't imagine that," Carter said.

"It'll happen sooner than you think," replied Grace. "Let's see, first thing I need to do is get y'all's driver's licenses and run a background check on y'all. Y'all ain't got nothin' to hide now, do ya'," she joked.

"Only that up until three days ago I was a cop," Carter joked back, eliciting a smile from Grace.

"Well, we ain't got anything to hide here, officer, pun intended," she said, as she lifted her arms straight out from her shoulders. The three of them laughed.

Connie took note that here she and her husband were, joking with a totally naked woman, and it didn't bother her. She thought that was odd, especially since they had just arrived at the nudist camp. As they planned the trip, she hadnt been worried about how

25

she'd do seeing naked people herself, she'd seen plenty of naked people in her thirty years as a nurse. She just wasn't sure how she would feel about seeing Carter around naked women. She knew he'd been in strip clubs as part of his work with the Kingsport Police Department, but that was different. That was work. She wasn't there watching his reactions. Now here he was, engaged in a normal, comical conversation with a totally naked, nice looking woman, and it really didn't bother her. Hell, Grace sure wasn't bothered being naked with them. She realized it wouldn't be long before the next step in this process took place; she'd have to take her own clothes off. 'So far, so good', she thought to herself.

Grace went back into the office, sat down in front of a computer screen, and entered the information off their driver's licenses while Carter filled out the forms she had given them. "I'm going to check on Thor," Connie said.

"He'll be fine, honey. Come here and help me finish this paperwork." Connie peered over Carter's shoulder as he went through the paperwork. He really didn't need her help, he just wanted her in the room with him. He read each section aloud, more to fill the room with noise than anything else. Connie answered as he wrote, although Carter was usually a word or two ahead of her on the form.

"You weren't joking when you said you were a cop, were you?" Grace asked when she came back out of the small office.

"Not at all, ma'am. And Connie really is a nurse."

"Yeah, I saw that" With you two around, we're all bound to stay safe and healthy around here."

"I certainly hope so, since we're the newbies around here," Connie said, again trying to emphasize the only nudist lingo she had picked up to this point.

Grace looked down and noticed they had finished completing their paperwork. "I'll tell you guys what, if y'all want to go ahead and get your camper set up, I've got you in spot E. Just drive around to the right, so past the swimming pool, tennis courts, and basketball court. You'll see the camping area on your left. You'll have to back into spot E, but there should be plenty of room. We only have one other camper in the campground, with it being Monday. Now if this was Friday, the place would be packed.

Here's a list of the rules and regs for y'all to take a look at. I'll send Jim around to your spot in a little bit to check on y'all and give you an orientation tour of the park."

"Sounds great, Grace," said Carter. "Uh, when do we need to get.....uhm..."

"Nekkid?" Grace finished his question. "Anytime you want. Like I said, the place is pretty empty, with it being Monday, so it's probably a good time to get accustomed to it. We give you a couple of hours to get adjusted, but to be honest, the quicker you get nekkid, the quicker y'all will start to enjoy it. Kind of like getting into the swimming pool, jumping right in is usually the best way to go."

"Thanks, Grace," Connie said. She looked at Carter, "Let's give this a try, sweetie."

"After you, my dear," Carter said.

****

They jumped into the Ram, Connie petted Thor, and they pulled around to the camping area as instructed. Connie spotted site E, and Carter pulled past it, let Connie out to guide him, and as he'd done many times over the past five years, proceeded to back into the spot. In typical South Carolina coastal plain fashion, the site contained no trees to provide shade. 'Well, I'm sure at one time this used to be a cotton field,' Carter thought to himself. After a couple of times of moving the Coachmen forward, then backward again, Carter finally got the fifth wheel where Connie wanted it. Both of them happy with their work, Carter hopped out of the Ram. He walked around to the back of the truck and began lowering the jacks on the Coachmen, in order to unhitch it from the Ram. As he did this, Connie walked behind the camper and began hooking up the electric, the water, and the sewer shorelines.

"Man, it sure is hot out here," Carter yelled back toward Connie. I think the high today back home is supposed to be about 80 degrees."

"Well, you can always get out of that shirt, you know," Connie said, almost daring him to do so.

"I'll take mine off if you take yours off", Carter challenged back.

Carter was a bit surprised not to hear Connie say anything back to him; she almost always had some comment to come back with. When he completed his task, he looked behind the camper and to his surprise, he saw Connie behind the camper, her white, medium sized breasts bared for all creation to see, her shirt and bra in her left hand.

"Your turn, big boy," she challenged back, a big smile beaming across her face. All she was wearing was her denim shorts and her sandals.

Carter just stood there, kind of dumbfounded, staring at his topless wife. Here was his wife of over thirty years, standing in an open field, with bare breasts. For the past year, he envisioned the two of them in this moment, but until now it just all seemed a fantasy. Now here, the moment seemed surreal. Carter gave his head a short, quick shake to snap out of his funk.

"No big deal," he said, half to Connie, half to himself, as he slid his polo style Mopar Performance shirt over his head, leaving him in his blue shorts and tennis shoes.

Connie seemed to be in control of the situation now. She walked up to him and gave him a kiss. "I bet the family jewels are still quite toasty," she chided.

Suddenly, Carter's fog cleared and he realized where they were and what was going on. He was not going to falter again; he would meet her challenge. "That they are, babe," he said, as he reached for the button of his shorts and pulled them, and his white Fruit of the Looms, over his hips and let them fall to his ankles. He stepped out of them, bent over, picked them up, and stood in front of his wife, wearing nothing but his Air somebodies. Carter danced a little dance as he spun himself in a 360. "Woooo!" he let out a Ric Flair sounding yell.

Somewhere in the back of his mind, a memory arose of a time in high school when Haysi High won the first track meet in the school's history. On the ride home from the meet, the boys had determined, one way or another, they were going to have a winning streak, even if they never won another track meet. So, the entire boys track team, with only a couple of members too scared to participate, took off through the center of Haysi, Virginia, naked as jaybirds, to celebrate their victory. Every one of them screamed a loud "Woooo!" as they took off through the town. The girls track team watched the boys in amusement, and the event went down in the lore of Haysi High School. Carter remembered how proud he was to have been a part of something so daring and risqué.

Connie was never one to be outdone. Without even a word from Carter, she quickly pushed her shorts and bikini panties over her hips and let them fall to the ground. She stepped out of them with her left foot, and with her right she kicked the clothing into the air and caught it. She stood there naked, staring straight at her naked husband, neither of them noticing that another couple was observing the entire scene from across the way. Now both of them let out a "Woooo!" together, as if to symbolize freeing themselves from societal norms. They walked to each other, hugged, not a sexual hug, but a "we did it" hug, and set about the task of finishing the setup of the Coachmen. Carter dropped the stabilizer jacks, while Connie got Thor out of the Ram, took him inside, turned on the air conditioning, and put the slides out. She came back out and got the tools from the storage bins to set the awning in place. When Carter finished with the jacks, he came around and helped her get the awning out. In less than thirty minutes, the camper was set up, the awning out, and their folding chairs were in place under it. Connie went inside and brought both of them a cold Bud Light from the Coachmen's fridge. They stood there, facing the Coachmen, beer in hand, taking in their home for the next week.

"Hi, guys." They both spun around as they heard the female voice coming from the golf cart stopped in the road in front of the Ram. Startled, they saw a naked couple getting out of the cart and coming their way. The man looked to be in his early sixties, balding on top, with mostly gray hair down on his shoulders. While not necessarily fat, he was a bit on the heavy side. The woman looked to be about fifty, slender with breasts that looked way too firm to be real.

"Couldn't help but notice you guys pull in," the male voice said. "We enjoyed the show; watching y'all set up. I'm Gil and this is Mary Ann."

"By all the 'Wooos!' and all the tan lines I see, I'd bet this is y'all's first time at a nudist place," said Mary Ann.

"You would be correct, we're newbies," Carter said, trying to show his command of the nudist jargon. "I'm Carter, and this is my wife, Connie."

"Well, welcome to Utopia, Carter and Connie," said Mary Ann. "Looks like y'all are getting off to a pretty good start," Mary Ann said, as her head exaggerated its look up and down their naked bodies.

"Well, when in Rome...," Connie said with a laugh.

"A day or two of sun and y'all will fit in just fine," Mary Ann replied. "Make sure to use plenty of suntan lotion on those new parts," she warned.

"Fur shure", said Connie, suddenly reverting back to her southwestern Virginia draw.

"What did you say your names were again?" asked Carter.

"Gil and Mary Ann," Gil chuckled. "Yeah, yeah, yeah, go ahead and laugh. We do all the time. It's probably the reason we ended up together. We actually met here. I won't say it was love at first sight, but it was love at first introduction. Gil and Mary Ann just had to be together."

"Oh, I've got to hear this one," Connie blurted out. "I've got a couple more chairs in the storage bin. Come on over and have a seat and tell us about it." Connie turned to get two more folding chairs from the camper while Gil went back and pulled the golf cart beside the Ram and grabbed their towels.

"Can I get y'all a beer?" Connie asked.

"Sure," said Mary Ann as Gil joined her and they walked under the awning. Connie came back out with a beer in each hand and Thor by her side, with a leash attached to his collar, but no one holding it.

"Well, you see, Gil had been coming here for years with his wife Sue, who had passed away from cancer a couple of years earlier. I had just been through a divorce and was here with one of my girlfriends on a dare. We were in the hot tub when we were introduced and of course the whole place goes ape shit, you know, 'Gilligan and Mary Ann' kind of stuff. All weekend, everywhere I went, all I heard was, 'Mary Ann, where's Gilligan'. My friend was the worst. Anyway, Gil and I got to talking to each other by the pool and discovered we had a lot in common. I decided to come back on my own a couple of weeks later. Gil told me I had to, that Mary Ann couldn't leave Gilligan stranded again. Before long, we were meeting here every weekend. From there, we became a couple, I guess; don't really know how that happened."

"So you guys ain't married?" Connie asked.

"Why, honey, no way," replied Mary Ann. "It's been five years now, and yeah, I love Gil. I'd do anything for him. But why mess up a good thing with a piece of paper and a couple of rings. We're happy, we're in love, and best of all, we're nekkid. What else could a girl ask for?"

"Mary Ann was really a lifesaver for me," Gil continued, telling his side of the story. "I was pretty down after Sue's death. I had been for a while, and I didn't even realize it. I hadn't even had a date since Sue died. Mary Ann rekindled love in my life. Quite honestly, I'm not sure I would still be here if she hadn't come along." He smiled and looked over at her. "Now tell us Carter, how did you ever entice this lovely lady to come here?"

"Wait, first I've got to ask, whatever happened to your friend, Mary Ann? The one who came here with you the first time?" Connie asked.

"She never came back. I tried to get her to a couple of times, but she never would. We're still friends, but she's not been back since that weekend. She ended up married to a guy who I think would kill her if he ever found out she'd been here. It happens with nudism, it's not for everyone."

"Well, I actually drug Carter here," Connie bragged. "My friend, Laurie, who's a phlebotomist at the hospital where I worked, came back from vacation telling me about a trip her and her husband had taken here. I couldn't believe Laurie had gone to a nudist colony. I kept asking her lots of questions and finally she gave me the website for Utopia and told me that Carter and I should check it out. It took some convincing, but I finally got my man down here." She nudged Carter's arm.

"Looks like he's doing ok to me," Mary Ann said, again giving Carter the once over.

31

"So far, so good, ma'am," Carter said with a smile.

"Laurie, was her husband named Bill?" asked Gil. Cute brunette, husband had a well trimmed beard?"

"That's them," said Connie.

"Gil never forgets a cute girl," Mary Ann said, looking at him with a smile.

"I didn't forget you, did I, honey?" Gil reminded her. "Hey, we'll let y'all finish getting settled in. We're having some hamburgers tonight, so y'all come over and be our guests. We're over here in the camper with the screened in porch and the nekkid sun goddess out front. Should have the burgers ready by six."

"Sounds great, Gil," Carter said. "We'd love to hear some more of y'all's nekkid stories".

Gil and Mary Ann said their goodbyes and drove the golf cart back to their camper. Carter looked at his naked wife. "I guess our first naked dinner date?" he asked.

"I guess so, sweetie," Connie said, as she got out of her chair, walked over to him, and gave him a big kiss on the lips. I guess we're fitting in ok. The fish near Morehead are all breathing a sigh of relief."

"Oh, they know I'm on my way. The governor has just granted them a stay, that's all."

****

Soon, Jim showed up in a four person golf cart at lot E. "You guys ready for a tour of Utopia?" he asked.

"Let's go," said Carter, as he and Connie started walking toward the cart.

"Don't forget your towels," instructed Jim.

"Got to get used to that," said Carter.

After getting their towels and a couple of beers, Jim, Carter, and Connie rode around the park, taking in all the things the park offered. Jim showed them where the pool and hot tub were located. He showed them the clubhouse, which held a bathhouse, an exercise room, a fifty inch flat screen TV, a dance floor with a DJ stage, a pool table, air hockey table, ping pong table, and a foosball table. It also contained a full kitchen. He showed them the tennis and basketball courts, the putt-putt course, the horseshoe pits, the sand volleyball court, and the one hole, par 3 "golf course", really just a flag set up at the end of a field. Carter noticed that there were a lot of campers that appeared to be set up permanently, and Jim explained that many members of Utopia rent their sites yearly and some come every weekend. He said the five mobile homes along the road were on land leased by the club and those people lived here full time; he and his wife, Nancy, the club's General Manager Doug and his wife Maggie, the gay couple Brian and Derrick, and two other couples, Rick and Judy, and Chris and Jane.

He went on to explain the rules of the park, most of them Carter and Connie had read on Utopia's website. First and foremost, nudity was required, weather and sunburns permitting of course. He stressed that Utopia was not a clothing optional park, where one could choose to either wear clothes or not. At Utopia, everyone was expected to be naked and needed a good reason not to be. He stressed that the park was a family friendly park. A good rule to follow was that if you wouldn't want your children to see you do it, then don't do it. He said Utopia was a nudist park, not a swingers club, that sexual advances would not be tolerated, and that sexual activity must be confined to one's own living quarters. He reminded again that all nudists must have their own towel to sit on, for sanitary reasons of course. Carter surmised that anyone who didn't understand this rule was simply nasty.

Jim also explained that Utopia was a co-op club. The members of the club were also the owners of the club. To become a member, you had to buy stock in the club, and the stock gave you the right to vote in club elections and to run for the club's Board of Directors. He said there used to be a lot of co-ops in the nudist industry, but a few big corporations had bought most of them out and ran them on a for profit basis. Carter hadn't realized that nudism was such a big business, and Jim informed him there were billions of dollars spent each year on nude recreation; everything from small resorts like Utopia, big ritzy retorts like Caliente in Florida, to nude cruises in the Caribbean. Jim was on Utopia's Board of Directors and one of his "jobs" was welcoming new guests and giving tours of the park. He liked doing it, as it gave him a chance to meet so many nice people.

After the tour, Carter and Connie were back at the Coachmen, each with a fresh Bud Light in their hand, sitting under the awning to avoid the direct sun in the still upper eighty degree heat. Thor was lying on the ground between them. Carter looked over at his beautiful wife, who sat across from him, totally naked except for her sandals, necklace, diamond ring and wedding band, and asked a silly question.

"You alright, babe?"

"Of course, sweetie. You think I'd be here right now if I wasn't?"

"Guess not," said Carter. "I just wanted to make sure."

"You know, it's funny, I'd forgot that I didn't have any clothes on. Seeing Grace, Jim, Gil, and Mary Ann so free without any clothes just kind of put me at ease. Hell, if I had clothes on, they'd be soaked with sweat and I'd be miserable. As it is, I'm sitting here under the awning with the man I love, the man I know will always protect me, not wearing a stitch of clothing. And I'm totally at ease with it. All I can think is, 'what took us so long to get here'."

Carter smiled a sheepish smile. "You're amazing, Cons".

"I know. As long as I'm with you," Connie said. "Hey, don't' we have a dinner date about right now?"

"Oh, shit, Gil and Mary Ann. I guess we'd better get over there. What should we wear?" They both laughed.

They put Thor on the leash, Connie grabbed them both a fresh beer, they grabbed their towels and the three of them walked over to Gil and Mary Ann's camper.

THREE

Thor was a big hit with Gil and Mary Ann at dinner; he usually was anywhere he went. Carter and Connie were always eager to show him off. They went through his standard routine of tricks; sit, down, play dead, stay, come, and so forth. Carter jogged back to the Coachmen, got Thor's toy, and had him fetch it, bring it back and place it in his hands. Then he told Thor to stay, threw the toy, and made him wait before sending him after it. After the exhibition, Gil snuck Thor a hamburger patty when no one was looking, he just couldn't stand to see the dog wanting one so bad and not getting anything. Gil figured, after all, he had earned it.

After dinner, the five of them walked around the park to help the burgers settle. Gil and Mary Ann showed them several things that Jim hadn't mentioned on the tour. They walked to the back of club, where Gil pointed out one of the trails leading through an area of woods and down to the creek, mentioning that it was called the "Minnow Trail", a reference to the Gilligan's Island ship, in honor of him and Mary Ann. They also had a chance to check out some of the more decorated and developed campers semi-permanently set up in the park; some with nude statues, some with frog or lizard themes, others with comical signs, and some beautifully landscaped. One was even decorated in honor of Porky Pig, painted pink with pig statues and a Porky mural on the floor of the deck. Carter couldn't help but compare Utopia to a well run small town. It seemed almost like Andy Taylor's Mayberry, only without clothes. When he thought of Floyd or Aunt Bea parading around Mayberry naked, he just chuckled.

As darkness fell on eastern South Carolina, a tired Carter, Connie, and Thor made their way back to the Coachmen. It had been a long day; they had driven seven hours, set up camp, had their first nudist experience, and met an interesting couple. Carter put Thor in his bed as Connie shut the blinds, not quite sure why, since they had been running around naked all afternoon anyway, but she felt they needed the privacy. Carter walked up behind her, leaned into her, reached his arms around her body, and cupped her breasts with his hands. Gently, he started to massage them, using his thumb and forefinger to rub her nipples. It must have been the latent sexual energy built up from seeing each other naked all afternoon, as each of them felt a passion they hadn't felt in a long time. Connie slowly stood straight up and turned around in Carter's arms to face him. Carter now felt the touch of her breasts against him, and she felt the hair of his chest against her. Their eyes met, and almost instantly so did their lips, in a deep passionate kiss. Carter moaned as their tongues danced together, and he squeezed her naked body tight against his own. She responded by reaching down and grabbing his checks into her hands and gently caressing each of them. As the kiss subsided, Connie took Carter by the hand and led him up the three steps leading to the bedroom of the Coachmen. Once there, another passionate kiss erupted, this time with them falling on the bed together. Carter broke the kiss, nibbled his way down her neck, finally reaching the soft skin of her breast. He took her nipple into his mouth, swirling his tongue around it. Connie moaned as her hand moved across his leg and found the manhood that she was searching for. Time seemed to stand still as they stroked, kissed, and caressed each other's bodies, finally building to lovemaking like they hadn't experienced in a long time. After what seemed like hours, they laid together in the still made bed, holding each other as their bodies tried to recover some strength. Carter slowly rubbed her breasts and stomach while his head lay on her shoulder, occasionally moving his head down slightly, gently sucking a nipple into his mouth.

"Wow," was the only word that escaped Connie's lips.

"Wow," Carter returned the thought, as he moved his head back to rest on her shoulder.

For another half-hour, they laid on the bed, holding each other in the afterglow of their sexual encounter, both of them trying to absorb all the passion they could from the moment. Finally Carter rolled over and they both got up, pulled down the covers, and fell into a deep sleep, feeling a sexual satisfaction neither of them had felt in a long time.

****

The next morning, Carter awoke about 8:00 am. He made the obligatory morning visit to the bathroom, then walked to the fridge and grabbed a can containing the day's first taste of Diet Dr. Pepper. As Connie began to stir from the bed, Carter sat down in his recliner and turned on his laptop and the Icom 7000 ham radio that sat on the small table between his and Connie's recliners. He turned on the radio, tuned it to a preset frequency, hit a button that raised the Tarheel antenna on the roof and hit the button on another box that tuned the antenna to the proper frequency. In less than a minute, Carter was listening to the Tennessee Navy-Marine Corps MARS statewide net. After a few minutes Carter held his microphone to his mouth and, pushed the key on the microphone, and said, "En en en zero Foxtrot India Lima, this is en en en zero Charlie Bravo Papa, portable, South Carolina, no traffic, over". After a few moments, the "traffic rep" was asked to send the traffic to the net. Carter made a few keystrokes on his computer as the noise from the digital signal on the radio, sounding like something from a late fifties science fiction movie, filled the room. A message for all Tennessee Navy-Marine Corps MARS members came across Carter's computer screen. Stations began acknowledging they had received the message by saying "This is, (their call sign), "Roger, over". When it was his turn, Carter responded with a "Roger" as well.

As Carter focused on his radio net, still not thinking about being naked, Connie slowly crawled out of bed and made her way from the bathroom to the kitchen, where she started her morning coffee in the two cup, Mr. Coffee, coffee maker. As the coffee brewed, she walked over to Carter and put her arms around his neck, rubbing her hands through the hair of his chest. "Hello, sweetie".

"Hello, babe," Carter said, as he looked over his shoulder, and then did a double take as he saw she was, as he himself was, totally naked. "Well, I see this wasn't just a dream after all," he said, as he took in her beauty.

"I don't know, I've dreamed about a night like last night for a long time now," Connie smiled.

Carter and Connie began their normal morning ritual when camping. They each ate a bowl of Special K, usually one of the fruit flavored kinds such as Redberry or Blueberry. Carter drank his morning soda and Connie had a couple of cups of coffee. They took a shower, separately due to the size of the shower in the Coachmen. Connie showered first, while Carter took Thor for his morning walk. While Carter showered, Connie packed a twelve-pack, soft sided cooler with Bud Light and a few wine coolers transferred into plastic bottles to make them safe at the pool. Carter carried the cooler and Connie grabbed a bag with snacks and sunscreen. They each picked up a couple of towels, and made their first trek to Utopia's swimming pool.

Upon arriving at the pool, Carter and Connie walked through the gate of the chain link fence surrounding the pool area. The pool was a half Olympic size, surrounded by lounge chairs. The two far sides had wooden decks with each holding three rows of lounge chairs. At first glance Carter determines that the area could hold approximately one hundred people, maybe a few more.

Being Tuesday, there were only twelve people at the pool when Carter and Connie arrived. Being a detective, by nature Carter quickly surveyed his surroundings. He noted two couples on the near end of the pool deck talking to each other; one couple in their sixties and the other about ten years younger. He noticed a group of five men in the far end of the pool at, standing in a circle talking to each other. Carter decided by their mannerisms that these guys must be gay. A lady sat alone in her lounge on the wooden deck across the pool, absorbed in a Nikki Heat novel. Carter noticed a couple with two children, a boy about eight years old and a pre-teen girl, playing in the near end of the pool. Connie moved to take a lounge near the two couples who were talking to each other. The couples' conversation immediately ceased, and they acknowledged Carter and Connie.

"Good morning," the older lady said.

"Good morning," Connie returned her greeting. "I'm Connie and this is my husband, Carter".

"I'm Jill," the lady replied. "This is my husband, Randy," she said, as she pointed to the older of the two men. "And this is Gene and Beth. We're all trying to get our sun in today before it gets too hot."

"Yeah, I know what you mean," Carter said as he sat the cooler down between the chairs he and Connie had chosen. He laid his towels across his chair, his body already moist with sweat from the walk to the pool. "The forecast is calling for nearly one hundred today."

"Yeah, that can toast you fast," Gene said. "I don't think I've seen y'all, you guys ever been here before?"

"Nope, first time. Can't you tell?" Connie laughed as she pointed to her white boobs.

"Those won't be that way for long, honey," Jill said. "The only white spot you'll have is where they sag."

"You know, I've threatened to duct tape mine up to get some sun under there," Beth chimed in, and the six of them laughed.

"Hey, duct tape can hold a race car together at two hundred miles per hour. I bet it could even handle those things," Gene laughed, and raises his arms in defense as Beth took a swat at him with her hand.

"Watch it, sucka'," she said in her best Aunt Ester impersonation, again eliciting laughter from the group.

"How long have you guys been coming here?" asked Connie. She had so many questions she wanted to ask, and decided this was as good a place as any to start.

"Gene and Beth were here at the founding of this place," Randy spoke up. "Back then, the swimming pool was a glorified mudhole. Jill and I have been coming here about eight years now.

"Y'all have a place here?" Connie's questions continued, as Carter handed her a wine cooler. The sound of a cold beer being opened soon followed.

"Naa, we just live over in Herbsville," Randy said. "We come over during the week to get some sun while the place is pretty quiet. Weekends are so busy, we usually don't bother coming anymore, except for the monthly board meeting or a really special event".

"Board meetings?" Carter asked

"Yeah, this is a co-op," Jill explained. "Most of us are part owners of the club. We elect a Board of Directors to run the club and they hire a Club Manager to oversee the day to day operation."

"Doug is the manager," Beth interjected. "He and Maggie live right up there along the road".

"Oh, ok," Carter nodded. "How does Grace fit into all this?"

"Grace works Monday and Tuesday, and one weekend per month," explained Jill. "Even working in Utopia, you need a couple days off. And Jim takes care of the grounds. He gets his lot rent free in return for keeping the grass mowed and things looking good."

"Sounds like a pretty neat system," said Connie.

"Oh, you ain't been here for a contentious Board meeting, yet," said Randy. "Things can get quite heated. Tempers can flare. A few years back Gene and I even had to break up a fistfight."

"Over what?" asked Connie.

"Which company to use to build the tennis court," he answered.

"Yeah, but it went deeper than that," said Beth. Those two and a few others were all involved in that swinging group."

"A what?" Connie's ears perked up.

"A swingers group," replied Beth. "You know, wife swapping, stuff like that. It's something all nudist clubs have to deal with from time to time. And we've been no exception."

"Yeah, we almost lost the club a few years ago when a swinger's club from Charleston decided it would be easier to take over our club than to start from scratch and develop their own. A couple of them even got elected to the Board here, and then all hell broke loose," said Randy.

"What happened?" asked Carter, as the topic grabbed his attention too.

"Well, over a period of about four years, they started, one or two at a time, becoming members here and either putting in campers or buying ones already here. Some of us figured out that they were swingers, but hey, what they do in their own camper is up to them, right? Well, before we knew it, they had almost fifty members here. Two of them got elected to the Board and they became quite brazen in their actions; having sex in the pool and hot tub, gang-bangs with men lined up outside the door of a camper, you know, stuff like that. Finally we all had to join together and take back our Utopia. We lost several of our good members during this time, and most of the swingers finally left, although there are still a few with campers here. But for the most part they stay to themselves now, and keep their activities inside their campers."

"Wow, I'd have never thought," replied Carter.

"Co-ops are hard to manage," said Jill. "I know, Randy was president of Utopia for three years. People squabble over little things and feelings get hurt. Most people don't want to get involved in running the club; they come here to have fun, not to be involved in club politics. That's why most co-ops never make it, or if they do, they struggle and end up selling to a big nudist corporation like Paradise Lakes. It's much easier to run the club as a dictatorship or an oligarchy than a democracy. That's why, after the swinger fiasco, we decided to hire a General Manager to run the club. Now, the Board only provides general direction for the club, the manager handles all the day to day operations and we can have fun. Doug has done a great job for us and Utopia is a fun place again."

"I don't know about y'all, but I'm about ready for a dip in the pool," said Connie, as she sat her wine cooler down and moved to get out of her lounge chair.

"Sounds like it's about time for a volleyball game," said Jill. "What do y'all think?"

"Too hot for volleyball for me," said Carter, who was getting up and following Connie to the steps of the pool.

"No, water volleyball," said Jill. "We've got enough people around the pool to play a game."

"Hey, if I heard 'water volleyball' count me in," came Mary Ann's voice from the gate.

In a matter of minutes, everyone except the lady reading the Nikki Heat novel was in the pool. A volleyball net was rolled out across the pool and floating ropes indicating the end lines were rolled across as well. Someone had fetched the volleyball from its storage area, and sides were chosen. Most couples had split up on different sides, as had the gay men and the two children. For the next forty-five minutes a rousing game of water volleyball filled the pool area.

****

After the water volleyball game and another round of sunbathing, Carter suggested he and Connie take on the eighteen hole championship putt-putt course. Carter's exact words were, "Hey Cons, I need to whup somebody at something today, you want to be my victim in putt-putt?"

"Since you asked so nice and humbly, my dear."

Carter and Connie walked to the office and checked out a couple of putters and golf balls, and picked up a Utopia scorecard. As they approached the first hole Carter told Connie, "Ladies first."

Connie's first shot put her within 2 feet of the hole and she quickly moved in and sank the putt for an easy par two. "Go ahead and start whuppin', sweetie," she said with a tone of satisfaction in her voice.

Carter placed his ball on the rubber square that imitated a tee box. He lined up carefully to hit his putt. As he looked up at the hole, he noticed Connie was standing behind the hole, right in his line of sight. "Hey, no fair! How am I supposed to concentrate on this shot with you standing there?"

"I'm just standing here, sweetie. I'm not bothering you, am ?"

"The hell you ain't! How am I supposed to concentrate on this shot with you standing there, naked, right behind the hole?"

"This ain't distracting you, is it?" she asked with faked innocence as she wiggles her body a little.

"It's just not fair," mumbled Carter, as he hit his shot to within three feet of the hole. "Well, missy, a makeable par putt anyway." Carter strutted confidently up to his ball, lined up his shot, and got ready to take the par putt.

"Oops, I dropped my pencil," Connie said as her pencil fell behind her and she turned around and bent over to pick it up. Carter had already started his backswing but caught sight of Connie out of the corner of his eye. His shot missed two inches to the left and just past the cup.

"Oh, so that's how we're going to play it, huh?"

"Carter, sweetie, I'm just here so you can whup me, remember?"

Carter tapped in his bogey putt. "I should have known better than to take you lightly, Connie Sykes."

By the time they reached the turn after the ninth hole, Connie had a two stroke lead. After the seventeenth hole, Carter had cut that advantage to one. Connie, feeling the pressure, made a three on the eighteenth.

"Awh, too bad, babe. To lead the whole game and lose it right here at the end."

Connie was a bit frustrated with herself, and it was evident in the tone of her voice. "Go ahead big boy. Let's see you sink this one."

Carter was also feeling the pressure now. He loved his wife, but he didn't like losing to her. The only disadvantage to being married to a competitive woman was that she really played to win, and often did. He lined up his putt, but he too succumbed to the pressure and hit the putt too hard. It hit the boards behind the hole and bounced back, leaving a four foot putt for a tie.

"You've got that left for the championship of the world, sweetie," Connie now teased a little, all the pressure on Carter.

"I can make this putt. After all the distractions I've had, I'll be happy to go to a playoff with you."

Carter moved beside his ball and took careful aim at the hole. The naked putt-putt bragging rights of the Sykes family were on the line. He focused intently on the hole, making sure not to look up. Then he saw Connie's shoes on each side of the hole and looked to see her squatting over the hole, staring straight at him with a smile. Carter stopped and stepped back.

"What's the matter, sweetie?"

"No, no, no," Carter said, shaking his head. "That's not fair. I've had to focus around your distractions all day, but this ain't fair."

"Is there a rule against it?" Connie asked.

"There has to be."

"I don't think so. I don't see it on the scorecard. No squatting over the hole, nope, not there," she said as she feigned looking over the card.

"But you're in my way."

43

"If you hit me you've missed the putt and I win anyway."

"Alright then, watch this. I'll sink this baby in spite of your distraction."

Carter did his best to focus on the shot as if nothing was unusual about it. Perhaps it was Connie's distraction, perhaps the pressure of the putt, perhaps a little bit of both. He grimaced as he hit the putt, he knew he had pulled his club back a bit. The putt stopped three inches short of the hole.

"I, am the champion, my friend," Connie sang to the tune of the Queen song as she sprang up from her squatting position.

"And you'll keep on cheating, 'til the end," Carter sang back.

"I am the champion, I am the champion."

"No time for cheaters," Carter yelled out.

"'Cause I am the champion….of the world."

After returning the putters and golf balls, they walked back to the camper for some lunch, and a break from the sun. Connie continued to brag about her victory, so Carter took Thor for a walk around the park for a break from her gloating. Connie made them some tuna sandwiches and mixed them each a drink. The three of them sat out under the awning, enjoying the beautiful afternoon, the sandwiches, and a second mixed drink. Connie knew she had rubbed her victory in enough, and as hard as it was, she didn't brag about it anymore. Both of them had had enough sun for the day, their formerly white parts now looked like the taillights of the Ram at night in a traffic jam. Connie grabbed a book to read while Carter sat at his ham radio and talked to several of his buddies in eastern Tennessee on forty meters.

While walking Thor, Carter had met up with Gil and invited him and Mary Ann over to the Coachmen to reciprocate the supper they had enjoyed together the previous night. Connie made lasagna, not the homemade kind she was famous for, but a frozen, store-bought dish heated in the oven for seventy minutes. She buttered and heated some garlic bread to go with it and broke out a big bottle of Wild Vines blackberry wine. 'No one will mistake this for a gourmet Italian meal,' she thought, 'but it is a pretty damn good camping meal, if I say so herself. Especially when the attire is so casual.'

It was about 6:30 when Gil and Mary Ann's golf cart pulled up to the Coachmen. Carter invited them under the awning; offering them a seat and a glass of wine. As they settled in, Carter walked behind the Coachmen and got a small card table from one of the storage bins. Once the table was set up, Connie brought everyone a tray with a paper plate, a paper towel, a plastic fork, and a plastic spoon. She and Carter went back in the camper and she handed him a paper plate with sliced garlic bread and he held the door as she came out with her oven mitts on, carrying the pan of lasagna. After each complimented Connie on the meal, they dipped some lasagna on their plates, grabbed a piece of bread, and dove in.

"Well, how was your first full day of nudity?" Gil asked.

"All I know is I am the Sykes champion of naked putt-putt. I beat his ass today. Who gave who the whuppin', sweetie?" Connie quickly responded, looking at Carter for his reaction.

"Distracted, huh?" Gil laughed. "I don't think I've ever seen a man beat his woman at their first game of putt-putt down here."

"Tell me about it," replied Carter. "Cons made sure she used all her attributes to the best of her ability." They all laughed.

"All's fair in love, war, and putt-putt," laughed Connie.

"Just remember, Connie, take every advantage you can," giggled Mary Ann. "Use what the good Lord gave you, girl."

"Trust me, she does," said Carter. "Hey, to change the subject here, we learned about the swinging issues the club had in the past. Heard they almost took this place over a few years ago."

"Well, between the swingers and the club's financial problems at the time, none of us were sure the club would hang on. I'm glad all that is behind us now. Sure, there's a few swingers around, all nudist clubs seem to attract them. But they keep their sexual activities confined to their own campers or homes. And they know better than to approach a guest."

"Financial issue?" Carter asked. "We didn't hear about those."

"Yeah, it got pretty rough there for awhile. The club bought the land on the other side of the woods and planned on building a nudist community back over here." Gil looked back and pointed behind him toward the woods. "We ended up having to sell off that land in order to keep the rest of the club going. Between the swingers trying to take the club over and the financial issues, the

45

club was torn apart. Randy hadn't done a very good job of dealing with either problem; I always wondered how he ever ran his trucking company after how poorly he ran this place. Then someone came up with the idea to hire a General Manager from outside the club to run it like a business and make the hard decisions that the club's members squabbled over for a year. That's when we brought in Doug. Now the financial issues are behind us. Heck, Doug's even got this place back to being a nudist club again. If you're here and it's above seventy-five degrees, you better be naked or have a wicked sunburn."

"So there were a lot of people running around wearing clothes?" asked Carter.

"Yeah, an offshoot of the swinging thing. You know, some sexy clothing is a lot sexier than a totally naked body, especially when it's gotten like this," Gil patted his belly. "Skimpy, sexy clothes leave a little to the imagination, and the imagination stirs the swinging."

"I can see that." Connie chimed in.

"Hey, you weren't the one distracted during the putt-putt game," Carter said.

"I didn't say I wasn't distracted, sweetie, just not to the same degree you were. You just don't know how to use your assets properly," Connie replied.

"That's nice to know," said Carter, with a smile.

As they finished supper and put away the dishes, twilight settled upon Utopia. Gil and Mary Ann went back to their camper and Carter, Connie and Thor went for a walk around the park. As the three of them walked, Carter and Connie hand in hand, with Thor leading the way on his retractable leash, Carter looked at his naked wife and asked, "I wonder if this is what the Garden of Eden was like?"

"I don't know, but if tonight is like last night, it'll give the Garden a run for its money."

Carter stopped, took his wife's face in his hands, kissed her softly on the lips, and didn't say a word. After walking to the camper, they made love once again, and while not quite up to the unbridled passion of the night before, it was certainly on the short list.

46

FOUR

Wednesday started much as Tuesday had for Carter and Connie Sykes; Carter on the radio, the two of them eating breakfast, taking a shower, Carter walking Thor. Connie packed a cooler and they walked to the pool about ten o'clock. Randy, Jill, Gene, and Beth were there, but the rest of the cast around the pool was different this morning. Carter quickly noticed that the tone around the pool was much different as well. It seemed Doug Westlake, Utopia's General Manager, did not show up at the office this morning. When Randy, Jill, Gene and Beth all arrived about 9:00, Randy went to Doug and Maggie's house, thinking he had just overslept. Maggie said he wasn't in the house and assumed he had walked down to the office as he did every other Wednesday. She retrieved the spare key, walked to the office with Randy, and opened it, thinking Doug may have locked himself inside to get some work caught up and lost track of time. Nothing appeared to have been touched. The papers Grace left on Doug's desk the previous day were still there for his attention. There was no sign of Doug anywhere.

"I'm sure there's some logical explanation," Randy said. Perhaps he had to go to town to take care of some business, a doctor's appointment, or something. I'm sure he'll be here soon."

"But his car's still here, Randy," Gene replied. "This just ain't like him. He would have at least told Maggie he was going to be gone for a little while. Then she would have run the office until he got back."

"Hi guys, what's going on this morning?" Carter asked. Gene explained the missing Doug and all the oddities involved.

"Sounds pretty strange to me," said Carter. "Has anyone talked to Grace? Has Maggie called his friends or family to see if they have seen or heard from him? Perhaps he just needed to walk down the road for a few minutes to clear his head and got sidetracked. I had a case once where we thought a guy just wandered off and he ended up leaving on a spiritual quest. He came back a week later when a cold spell hit and his Walmart

47

sleeping bag didn't keep him warm. I suppose the cold air gave him all the spiritual awakening he needed."

"No, not yet." said Randy. "Those are good suggestions though. Who are you, Columbo or somebody?"

Carter realized that yesterday they never had the usual conversation about what each of them did for a living. He thought that was odd, since that's usually the first thing people talk about. These folks could be doctors, lawyers, or Indian chiefs for all he knew. "Well, almost," he said. "Up until Friday evening, I was a detective on the Kingsport, Tennessee Police Department. I don't guess I've got the raincoat thing going on though, so you wouldn't have known." The attempt at humor didn't go over as well today as it would have yesterday morning.

"Where's Maggie now?" asked Connie.

"In the office," replied Beth.

"Well, why don't we get her with Columbo here and see if they can have any luck tracking him down, if that's ok with you, Columbo?" In spite of the situation, Connie was having fun picking on Carter about his new alter ego.

"Guys, we're jumping the gun a little bit here," Carter told them. "In the vast majority of cases like this, the person just had to step out for a few minutes and got detained. Let's give him a couple of hours and see if he calls or comes back. If he's not back, or we haven't heard from him by noon, then I'll get with Maggie and we'll start trying to track him down." They all agreed, not because they wanted to, but because they really didn't know of a better way to proceed. It just wasn't like Doug to not be where he was supposed to be. This whole situation just felt like something was wrong.

Everyone's eyes seemed to anxiously watch their watches until noon rolled around. Jill walked to the clubhouse and checked with Maggie, who was trying to focus on the office, but there was still no sign of Doug. The worry was beginning to show on the face of the attractive woman with wavy, medium length, black hair. "He didn't say anything last night about going anywhere," she said. "He would have told me something, it's just not like him."

"Honey, we're going to get Carter to help us locate him." Jill said reassuringly. Carter told us he was a retired detective in

Tennessee. Why don't you call Grace and see if she'll come in and handle the office while you and Carter talk and make some phone calls?"

"Sounds good to me, Jill. I don't think I can take this office anymore this morning. I'm really starting to get worried now."

Within ten minutes, Carter and Maggie moved into the back room of the office and they began making the usual first round of calls; police department, hospital, parents, children, golfing buddies, etc. None of them had heard from Doug. After an hour and a half of exhausting the list, Carter and Maggie had laid out on the legal pad, he finally asked the question he always hated to ask a wife in a missing person case, "Maggie, do you know if Doug has a girlfriend?"

Maggie hesitated just long enough to let Carter know there was more to her answer than he was going to easily get out of her. "No, no, not that I know of."

"Why the hesitation?" asked Carter, staring her straight in the eye. The fact that both of them sat in the office buck naked had long ago lost its luster. Carter Sykes was now in his element, interrogating a person of interest. "If there's anything I need to know to help find your husband, you need to tell me now, Maggie. I've been a detective for thirty years, and a pretty good one at that. I will find out sooner or later. It'd be better if I found out sooner." Carter rarely saw this line produce the desired results, but he always felt obliged to give it a try.

"There's nothing going on, sir." Maggie replied, the word sir showing that she now understood that Carter was questioning her.

Carter thought, 'That's her story and she's sticking to it.' "Like I said, it will all come out in the end, Maggie"

"Shouldn't we call the police or something?" she asked, obviously trying to get the attention off of herself.

"Doug's only been missing for five hours Maggie. Unless y'all have a pretty tight relationship with the local cops, there's not much they're going to do until tomorrow." Carter waited for her reaction. He could see the wheels turning in her head, most likely pondering either the Westlake's, and the club's, relationship with the local police or her husband's involvement with another woman, or both. Carter guessed the relationship between the local police in a small, southern town and a nudist park wasn't very good. He also knew by her hesitation that there was something to the other woman scenario; he just didn't know what it was yet.

"I don't guess Ralph would be too inclined to help us if he didn't have to," Maggie finally said.

"I take it Ralph is the local law enforcement around here?"

"Yeah, Ralph Tedder is the sheriff. As you can imagine, with us being a nudist park our relationship with Ralph is strained at best. Although we break no laws, most locals really don't like us being here."

Carter was glad to know he still had his instincts working, even in his retirement. This gave him even more faith in his new theory that there was another woman involved. "Well, without anyone else to call, I guess we've done all we can do until Doug comes back."

"You sound pretty sure he will."

"I've been a detective for a long time, Maggie. They almost always do in these kinds of cases." The look on her face let him know that she knew exactly what he meant; cases involving a mistress. But just for good measure, he said, "Who knows, maybe he went hiking on the Appalachian Trail." Carter was in South Carolina; he just couldn't resist alluding to the former Governor. "I'm ready for some lunch and I'm sure you could use something too."

"Yeah, I guess I could," said Maggie, almost relieved that Carter was giving her a break and not pushing her further on the other woman angle.

"Let me know if you hear from him, ok."

"Ok Mr., uh, Carter. Thanks for your help in trying to find Doug."

"Glad I can help, Maggie. I'm sure he'll turn up soon." With that, Carter left the office. He checked the pool and was told Connie decided to walk back to the Coachmen for lunch and a break from the sun.

****

"Enjoying your vacation, sweetie?" Connie asked Carter as he stepped into the Coachmen.

"You know Cons, people are people, no matter where they are; whether they're clothed or naked. We spend nearly two hours making a list and calling nearly everyone they know, and the minute I mention a mistress, she hesitates and denies one exists. He'll turn up in a day or two, they almost always do."

"But his car's still here, sweetie. Where did he go without it? He didn't run off for a rendezvous on foot."

"Easy, they took her car. As for clothes, he may have a stash at her place. It's hard to say, but this fits the pattern. It wouldn't surprise me if she's calling his mistress right now, trying to run him down."

"Well, I hope so. Everyone at the pool is nerve wracked. And it's only going to get worse when the weekend gets here." She offers him a chicken wrap she had made for lunch.

"Unless his mistress has got a whiz wheel in that thing, he'll turn up before the weekend is over. He'll get a guilty conscience or start thinking about what all it is costing him; his life, his job, his friends, his money, his pretty wife, his things. Happens all the time. Hey, this is pretty good, thanks Cons." Carter nods toward his wrap.

"You're welcome, sweetie. I couldn't let my hubby go hungry when he came home from work, now could I? I hope you're right about Doug."

"Trust me; he'll turn up by the weekend."

****

With all the excitement of the day, Carter and Connie decided to eat a simple dinner together that evening. Carter knew that if they ate with someone else at the club, the topic of conversation would be the disappearance of Doug Westlake. Carter didn't want to go into all he had learned from Maggie. He knew at the end of the day, the truth would come out. He just didn't want to be the one to expose it.

After dinner, Carter wanted to get in a set of tennis. He had been destroyed at putt-putt, and knew that the distractions he would encounter at tennis wouldn't be as bad as those on the putt-putt course. In tennis, they would, after all, be on the other side of the net, not hovering over the hole. Tennis was his game. In college, he played on Clinch Valley's conference championship team his senior year. He and Connie started playing before they started dating in college, and he always won. Every now and then he'd let her get close, but he just couldn't bring himself to purposefully lose. Sometimes he wondered why she kept playing him, but she nearly always jumped at the chance for a set. He knew after the putt-putt fiasco she'd think she actually had a chance this time, and he knew he would redeem himself, and the entire male gender.

They walked to the courts together, Connie carrying her K-Mart purchased Wilson racquet and Carter carrying the Yonex he bought at the Appalachian Athletic House back in the '80s. Connie had her hair back in a pony tail, which Carter had always thought was so sexy, even in her normal tennis attire; even more so with her wearing not a stitch of clothing above her ankles. Carter was doing his best Johnny Mac imitation, wearing his headband like he did three decades earlier. Connie played hard, like she always did, giving it all she had; but even with all the distractions she could muster, Carter was still able to secure a 6-3 victory. After his final cross court forehand winner, Carter began his victory dance as he approached the net.

"Still the King," Carter yelled, self-proclaiming his greatness. "King Carter, that's me."

"Of tennis, maybe, but I'm the queen of putt-putt, remember?" Connie reminded him.

"I think they have putt-putt courses in old folks homes, don't they, honey?"

"You better get some practice in then, sweetie. You'll be the laughing stock of the nursing home when I kick your ass."

They gathered up their racquet covers, put the tennis balls back in the can, and walked toward the Coachmen; Carter still boasting over his tennis victory and Connie still countering with her putt-putt prowess. "Tomorrow, the Sykes Cornhole Championship," Carter announced.

52

"You're on, sweetie." Connie smiled, thinking about the distractive techniques Mary Ann had given her for cornhole.

They arrived back at the Coachmen just before dark. Connie finally agreed that as the loser of the tennis match, she had to take Thor for his walk. "It'll beat hearing you gloat," she told him as she gave in. She put on Thor's harness and grabbed the maglite out of her purse as they headed out the door. Carter grabbed a beer and settled down at his recliner and flipped on the TV, the first time it had been on since they arrived at Utopia.

Connie decided since it was Wednesday and there was no one in the park except Gil, Mary Ann, Jim, and Maggie, she would let Thor walk without his retractable leash. He would wander ahead twenty or thirty yards and turn around and run back to her, going past her and circling back again. This went on for about five minutes until they reached a part of the park they hadn't been to yet. They walked into the woods leading down to the creek. She knew they were close to the creek, and Jim had warned them the club's property ended there, a result she had later learned, of the financial troubles the club had faced several years before. Thor went ahead, but this time took off running, barking at something. She called him, but Thor's instincts had kicked in; he kept barking at his discovery. Like his dad, he had found something and he just had to check it out. "These damn Sykes men," she muttered. "All they want to do is investigate."

Down in the woods, by the creek, at the border of the land that was to have been the nudist residential community, Thor had found something. His hackles were up and he was barking intently, looking back at Connie, then back at the object of his attention. Connie instantly recognized that this behavior was different than Thor's usual rabbit chasing bark. She walked up to him to see what had gotten his attention. Darkness had settled upon Utopia so Connie pointed the mini maglite's beam on the ground in front of Thor. He instantly jumped backwards.

"CARRR-TEEEEERRR!"

FIVE

When a fully clothed Carter and Connie emerged from the Coachmen around 10:00 am the next morning, Herbsville's two police cars sat outside the office of the Utopia Sun Club. The Sykes' both knew it was going to be a long day.

After their discovery the night before, Connie and Thor ran back to the camper to get Carter. The body they found was lying behind a tree in the woods that separated Utopia from the outside world. Carter looked over the scene without touching anything. He assumed the body Thor found was that of Doug Westlake; it was male, naked, and lying face down. On the body's backside, Carter saw no sign of what might have caused the death, but did notice the ground around the body's chest was darkened. Carter assumed this was from bodily fluids from the deadly wounds. Since there was no cell service at Utopia, Carter knew his only choices for calling in the discovery were the homes along the road. Westlake's house was out of the question, it was not his place to tell Maggie what Thor had discovered. He went to the house of Brian and Derrick, obtained their promise to let the police tell Maggie, told them what Thor had found, then used their phone to make the call to 911. He instructed the gentlemen not to go to the scene, reminding them the police could do their work best with the scene as undisturbed as possible. Just before midnight, a police cruiser arrived at the Utopia Sun Club and used his emergency pass code to quietly enter through the gate. Carter thought it best to throw on a pair of shorts and a t-shirt while awaiting the police. He met the local law enforcement outside the office.

"Carter Sykes, Kingsp..." Carter caught himself before saying Kingsport PD, and held out his hand. He made a quick appraisal of the cop: about the same height as himself, chubby midsection, thinning and receding hairline, probably early to mid sixties. 'Stereotypical southern sheriff.' he thought.

"Sheriff Ralph Tedder," the cop introduced himself, shaking Carter's hand. "Where's the body."

Carter got in the patrol car and directed Tedder to the path leading to the body. After walking to the scene, the sheriff asked, "Y'all disturb anything here?"

"My dog found the body, but I don't think so, not beyond the usual sniffing, anyway."

"Doesn't look like it," Tedder said, shining his powerful light at the body. "Were you the first person to discover the body?"

"No, sir, my wife, Connie, was. She's back at the camper with Thor, our dog."

"Well, does Maggie Westlake know that her husband is dead?"

"No, sir," said Carter, his suspicions that the dead body was indeed Westlake's confirmed.

"Well, I'll get this place taped off and call this in to the State Police. There's not much I can do here until they have a chance to do their thing. As much as I don't want to, I guess I need to go to the Westlake's house and inform Mrs. Westlake of what your dog has found."

"You gonna have anyone stand guard until state gets here?"

"Hell, son, it's me and Sam Mitchell here in this town. I can't have one of us staying up all night, especially not here in the middle of a nudist colony. Hell, Sam's wife would kill him dead as Westlake, here if she knew he was out here."

"That's it for the force?"

"That's it. Normally the biggest crimes around here are some teenagers racing on Saturday night and a delinquent cat that has got itself stuck in a tree. That's why I hired Sam; he's a hell of a tree climber." Tedder laughed.

"But there's a chance that whoever committed this crime could come out here and remove evidence."

"Why are you rushing to conclude this is a crime scene? This man could have had a heart attack back here while taking a leak for all I know."

"Well, he would have had to have taken a leak with blood flowing out his chest, then. Look at the darkness in the sand coming from under the chest." Carter said as he pointed his mini-maglite around the dead body. "Hundred to one that's blood. My experience has shown that where there's a dead body and blood, there's likely to have been a crime."

"Your experience? Who the hell are you, Columbo?"

'What is it with the Colombo thing around here?' Carter thought. "Detective Carter Sykes, Kingsport Tennessee PD, retired," he said, with a bit of pride.

"Only two problems, Columbo. First, this ain't Tennessee, and second, you're retired. Now, I suggest you leave the current detective work up to those of us who have jurisdiction and who are currently carrying a badge."

Tedder's remarks reminded Carter of his dad telling him he couldn't rebuild the carburetor on the '63 Valiant when he was twelve. It was all he could do to bite his tongue and keep quiet He knew cops had a way of being territorial, but all he was trying to do was help. He didn't want to, but he knew the best thing for him to do right now was to say "yes, sir", go back to the Coachmen, and check on Connie. So that's exactly what he did.

****

A couple of minutes after they emerged from the Coachmen, Carter noticed two late model Dodge Chargers with state tags stop at the office. "The state's here," he told Connie. "They'll be going over the crime scene." A few minutes later, Tedder led them into the woods and to the body. Carter was hoping rural areas in eastern South Carolina didn't get the rookie crime scene investigators like his native Virginia coalfields. Within an hour, they had gone over the scene, bagged the body, and left the park. "Yep, I know where the South Carolina rookies get their start," Carter told his wife.

"What do you mean?" she asked.

"These guys are young, barely out of college. Neither had on a wedding band. I watched them enter the crime scene. They just walked up to the body, didn't take time to get the overall picture of their surroundings. They probably didn't mess anything up, but they definitely didn't learn all they could have either. We'll take a closer look at the scene this afternoon and see what we might find."

"We will?" Connie questioned.

"Of course, it might be valuable later on."

"Carter, you're not a cop anymore," Connie said to him sternly.

"But I'm only barely retired. Besides, Tedder is going to need some help."

"Leave it alone, Carter," Connie warned him. "This is supposed to be a fun, relaxing vacation

."

****

Tedder had turned one of Utopia's rental campers into an incident command center for the day. First, he brought Maggie into the makeshift office. Over the course of the morning, he would talk to everyone who had been at the club the past two days. Some went into the meeting naked, others wore clothes. One of the first he talked to was Connie, since she had been the human who discovered the body. Later that day, he brought Carter over to his new interrogation room.

"What did you see last night?" Tedder asked Carter.

"Same thing you did, Sheriff. I saw the body. I looked the scene over the best I could without touching anything. It was dark, so what I could see with the maglite was limited. There didn't appear to be any obvious signs of struggle, though it was hard to tell with that little light. It looked like someone had partially covered the body with leaves and twigs. I noticed the darkened dirt coming from under the upper torso, which I reasonably believed was blood. It was pretty obvious the body had been there a day or so."

"Are you telling me you never moved that body?"

"Of course not, Sheriff. I've been...I was a detective for thirty years, I know better than to do that."

"You knew too much last night for me. How'd you know that was Doug Westlake? How'd you know he had been shot in the chest?"

"'Because the evidence was there. It was easy for anyone to see. We all knew Doug Westlake was missing yesterday; he didn't show up for work and his wife was worried about him. I assumed he had run off with his mistress, maybe to Argentina for all I know." He couldn't resist another chance to make fun of South Carolina's former governor.

"Where did you get this mistress thing from? Far as I know, he didn't have a mistress. Maggie never mentioned one."

"Did you ask her?"

"Of course I did. She said 'no'."

"She's lying to you, Sheriff."

"Now what makes you think that, Columbo? No one else seems to know about a mistress either."

"Because yesterday, everyone was concerned about Westlake not showing up for work. Maggie and I were calling the usual suspects; family, friends, associates, you know the drill. When no one knew where he was, I asked her about another woman and she hesitated before denying one existed. She hesitated long enough that I knew she was hiding something. Quite honestly, after her hesitation and denial, I assumed Doug was off with his mistress and would show up soon enough. I just didn't expect to see him show up dead."

"Bet you could tell what kind of gun it was killed him, too, Mr. big city detective."

"No, but if I was guessing, I'd say it was probably a .38. Easiest to obtain, hardest to trace."

Tedder raised an eyebrow at Carter's correct assumption. His tone began to soften. "What else have you figured out, Columbo?"

"I'd guess Westlake knew the killer, I didn't see any signs of struggle or an attempt to run. Looked like someone had rolled the body and covered it up with leaves and twigs. That's about it from the crime scene. From the few people I've talked to, it seems Doug was well liked around the club. From what I've been told, he came here when the club was in a crisis, both internally and financially, and brought it out of it. That's about all I know at this point, Sheriff."

"I'd assume the murderer had to be someone here, since the murder occurred on the property," Tedder deducted with pride.

"Not necessarily. A jealous husband could have come to confront Westlake and Westlake could have led him to the woods for a more private place to have their discussion. Westlake could be involved in drugs and the privacy of a wooded area in a nudist park on a weekday would be a great place for an exchange. Maggie may have found out about the affair and lead him here to kill him instead of having a mess in the house." There's lots of possibilities we haven't ruled out yet. There's lots of angles we need to look at. If it were me, I'd pursue this other woman angle until it fell apart, though. Maggie is still trying to hide it, so we need to find out why."

"When are you heading back to Tennessee?"

"Planning on leaving Monday. But I'm retired now; I have no clock, no job, no worries, no money," Carter had been waiting to quote the famous license plate ever since he first announced his retirement. "And here, I have no clothes," he laughed.

"So, y'all will be here for a couple days if I need to ask you any more questions?"

"Either here or in town getting a few things. Of course, I can't guarantee you'll find me wearing anything."

"That was a visual I didn't need," Tedder laughed. "Now get on out of here."

Carter got up and turned to leave, then stopped and turned back, facing Tedder. "How long until you get the forensics report?"

"A couple of days, maybe Monday. I'll let you know what I find."

"Thanks, sheriff. Being curious by nature, I'd kind of like to know where this whole investigation leads. You know, see how good my hunches are."

Tedder purposefully waited to make Carter Sykes his last interview at Utopia. He wanted to get all the information he could before questioning a trained detective. He wanted to see if Carter had seen anything that he and the state boys had missed. Indeed, Carter had. Tedder knew the mistress angle was a viable one, and was the best lead he had so far. Unless something unexpected came up in the forensics report, it might be the best lead they'd get in the investigation. After interviewing Carter, he packed his gear into his marked Taurus and left Utopia.

From his conversation with Tedder, Carter knew the sheriff had a good heart, but was in over his head in a murder investigation and needed help to solve this case. He had seen that overwhelmed look in rookie detectives many times before. Carter also knew Tedder wasn't likely to get top notch help from the state. In an era of budget cuts and expanding caseloads, a murder in a nudist colony in a rural South Carolina town was not going to get a high precedence. While no one would say it publicly, the general attitude would be the SOB got what he deserved for running a place like that. He hoped the sheriff had softened enough to let him provide some guidance while in the area.

As he walked back to the Coachmen, Carter instinctively checked his smartphone, but there was no signal. No wifi, no 3 or 4G signal. Without the internet, Carter was severely limited in things he could check online concerning this case. He grabbed a Diet Dr. Pepper from the fridge, sat down in his recliner, reached out and hit the power button of the Icom 7000. Then he got an idea. He knew where to start his investigation. He reached up and turned on his laptop and took a couple of sips of soda while the computer booted up. Once it completed its cycle, he clicked an icon labeled RMS Express and waited a few seconds for the program to appear on his screen. Once the program was ready, he clicked on 'message', then 'new message', and wrote an email to his friend and partner in Kingsport, Tony Ward. Since the email was going over the limited bandwidth of high frequency radio, Carter kept the email short and to the point:

....

Hi Tony, Carter here. No internet, no cell phone service, using ham radio. Got a murder here in this modern day Mayberry sized town. Need info on the deceased, Doug Westlake of Herbsville, SC and his wife Maggie. Reply to this Winlink email address, not my regular address. Keep info as concise as possible, no photo attachments. I'll be receiving it over the radio.

Thanks, Carter.

Carter posted the message to the outbox and hit the "Open Session" tab on the RMS Express program. A few clicks later, he hit the "start" button and his radio transmitted a short burst of noise, sounding like a fax machine, only different, came from his computer's soundcard. Again it transmitted the same noise and this time a similar noise was received by the Icom, indicating another computer had been contacted. In seconds, the two computers became intertwined in a digital dance by controlling the radios that transmitted their alien sounding messages. This dance continued for about three minutes, until Carter's radio transmitted "de KA4CS" in Morse code. The other radio responds with "de WD9FHP" in Morse code, ending the communication. Carter closed all the boxes of the RMS Express program and went through the process of shutting down his computer. He turned off the Icom 7000. His email was gone, and he'd check for Tony's reply in a couple of hours or so. He got up, walked to the kitchen, and tossed his empty can into the trash. Now it was time to get a beer, get his clothes off, and try to enjoy the rest of his vacation.

SIX

For the first time since he'd been at Utopia, Carter felt weird taking his clothes off. He noticed this feeling and surmised it was because he had been doing something akin to his normal work routine, where he always wore a shirt, tie, and slacks. He had just finished discussing a case with a fellow law enforcement officer, something he would never dream of doing while buck naked. But he wasn't on a case, not his case, anyway. He was on permanent vacation, retirement. What was he doing sending emails to Tony? Why was he looking for information? Sheriff Tedder was the law around here. It was his case, his responsibility. Carter knew he needed to back off. But he also knew that Tedder was out of his league, he could see the small town sheriff couldn't handle a murder case alone. It wasn't necessarily Tedder's fault, he seemed to be a good man. But he was undertrained, understaffed, and didn't have the resources to conduct a proper investigation. Carter saw the rookies the state sent down to process the crime scene. He knew these men would do what they had to do, but would not become personally invested in a murder in a nudist park in the middle of nowhere. Carter had the sneaking suspicion that if this case was going to be solved, he was going to be a part of solving it. Probably a big part.

Carter walked up the sandy road toward Maggie's house when he saw Connie heading toward him. She had been with Maggie, helping her call her mother, her daughter in college at Wofford, Doug's parents, and a couple of friends to inform them of Doug's death. Her main objective was to keep Maggie away from the crime scene and all of the police activity in the park. From her time working with anxiety patients, she knew if Maggie had a visual of the crime scene the trauma of losing her husband would be much harder to overcome. Connie knew if Maggie saw where Doug had died, it would haunt her dreams for a long time. She also knew Maggie needed support. She knew Maggie had a long, hard road in front of her. It really wasn't Connie's job, she didn't know Maggie at all; in fact, she had barely spoken to her. But she knew she was trained and equipped to help, as she had done so many times as a nurse. Finally, Jill and Beth came to the Westlake house and took over the job of sitting with Maggie, allowing Connie to go back to the Coachmen, take a break, and get some lunch.

"Saw the sheriff leave," Connie said, as she approached Carter. "Are they finished here today?"

"Yeah, they've got all they're going to get from here, despite what they might have missed."

"Jill and Beth came up so I could take a break and get some lunch."

"Nice job keeping her occupied while all this was going on, babe."

"She needs someone right now, anyone, until her family can get here. After the sheriff finished interviewing me, I figured it was the least I could do. You find anything out yet?"

"Why do you think I'd be trying to find anything out?" Carter innocently asked.

"Sweetie, how long have we been married? Thirty years, that's how long. You don't think I know you by now? You're already into this thing waist deep and heading as fast as you can toward the deep end. I could read your face when you saw this poor sheriff in this one horse town. If I didn't know there wasn't any wireless internet or cell phone service here, I'd swear you had already contacted Tony."

"You forget, dear, I am a ham radio operator." Carter smiled, admiring both his wife's detective skills and his ingenuity to overcome technical obstacles.

"I should've known," she said. "Let's get to the camper, I need a drink. We do have some Admiral Nelson in the cabinet, don't we?"

"And a fresh bottle of diet Cranberry Splash Sierra Mist," Carter added.

"Good, I need a strong one."

"Hey, did Maggie say anything about her husband's mistress?" Carter asked, changing the subject as they reached the Coachmen.

"No, she didn't. Are you still on this mistress kick?"

"Yes, because I asked her yesterday and she lied about it. If there was nothing to it, she wouldn't lie about it."

"You've got to be sure before you make accusations."

"Cons, she denied it, of course; they always do at first. But her hesitation told me that she is hiding something. I'm hoping now, now that Doug's dead, maybe she will tell us the truth. Even if the mistress has nothing to do with the murder, it would make the investigation easier if we knew everything up front."

Connie poured the spiced rum into her ice filled plastic glass and reached for the soda. "You think anyone else knows?"

"I'm not sure if anyone here knows or not, but I can't just say 'Kingsport PD, I need to ask you a few questions'. We need to be a bit more discreet in finding out."

"We?"

"Of course, Cons. Haven't you always wanted to be my partner?"

"No, I've always dreamt of being a little bit more like your wife, more like Rock Hudson and Susan St. James. I know you've always wanted to be Rock; at least until you found out he was gay."

"Yep, that's us, Cons, *McMillan and Wife*".

"Yeah, but you're retired now, Rock. You're not a police commissioner. We're on vacation, sweetie, not undercover."

"No, we're on an adventure, babe. And one never knows where a true adventure will lead. It seems this one has led us right into the middle of a murder."

"And you can't walk away from it, can you?"

"Have I ever?"

"No. And you know I've always supported you, sweetie, even when I really didn't want to."

"More than any woman should have, babe." Carter thought of the many times he hadn't been there for her because he was trying to solve a case.

"Well, let's see where this adventure leads, then. *McMillan and Wife*." Connie raised her right hand over her head and Carter slapped it with his.

"*McMillan and Wife*," he replied.

****

65

Needing to relax a bit after lunch, Carter, Connie and Thor walked around Utopia, which was now nearly deserted. It was, after all, a Thursday afternoon, the day after a dead body was discovered in the park. The place literally had every cop in town here this morning. It wasn't that being in a nudist camp was illegal, it was just that people in general often didn't feel comfortable around police, especially with the cops asking them questions as they are trying to relax in the buff.

For the most part, Carter, Connie, and Thor had the place to themselves. Only Maggie, Grace, Jim, Randy and Jill, Gene and Beth remained on the grounds. The only person they saw on their walk was Jill, she was taking a small, half-full bag of garbage from Maggie's to the dumpster. Even Jill didn't slow down to say hello, her mind seeming focused on the task at hand.

"What do you think, sweetie?" Connie asked.

"About the murder?"

"Yeah. Got any ideas about what happened or who did it?"

"Not yet. Probably won't until I know more about the mistress. But with the murder happening here in the park, it doesn't fit the typical 'woman scorned' scenario. I can't imagine a husband or boyfriend coming here to confront Westlake, much less to take him back in the woods and kill him. But ya' never know. Heck, I thought Doug was out running around with another woman, shows how much I know. Right now, without knowing more about the mistress, all we have is stimulation, pure stimulation, as Jay would say. I'm hoping Tony's inquiry into just who Doug Westlake really was will shed some light on things.

"This is all just all so crazy." Connie said. Here we are, retired less than a week, our first adventure of our new lives, and what are we doing? Looking into a murder. It's just all so surreal."

"Well, maybe we were meant to be here, Cons. And if we were, this will truly be the adventure of a lifetime."

"I guess so. I was just planning a little more pool time and a bit less murder solving time."

"The best laid plans of mice, men, and naked ladies," Carter paraphrased John Steinbeck. They both laughed.

The conversation turned to other subjects, such as the people they had met, what if felt like to walk naked and free, why they hadn't tried this years before, and so on. After an hour of walking and talking, the three of them arrived back at the Coachmen. They stopped before going into the camper, knowing that when Carter went inside, the first thing he was going to do was flip on his ham radio and attempt to check his Winlink account in hopes of having an email from Tony waiting for him. As they walked in, Carter headed for his recliner and Connie to the kitchen to get them both a drink, as the heat had drained them, even on a leisurely walk. Even Thor went straight for his water bowl. In a few minutes, Carter had his computer connected to another via amateur radio, and the digital dance ensued as the computers passed information over the forty meter band. Carter walked to the bathroom and just before he returned he heard his radio send the familiar 'de KA4CS' in morse code, indicating the communication was complete. He closed the session and sure enough, sitting in the inbox was an email from Tony.

....

Message ID: I2UN3TQ1ORKI
Date: 2013/06/20 20:18
From: tony.ward@kpd.tn.gov
To: KA4CS
Source: tony.ward@kpd.tn.gov
Subject: Re: Doug Westlake

Hey man,

Where in the HELL are you and what in the HELL have you gotten yourself into? This Westlake is into some pretty weird shit man. W/O sending the entire file, here's the crux of it.

Westlake is the manager of a NUDIST COLONY called Utopia Sun Club. He has been employed there for 5 years now.

Before Utopia, he was a real estate developer in the Greenville/Spartanburg SC area. Looks like he was pretty successful.

Now get this one...He and his wife Maggie are members of a group known as "Carolina Couples and More". I checked this group out on the internet before sending this email. Carter, this is a SWINGERS group, one the largest in the Southeast. Westlake and his wife are knee deep into it too. Seems like Carolina Couples has groups that meet in Charlotte, Charleston, and the Raleigh area for the purpose of swapping wives and group sex.

Man, what the HELL are you and Connie up to? I trust you man, but whatever is going on, you and Connie be careful. You can't make a call on the radio and have half the cops in Tennessee backing you up anymore.

BTW: We got the dealer that punk kid turned you on to. He won't be putting any shit on the street for a long time. It's not the same without you man. We all miss you. BE CAREFUL.

Detective Tony Ward
Kingsport Police Department

....

Carter leaned back in his recliner with his hands behind his head. "Well, Cons, looks like we got some answers...and of course, a few more questions."

"What is it, sweetie?"

"Remember the other woman?"

"Yeah?"

"Turns out there were many other women. And probably many other men for Maggie too."

"What are you talking about, Carter?"

"Seems like the Westlakes are members of a group called "Carolina Couples and More". This is one of the biggest swingers groups in the Southeast."

"I thought Doug got rid of the swingers here at Utopia?"

"Yeah, me too. Now I know why Maggie hesitated when I asked her if there was another woman. I wonder what Maggie will have to say when I ask her specifically about Carolina Couples."

"Now Carter, you're not a cop anymore. You can't just go asking these types of questions."

"I guess not, but I know someone who can. Ralph Tedder can. I've got to talk to him in the morning. Don't we need a few things from town anyway?"

"I'm sure I can find something we need."

"Sounds great. Off to Herbsville we go in the morning," Carter sang, making up a tune.

****

The next morning, Carter and Connie follow the GPS directions along the flat, straight back roads leading to Herbsville, South Carolina. Herbsville is a town of about five hundred people and is the county seat. Originally settled in the late 1600's, Herbsville served as the trading headquarters for the cotton farmers in the area. After the Civil War, the area around Herbsville was worked mostly by sharecroppers, and the town declined. The town is now about a third white, half black, and the rest Latino, although one wouldn't know it by the visitors at Utopia. Carter and Connie had yet to see a non-Caucasian at the sun club.

Carter drove the Ram through the one stop light in town, actually the only stoplight in the county, and saw the Civilian Conservation Corps looking Sheriff's office building on the left. Luckily there were a couple of parking spaces open just past its front door. Carter wouldn't have liked parallel parking the big, Mega Cab Ram into a spot designed for a small car.

Carter walked to the front of the truck and put a dime in the meter. Connie commented on how long it had been since she'd actually seen a parking meter. For a brief moment Carter's mind went back to his childhood and the parking meters that lined the streets of many southwestern Virginia coalfield towns. He even envisioned the meter maid writing parking tickets for those who didn't put coins in the meters. 'How times have changed,' Carter thought. Now the meters are all gone, and most towns would love to see cars lining their streets again. Instead, they're all at the Walmart in the bigger towns thirty miles away. Carter is sure the same thing will happen to Herbsville, if it hasn't already. Carter reached for Connie's hand and the two of them walked side by side, hand in hand, into the sheriff's office.

"Hello Sheriff Tedder," Carter announced their presence to the sheriff sitting behind the desk.

"Somehow I knew I'd be seeing you down here, Columbo. I'd ask what brings you down here, but somehow I already know. Hello, ma'am," the sheriff stood up, acknowledging Connie's presence.

"Nice to see you again, sheriff," Connie said

"What do you know about Doug Westlake?" Carter got straight to the point of the visit.

"I know the son of a bitch came here five years ago and kept that damn nudist colony from shutting down. We thought we had 'em. They owed thousands in back taxes, and that's just to the county. I know the state was after them, and I heard the feds were, too. Westlake came in here and cleaned up the whole mess. At least he had to sell that land they owned where they planned to start a naked housing development. Worked something out with some corporation to buy that land and keep the colony afloat."

"Ever hear of 'Carolina Couples and More'?"

"Nope."

"Any idea what Westlake did before he came here?"

"No, but I should have the report about him later this morning. Where are you going with all this, Columbo?"

"Sheriff, I received some information on Doug Westlake in an email via ham radio. Westlake's not exactly what he appears to be. If I'm guessing correctly, his alternate lifestyle may have led to his death. We can solve this case, but we need each other. You see, I grew up in a small town in the Virginia coalfields. I know first hand how small towns work. I need your knowledge of the community and trust the people have in you. You need my thirty years experience as a detective. You won't solve this murder without me, and I don't think I can solve it without you."

"You know, Columbo, you're probably right," the sheriff admitted. For twenty years I ran the hardware store in town, until Lowes built a new 'home improvement center'," Tedder made the quotation marks with his hands, "just on our side of Lewiston. People just assumed they were getting a better deal because they were buying from big ol' Lowes instead of the small town guy. So I shut down the hardware store that my great granddad built. I knew everyone in town, and decided to run for sheriff when Williamson retired. It was an easy victory and a pretty good job. I get along well with the whites and the blacks; both had been customers in the store and quite honestly, I didn't care about the color of a man's skin, just the color of his money. I could deal with the teenagers racing on Saturday night and the old ladies whose cats got themselves stuck in a tree. Every now and then somebody would steal something and we'd figure out who did it; wasn't too hard, they'd usually either try to sell it, or get drunk and brag about it. Some guys here in town grow and sell a little weed, but they don't hurt anyone and we generally leave them alone as long as that's all they're into, and don't sell it to the kids. Hell, you ever seen anyone get into trouble when they're stoned, Columbo? This is the first real crime we've had in the seven and a half years I've been sheriff. Oh, except for when some idiot from that nudist colony brings his wife into Taylor's Grocery and tries to get her to show her tits and ass to all the customers; some people in town think that's worse than this murder. Well, anyway, right now I'm here waiting on the state to send me some report I don't have any idea what to do with. To be quite honest, I need a man like you on this case, Columbo. Hell, if you weren't going back to Tennessee, I'd deputize you."

"Well, Sheriff, I'm going back to Tennessee, but this is the twenty-first century. Let's catch us a killer," Carter said with a smile.

"Sounds good to me. Hell, if I have an unsolved murder on my record, somebody will decide to run against me in the election this fall and I may actually have to get a real job. It's a long drive everyday to Lewiston to work at Lowes," Tedder chuckled. "Where do we start, Columbo?"

"First, we start by calling me Carter, not Columbo."

"Yeah, he thinks of himself more as Rock Hudson in *McMillan and Wife*," Connie couldn't help but chime in.

The Sheriff chuckled, "Rock? Wasn't he gay?"

"Thanks, Cons," Carter sighed.

"Secondly, do like you'd do if this were a burglary. Ask a few questions around town and see if anyone starts bragging about this murder. Third, get all the info you can on Doug Westlake, Maggie Westlake, the swingers club, and any financials you can find on the Utopia Sun Club and the Westlakes. I'm sure as a small town sheriff, you've got great connections with the local judge."

"I hope so, he married my daughter," Tedder laughed. "I'll get right on it, but with today being Friday it might take a couple of days to get all this info. This isn't New York City, ya' know." Tedder said New York City in his best barbeque sauce commercial voice. "What are you going to do the next couple of days?"

I'm going back to Utopia and finish my vacation, running around naked with my wife," Carter said, trying to provoke the Sheriff a bit after his gay comment. "I want to listen and ask some questions there and see what turns up. I've learned a lot about the history of the club the past few days without even trying. With the place packed for the weekend, and me actually trying to find out some info, I should find out even more. People do get drunk and brag nudist park too, you know."

"Yeah, I guess so. This will be a first, a naked detective. I don't guess you'll have your raincoat on?"

"Hey, maybe we can start a trend," Connie joked.

"Oh, one more thing. We need to question Maggie Westlake down here at the station. We need to find out what she will tell us about their involvement with Carolina Couples. I've got a feeling that somewhere in this case, the Carolina Couples are going to be a big part of the puzzle. Her hesitation and lie when I asked her about the other woman isn't coincidental, you know. Can we arrange for a visit with her Monday morning, before I head back to Tennessee? I don't want to do it before the funeral, and I want to leave town right after the interview."

"Sure thing. I'd like to hear more about this swingers club thing myself."

"Cell phones don't work up at Utopia, and neither does internet, so you'll have to contact me via email over my ham radio. You do have email here, don't you?"

"Yeah, us poor redneck hillbillies have email and, indoor bathrooms, too," Tedder said in his best exaggerated southern drawl. "What's the address?"

Carter wrote down KA4CS@winlink.org on an old business card he had in his wallet and handed it to the sheriff. "I'll check it two or three times a day. Send me what you find out, just don't send any pictures or big files, this is ham radio, not NASA. I'd program my radio to your frequency, but I don't want every police wannabe in the county finding out about this murder investigation."

"Sounds good, I know we've got plenty of scanner listeners around here. Some of them always beat me to the trees when the cats get themselves stuck. Now you and your wife keep your clothes on until you get back inside that gate. I'd hate to have to arrest you."

"No problem, Sheriff. I won't be showing my assets in the grocery store, no matter how hard Columbo here tries to get me to," Connie laughed.

"That's a good thing, ma'am," Tedder laughed with her.

Carter and Connie left the sheriff's office, returned to the Ram, and drove to Taylor's Grocery where they picked up some supplies for the weekend.

"Wish you'd worn a short dress to town now, babe?" Carter asked, as Connie bent over to get an item off the bottom shelf.

"You heard the sheriff. I'd just tell him you forced me to show my ass; that you were the Godfather of the exhibitionist ring. He'd lock you up and me and Thor would take the Ram and Coachmen and run around nekkid all over the country."

"Think you got it figured out, huh?"

"Yep."

"Well then, just keep your britches on until we get back to Utopia."

"Yep, then you'll get to see it all." Connie smiled as she walked up the aisle.

SEVEN

After picking up groceries and stopping at the liquor store, Carter and Connie went back to the Utopia Sun Club. As they approached the gate, Carter noticed a red Ford Focus with a Wofford sticker parked outside Maggie Westlake's house.

"Looks like the Westlake's daughter is home," Carter said.

"That's good. She and Maggie need to spend some time together right now. They'll need each other."

Carter thought back to when his own father passed away forty years ago. He remembers the struggles his mother had, even with all the family support around her. He could only imagine what it's like to go through the grieving process with no family and only the support of a mostly transient nudist community. His heart went out to Maggie Westlake, and in a way, he was sorry he was going to have to ask her the questions he was going to ask her Monday morning. But he learned a long time ago how to put his personal feelings aside and proceed professionally with an interview. He knew if he was going to figure out what happened to her husband, he had to have the answers to his questions. Hell, as far as he knew, Maggie might be right in the middle of the murder.

Carter's mind was brought back to reality when he looked over at Connie in the passenger seat of the Ram. She has taken off her shirt and bra and was holding them in her lap.

"Couldn't wait, could you?" he teasingly asked.

"Why should I?"

"Good point."

Carter parked the Ram and watched as his wife hopped out of the truck and walked toward the Coachmen, wearing nothing but her shorts, her sandals, and a smile, she looked back over her shoulder at him sitting in the truck. All he could think about was how lucky he was. How lucky to have such a beautiful wife. How lucky to have someone so comfortable with herself. How lucky to have someone so playful, yet so loyal. He was aware of all the stress his job put on their marriage over the years; the hours, the mood swings, the midnight calls, the shady places he had to go in

75

search of bad guys, the long nights she spent worrying about him. And yet, she endured it all. Here she was, thirty years later, still as playful and carefree as if they were in college, maybe more so. What had he done to deserve her? Then, almost as if on cue, a voice in his head said, 'you chased down and caught some very bad people. There's a reward in that.' Carter knew it all right. He didn't need seventy-two virgins, Connie was the perfect reward for him.

****

Once the groceries and supplies were put away, Carter and Connie grabbed a cooler full of drinks and walked up to the pool. It was Friday, Carter was hoping there would be more people coming in today and figured Doug Westlake's murder would be the topic of conversation around the club. He was hoping to listen and learn as much as he could. He might even hear some theories surrounding the murder he hadn't thought of yet. He told Connie this was kind of like going undercover, they were trying to find out as much as possible without anyone knowing they were looking for information. They had to blend in, get all the info they could get with their ears, and say nothing with their mouths.

When they opened the pool's gate, they were rather shocked to see Maggie Westlake standing in the pool near the steps with a stunning young woman, who they deducted must be her daughter, along with Randy, Jill, Gene, Beth, and a couple others they didn't recognize. Carter and Connie put their cooler and towels down in a pair of empty lounge chairs and proceeded to the steps of the pool. It was already more than ninety degrees, and just the walk to the pool caused Carter to work up a sweat.

"Hey, guys." Connie said effortlessly.

"Hi, Connie," the chorus of voices rang out.

"Where y'all been this morning?" asked Jill.

"We had to go to town and pick up a few things. There's certain things you don't want to run out of." Connie replied, realizing she wasn't telling a lie, but wasn't telling the entire truth either. "Herbsville's a cute little town."

"Yeah, we were out of industrial strength beverages," Carter spoke up, now on the first step of the pool with a drink in his hand. "You know, I kind of thought running out of alcohol at a nudist park would constitute a national emergency, and FEMA might send a team out here if we didn't replenish our stock."

"This has to be your daughter," Connie said looking at the beautiful, young woman standing beside Maggie. Emily Westlake was a senior at Wofford College in Spartanburg, South Carolina. She was about five-six, shoulder length brown hair, a very cute Sally Fields type face, and a body that many movie stars bought their plastic surgeon a Corvette to acquire.

Before Carter finished thinking it, he blurted out, "What are you doing at Wofford?"

Emily seemed to take him to mean 'What are you studying'. "Library Science," she replied.

"If you had been the librarian at my library, I would have spent a lot more time there," one of the men in the group said, only half joking.

"Yeah, but you wouldn't have been looking at any books," retorted the woman Carter assumed was his wife.

"No, I meant 'Why Wofford?'" said Carter. "Why not a big university like South Carolina or Clemson?"

"I spent most of my high school in Greenville until we moved here five years ago," Emily replied. "A few of my friends went to school there, and I wanted to go to school with them. They have an outstanding library science program, and I love the new library scene, especially all the digital media available today. Lots of new jobs, too. Many of today's librarians are retiring rather than dealing with learning all the new digital technologies, so I'm ready to take their jobs and move forward."

"Sounds like a great plan to me," Connie said. "The hours are better than being a nurse, let me tell you."

"Yeah, but not as good a chance to meet a doctor, honey", Beth said with a laugh.

"No. just a Professor, maybe a Sean Connery type," another lady said, which elicited a round of 'oohs' from the other ladies.

Grace came to the gate and told Maggie and Emily that they had a phone call in the office. They got out of the pool; each grabbed a towel, slipped into their flip-flops, and walked toward the office.

"How are they handling things?" asked Connie.

"They seem better than I expected," said Beth. Emily is a strong young lady with a good head on her shoulders. Would have graduated first in her class had she been here long enough. They said her senior year didn't give enough of a sample to make her eligible for honors. I think they just wanted to make sure a local girl got the award."

"So, she was here for a year after the Westlakes came to Utopia?" Carter asked.

"Yeah," said Randy. "A little shy at first, but she came around to nudism before long. As you can see, she has no problems with it now."

"I think her year touring Europe had a lot to do with that," Jill added.

"How could her parents afford for her to go to a private college like Wofford and tour Europe on what the manager of a small nudist park earns? Unless y'all were paying Doug more than I imagine." Connie asked the question Carter was thinking.

"I reckon her grandparents left her a trust fund for college," Randy said.

"Clinchfield Coal Company had a trust fund waiting for me," Carter said. "Go to work in the coal mines and trust us to pay you." Everyone chuckled. "I turned that one down."

Emily came back to the pool. "That was the funeral home. They called the office when they couldn't get us at the house. The funeral is set for tomorrow night at 6:00 pm. We wanted it this weekend so more of the club's members could attend and they worked it out for us."

"That's great, honey. Anything we can do for you right now?" Beth asked.

"Not right now. Mom's gone back to the house for a bit, and I'm going to join her there. I think it did her good to come out and sit with y'all for awhile. Make sure all the members know about the funeral as they come in this afternoon, ok?"

"Sure thing, honey," said Beth. "Just let us know if you or your mom need anything. We'll check on y'all in a little bit." Emily grabbed their other towels and pool bag and walked back to her mother's house.

"I'm glad she's here with her mother. I'd be scared to death to know that my husband just got shot, basically in my backyard," Connie commented.

"Yeah, I would be too," Beth added.

"I think she'll be ok. Doug had a .38 that he kept in the house," Jill said.

"He kept a .38?" Carter asked, making sure he heard correctly.

"Yes, sir. He let me and Randy know about it not long after he came here. I reckon Maggie knows how to handle it pretty good too."

'Interesting,' Carter thought to himself.

Carter and Connie sat at the pool until about 2:30, finding out more about Emily, Maggie and the Westlake family's move to Utopia five years ago. Carter was intrigued knowing Maggie had access to a .38; in his mind made her a prime suspect, especially given what he knew about their swinging history. One thing he couldn't figure out, though. No one at the pool seemed to know anything about the Westlake's swinging. At least if they did, it was never brought up. He also knew other bits of the pool conversation would become important to them as their investigation continued and the pieces began to fall together. The more info they had, the more they could tell what fit and what didn't make sense. As an investigator, he always looked for things that didn't make sense.

****

While Connie fixed a couple of sandwiches for lunch, Carter checked his email via his amateur radio and began compiling his notes. Westlake was a successful real estate developer who got out of it to manage a nudist club, moving his wife and daughter the year before she graduated high school. Something about this just

79

didn't add up, on several levels. Carter put a question mark in his notes. The connection with Carolina Couples while Doug was instrumental in getting swingers out of Utopia didn't make sense either. Another question mark. Carter really wanted the answer to that one. He asked himself whether his curiosity about the swingers club was with how it played into this case or because it had an outside the box sexual theme. Carter decided it probably was a little of both, but knew he needed to make sense of the swingers issue in order for this case to come together and move forward. Next, he put in his notes that the Westlakes had a .38 and Maggie knew how to use it. Carter put 'opportunity' beside this note. He wished Taylor's had carried white poster board so he could set up a makeshift murder board in the living room of the Coachmen, but they didn't. Setting up a murder board would have been dangerous, anyway. All he needed was someone stopping by and seeing details of Westlake's murder on a board in his living room. The way people talked around the pool, if one person found out he was looking into the murder, the whole club would know within an hour. That was one way to assure he wouldn't get any information from anyone. He had to keep his investigation secret as long as he could. He knew it would be out of the bag Monday morning, after he and Tedder interrogated Maggie, but by then, he figured he would have all the information he was going to get from his undercover work here. While he could keep his investigation a secret, Carter had to assemble all the information he could get, organize it, and see what questions were left unanswered, what didn't make sense, then proceed to try to find the answers to those questions. Once he did this, he usually understood who the murderer was and why the crime was committed. Then all he had to do was see if the evidence could prove it beyond a reasonable doubt.

Carter had a hard time drinking his beer while eating his sandwich. He never drank on a case, except for the couple of times he went undercover in a bar; and then only to avoid raising suspicion. He didn't want it to dull his senses or cause him to miss a vital detail. It didn't seem to bother him at the pool; after all, he was enjoying his vacation and doing his undercover work at the same time. But here, working on his notes, drinking a beer just didn't seem right. Carter decided, since the beer was open, he would finish it, rationalizing that it was just plain wrong and un-

American to waste a good brew. But he would not have another until his work with the murder notes was completed.

Before they went back out, Carter took one more check of his email. Not long after the radios began their dance, Carter could hear the change in tones, indicating he was receiving an email. 'Tedder or Tony?' he thought, as he waited for the agonizingly slow connection to end and the information to appear on his laptop's screen. As Connie called him a second time to come on, he glanced at the screen to see Tedder

sent him some info on Westlake Realty Corporation, undoubtedly Doug's real estate company before he came here. He'd take a look at it over supper when he had time to study it in more detail. Right now, he didn't want to frustrate that naked lady calling him from outside the front door.

The afternoon and early evening proceeded pretty much as planned. Many club weekenders came in and were shocked to learn of the murder of their friend right here on Utopia property. Not much, if any, new information surfaced. Gil and Mary Ann had returned and invited Carter and Connie over to their place for dinner and a campfire. Carter quickly turned down the dinner part of the invitation, knowing he needed to look at the info Tedder had sent him. But Connie quickly accepted the campfire offer. It had been years since she'd been to a campfire and was quite girlish about accepting the invitation. Carter was glad she did, as it provided an opportunity for him to gather information about the Westlakes.

While Connie fixed supper and drinks, Carter focused on his laptop and opened the email he had received from Tedder. Tedder's information showed that Westlake was making a quarter million per year after taxes in Greeneville before the real estate bubble burst. Carter knew that meant his real income was actually much higher. In 2008,however, Westlake had barely cleared fifty grand and sold his half million dollar home for $350,000, probably a pretty good price considering the real estate climate at the time. Carter could see how the business climate influenced Westlake's decision to come to Utopia, but still couldn't shake the feeling that there was something here he didn't know about yet. 'A man making a quarter million per year just doesn't take a thirty thousand dollar job, unless there's an opportunity associated with it,' he thought. But what was that opportunity, and how was Westlake, who had just lost a hundred fifty grand on his house, going to take advantage of it? Carter surmised, given Westlake's background, this opportunity had to involve real estate.

****

As darkness fell on Utopia, twelve naked couples, a couple of naked single men, and a naked dog brought their lawn chairs and coolers filled with their beverage of choice to Gil and Mary Ann's camper for a campfire. For over an hour, they talked, then someone broke out a joint and began passing it around. Carter immediately recognized the smell of marijuana, as he had been around it in some of his investigations. When the joint came to Connie, she stared at it, looked at Carter, then toked lightly on it. Someone saw her and called out, "Girl, take a hit of that thing." Connie obeyed, drawing deeply on the joint. She then passed the joint to Carter. Carter stared at it; he had never as much as smoked a cigarette, much less marijuana. For Carter, it was gut check time. He had arrested people for using pot because it was against the law, but he never really saw the problem with using it, as long as it was in a setting like he was in now. But it was still illegal, and in the end, retired or not, he was still a cop. He just could not reconcile himself to using an illegal drug. He passed the joint on to the person on his left.

The campfire talk was lighthearted. People seemed to talk in groups; some people discussing the murder, some their weekend plans, others baseball or NASCAR. For Carter, the most interesting topic was when each person began talking about what they did, or no longer did, for a living. Carter saw this not only as interesting conversation, but as an opportunity to get to know more about who these people were in their normal lives. The fact that alcohol and pot lowered their inhibitions didn't hurt either.

"Well, I owned Hartland Trucking," started Randy. "Drove an eighteen wheeler for thirty years. Started out with one truck and ended up with fifty when I sold the whole damn company a few years ago to a big corporation out of Texas for more than the company was worth. Jill and I had gone on a couple of trips to St.

Martin, and decided we wanted to be close to a nudist park and be in a warmer climate than central Ohio. The places in Florida, with their high class attitudes, didn't suit us working types. Hell, I'm a truck driver, not some high class corporate executive. We found Utopia and fell in love with the small town atmosphere of both the club and Herbsville. So here we are."

"Well, I can't touch that," said Gene. "You see, I retired from McDonalds." The whole campfire broke out in laugher, with some saying 'McDonalds?' under their breath. "Yep, Mickey D's, that's me, flipping burgers," Gene laughed. Actually, I worked at the corporate headquarters. I ain't never flipped a burger in my life, just ask Beth. I was a vice president in charge of vendor contracts, making sure we got the best deals on hamburger meat, drink cups, napkins, and those little packs of ketchup. Hell, Beth laughs, saying I couldn't make a hamburger if I tried. But I do know what that special sauce really is."

"Yeah, we do too. Thousand island dressing," blurted out one of the single men.

"Man, I thought it was a bigger secret than that," laughed Gene.

"I'm retired from the Navy," said Gil. "Twenty-five years. Made it to captain. One hell of an adventure, let me tell you."

"And not a bad retirement plan either," added Mary Ann.

"I got to travel all over the world. Spent time in South America, Japan, Korea, the Mediterranean, even visited Australia. Always lived near the ocean. Great life for a single guy, tough on a marriage. Saw many marriages fail, though, somehow mine survived until Sue passed away."

All eyes then turned to Carter. "Well, don't get all nervous now, but this time last week I was a cop." A couple of people laughed. "No, really, I retired last week as a police officer with the Kingsport, Tennessee Police Department." Carter made sure not to use the term 'detective', knowing people would associate police officer with an uniformed cop rather than a detective. Thirty years on the force. And here I am a week later, sitting here nekkid with you rascals."

"You ain't gonna' bust us for that joint, are you, man?" someone asked.

"SWAT team's got the place surrounded right now," laughed Carter. "No, man, I couldn't if I wanted to, I'm retired now." He looked over at Connie with a smile. "Besides, I'd have to bust this wonderful lady right here, and I don't think I could make it without her."

"I'm a retired nurse," Connie announced to the group. "Spent thirty years trying to put the bad guys that Carter busted back together so the DA could throw them in jail."

"Why didn't I get a nurse that looked like you when I was laid up in the hospital?" a man blurted out.

"Because I would have killed you if you had," his wife said as she popped him on the side of his head with an open hand. Everyone laughed.

The conversation continued around the campfire until about midnight. Finally everyone started heading back to their respective campers with their coolers and lawn chairs in hand. Several left with a noticeable, drug induced wobble in their gate. Most everyone at the campfire had a permanent camper site at Utopia, although one other couple besides Carter and Connie was camping in the RV area.

"How was that toke?" Carter couldn't help but ask Connie as they walked with Thor back to the Coachmen.

"I had dreamed of doing that for so long. But I couldn't. I couldn't risk getting caught in a random drug test. Or I couldn't risk getting busted by you. I don't know if I felt anything, but I had to do it."

"Yeah, I know, babe. I have to admit, I thought about it, too. Just couldn't bring myself to do it. Thought it would be too hypocritical of me after having arrested people for doing the exact same thing. And trust me, if I had busted you, you would have enjoyed it."

"Is that right? Did all the women you arrested enjoy it?"

"Only the special ones. And you would definitely have been the most special."

"I love you, sweetie," Connie said and reached up and gave Carter a kiss on the lips as they reached the Coachman.

"I love you too, Cons, more than you'll ever know." He sat the chair down, put the cooler in the seat, then wrapped his arms around her, their naked bodies caressing under the awning of the Coachmen.

"Let's take this inside," whispered Connie.

"Ruff," Thor agreed.

EIGHT

When Carter and Connie walked to the pool the next morning, they couldn't believe how many people were there. They noticed all the activity in the RV and tent camping area; RVs being parked, tents being set up. They knew day guests would come to the club and attend Doug Westlake's funeral that evening. By the time they reached the pool, nearly every lounge chair was taken. Several pre-teen children were playing in one end of the pool and one man was in the water calling out, "Volleyball, volleyball, you lazy bums." Connie spotted Maggie and Emily sitting in chairs near the far corner of the pool area, with an ever-changing crowd offering their condolences gathered around them. Connie tapped Carter on the arm when she spied a couple picking up their towels and vacating their back row lounges. They made a beeline to claim the chairs, as there was little hope for another place to sit.

For Carter, this was the perfect people watching experience. There were people of all ages and sizes hanging out naked, enjoying a beautiful, South Carolina summer day. Some were laying on lounge chairs simply soaking up the sun. Others were engrossed in a book, either printed or on a tablet. Carter could see children coming out of the pool and running to their parent's lounges, wanting something to drink and being handed a boxed fruit drink with a straw emerging from the top. Carter noted a few single men, but most people appeared to be in a couple or a family. Besides the lack of bathing suits, this could have been any other pool in America on a hot Saturday morning. Carter also noticed there were almost no tan lines to be found anywhere. He looked at Connie and saw even she had lost her tan lines. The past few days in the sun, along with lots of sunscreen, had given her bikini lines a nice tan. He knew she would be disappointed because she wouldn't be able to tell how dark she really was without the white lines as a reference point. And she wouldn't be able to show off to all her friends back home.

As the day continued, many water volleyball games were played, with another team always ready to jump in to play the winners. Outside the pool's gates, the cornhole boards were set up and a rousing cheer could be heard when a bag fell through the hole. Several men were deep into what appeared to be the world championship of naked horseshoes. Some clothed teenagers, three girls and two boys, were playing a casual game of horse at the basketball court. At first, Carter thought it odd that the teens were clothed, but then remembered how awkward he felt at that age. Sometimes he still felt awkward, and he was in his fifties.

When Connie noticed the cornhole games, she tapped Carter on the arm. "Hey, sweetie, don't forget we've got a cornhole challenge, you and me. The final leg of the Sykes Naked Athletic Challenge."

"Yeah, I know. Looks like they're all playing teams."

"I'm sure we will be able to find another couple to team up with," Connie said confidently.

"It don't matter, babe, just get ready to take your whuppin'"."

"I don't mind taking a whuppin' from you, sweetie, but it ain't going to be at cornhole," she chuckled.

After three and a half hours of sun, water volleyball, and idle chit-chat with those lying nearby, Connie decided it was time for lunch, so she and Carter took their towels and cooler back to the Coachmen for a bite to eat. Carter walked Thor, then took the opportunity to check his email on his radio.

"Hey, got an email from Tony," Carter called to his wife across the camper after the digital noise subsided and the morse code identification ended. "Looks like he's got some more info on Carolina Couples." He paused while he read the message. "Tony contacted the Greenville PD and it seems that a few years back they used to meet quite regularly at the home of, get this…"

"Doug and Maggie Westlake," Connie blurted out.

"You got it, babe. Seems when Doug sold his house, the group could never find a place to meet. Greeneville area upscale hotels didn't want to rent an entire floor to them. So they started making the drive to Charlotte, where that group had established relationships with an upscale hotel manager."

"So where'd Doug and Maggie go?"

"Looks like they drove to Charlotte for events. I would think it would be kind of hard to leave the people you had been screwing around with cold turkey like that."

"This whole thing just seems odd to me," Connie said, half aloud, half to herself. "How could they go from hosting swingers events in their own home and then come here and clean this place of its swingers problem? There's something that's not right here.

"I agree. It just doesn't add up. There's something we're missing here. But I've got a feeling this is the sixty four thousand dollar question, babe" Carter reached for his murder notebook and jotted down Connie's statement almost verbatim.

"Sixty-four thousand, adjusted for inflation," Connie added.

****

That evening, Doug Westlake's funeral was held at the Morton Funeral Home, in downtown Herbsville. The funeral home was a converted two story brick house, no doubt built by one of Herbsville's wealthy cotton families. The exterior of the house had been restored to its grandeur of one hundred fifty years earlier. The large front lawn was beautifully landscaped and a large oak tree remained its centerpiece. On the right side was a drive leading to the garage where the Cadillac hearse was kept. A wide walkway led from the street through the front yard to the double doors that had been added to aid traffic flow into the funeral home. Inside, the large service room was the focal point, serving as a place where funeral services could be held if the deceased didn't have a church or other place for the service. The upstairs was used for office space, the rest of the house for a casket showroom, and storage areas. The renovator of the house had taken great pains to assure it retained its original identity while being transformed into a modern, functional funeral home.

As they walked toward the front doors, Carter began to focus on the people attending the funeral. He was glad to see the slacks and polo shirt he brought with him 'just in case' didn't look out of place, nor did Connie's long sundress. The only people wearing neckties were the employees of the funeral home. He noticed groups of people gathered together talking, and it wasn't hard to pick out the general topics of conversation; how Doug was murdered, how Utopia would handle losing the General Manager who had saved them from financial doom, how Maggie and Emily would make out, and who all the people attending the funeral were. Carter and Connie nodded and said a low "hello" as they walked past these groups, making their way through the line to greet the widow and daughter, and to view the body of Doug Westlake for the second time.

In true nudist fashion, Doug was buried in his birthday suit. Only half the casket was open, but it was obvious from the half the body didn't have anything on. The mortician did a remarkable job of repairing the hole left in Doug's chest by the fatal gunshots. The body looked at peace, despite the violent way the life that had once lived in it ended. Carter never knew Doug Westlake, and figured the viewing was as close as he'd get to getting a visual of the man whose murder he was trying to solve.

Carter didn't like going to funerals, yet he often attended the service of those whose murder case he was investigating. He always hoped for some insight into the person. He used the time he spent in front of the body to make a vow to the person who had at one time occupied it; to do everything in his power to find the person who ended their life. As Carter viewed Doug's body, he made this vow to him as well. Somehow, Carter felt that Westlake was aware of the silent vow he made while staring at his body.

After viewing the body and walking outside, Carter began noticing that while most of the people at the funeral were from the nudist club, there was a contingent who just didn't fit in with the nudists. These people were not as tanned. Their clothes were fancier, more chic. They weren't talking and mingling with the ones he knew were from Utopia; they stayed in their own group, talking in quiet whispers. He just couldn't put his finger on it, but he knew they were not part of Doug's most recent life as a nudist park manager. Some, he deducted, were people from his life in Greenville as a real estate developer. These weren't hard to spot, talking about knowing Doug and business dealings they had with him. But the whispering group didn't even fit in with them. The women, especially, were dressed more risque than either the Utopia group or the real estate group. Most of them were very well groomed; wearing expensive watches and jewelry.

"I bet those folks are from that swingers club," Connie whispered, moving her eyes toward a group of them without evening moving her head.

"I'll bet you're right," Carter said, a little surprised at Connie's observance and deduction.

"I'm surprised they showed up here," she whispered.

Carter knew that their presence here meant they were much more important to the Westlakes than distant acquaintances, or friends from years gone by. Someone had to tell them of Doug's death. He realized this meant they had an ongoing relationship with the man who had cleaned Utopia of them over the past five years. He also realized solving Doug Westlake's murder was going to take a deeper understanding of Carolina Couples and More than he wanted to think about.

****

Sunday at Utopia was very similar to Saturday up until mid afternoon, when the crowd began clearing out. All the transient RVs pulled out except for the Sykes' Coachmen and a Sandpiper travel trailer. By about 4:00 pm the pool area was down to a couple dozen people. A clothed teenage boy and girl were shooting hoops on the basketball court. Even the vast majority of permanent campers appeared to have been vacated, with no cars in the parking spots. Everyone seemed reluctant to leave, most waiting to put their clothes on until the last possible moment. But each person had to get back to their normal life. Utopia seemed to be just a deviant escape from reality for most of these folks. Come Monday morning, you wouldn't know them from anyone else in society, unless you undressed them and looked for their tan lines.

Carter knew the departure of the crowd meant he needed to get ready for his own trip to town the next morning. He and Connie went back to the camper, but this time Carter had work on his mind. Connie made a drink and offered Carter one, but he turned it down. Seeing the people who didn't fit in at the funeral had raised his interest even more in the Westlake's Carolina Couples connection. As he sat in his recliner trying to jot down some notes for tomorrow morning's interrogation of Maggie, he went over and

91

over in his head the questions he would use to start the conversation about the Carolina Couples. He knew when he walked into Sheriff Tedder's office tomorrow, he had to be ready to get all he could out of Maggie Westlake.

Just as he laid down his notebook to take a break, he heard the now familiar voice of Mary Ann announcing her and Gil's presence at the front door of the Coachmen. "Hey, y'all decent?" she said in her southern drawl.

"No, come on in anyway," Connie answered with a chuckle as she opened the door.

Carter was shocked to see a fully dressed Gil and Mary Ann. He realized he had never seen the two of them with their clothes on. 'They are somebody's next door neighbors most of the time,' he thought. 'I wonder if the neighbors know where they go on the weekends.'

"Y'all leaving?" asked Connie.

"Yeah, we've got to get back for a few days. Just wanted to take a moment to stop in and say goodbye. I know y'all are leaving tomorrow."

"Oh, I hadn't thought about how much I'm going to miss y'all," Connie said.

"Give me your phone number and email and at least we can stay in touch."

Connie and Mary Ann exchanged email addresses and put each other's phone number in their phones while Carter and Gil shook hands and said their goodbyes. Gil told Carter to come back soon, but both men knew it would be a long time before they saw each other again. Finally, Carter and Mary Ann and Gil and Connie exchanged hugs, Gil petted Thor, and they walked to the Chevy Malibu they had parked in the road in front of the Coachmen. The four of them waved goodbye as Gil and Mary Ann drove off.

"I'm going to miss them," Connie said.

"Yeah, me too," replied Carter. "Good folks."

"Yeah, and they really do love each other. They each need the other, and that just brings them closer together. I just wish they would get married."

"Cons, they're happy like they are."

"I know, but still, it would be cool to come back down here for a wedding, wouldn't it?"

"I guess so, babe, I guess so." Carter knew his wife well enough to know that she would start something, even if she had to do it via email and Facebook.

****

Monday morning rolled around and Carter knew Tedder would have Maggie in the office at 9:00 am. He and Connie left Utopia at eight and drove to Herbsville to visit the town's only fast food restaurant, Hardees. Ever since he was a kid, Carter loved Hardees' steak and egg biscuits. It had been a long time since he had eaten one, though. Connie was always after him to eat healthier, and at nearly six hundred calories each, the steak and egg biscuit didn't qualify as healthy. This morning, he was determined to get his fill of them. After devouring his biscuits, he and Connie made their way to the sheriff's office. They parked the Ram behind the building, out of sight of main street. They decided it was best if Connie wasn't involved in the interview/interrogation of Maggie, so she walked downtown Herbsville to do some sightseeing and maybe a little shopping for a souvenir. Carter went inside to wait.

Sheriff Tedder had asked Maggie to come to the office for an update on the murder investigation and she was right on time. As she walked into the Sheriff's office, Carter could tell that she was physically and emotionally drained from the stress of the last few days. While Carter felt sympathy for her and all she was going through, he knew her weariness made his job of extracting information from her easier.

Tedder invited her into his office, which was doubling as the interrogation room. She was surprised to see Carter sitting at the table, and gave him a puzzled look as she took the seat Tedder offered her across the table from him. Carter noticed how smooth and accommodating Tedder was to Maggie. 'The ol' boy's not so bad after all,' he thought, and took Tedder's demeanor as his key to play bad cop.

"Mrs. Westlake, I've asked Mr. Sykes to sit in with us today. As a police detective in Tennessee, he has lots of experience in solving murder cases," Tedder explained Carter's presence. "I'm hoping his experience will help shed some light on your husband's case."

"Good morning Maggie, thank you for joining us," Carter said.

"You're welcome, Carter. What do y'all know about who killed my husband?" she asked, rather matter of factly.

"We're hoping you can give us some information to help us find the killer," Tedder answered.

"How can I do that, sheriff? I told you what I know at the park the morning after...." Her voice trailed off.

"By being honest with us, Maggie," Carter began. "For starters, you didn't tell us that you and Doug had a .38 in the house."

"I didn't think it was important," Maggie replied. "In South Carolina, most people have a gun or two in the house."

"Yeah, most people in Tennessee do too. But usually it's not the same caliber as the murder weapon."

"Well, to be honest, I don't even know where Doug's gun is. I looked for it in the nightstand drawer where I thought he kept it, but if wasn't there. After Doug's body was found, I was going to get it out, just in case the killer came back. but it wasn't there. Doug made me learn how to shoot it, you know. Emily and I looked for it, but we couldn't find it anywhere. Maybe I should go home and take another look around for it."

"Might not be a bad idea," Tedder chimed in.

Carter watched closely. Something in the way she readily admitted to knowing about the gun and being able to shoot it told him that she wasn't hiding anything here Carter had seen her try to cover something up, and this didn't look the same. He kept the gun in the back of his mind, but decided to go after the information he really wanted to know about. "The other day, when we thought Doug was simply missing, I asked you if there was another woman. You said 'no'."

"That's right. Doug wasn't having an affair."

Carter could tell she was choosing her words carefully. "But there's more to this story than you're telling us, isn't there Maggie?"

"No, Doug and I were happily married. He wasn't cheating on me."

"But there was another woman, maybe even other women, wasn't there, Maggie?"

"He was a faithful husband and a good father," replied Maggie, not wanting to lie. She had a bad feeling about where Carter was going with this line of questioning, but she wasn't going to just give anything away. If Carter wanted to know anything, he was going to have to lay his cards on the table. Carter was happy to oblige

"Maggie, we know about Carolina Couples and More. How long did you really think it would take us to find out?"

"Find out about what? What the hell are y'all talking about? Ralph, what's going on here?" She looked to Tedder for support, but the sheriff sat there quietly, letting Carter conduct the interview.

Carter reached behind him and took a small stack of papers off the shelf that tied the Westlakes to the Carolina Couples. He dropped them on the table in front of Maggie. "This is what I'm talking about," he said, a bit more forcefully now. "Carolina Couples is a swingers group, located throughout North and South Carolina; in Charlotte, Charleston, Raleigh, and Greenville. But you already know this, Maggie. Because you and Doug were a part of them, an integral part. When you kept denying the other woman, how long did you really think it would take us to find out there were actually many other women…and men."

"Doug told me there was no way in hell the cops in this little town were going to find out about Carolina Couples." She looked at Tedder as if he were a fifth grader. "I didn't want anyone to know what Doug and I had done in our past life."

Carter quickly realized that she was still denying their current involvement wth the swingers group. "Well, this cop didn't find it," Carter touched his chest with his index finger. "But my partner from Kingsport sure did, Maggie." Carter's tone softened suddenly, "We believe that your ties to the Carolina Couples may have led to your husband's death. We need to know how deeply you were involved in the group. We need to know names of people you were close to. We need to know everything you know about everyone in Carolina Couples. I'll bet there's some connection to Carolina Couples and Doug's death."

"You don't know anything about these people. How the hell can you make a statement like that?"

"I know more about them than you think. Maybe not these exact people, but their type. Trust me when I say I've had firsthand experience here."

"You don't know shit." Maggie was now raising her voice as her face turned red and angered. "Hell, I've fucked these people. I've sucked their cocks and ate their pussies. These are my friends. We swore an oath that what we did was done in private, in complete confidence, that we would protect each other's identity and privacy. Doug would roll over in his grave if I gave you any information about our friends. I'll be damned if I'm going to turn on my friends. These folks did not kill Doug. You're barking up the wrong tree, mister."

"Maybe not, Maggie," Carter said calmly, despite her outburst. "But there's a connection somewhere. I don't yet know what it is, but I will find it. It will be easier to find Doug's killer, regardless of who did it, if you cooperate. If you cooperate, I won't have to waste time looking into all your Carolina Couples friends' private lives. But if you don't cooperate, I will do this the hard way. I've done it for many times, and trust me, I know how."

"Well, you're going to do it without me. Now, am I being charged with anything? Do I need a lawyer? If not, then I'm going home. This is bullshit," she said, as she looked at Tedder.

"No, ma'am, you're not being charged with anything," said Tedder. "We really appreciate you coming down here and talking with us. I'll contact you if there's anything else we need."

"Just get your ass out there and find my husband's killer, Ralph. And get this son of a bitch the hell out of here before I file a lawsuit against the both of you." Maggie grabbed her purse and headed for the door of the sheriff's office.

"What the hell just happened there?" Tedder asked.

"We just got all the information we were going to get from her, sheriff," Carter said with a bit of pride in his voice. We now know that the Westlakes were tied deeply to people within the Carolina Couples. We know these ties go deeper than just a good roll in the hay every now and then; these people really mean something to them. I'll bet my right nut that solving this case is going to involve getting to know more about the Carolina Couples and the role that the Westlakes played, and probably still play, in the group."

"How are we going to find this information out without help from Mrs. Westlake?"

"Somehow, we're going to have to get inside the group. See how it works. Meet the people. If I were still on the force I'd send an undercover cop couple to infiltrate the group. There's always some crazy cops out there looking for weird assignments, they thrive on them. You think Sam Mitchell and his wife might do it?" Carter asked with a straight face.

"You trying to get us both killed, Columbo? Somehow I don't think Sam Mitchell's wife is going to let him eat another woman's pussy in order to solve any murder." They both laughed.

"Give me a few days, I'll think of something. I've only been retired ten days now, not much more than a vacation. I'm not letting this one go, sheriff, paid or volunteer. I stood before Doug Westlake's body and made a promise I'd find his murderer. And that I intend to do."

"Tell me what you need, Columbo. I told you, I'm pretty close to the judge around here. Just keep me informed of what's going on."

"Don't worry, sheriff, I'm on your side here. I'm heading back to Tennessee after I leave here. Here's my cell phone number, it's always on me, as well as my regular email address," Carter said, handing him a business card. "If you come across anything, even minor, let me know. We'll need all the pieces to solve this puzzle."

"Thanks, Columbo. I'm curious; solving this case somehow sounds personal to you."

It is, my friend. Trust me, once we solve this case, I'll explain it all to you."

"Good enough then. Be safe going back to Tennessee."

Carter left the sheriff's office and walked behind the building where he saw Connie coming down the street from her sightseeing trip carrying a bag in her right hand.

"Hey, sweetie, how'd things go," she asked as she came up beside him and grabbed his hand.

"Not as good as I'd hoped, but as good as I expected, I guess. We did get some info to work on. Come on, I'll tell you about it on the way back to the campground."

Carter opened the door for her, and she jumped in the passenger's seat. He walked around to his side and hopped in. They both buckled their seat belts and Carter turned the switch that brought the HEMI to life. As they drove back to Utopia, he filled Connie in on the interrogation of Maggie Westlake.

By the time they got back to the Coachmen, the morning sun had risen in the sky and the Ram's thermometer said the temperature was already an oppressive ninety-three degrees. They had put up the awing and packed up most everything the night before. All they needed to do at this point was to unhook the Coachmen's shore lines and hook it up to the Ram.

"I'm getting out of these things as long as I can," Connie said, as she jumped out of the Ram and pulled her shirt over her head.

"Yeah, it is rather warm," replied Carter as he, too, removed his shirt and reached down to unbuckle his belt.

"I'm going to take Thor for a walk while you get the camper hooked up, sweetie," Connie told him as she stepped out of her shorts and panties.

"Why do you get to walk the dog and I have to do the dirty work?" Carter complained.

"Because of that thing right there," she giggled as she pointed at his penis.

"Sometimes I like that thing, but sometimes it's a pain in the ass," Carter mumbled, purposefully loud enough for Connie to hear.

"That's what I say about it too, sweetie," Connie laughed as she opened the door of the Coachmen and said hello to Thor.

****

98

As they left the park, Carter stopped the Ram in front of the office to see if there was anything they needed to settle before leaving. He left the Ram's engine running as he and Connie walked into the office, both of them fully dressed for the trip home.

"Awh, you guys leaving?" asked Grace, coming from the back room.

"Yeah, got to head back to Tennessee," replied Carter.

"We're going to miss y'all around here. It seems like everyone is leaving this morning. Emily just took off a few minutes ago going back to Spartanburg."

"Already?" asked Connie.

"Yeah, I thought she was staying a couple more days, but she said she had to get back to take care of some things there. I was hoping she'd spend some more time here with her mom, but I guess not."

"Anything we need to do before we leave?" asked Carter.

"No, everything looks good. Just go ahead and make reservations for next time."

"I'll do my best to get him back here," Connie said. "It took me a year this time; maybe it won't take as long to talk him into it again."

"Yeah, I never did get to whup you at cornhole," Carter reminded her.

"Good. Now we have a reason to come back. Grace, take care. I hope we'll be seeing you soon."

"You guys have a safe trip back to Tennessee."

Carter and Connie got back in the Ram and drove toward home. Carter looked at the Westlake's house as they left the park and noticed that Emily's car wasn't there.

"It sure is odd that she'd head back to Spartanburg so soon. I can see it if school was in session, but in June? A part-time or seasonal employer would understand her taking a few days off to be with her mom after her father's murder. Just odd."

"It seems this case has a lot of odd things," Connie commented.

"Yeah, it's different, that's for sure."

"In the end, it will fit together like a jigsaw puzzle," Connie said with confidence in her husband's detective skills.

"It just seems like this one has a thousand pieces," Carter said as he reached for the Ram's radio. He hit a button and the Scorpions' "*No One Like You*" came across the Ram's speakers. Carter turned the volume knob to the right.

Part Two

Just A'Swingin'

NINE

"Where in the hell have you been, man?" Tony Ward asked when he saw Carter Sykes enter his office at the Kingsport Police Department headquarters. "Sending me shit that leads to nudist colonies and swingers clubs. Either you're jerking my chain or you're into something pretty damn deep. I sincerely hope you're just screwing around with me, man."

"Good morning to you too, partner. Awh, we had a great trip, thanks for asking. Cons and Thor are doing just fine. I knew things would be different without me being here. I sure do miss y'all too," Carter replied sarcastically.

"You know what the hell I'm talking about, man. Where the hell have you been?"

"Come on, sit down in your office. We need to talk".

Carter walked into the office behind Tony like he had done so many times over their careers. But this time was different. Carter was not a cop anymore. His retirement seemed to ever so slightly change the relationship between the two men. Carter was a bit more laid back, Tony a bit more down to business. It probably wasn't noticeable to outsiders, but Carter and Tony, who had worked together for the past ten years, could tell the difference. Carter shut the door behind them.

"Ok, what the hell is going on?" Tony demanded once they had settled into his office.

"It's gonna' sound a little funny at first, but it gets serious," Carter explained. He had been thinking of how to open this conversation ever since he and Connie got back home. He recalled how Maggie Westlake tried to skirt the other woman question and determined avoidance wasn't a very viable alternative to use with Tony.

"I'm all ears," Tony said, alluding to the famous Ross Perot line.

"About a year ago, one of Connie's coworkers told her about taking a trip to a nudist camp down in eastern South Carolina.

103

After a year of discussion, we decided it would be our first trip after I retired. So off we went."

"You sly dog. See anything nice?"

"Of course. I was with Cons," Carter smiled.

"Ok, ok, mister perfect husband. This is Tony here. You can tell me. How was it, man? Babes everywhere, right?"

"Oh, there were some great looking gals," Carter recalled the image of Emily Westlake stored in his mind. "But quite honestly, most of them were about our age. Several families with kids down there, too."

"Oh shit, man. Why couldn't my dad have taken me to one of those places when I was fifteen?"

"Because you wouldn't have liked it. Remember how awkward we all were about our bodies back then? Hell, gym class was uncomfortable. All the teenagers tended to hang out together and they all wore clothes, except when they were in the pool. Anyway, the nudity thing really became no big deal. Everybody was naked. It was the freedom that mattered most."

"Ok, so if everything was so innocent, how the hell did the swingers club come into play?"

Carter explained about the Westlakes and their connection with Carolina Couples. He explained about Maggie Westlake's hesitation and then her bucking his questions about Carolina Couples. He went into only as many details as he thought necessary to give Tony the picture of what had happened.

"So you and Cons were running around nekkid, but weren't having sex?"

"Only with each other," Carter smiled.

"With a woman like Cons, that ought to be enough for any man," Tony said, as a compliment to Carter's wife. He decided to move the conversation forward. "So, what do you know about the murder at this point?"

"Well, it's more like I know a lot of shit, but it don't make a whole lot of sense yet. I know Doug Westlake came to Utopia and cleaned the club of its swingers problem, but yet he himself had been, and was until his death, heavily involved in swinging. I know he left a quarter million dollar a year income to take a job making roughly thirty-five thousand. I know the real estate market died but, hey, there was still more money in real estate than what a small nudist park was paying him. I know he took a hundred and fifty grand loss on his half million dollar house in order to make the move. I know he left the nice sized town of Greenville, South Carolina to go to a one horse town like Herbsville. I know Maggie's husband is dead, and she's more concerned with her pact with the swingers than she is in finding her husband's killer. And I know the Westlake's have a gorgeous daughter in a private school studying library science on a nudist park manager's salary. None of this makes sense, yet"

Well, you know, man, when one piece starts to fall into place, the whole damn puzzle will follow suit. And quickly."

"Yeah, but I've got to make that first piece fit."

"Sounds to me like the first place to look is at that swingers club," Tony said.

"I was afraid you were going to say that."

"One thing you ain't found yet, that's the money trail. You know there has to be one. Else Westlake wouldn't have left Greenville. When you find it, and put it together with the sex trail, you'll probably find your killer."

"The money trail," Carter half mumbled, half asked. "You're right. Besides not understanding why Westlake left his job and sold his house, I haven't thought much about the money trail. Hell, I didn't even quiz Maggie about why they left Greenville. I've been looking at it as a crime about sex. It probably has just as much to do with money as it does sex."

"Ahh, my Republican friend. Remember the lessons of my good friend Ross Perot. Follow the money. A man without money is a man who ain't worth killin'. Sounds like this Westlake feller had some kind of plan to make some money. And I would guess some big money."

"Ross Perot never said that. And when did you two become buddies?"

"Maybe not, but he would have if he'd been a detective. Somewhere in this case there's a money trail to go along with the sex trail. And I'll bet it all leads back to when the nudist club was in financial straits. Let's look at what happened. Westlake comes in and somehow straightens out the clubs financial issues. At the same time, he deals with the swingers, while remaining a swinger himself. I might be wrong, but I'll bet somewhere there's a connection. Maggie tried to hide the swinging, but I bet there's some money somewhere she's hiding, too. Find out where the sex and money meet, and I'll bet you find your killer, grasshopper."

"Good thought, Tony. Why didn't I think of looking more closely at the money trail?"

"Because you were in the middle of the fight. You're forgetting, nobody sees the whole picture when they're in the middle of the battle. Remember, the best fighters in the world fight for three minutes. Then they go back to their corners. Why? A break? Hell, they don't need to rest; these guys have trained, or at least should have trained, to fight thirty rounds. They go back to their corners to talk to their managers. They only see what's right in front of them; their manager gets a wider view of what's going on. The manager sees the whole picture. You're too close to this fight, man. Hell, your dog found the body. You're not going to see everything that's going on. Plus, I'm sure the subject matter brings up some personal issues for you."

"I guess you're right, Tony. So it seems now that we have two possible scenarios to follow. First, we look at the swingers club angle, the sex angle. And we also need to look at the money trail. What did Doug Westlake do to get Utopia back on its feet? And why did Westlake take a meager job in a one horse town? What was in it for him?"

"Not we, brother, but you. I've got too much to handle with the KPD. Remember, I had an experienced detective, one of the best in the business, retire on me. I heard he ran off to some nudist colony. I can't be working my cases and one for Andy and Barney too."

"Hey, I understand, man. Let me get Tedder on board with the money trail theory and see what he can get for me. He should be able to access all the records we need to run this down. In the meantime, I've got to figure out how to get access to that swingers group."

"Good luck on that one, man. I'd offer to help with that, but Suzie would have my ass for even mentioning a nudist colony. If I told her about a swingers club she'd cut my dick off and hand it to me in a pickle jar." Both men laughed at the thought.

"Thanks for the help, Tony, but I don't want to see your dick in a pickle jar."

"No problem, man. That's what friends and partners are for. But Sykes, be careful, man. Seriously, be careful. When it comes to either sex or money, people can get violent. Put the two together and it's a powder keg. Someone has already killed one man over this. I doubt they would hesitate to kill again."

"I'm not planning to do anything stupid. I'm retired, remember. No need to put my life at risk."

"Yours or Connie's, man. Keep in mind that she's into this as much as you are.

****

For both Carter and Connie, it was nice to be back in their home. They had a great RV, with lots of room, plenty of creature comforts, and they thoroughly enjoyed most of the places they visited. But as nice as it was, it still wasn't home. Many times they talked about selling their house when they retired and becoming RV nomads. Connie envisioned a life like that of David Banner *of The Incredible Hulk*, roaming around the country, going from town to town, trying to find and control that green monster that lives within. Instead of a backpack, she and Carter would have the Coachmen, pulling it from town to town in search of adventure and greater insight into who they really were. Carter just couldn't bring himself to do it. Perhaps it was having such a nice, middle class home after growing up dirt poor in the Virginia coalfields. Perhaps it was his love of cars, especially Mopars, and he knew he would have to give up his prize automotive possessions if they hit the road. Carter always wanted adventure, but was not going after it by sacrificing the existence and security he and Connie had built over the years. Adventure a week or two at a time was enough to satisfy his itch, at least for now.

When Carter got home, Connie had just returned from the gym. She had made a promise to herself to get into better shape, and she meant to stick to it. Today was her first day at the gym in a couple of months, but she was determined it wouldn't be her last. She really didn't know why she didn't go more often, she now had plenty of time. While she definitely didn't look bad for a woman in her mid-fifties, she knew she needed to tone up. As she came into the house, she removed her shirt, which was still wet with sweat, and her sports bra. She heard the Ram pull into the driveway and decided it would be fun to surprise Carter. She walked into the kitchen, poured herself a glass of diet Coke and walked back into the living room just as the door opened. As Carter walked in, he saw Connie standing there in her black workout shorts, white Nike tennis shoes, and her auburn hair pulled back into a pony tail.

Carter shut the door behind him without taking his eyes off his wife. "I see you're taking this nudist thing seriously, babe."

"Damn straight," she said with a straight face. "Here in a few minutes I thought about mowing the yard, after I get these shorts off, of course."

"Want me to help you get 'em off? I'm sure the neighbors are anxious for you to get started. I bet Clem will grab a beer, have a seat on his patio, and watch," Carter said, referring to his next door neighbor.

"I can handle that just fine, kind sir." They both started laughing. If there was one thing that Carter loved most about Connie, it was her ability to go mano a mano with him when it came to joking about sexual topics. It was rare he flustered her; she could hold her own with just about anyone, under the appropriate circumstances, of course. And for Connie, it wasn't just talk. After all, she was the one who had first kissed Carter. she was the one who initiated their first sexual experience together. she was the one who came up with the idea of going to the nudist park. Carter knew Connie was a very faithful and dedicated wife. Never in their thirty years of marriage had she given him any reason to doubt her. But she was, well, a fun woman. For Connie, sex was something to be enjoyed by a loving couple. And she intended to enjoy it with Carter. If they could enjoy sex together, there was no reason for either of them to stray, she reasoned. And Connie Sykes was going to make damn sure that her man never had a reason to want another woman.

"How's Tony?" she asked.

"He's fine. Just wishes he had seen you at the nudist park."

"Awh, shit. You didn't tell him about our trip, did you?" Connie asked, already knowing the answer.

"Didn't have much choice, babe. If I'd hee-hawed around it, he wouldn't have stopped until he got the answer. I figured the straight forward approach was best."

"Yeah, but now he'll never let me live it down. Every time I see him, all I'll hear about is getting naked."

"Well, just nip him in the bud. When he starts, just invite him and Suzie over for a nudist party. He'll squirm out of that one real quick.

"Yeah, not a bad idea. But I'm just afraid you'd egg him on. It wouldn't bother you to see Suzie naked."

"Listen, I saw Emily Westlake naked. If I can handle that, I can handle just about anything."

"Well, you've got a point there. That girl was drop dead gorgeous. She could be in movies."

"And yet she's in library science. Another thing that doesn't make sense to me."

"Does everything have to make sense to you, sweetie?"

"It always does, Cons. In the end, it always does. If it doesn't make sense, then there's something wrong with the story. And if there's something wrong with the story, then I'm missing something."

"Well, what did you and Captain Pervert decide about the Westlake case?"

"Basically, there's two angles to this whole thing. Tony actually recognized the money angle. 'Follow the money trail,' was his mantra. I'm going to get 'hold of Tedder and see if he can use his resources as sheriff and father-in-law of the judge to get the information we need to check into the financials of all involved, including Utopia. Then, of course, there's the sex and swingers side of this case. You know, nothing excites violence like sex and money, except for money and sex. Somehow, we've got to find out what is going on inside the Carolina Couples and how Doug and Maggie continued to fit into the group after he began cleaning house at Utopia. Tony agrees there's a good chance the answer to the murder lies there. He figures the money and sex are somehow connected. He thinks when we find where the two trails intersect, we will find our killer."

"Can you get a couple of undercover cops to infiltrate the Carolina Couples?" she asked.

"Maybe, if I was a cop and if the case was in my jurisdiction. But I'm not a cop anymore. I don't have access to undercovers. And Tony can't pull any for me, this is a South Carolina murder. It's not in his jurisdiction. And somehow I don't think Sam Mitchell's wife is going to go undercover to a swinger's club with him."

"Not from what I hear about her, anyway," she laughed.

"We've got to find a way inside their group in order to get to the bottom of this case. I just don't know how."

"Well…if you want something done right….," Connie stopped her thought.

"What are you suggesting, Cons?"

"Well, we do have plenty of time on our hands now that we're both retired. And we're not that old yet, are we? Is there any reason why we can't become a Carolina Couple, at least long enough to get inside the group? I'm not advocating we have sex with other people. I'm just saying that we could become the undercover cops we need to solve this case. I bet Rock and Susan would do it."

TEN

"Not just no, but hell, no," Carter said, as forcefully as he knew how.

"Why not?"

"Connie, you're talking about a swingers club. Do you know what these people do?"

"Yeah, I know, sweetie. And I'm definitely not advocating having sex with other people, no way! But we can go, watch what's going on, and try to get the information we need. What's the worst that can happen?"

"It's not that simple, Cons. These folks just don't let you walk in the door. And they sure as hell don't just start talking to perfect strangers. Now they might fuck a perfect stranger, but they're not going to start giving out secrets. Of course they could find out who we are and why we're really there. Now that would be pretty, wouldn't it?."

"I didn't say we wouldn't have to do our research. But I think we could pull it off. If we don't succeed, well, what have we got to lose?"

"Ask Doug Westlake," Carter reminded her.

"Oh, I hadn't thought about that." Connie's enthusiasm waned a bit.

"I know you haven't, babe," Carter softened his tone. "The person or persons who killed Westlake could very well be a part of the Carolina Couples. If we are even able to get in the door and show up asking questions about his murder, do you seriously think they would just let us walk away, especially if we started getting close? Remember, I'm not on the force anymore. I don't have backup."

"Probably not." Connie realized Carter made sense. "I'm just trying to find a way that we can solve this case. We need to find out more about the Carolina Couples. It just makes logical sense that we try to get in and find out more."

"Well, it doesn't to me. Some of these people are just perverts. But some are the crème de la crème of society. They didn't get there by letting people just walk in and get the information they want. They got there by being ruthless. A person getting in their way is not another person; he's something to be dealt with. I know these types all too well, honey."

"Ok, sweetie, ok. Don't get so worked up. It was just a suggestion."

" I'll talk to Tedder. Maybe he has access to a pair of undercovers who can help us infiltrate the Carolina Couples. Maybe the state of South Carolina can supply a couple."

"Ok, sweetie." Connie saw this conversation wasn't going the way she had hoped and knew it was time to change the subject. "How 'bout I fix us a drink. Maybe we can take off our clothes and play Utopia?"

Carter shook his head and grinned. "What am I going to do with you now? Next thing you know, you'll have us selling the house and building one in one of those nudist neighborhoods Utopia was planning."

"Well now, you may have come up with a pretty good idea." A smile crossed her face.

"Oh no. You ain't putting that idea off on me. I think we'll be fine right here."

"Well, have you at least thought about a privacy fence or hedge for the backyard? I kind of like not having any tan lines." She glanced down at her newly tanned breasts.

"Well, apparently you've thought about it," he laughed. "And yes. I am enjoying your tanned boobs. You could be my new superhero, Naked Woman."

"Naked woman, huh? And where would my NW go?"

"On your headband, of course," Carter said, starting to form a new comic book character in his imagination.

"And what would my super powers be?"

"You'd be able to stop any man dead in his tracks. Let's see..." Carter thought for a second. "...a crook is committing a crime. In pops Naked Woman. Boom, it's over. He's so stunned by her beauty, he can't move a muscle. You call the cops on your special watchphone and they take him off to jail."

"And who would you be?"

"Me? Hmm, I'd be your loving husband who has no idea of your secret identity. I'd think you were just a mild mannered housewife while in reality you were out saving the world." Carter pauses a second. "And of course I'd be the cop who always shows up to arrest the crooks you catch. I'd never recognize that you were Naked Woman because of your super powers. Hey, look what a pair of glasses did for Clark Kent."

"Could be truer than you think, sweetie," Connie said, holding her arms out in front of her, like superman flying.

"Don't think I don't know it," Carter said with a sense of pride in his wife. "I guess I better at least think about that hedge then."

"Better hurry before I lose this tan. Naked Woman's powers go away if her boobs turn too white."

"Is that right?"

"Makes sense to me," Connie said. "Let me get those drinks."

****

"You mean to tell me you can't get access to any undercovers to infiltrate the Carolina Couples and try to get the information we need to solve a murder?" Carter Sykes asked Sheriff Tedder over the telephone; his frustration evident in his voice.

"I'm telling you, Columbo, I would have to pay for them out of the Herbsville sheriff's budget and there's no way I can do that. If I were trying to solve the murder of a regular citizen, maybe, but not for trying to solve the murder of the head of that nudist colony. Most of the county would just as soon see the whole damn place closed down, anyway. I want to solve this case; I don't want this murder on my record. But I can only do what I can do. I can get you the financial records you want; that's not a big issue. But I can't afford to spend a ton of money on undercover cops. Especially not in this economy. Everyone is watching every penny that's being spent. Now if you can tie this murder to Homeland Security, that's a different story. But nudists and swingers? That ain't gonna fly in Herbsville, South Carolina."

"Alright, alright. I understand. We've been fighting budget cuts here in Kingsport for the last five years now. Remember, this

113

here ain't New York City either. We're just a small city making it on coal and Kodak. Obama's against coal and there ain't nobody buying film anymore. Sounds like we need to come up with some angle where these swingers are a threat to national security then?"

"Maybe Ron Jeremy can dream us up a scene," Tedder laughed. "While I'm waiting on Ron Jeremy, I'll try to get the financials on Utopia and the Westlakes. Let's hope there's something in there that can help us and we don't have to worry about the swingers."

"I hope so, Tedder, but I'll bet we have to put together both the swingers and the money angles to this murder. When we find where these two trails cross, we will find the killer. Thanks for doing what you can."

"No, Columbo, thanks for all your help. Like I said, I wouldn't be this far without you. Keep working with me. Let's see what we can do."

"Ok, Tedder. Get me the financials. We'll see what we get. Goodbye."

"Watch for my email. Talk to you soon, Columbo."

Carter hung up the phone and hung his head. He knew he might get some info from the financials he requested from Tedder. But he was sure that information would point back to the Carolina Couples. He knew, somehow, he was going to have to find a way into that organization. But how?

****

Back at home, Carter Sykes, now retired, had to figure out what to do with himself. Sure he had the Westlake case to work on, but it was three hundred miles away. What he could do on it was limited by both distance and access to information. He hadn't really considered his daily post-retirement life; his life had always revolved around his work schedule. He thought he'd have time to play on his ham radio and have real conversations with people all over the world, more than just the "59 QRZ" he usually heard in contests and from DXpeditions. But as nice as it was to talk to foreign countries at four in the morning or two in the afternoon, there was only so much chair time a man could take, especially a man who had always been active. After thirty plus years of ham radio, most of the countries he still needed to work were uninhabited places that would require a DXpedition, a group of ham radio operators visiting such a place just to make contacts from it. Carter thought that one day he might like to go on a DXpedition, but that didn't make his everyday life more exciting.

So, at Connie's urging, Carter began to actually think about either a hedge or a fence for the back yard. He had to admit, Connie's tanned body was pretty sexy. It was strange seeing her with a golden tan all over. He was sure by her comments and actions they would be taking the Coachmen back to a nudist park in Florida again; maybe to one of the big resorts like Cypress Cove or Lake Como. Maybe as soon as this winter. Even he could use a break from the cold and snow. He would like to be able to keep a little of his all over tan as well. So he thought about the fence. He would walk outside and walk off where the fence would go, only to think about his neighbors wondering what the hell he was doing putting a fence around his backyard; and what he was doing behind that fence. 'Who the hell cares what they think,' Carter would say to himself. 'I reckon I do,' he'd answer back.

Other bits of his spare time had focused on the Carolina Couples. He had gone to their website and looked around at least a half dozen times. He was hoping against hope for something that would help him in the Westlake investigation, but knew he wouldn't find anything. He saw the basic information that Tony had provided. They seemed to have three distinct groups; the Charlotte group, the Charleston group, and a group in the Raleigh/Durham area. They rotated their meetings between the three locations, with occasional meetings elsewhere. For instance they had an event planned in Blowing Rock, North Carolina in July, a location which affirmed Carter's thoughts of the ritziness of the group. It seemed the Charlotte group had an arrangement worked out with an upscale local hotel where they could rent an entire floor one weekend per month for an event. In Charleston they owned a house that was their 'play house'. Here, they charged a cover charge and had food and alcohol for sale on site. If a couple was going to get into their scene, this was probably the easiest, since the Carolina Couples were basically running a business from this location. They wouldn't want to turn down the money. In the Raleigh area they had a couple of hotels they alternated between, but something told Carter that their relationships with these hotels wasn't as strong as in Charlotte. According to their schedule of events, it appeared they had to dodge University of North Carolina, NC State, and Duke football and basketball weekends. 'Only God knows why,' Carter thought, 'The three of them put together can't hold a candle to the Tennessee Volunteers.'

Why he kept looking at their site he really wasn't sure. After the second time he knew there wasn't anything there. He had been through all their information and even looked at most of the profiles of couples that were open to public view. Most of the profiles were available only to members. Perhaps he was simply trying to find out all he could about their group, with the hope that something he would learn would help him in the Westlake case. Hell, he had even read reviews of the group on several swingers' websites. Most every piece of information on them had came up on his web searches, not on their site. He even found an archived news story aired several years ago by a Raleigh TV station entitled Raucous Raleigh. He kept telling himself information was all he was after, but he knew all too well he wouldn't find what he needed on the internet. What he really needed was to get inside the Carolina Couples.

But he knew there was no way in hell he was going into anything like this with Connie. Sure, he had enjoyed their nudist experience immensely, mostly from being able to spend time naked with her. But nudism and swinging were far from being the same thing. In nudism, people were simply without clothes, doing the same things they'd do on any other camping trip anywhere else in the country. They were just doing them naked. The whole time they were at Utopia, no one tried to hit on Connie. If anything, people were more careful about their words and actions than in a clothed environment. They played putt-putt for God's sake. At these swingers clubs, the idea was to have sex with somebody, pure and simple. And preferably somebody who wasn't your spouse. This wasn't Carter, and he knew damn well it wasn't Connie either. They were college sweethearts and had been together their entire adult lives. He wanted her desperately, but he didn't want anyone else. He knew she didn't wanted anyone else either. She liked to

116

play, to joke, and to have fun. She liked to prod him a little bit when it came to sex, but mostly because he had grown up sheltered and remained relatively shy about the subject. To be honest, he loved her sexual playfulness, even thought it embarrassed him at times. It made him feel wanted, loved. And while he had finally agreed to go to the nudist camp for the experience, to say he had done it, he knew neither he nor Connie would ever cross that boundary and have sex with anyone else. That was a sacred bond between the two of them.

'So why am I still on the Carolina Couples website?' Carter kept asking himself. 'Because I need to get inside the group to get the information I need to solve this murder,' he kept answering.

****

Connie was delving into the internet presence of the Carolina Couples herself. Carter's warnings to her had been stern. But she was no internet rookie; she realized the outward appearance this group carefully placed on their website was their public appearance. Even a car salesman, specializing in crappy used vehicles, made his cars out to be the best value on the market in his ads. But deep in her heart, she knew this murder investigation she and Thor had unleashed when they discovered the body of Doug Westlake provided her a chance to help Carter solve a crime, a murder at that. In reality, for years she had secretly dreamed of her and Carter being a team like *McMillan and Wife*. She didn't want to be the unseen wife in the Columbo series; she wanted to be Carter's partner in solving this crime.

Moreover, she thought they could really pull off this swingers thing. No, she would not have any form of sexual relations with another man, or woman. She was Carter's; she had been since their first kiss. She had been in love with him for her entire adult life; if she was honest with herself, she knew she loved him even before that first kiss. She knew even though they were in their fifties now, she still looked pretty damn good. And while Carter was an average looking fifty something man, she knew he'd clean up well. With a few expensive touches, which he always denied her the opportunity to provide him, she could make them out to be a well-to-do couple out for adventure. She knew they could pull this thing off, and do it without sacrificing their marriage. In fact, getting through it might even make their trust in each other, and their bond, stronger, she reasoned. All she had to do was convince Carter to help her come up with a plan.

Connie clicked on the 'Upcoming Events' button on the Carolina Couples website and saw they were meeting for their 4th of July bash in Charlotte. Connie read the itinerary. Dinner and drinks in the hotel restaurant Saturday evening. A 'meet and greet' would follow at the bar. This all seemed innocent enough. Afterwards, the party would start. She concluded that's when the activities would begin. Connie had a pretty good idea what those activities would be. She thought this itinerary provided the perfect opportunity to get to know some of the people in the Carolina Couples, especially during the meet and greet. She envisioned them getting a room in order to fit in. She knew they had to fit in. they could always return to their room when the 'activity' reached a point that they were not comfortable. 'Get our information and get the hell out,' she thought. She thought they could pull this off without being recognized as 'narcs'. She had no doubt Carter, with his years of experience in law enforcement, would do just fine.

The main thing would be getting the information they needed in one visit. She realized they might not get another chance. From what she read on the website, she thought they might be a little patient with them since it was their first visit with the group. But she knew if they had to go back again for more information, someone would start pushing them to join in, to do something they weren't prepared to do. She knew they had to play their cards right the first hand. There was little room for error. She had three days to convince Carter to actually do this. Three days to get ready for their crime fighting adventure. Now she had to lay out a plan to convince Carter. She had always heard the way to a man's heart was through his stomach, so it was time to fix his favorite dinner in the world. Then she would lay out her case for infiltrating the Carolina Couples.

Connie thought about emailing the Carolina Couples on their 'Information' link, but decided it was best for her to wait until Carter was onboard with the idea. She didn't want to make a mistake and say something wrong or ask the wrong questions. She didn't want to give Carter any additional reason to say no. Besides, she knew that he would know how to handle the details of their undercover escapade.

She knew what her next move had to be. Within minutes she was headed to Food City, where she picked up everything she needed for two of her husband's favorite dishes; oysters and fried yellow squash. She didn't eat oysters, so she added in some shrimp for herself, and some slaw to go with the dinner.

. Carter was across the mountain in Boone, North Carolina, taking a look at a '58 Plymouth Fury he had come across. At first, she couldn't understand why he kept talking about Christine. So he explained to her a '58 Fury was the car from Stephen King's book, and the movie, of the same name. She should have known. Carter had tricked her into going to watch the movie on their honeymoon. Who in their right mind wanted to see a horror movie about a car on their honeymoon? 'Carter Sykes, that's who,' she laughed under her breath. She knew Christine would take him away for most of the day, so she figured she had until early evening before he got home. By 5:30 she finished the last of the squash and it was a good thing, she heard Thor bark as the Ram pulled into the drive.

"Wow, is that fried squash I smell?" was the first thing out of Carter's mouth when he walked into the house.

"Yep, sure is, sweetie. I figured you deserved it." She came around the corner wearing nothing but her oversized "beep beep" shirt with a picture of the cartoon Road Runner on it. Carter had bought this for her when he and Tony attended the MOPAR rally in Carlisle, Pennsylvania a couple years ago. She knew after spending the day looking at Christine, it would get his attention. She was going to pull out all the stops on this one.

Carter stared at his wife. "I'm surprised you're wearing road runner. I expected to find you au natural."

"Well, I have been cooking a little bit. But I can remedy this situation if you prefer." she reached her hands down and grabbed the bottom of the shirt.

"No, no, babe, that's ok. You know I've always thought you looked so sexy in that shirt."

"You'd think Aunt Bea was sexy if she was in something associated with MOPAR."

"Probably," he laughed. "She'd have looked pretty damn good driving down the road in that Fury I saw today." Carter nodded his head.

"Here I am, slaving in the kitchen, fixing your favorite supper, and you're out dreaming of Aunt Bea driving around in a Plymouth Fury. What am I going to do with you?

"I'm sure you'll think of something. You always seem to."

"I'll do just about anything it takes, sweetie." A big smile formed on Connie's lips as Carter came over to her and gave her a passionate kiss.

"Ok, I know something's up. I don't get fried squash every day."

"And oysters, too."

"Oh, no. I'm in deep trouble now."

"Probably. Now come on in and let's eat while it's still fresh." Connie grabbed Carter's hand and turned around, leading him into the kitchen.

Over supper, Connie laid out her plan to infiltrate the Carolina Couples. At first Carter kept interrupting her and she kept responding with "Hear me out, sweetie. Just hear me out." She wasn't going to give up easily. Playing to his cop ego, she stressed that she knew they could do this, but it would take his years of experience at such operations while on the force.

After his initial interruptions, Connie began to lay out her thoughts as he ate. Now, instead of interrupting her with objections, he interrupted her with "umms' and comments about how great the dinner was. Connie persisted, and by the time they finished dinner, she had laid her plan out to him. He still didn't think she recognized the danger involved. He was glad she hadn't sent off the email for information, as they couldn't afford to be recognized by anyone in the Carolina Couples; especially someone who may have seen them at Utopia. He tried to scare her by telling her that if something went wrong, getting out of there wouldn't be their only problem, staying alive after getting back home could very well be a bigger issue. He reminded her the person who killed Doug Westlake didn't do it at a swing club, but did it at his home, in his own backyard. But as he listened to her plan, h e realized it was their best shot at getting the information they needed on the swingers group. He knew Connie was smart and could handle herself. But he also knew their best laid plans could go wrong. All it would take was the wrong person in the wrong place at the wrong time. His mind began thinking how to minimize any danger. It seemed Connie had worked most of the plan out, all Carter needed to do was touch up the fine details. He knew Tony would help them get the fake identities they would need in order to keep from being recognized in background checks. The big question was, was he actually willing to go along with Connie's plan? Was he willing to actually participate in a swingers event? With Connie? He knew the dangers all too well. He knew he could be putting his wife face to face, or worse yet, cunt to cock, with a cold blooded killer. He knew damn good and well the word rape didn't exist at a swing club, everyone was there to fuck, nothing less. Except him and Connie, which made it even more dangerous.

But he also knew he kept looking at the Carolina Couples website. He realized he and Connie going in themselves was probably their only chance to get the information they needed to piece together Doug Westlake's murder. The question was, is solving a murder case worth the risk? Carter knew he might also have to wrestle with some personal demons, demons he hadn't dealt with in many years. Demons Connie wasn't even fully aware of. In the end, he knew he had to give it a try, especially with Connie so gung-ho about the operation.

As Connie finished her plea, Carter said, "Babe, if you're serious, really serious, we'll give this a go. I don't see much other way to move forward with this investigation. But we're going to do this right. We'll get Tony to set us up with fake ids. We'll get the info we're looking for, and we'll get the hell out of there. When I say 'let's go', we go, no matter what. Ok?"

"Sure, sweetie. I trust you or I wouldn't even think of this. But we can do this, I know we can. We can solve this murder. I've wanted to be a part of one of your cases for years, and now I've got my chance. I'm not going to blow it by being stupid."

"Alright then, babe, let's so swingin'."

ELEVEN

After supper, Carter sat down at his computer to check his email. He was expecting an email from Sheriff Tedder with the financials he needed on the Westlakes and on Utopia. Tedder did not disappoint. In the middle of ten messages in his inbox was one from "Sheriff Ralph Tedder". Foregoing the others, Carter clicked on Tedder's.

....

Hello, Columbo. Hey, I'm a poet, "hello Columbo", get it? Here are the financials you wanted on the Westlakes and on the Utopia Sun Club. Very interesting. I'm no financial expert, but even I can sense something fishy here. Let me know what you think or if you need anything else.

Sheriff Ralph Tedder

....

Carter saw two attachments, one for the Westlakes and one for Utopia. He opened the one for the Westlakes first. In the file, he saw Tedder had gone back six years, prior to Westlake moving to Herbsville. This was good thinking on the sheriff's part,. 'The ol' boy has more sense than he gives himself credit for,' Carter thought. The extra year would give Carter a picture of what Westlake's financial life was before the economic downfall and the move to Herbsville. He clicked on Utopia's attachment and saw the same thing, a six year history. This would allow Carter to examine the mess the nudist club was in before Westlake came in and got them out of trouble. Carter typed a quick reply:

....

Thanks Sheriff. Let me look these over and see what I can get out of them. I'm not a financial expert either, but I've been through

123

quite a few cases that relied heavily on financials over the years. If I have questions, I've got a resource or two at the department I can use. I'll be in touch soon.

BTW, we're devising a plan to get inside that swingers club. Hopefully, with the financial info and what we learn from the swingers club, we can figure this thing out.

Carter

....

Carter almost added "Detective, Kingsport Police Department" to his signature line, but caught himself in time. It felt strange not doing so. It was now a fact of life; he was no longer a cop. He knew he had to accept that fact, at some point.

Carter began looking over the Westlake's financial report. The federal income tax returns showed in 2007 they brought in over a quarter million dollars in taxable income. This wasn't news to Carter, but Carter noted the amounts he had written off pushed their gross income to somewhere in the half million dollar range. Carter felt a tinge of jealousy, he and Connie combined hadn't made a fifth of that. Brokering a commercial development near Anderson, South Carolina and a new residential development near Landrum accounted for a big chunk of that income. Carter guessed those guys who invested in those projects in '07 now wished they had their money back. Westlake's income fell sharply in '08 as the real estate crisis took hold. His pre-tax income fell to one hundred grand, and by the end of the year he was dipping into his savings to pay the mortgage on his half million dollar house. It looked like '09 left Westlake with a pre-tax income of seventy –five grand, from the closure of his real estate development business and his pro rated thirty-five thousand dollar income as the General Manager of Utopia, a position he assumed in May. Funny, he really hadn't lost anything from the sale of his home, which Carter assumed he had taken a beating on. Seemed Westlake had bought the house at a steal in 2004 and the loss he took was from its peak value of a half million in 2006, not from what he paid for it. He actually got a pretty good price for it in early '09, given its market value. He was obviously pretty good at working deals in the real estate world. From there on, his income was pretty steady at thirty-five grand per year, plus the money he made from stock sales as the markets recovered. Westlake had been smart enough to buy quite a few stocks when the Dow hit seven thousand, knowing it would eventually come back. Upon noticing the stock purchases, Carter realized that the money coming from savings was not to pay bills, but rather to invest in stocks. He thought back to how he had contemplated investing in the market at that time, but was afraid to take the risk. 'That's what separates the rich from the middle class,' he thought.

Except for the change in profession, nothing looked out of place. Westlake looked squeaky clean. Too much so for a man grossing over a half million per year with half that money going into deductions, Carter decided. But one question kept nagging Carter. How did Westlake find out about the Utopia job? Carter couldn't find anything linking him to nudism prior to him taking the position, not even an American Association of Nude Recreation membership. He did see many financial links to the Carolina Couples, though. Moreover, his Carolina Couples ties continued long after his arrival at Utopia and his cleaning the club of swingers. 'Odd, to say the least,' Carter thought.

Next, Carter opened the financials of the Utopia Sun Club. The first thing he examined was the tax mess of 2007 and 2008. 'Wow,' thought Carter. 'This was one hell of a mess.' Local property taxes not paid. State sales taxes were not only not paid, but the required reports were not filed. Federal and state withholding forms were not filed and the taxes weren't paid. Carter saw where Utopia had failed to even file federal or state income tax returns for a couple of years. 'How was it that one of the branches of government didn't come in and take this place over?' Carter thought. He knew the local government wanted the nudist club shut down; surely they would have come in and taken the land for the taxes owed. A quick tap of a few keys on his adding machine told him that by the end of 2008, the Utopia Sun Club owed a total of thirty thousand dollars in back taxes alone. Add in penalties, fees, and interest and the amount owed to governmental agencies totaled over a hundred grand. A quick look at the club's income showed the club didn't have the revenue stream to pay that money.

It appeared the land the club itself was located on was owned outright by the club, no mortgages or liens. But in 2004, the club bought an adjoining one hundred acres of land. Carter assumed this was the land the club planned to develop into the nudist community they learned about during their visit. The land was financed at a bank in Darlington. That a local institution didn't handle the financing would have been interesting, except Carter knew no bank near Herbsville would finance anything for Utopia; they all wanted the club gone, not expanding their land holdings. Cater also noticed the selling agent was from Charleston, again making sense, since he doubted any local agent would even accept an offer from Utopia, regardless of their legal obligation to do so. They owed approximately twenty thousand dollars on this land at the end of 2008. Carter noted that despite not paying their taxes, the club had done an excellent job of paying off the mortgage. The original loan had been eighty grand in 2004. "Why would they pay ahead on the mortgage and forego paying the taxes?" Carter mumbled his question to himself.

The next thing Carter saw was where the land designated for the nudist community was sold to The Dawson Corporation for forty thousand dollars right after Doug Westlake came aboard as General Manager. 'Dawson got a steal,' Carter thought, 'even with land prices being depressed at that time. How the hell did a real estate developer like Westlake let that happen?' The Dawson Corporation had apparently paid cash for the land and Utopia, with all it's financial issues, needed the cash. 'Still yet, one would have thought that a man with Westlake's real estate experience would be able to get a better price for that land, especially after what he had done with his house,' Carter thought, while pondering the transaction. There was no indication who the Dawson Corporation was or what they intended to do with the land. Carter also found this odd, as he would have thought Utopia would want to know who their new neighbors were, regardless of their financial straits. After all, they wouldn't want BMW building a plant next door to their nudist park. That would shut them down quicker than the tax man. Carter figured Westlake had some knowledge of The Dawson Corporation. He could smell a rat somewhere here.

126

Carter ran a quick web search, but only pulled up a lot of references to *Dawson's Creek*, nothing for the Dawson Corporation. He got a gut feeling he would have to obtain info about Dawson in order to find Westlake's killer.

In what appeared to Carter to be a small miracle, Westlake apparently worked out a deal with all levels of government to settle with Utopia for actual taxes owed. The feds, the state, even the locals, had waived any interest or penalties against the club. That meant the twenty grand equity the club received from the land sale paid off all but ten thousand dollars of their tax obligations. But where did the other ten grand come from? Carter found a ten grand deposit during '09, not long after Westlake came on board, but oddly, no indication as to where, or who, it came from. Apparently, Utopia had someone who wanted to see it stay afloat bad enough to donate ten grand, anomalously, or course.

As Carter continued to study Utopia's financials, more questions came to light. From his conversations at the pool, he thought the club was doing well now. But the financials showed new tax liens filed against the club just in the past three months. These liens were for taxes going all the way back to 2010. He looked at the bank statements and saw where the club was paying the taxes. Every quarter, a check for taxes was paid to Sam Collins, a CPA that a quick Yahoo! search showed was in Rock Hill, South Carolina. Carter realized Westlake probably wouldn't have trusted anyone locally and figured Collins and Westlake had business ties previously. But what was Collins doing with this money? He obviously wasn't paying Utopia's taxes with it. And knowing that the money had been paid, why didn't Westlake do something about it when he got the first tax notice? 'Or maybe he did and got murdered for it,' Carter thought. There was definitely more to this money trail than he had expected to find.

As he was getting ready to make some notes on the next round of financial information he wanted Tedder to get a warrant for, he looked up and was shocked to see Connie standing at the door to his home office. She was totally naked, with her right hand on her hip, her left hand by her thigh. "Do you realize it's after midnight, sweetie?" she asked him. Carter looked her over and again noted her lack of tan line. For Carter, Connie standing there was one of the most beautiful sights he had seen anywhere. He glanced at the clock on his computer screen. "Oh, man, no I didn't, babe." I guess I just got caught up with these financial reports."

"That's ok, sweetie. Come on to bed, we've got a big day tomorrow."

"What kind of big day? I don't know of any plans?"

"You'll see tomorrow. Now come on to bed," she sounded more forceful than before.

"I'll be there in a few minutes. Let me finish thus thought."

"Alright, but don't make me come back in here again." Carter knew he better not.

As Connie walked away, Carter closed Utopia's financials and hit reply on the email from Tedder.

....

Thanks Sheriff. Very interesting info, especially on Utopia. Any idea who this Dawson Corporation, the group that bought Utopia's land, is? Any idea what they intend to do with this land? I'd love to take a peek at their financials as well. We need to know more about them. It might answer a few questions. And we need to take a closer look at Sam Collins; the CPA in Rock Hill who it appears was supposed to be making the tax payments for the last three years. If you can get me his financials we can find out where Utopia's tax money is really going.

Connie and I have some undercover work to do this weekend. I'll try to get you a full report of where we are in the investigation early next week.

Carter

....

He hit the send button and closed out of Outlook Express. He was tired, and he definitely didn't want to face the wrath of Connie coming back to get him. He walked to the kitchen, grabbed a quick drink of Diet Dr. Pepper straight from the bottle, and went to bed.

TWELVE

The next morning, Carter and Connie arrived at the Kingsport Police Department and found Tony Ward interrogating a man involved in an assault the night before. Carter knew these things usually didn't last long. It wasn't like a murder case where the person being questioned was facing life in jail, or worse. Typically someone facing a lesser crime like assault would cave quickly in the hands of a skilled detective, either confessing or spilling the beans on someone else. Interrogation had been Carter's strong suit during his career. He enjoyed having a suspect in the hot seat and probing into the criminal's mind for the answers he needed. He knew Tony was a more than capable interrogator as well and could handle this one just fine. He and Connie made themselves at home in Tony's office and waited. Fifteen minutes later Tony walked into the room and dropped the file he was carrying on his desk.

"Connie, what a pleasant surprise," Tony said enthusiastically.

"Hey, Tony," replied Connie with a smile. "Are you having fun in interrogation?"

"Not until I saw you. My day just got a thousand percent better. I think I do need to interrogate you, though."

"You know I've been interrogated by the best." She looked over at Carter. "I'd just plead the fifth. And probably lawyer up too."

"Yep, that's what she'd do all right, lawyer up." Carter said, remembering how he always tried to work her in their arguments, only to have her end the discussion.

"Oh, hello Carter. I guess I was mesmerized by your beautiful wife." He looked back at Connie.

"Yeah, I know the feeling," Carter said. He really did know what Tony meant. "I've been mesmerized by her for a long time. Hey, we need your help."

"What can I do for my partner?"

"Remember I told you about trying to find some undercovers to go into that swingers club? Well, that ain't going to happen. So we're left with two choices; forget it, or do the job ourselves.

129

Looks like Cons and I are going to be a couple on the wild side, this weekend."

"You're not seriously considering going to a swingers club, are you?" Tony knew his partner and already knew the answer.

"We're not going to have sex with anyone, if that's what you mean. But we've got to find out more about this club and its connection to Utopia. All we need from you is for you to set us up with fake identities."

Tony Ward did all he could to try to dissuade Carter and Connie from their plan. Finally, after realizing they were intent on going through with it, and he was convinced they had carefully thought through the plan and the consequences, he set them up as Marty and Debbie Calloway of Abingdon, Virginia. They owned Calloway Mining Corporation LLC, a group of coal mines located in Wise, Dickenson, and Buchanan counties in Virginia's coalfields. The coal business had been very good to the Calloways, allowing them to become multi-millionaires. Debbie volunteered with Hospice of Washington County, Virginia. These identities had been used before by police in both Virginia and Tennessee. They were already set up in the system as real people, so if anyone ran background checks on them, they would be there, and be clean. Tony would have to get the Captain to go in and change Marty and Debbie's physical description to match Carter and Connie, but he and Carter both knew that wouldn't be a problem. These identities seemed especially suited for the Sykes', since Connie was a nurse and Carter, having grown up in Haysi, knew the coal business quite well

"So Carter, or should I call you Marty, what car are you guys going to take to your first swingers event? That Ram with the airbrushed badge probably ain't the best choice."

"I thought we'd take the TC," Carter said without hesitation. "I figure it should be an icebreaker."

"Hey, that's a great idea, man. Only what, about six thousand of those things built?"

"A touch over seven." Carter didn't want to sound like a pompass ass and give the exact number. Ours is one of about five hundred with the Maserati engine and the Getrag trans."

130

"See, we've already got the conversation going, This is the first part of this whole thing I really like." After a few keystrokes, Tony left the room. When he came back, he handed Carter Marty and Debbie's Virginia driver's licenses. "I'll have your plates and registration this evening. Since this isn't a KPD case, I can't issue the credit cards for Marty and Debbie. You'll have to use cash to pay for anything at the club. Put it off on wanting to be discreet and you should be fine."

Carter looked at the licenses, handing Connie the one for Debbie. "Hey, Cons, I'm two years younger than you," Carter beamed proudly

"Remember, sweetie, this is a fantasy."

"You guys get out of here. You're now in the system, practice using these IDs. Go ahead and become Marty and Debbie. The more you use these identities now, the less chance for a slipup this weekend."

"I just hope Cons can avoid calling out 'Carter, Carter.'" Carter couldn't pass up the joke.

Connie punched him in the arm. This time it was her who was a little embarrassed. "I'm always under complete control. It's you I'm worried about."

"Y'all take your fantasy on out of my office. It's more than I can stand," said Tony

"Thanks, man. I owe you one," replied Carter, as he and Connie turned for the door.

"If you get hooked up with a twenty-five year old blonde, you owe me two." Tony said, with a laugh.

"He'll only owe you one then. The only thing he's getting hood up with is..." Connie looked at her driver's license and made the calculations in her head, "a fifty-three year old with auburn hair. That's more than he can handle, anyway." She grinned.

"I'll take that anytime," laughed Carter as they walked out of Tony's office.

****

131

After they finished with Tony, Connie had Carter stopped at Julian's salon, the most upscale and expensive hair styling salon in Kingsport. "Why are you going in here, babe?" Carter asked.

"I'm not, you are," Connie answered him.

"What? Huh-uh. There's no way in hell I'm going in that place. No way."

"You were the one who said we were going to do this right," Connie said, using Carter's own words against him. "Do you think Debbie Calloway is going to let her millionaire man look anything but his best? With a new haircut, and hair plucked from the right places, heck, you'll look just like Rock Hudson."

Carter grumbled a bit, because he hated spending money on stuff like this. But he knew Connie was right. He couldn't go into the Carolina Couples event looking like a middle class working man. He had to look like a million bucks, literally. He finally resigned himself to going into Julian's.

In a couple of hours, and one hundred fifty dollars later, Carter Sykes emerged from Julian's looking like a new man. "Hell, they cut hair I didn't even know I had," he said.

"Welcome to the world of the rich and famous, sweetie," Connie told him as he settled into the passenger seat of her Dodge Avenger.

"Rich and famous' ass, I just left a new forty meter vertical in there. And in two weeks you'll never know I visited the place."

"But you look so good, sweetie. You never know what it might get you tonight," Connie teased. "How about Applebees for lunch, my treat."

"It'll have to be your treat. I spent the next two month's lunch money on this damn haircut."

Carter and Connie both knew the young lady who waited on them at the restaurant. "Good afternoon, detective. Do you and Mrs. Sykes have some big plans the weekend?"

"Why do you ask, Patty?" Carter was wondering what she knew.

"I've never seen you all snazzed up like this before. Look at that haircut. You look like a million dollars."

"Actually, only a hundred and fifty."

Patty laughed, getting the meaning of Carter's reply. "What can I get y'all to drink this afternoon?"

****

The next stop for Carter and Connie was the Fort Henry Mall. 'Well, at least I'll be comfortable here. I know my way around the men's department at Belks.' Carter thought, as he turned and walked toward the Belks entrance.

"Where ya' goin', sweetie?" Connie asked him.

"Well, I just assumed we were going to Belks to get something for the trip."

"We're getting something for the trip all right, but not at Belks. There's a great men's store in here called Hiram's that will leave you dressed to kill Saturday night. Oops, maybe not such a good choice of words for a murder investigation," Connie chuckled.

Carter laughed, "It's ok, babe, we're not going to kill, we're only going to catch a killer. But I hear that Hiram's is very expensive. Tony got a shirt there one time, eighty dollars, just for the shirt."

"You are a wealthy millionaire, Marty Calloway; you've got to look like one. Belks ain't gonna cut it for you on this trip."

"Oh, boy. I guess I can forget about Christine."

"Now who's Christine?" Connie said with a tinge of feigned jealousy.

"That '58 Fury I went to look at the other day, remember?."

"Oh, I remember. Maybe I'll make it worth your while, Marty." Connie gave her husband a seductive smile.

"You said that before the haircut, babe."

About an hour later they left Hiram's with Carter being the not so proud owner of an upper end light blue Tommy Hilfiger button up shirt, khaki slacks, and a pair of very expensive shoes, some brand he had never heard of before. He also picked up a new belt, new designer socks, and even designer underwear. Carter didn't even know they made designer socks and underwear, and now he owned a pair of each.

"Where in the hell am I going to wear designer underwear? And who the hell is going to see it?" Carter grumbled as they walked back to the car. Before Connie could speak, he remembered the answer to his questions.

"You're not going to wear them anywhere, sweetie. But Marty Calloway is going to wear them to a swingers club. They might actually get seen, and admired, there."

"Carter Sykes gets to spend the money on them and Marty Calloway, a multi-millionaire, gets to wear them for a bunch of horny women. Figures."

After leaving the mall, Connie knew Carter had done all the grooming and shopping he could take for one day. He was, after all, a simple mountain man. All this fancy stuff just wasn't for him. But she knew he could pull off being rich for one night. After all, he had done similar gigs many times before. She figured he was actually looking forward to the challenge. She also knew that he knew he had to pull this off to solve this murder. But besides solving the murder, there was too much to risk if he didn't. Or if she didn't.

****

Connie drove them back home and they both sat down at Connie's computer. She opened her browser and hit the bookmark she had created for the Carolina Couples website. She clicked on the 'Contact Us' tab along the left side of the page. A new page loaded, with a snail mail post office box and an email form to fill out for more information about the group. Connie got out Debbie Calloway's driver's license and began to type in the information the form asked for:

Name: Marty and Debbie Calloway
Address: 322 Oak St
City: Abingdon   State: VA
Zip: 24210
Age: 45-54

How can we help: Hello. We are Marty and Debbie Calloway from Abingdon Virginia. I, Debbie, came across your website and have finally convinced my husband Marty to try one of these lifestyle parties. I see your July 4th event is scheduled for this weekend in Charlotte, which would work perfectly for us. What do we need to do to get the information to attend our first lifestyle event? I'm afraid if we miss this one, he'll back out on me again.

....

"Sounds good, babe, glad to see that you talked me into it," Carter chuckled. "Go ahead and hit the send button. I'm sure someone will get back with you this evening, especially with the email coming from a woman. Too bad you couldn't include your pic; they'd be back in touch in ten minutes."

"You seriously think it would take them ten minutes?" Connie said, as she hit the send button. The next page appeared, thanking them for the inquiry and said someone would be back soon with the information they requested. Connie noticed she was sweating. For the first time, she was nervous about this undercover operation. She had never lied about who she was before. Nor had she contacted a group of people using her false identity. And these people would be expecting to have sex with her. She knew she would have to get used to being Debbie Calloway, but she also knew she wouldn't get used to someone else wanting to have sex with her.

****

Later that afternoon, Connie left to meet her friend, Jenny, for her part of the shopping. She knew she needed something classy and sexy for the event and knew Jenny was the right girl to help her pick it out. Jenny was in her mid thirties, single, and dated fairly often. She was used to dressing up to go out for an evening at some of the Tri Cities better hot spots. She knew Jenny would help her pick out the perfect outfit for her and Carter's 'special event'.

Connie met Jenny at the Fort Henry Mall. This time they stopped in several high end ladies' boutiques. After a couple hours of shopping, Connie ended up with a black, mid-thigh skirt; a red, shoulder-less, low cut blouse;, a matching red, strapless push-up bra; a matching lightweight wrap to cover her shoulders and chest when a bit more conservative look was required; a pair of red, thigh high fishnet stockings; and black thong underwear. She chose a pair of black mid calf three inch heeled boots to top off the look. She thought about a black purse, but decided she wouldn't have her purse with her when she was wearing the outfit at the event.

"Girl, I don't know what your plans are this weekend, but someone is definitely going to appreciate you," Jenny responded to seeing Connie in full attire.

"Think I look ok?"

"Ok? That's the understatement of the year. You look fabulous. I'm just glad I'm not having to fight you for attention from the men."

Connie chuckled, "I guess this is the look then."

"Damn well better be, girl. That Carter Sykes will certainly know he's a lucky man. And so will everyone else who sees y'all together."

****

Carter's job for the afternoon was to get their yellow with black top Chrysler TC by Maserati ready for the trip to Charlotte. Carter and Connie bought the TC new in 1989. Carter just had to have one after he heard about them. They had traveled to Nashville to order one since the local dealer was unable to get one of the limited production models. This car had the "Maserati" turbocharged 2.2 liter four cylinder engine and German Getrag five speed manual transmission. Carter was pleasantly surprised to be able to get the car in yellow, as the color was not available with the Maserati engine. Best he could find, his car/color combination didn't even show up in the official sales data released by Chrysler. Over the years Carter had updated the engine with a new turbo, new exhaust, and new fuel injectors to give it about two hundred seventy horsepower; a fairly respectable number for a four cylinder these days. The car only had 30,000 miles on the odometer; they only took it out for special events like anniversaries, police balls, and the East Tennessee Mopar Show held at the Bristol International Dragway each September. Carter definitely thought their infiltration of the Carolina Couples qualified as a special event.

He washed and waxed the TC, dressed the tires, took off the hard top and cleaned the cloth top, figuring if the weather was ok they'd drop the top when they came into Charlotte, making an even better entrance. He conditioned the dash and the hand stitched leather interior. Next he checked the oil and other fluid levels. He checked the tire pressure and set all four to thirty-five pounds. Carter had nearly completed his work when Connie rolled in.

"Nice set of wheels, Marty."

"Maybe I'll take you for a ride sometime, Deb."

"Maybe I'll let you."

"What did you get for the event?"

"You'll find out Saturday night, sweetie. I can't show you everything. There has to be a little mystery involved or this whole thing will look over planned. We wouldn't want that, would we?"

"Just a quick preview?" Carter pleaded.

"Saturday night, sweetie."

"I guess Saturday night will be full of surprises then."

THIRTEEN

Connie was anxious to check her email to see if she had received the information she requested from the Carolina Couples. She put her new clothes away, set the oven to preheat for a frozen D'journo pizza, and went to her computer. She opened her browser window and her Yahoo! home page appeared on the screen. She clicked on 'mail' and saw she had two new emails in her inbox. She clicked on her inbox to find that one was indeed from the Carolina Couples and one was from 'Mary Ann'. Was this the Mary Ann from the nudist park? She clicked on that email first and found out it was indeed nudist Mary Ann. She read through the email and about the time she finished she heard the buzzer tell her the oven was ready. She walked to the kitchen and put the pizza in. About the same time she heard the door open and Carter came in from prepping the TC.

"Hey, sweetie, I've got an email here from Mary Ann."

"Mary Ann from Utopia?" Carter asked

"Yep, that Mary Ann."

"What did she have to say?"

"Just that everybody is still in an uproar over the murder of Doug. She said it will probably take a while for the place to get back to normal."

"Did she say who was running the place now that Doug's gone?"

"Yeah. She said Randy had taken over on an interim basis, since he had run it before Doug arrived. Said he'd run it until they find a new General Manager. She said Grace was working an extra couple days per week so Randy didn't have to put in five days per week."

"Well, that's interesting. Randy was the president when the tax situation went down. Did she mention any prospective new GMs?"

"She didn't mention anyone."

"I'm interested to find out what they have in mind. I doubt it will connect to the murder, but you never know."

"Hey, I got a reply from Carolina Couples, too. Haven't opened that one yet though. You ready to see if we're in?"

"Hold on a minute, I'll be in there to read that one with you."

"Check that pizza before you come back here."

Ten minutes go by as Carter cleaned up from his work on the TC. He came back in and checked the pizza. "It's done," he yelled to Connie. "I'll take it out. Be there in a second."

When Carter walked into the room, Connie had the Carolina Couples email pulled up ready to read. Carter pulled up a chair beside her and she began to read it out loud as they both read the screen.

....

Hello Marty and Debbie,

I'm glad to hear of your interest in Carolina Couples and More. We strive to have the best events in the lifestyle. As you can understand, many of our members require the utmost discretion. As such, we have certain rules that must be followed at our events.

First and foremost, No" means "No."

Yeah, right," Carter mumbles

All members and guests are referred to on a first name basis. Only give out other information, i.e. phone numbers, email addresses, or physical addresses at your own discretion." Connie paused for a second. "At least I won't have to remember Calloway."

No recording devices, either video or audio, are allowed at any event. This includes cameras. Cell phones and other mobile devices are required to be kept in your own vehicle or your own room.

140

A background check is required of all prospective guests. To speed the process along, you can submit your information on our 'background check' link at the bottom of this email. There is a one-time fee of $25.00 to cover the cost of the background check."

I should have know, another fee," Carter mumbles again.

The event cover charge is $100.00 per couple or single. This does not include room, drinks, food, or other fees. This charge covers the club's costs of putting the event together.

Once your background check is complete, you will be able to register for the event. The $100 cover charge is due when you register. We will give you the location of the event by email after you register.

We're looking forward to meeting you guys this weekend.

Sam,
Carolina Couples and More.

....

Connie leaned back in her chair. "Glad we got these fake ids from Tony," Connie said. "Should I click on the link and get the background checks started?"

"Gonna have to I guess, babe. That is, if we want to get in. I picked up a prepaid Visa in Marty and Debbie's name just for something like this. The more I see, the more I know we're on the right track. Last night, in going through the financials, I found a CPA in Rock Hill named Sam Collins, who just happened to be Utopia's CPA, It seems Sam wasn't paying the taxes he was receiving from Utopia. I'd bet my ass that this Sam in the email is Sam Collins the CPA. If I'm right, we'll confirm it Saturday night."

141

"Well, let's get a head start," Connie said enthusiastically. "If he's a CPA in the Charlotte area worth his weight in crap, he'll have a webpage with his picture on it." She had already opened up another browser window and typed 'Sam Collins CPA Rock Hill SC' into the Yahoo! search box. The results popped up and quickly Connie found the page she was looking for. "There's our guy, sweetie. I'll bet that's an old picture though," Connie said as she looked at the picture of Sam Collins, who appeared to be about forty years old.

"Good work, Cons. We'll read his page and get all the info we can on him before the event. At least now we know what he looks like. Go ahead and send Marty and Debbie's info for the background check and let's get our invitation to go swinging."

"Already on it, sir." Connie said, mockingly adding the "sir" to correspond with Carter's commands. She dug Debbie's driver's license from her purse. "Give me Marty's license and that credit card sweetie."

Connie typed the requested info into appropriate boxes on the Carolina Couples' background check page. She figured by tomorrow they would have their invitation to the event. Then they'd be set, and ready to ride to Charlotte Saturday morning.

****

After taking a few minutes to eat the pizza, Carter and Connie spent some time getting a better understanding of who Sam Collins was, or at least who he portrayed himself to be, on his webpage and Facebook page. They found Collins was indeed a successful CPA in Rock Hill, had a wife, two children; one grown and one in college. He had graduated from the University of South Carolina in 1982, thus putting him in his early fifties, if he graduated at twenty-two.

"I knew that pic was pretty old," Connie said.

"Most of them are," Carter replied. "His is actually closer to the truth than a lot we see."

After they finished with Collins' website, Carter went back to his office to check his email. There he found another email from Sheriff Ralph Tedder, the email he was hoping to get.

Disregarding the three other emails in his inbox, Carter opened Tedder's email. There he found an attachment titled 'Dawson Corporation' but saw nothing on Sam Collins.

·········

Hello Columbo,

Here's the financials on Dawson. You'll know as much as I do about this group when you read them. Got to convince the judge to give me the warrant on Collins. He's concerned that because Collins is a CPA this could lead to a fishing expedition which he wants to avoid at all costs. He's very concerned about the privacy of Collins' clients. If you can provide more info on why we need Collins' financials let me know, it'll help.

Sheriff Ralph Tedder

··········

Given what he was now speculating about Collins, Carter wanted Collins' financials more than ever. Going through Dawson's financial report would probably keep him busy tonight, though. More importantly, he didn't want to raise Collins' guard before he could talk with him. He quickly replied back to Tedder:

···········

Thanks Sheriff. I'll look through Dawson's stuff and see where that leads. We will need Collins' records though, specifically related to Utopia, Westlake, and Dawson, if there are any. I'll bet my ass there are. But don't do anything until Monday. Don't even make another request for Collins' records until then. I think we will be meeting him Saturday night at the swingers club and don't want to throw up any red flags before then. Hopefully I can be more specific as to our scope after this weekend.

....

Carter sent the email, walked to the kitchen, grabbed a soda, and dove into the financial information on The Dawson Corporation.

The first thing Carter looked for was what exactly The Dawson Corporation was, especially since he couldn't find one reference to them on the internet. In the info Tedder sent, Carter found Dawson had been set up in late 2008 as a real estate holding corporation. 'Interesting,' Carter thought, almost aloud. 'Why would anyone set up a real estate holding corporation as the real estate market was tanking? I wonder what, or who, this corporation was hiding?' A moment later his eyes came across the answer. The president of Dawson was none other than Emily Westlake, with Chad Collins listed as the corporation's secretary. Carter's eyes lit up.

Carter had an idea. He quickly opened a new Internet Explorer window and went to 411.com. Once there, he typed 'Sam Collins, Rock Hill, SC' in the appropriate boxes and hit enter. Collins' address in Rock hill came up, but his phone number did not. But Collins' phone number wasn't what Carter was looking for. He looked under 'associated people' and there he found Chad Collins. "Bingo," said Carter aloud.

Carter's attention returned to the financial report. To date, Dawson's only real estate holding was a one hundred acre plot in Herbsville, South Carolina. "Wonder where that is?" Carter asked himself cynically. He saw where the corporation had paid to have the land divided into ¾ acre lots. Carter noted several periodic one thousand dollar deposits by Dawson. He also noted there were a few ten thousand dollar deposits. Finally he saw his first trend. Starting in 2010, after the 15th day of each quarter, there was a deposit made to the account. The amounts varied, more in the summer, less in the winter, but there was always a deposit. "Ten to one I know where that money's coming from." Carter thought out loud. He minimized the Dawson information, clicked on the email he received from Tedder containing Utopia's financials and opened the file. At first he didn't see it. No amounts from Utopia matched the Dawson deposits. They were all much smaller. Then he had an idea. He added up the payments by Utopia that dealt with taxes before the 15th of each month. Sure enough, the amounts that Utopia was sending Sam Collins for taxes and the amounts that were being deposited into Dawson's account matched perfectly. Westlake and Collins were taking Utopia's tax money and using it to fund Dawson. But except for local property taxes on the hundred acres adjacent to Utopia, which only amounted to about a thousand dollars per year, Dawson had no expenses.

Carter got up, walked to the kitchen, and mixed himself a Jim Beam and diet Coke. He sat back at the desk, took a long sip of the industrial strength beverage, leaned back in the chair, and stared at the computer screen. "What in the hell was the game here?" he asked himself. If Westlake and Collins just wanted to steal from Utopia, they could have just as easily had Utopia make a payment to The Dawson Corporation every so often for a service that was never performed. That could have gone on indefinitely. But this scheme of diverting tax money into Dawson's account through Collins' accounting firm wasn't designed to throw off an investigation. Even worse, anyone could see that this scheme was limited. Sooner or later, the tax authorities were going to move in and once again demand payment, or else. Westlake knew all too well, his first order of business when he was hired had been to clean all the tax mess up, which he did in remarkable fashion. And Carter thought it funny that although it was not obvious without some research, it was not all that hard to find that the Utopia's tax dollars were going to fund Dawson. No, there was more going on here than just trying to steal from Utopia. It was almost like Doug Westlake and Sam Collins were trying to steal all the money they could and slowly put Utopia into a position it could never recover from. As he thought through the process, Carter realized what was going on. Collins and Westlake were trying to destroy the Utopia Sun Club.

****

Friday morning Connie poured the morning's first cup of coffee, then sat down at her computer to check her email. She was disappointed; there was nothing in her inbox from the Carolina

Couples. She wasn't worried yet, she knew the Carolina Couples had to run the background checks before they sent their invitation. She also knew they needed that invitation to get in the event tomorrow night. Without it, they were probably a month away from connecting with their newfound friends.

"What's ya' doing, babe?" she looked over her shoulder to see Carter standing at the door of her home office.

"Checking my email. I was hoping to have our invitation to tomorrow night's event."

"I figure mid-morning if they're going to run the background check. Check it again about ten. I've got some news to fill you in on from the financials I went over last night. A good partner always keeps his partner in the know, ya' know."

"Ya' know I know," she laughed.

"I know," Carter chuckled back.

Carter proceeded to tell her the information he found in the Utopia and Dawson financials. He made a special point of pointing out Sam Collins was involved in this whole thing, probably at a pretty high level. He hadn't run any calculations yet, but figured there was a lot of money involved, well into the millions once development costs were considered.

"What do you think it all means?" she asked.

"Well, there's definitely a connection between Westlake, Collins, and Dawson somewhere. Just the fact that Chad Collins and Emily Westlake are the officers of Dawson tells us that. If my gut is right, the Sam who signed your email is Sam Collins. And I'd bet my ass he'll be at the event tomorrow night."

"Do you think Maggie Westlake will be there?"

"You know, I hadn't thought of that," Carter stopped and thought for a moment. "I wouldn't expect her there this soon after Doug's death. Not at a big event like their 4th of July celebration anyway. I would expect her to reappear at a smaller, more intimate, event. But if she showed up that would be the coup d'gras to allow us to go into all their records. Not to mention that seeing us there would shock the shit out of her. She might say or do something stupid."

"And it would blow our cover," reminded Connie.

"The way I figure it, we ain't got but one shot at this anyway, Cons. I don't want to blow our cover, no. But I won't drag you back into this environment a second time. We might get by with saying 'we're just seeing what all this swinging stuff is about' once. I don't think we'll get by with it again. After the first time, it'll be 'put out or get out.' That's why I said, when it's time to go, it's time to go. If you say 'Let's go', then I'm heading out, no argument, I promise. If I say 'Let's go', then don't ask why, just grab your stuff and let's get the hell out of Dodge."

"Roger," Connie said, partly as an ice-breaker, partly to let him know that she understood the seriousness of the situation. "Remember one thing, sweetie, no matter what happens, I love you."

"I love you too, babe. And we ain't gonna let anything happen. I'm trying to scare you, because this can become dangerous. At the very least, Collins knows a murder has already been committed. If he was involved, then another one would just be collateral damage. If you want to back out, we ain't lost anything yet. I'll take you out somewhere nice in the TC tomorrow night. We'll wear our new clothes and style and profile."

"I'm not going anywhere around here wearing what Jenny and I picked out."

"Dressed to kill, huh?" he laughed.

"You bet your ass. Opps another bad choice of words."

"Yep, a bad choice of words, babe."

****

Carter drove the TC to the police department to pick up the Virginia license plates and registration. The TC needed a good drive before the trip, it hadn't been out of the neighborhood since last New Year's Eve when he and Connie took it to a party the Commissioner of the Johnson City police force threw for officers throughout the Tri-Cities. He loved to drive this car. Sure, it was twenty-four years. He knew today's cars, with new direct injected engines performed better. But he had made some upgrades to the Maserati 2.2 liter turbo to help it hold its own. The Getrag transmission was still a smooth shifting gearbox. And most of all, it still turned heads, especially when they saw the 'by Maserati' on the emblem. Every time he got in the car, Joe Walsh's *Life's Been Good* ran through his mind. Carter was counting on heads turning in Charlotte tomorrow night.

"Whoa, who the hell got a hold of you, man, the style police? You look like a million dollars with that haircut," Tony exclaimed when Carter walked into the station.

"Nope, only a buck fifty." It was becoming Carter's pat answer.

Tony again tried to talk Carter out of going to the Carolina Couples event and Carter assured him that if there was any danger at all they were out of there. Carter and Tony went over the information he had found in the financials, as they often did when they were both detectives, just to get another perspective on the case. Tony agreed with the deductions Carter had made. He too felt that there was some reason Westlake was setting Utopia up to fail, and told him to look for the answer to that question during the event. He postulated that the swingers club and the failure of Utopia were probably related somehow, especially with Westlake and Collins being involved in both.

"Man, you be careful. This whole damn thing is scary. Big money and wild sex are a recipe for trouble. We're talking one person already dead and what appears to be millions of dollars on the line," Tony said, deadly serious now.

"Yeah, I know. I can handle myself. I'm worried about Cons. She's a smart girl and all, but she's never done anything like this before. Never been undercover Do the wrong thing, say the wrong thing, and, well, you know, things can turn bad quick."

"Remember what happened to Nash over in Bristol a couple of years ago. Poor son of a bitch will never be the same after that beating he took in that bar. Keep her with you at all times, man. Don't let her out of your sight. She's a damn good looking lady; clever, and funny as hell. I don't care if she is over fifty, fifteen minutes after y'all arrive, there won't be a man in the place who won't want to screw her. And most of these guys are used to getting what they want."

148

"I know. Trust me, I know. But I also know we both want to solve this murder. She wants to be part of the team, like McMillan and Wife. If we can pull this off...."

"I know, I know, McMillan and Wife. I've heard it from her a million times," Tony interrupted. "But Rock and Susan didn't go to no damn swingers clubs together. And this ain't no fuckin' TV show, man. There won't be any commercial break when things heat up. You won't have a chance to catch your breath and regroup."

"That's only because there were only 6 episodes per year. Give 'em a twenty-two episode run and the writers would have eventually put them in a swingers club."

"One more thing, man. Are you sure this is about solving THIS case? It's not about revisiting your dad's murder, is it?"

Carter was almost mad at Tony for asking, but he understood the reason he did. "I don't know. It's brought back a lot of bad memories and emotions, most of which I thought I had packed away. Dad's murder might be one of the reasons I want to get the SOB who did this. It's been forty years, and I still don't have all the answers to his case yet. But I do know that no matter how much of a scoundrel Westlake may or may not have been, he didn't deserve to have another person end his life like this. No one does. That's why I'm a cop, right?"

"Be careful, man. That's all I've got say, be careful."

"We will, Tony. You know I can't let anything happen to Cons. She's my life, man"

****

Connie just couldn't wait for Carter to return. At ten o'clock she checked her email again. In her inbox was a message from the Carolina Couples. She clicked on it.

....

Hello Marty and Debbie,

Carolina Couples and More is excited to have you join us this weekend in Charlotte, NC. You can pay your $100.00 cover charge online at our website via credit or debit card. Simply go to click the link below and enter your payment information. Remember, this does not cover your room, meals, or other hotel charges. You will need to make arrangements with the hotel for any services they provide.

This weekend's event will be held at the Uptown Suites and Hotel in Charlotte. You can make reservations by calling 888-432-8399 or online at the link I have provided below.

Make sure to request the 5th floor when you make reservations to make sure you are in the center of all the activity. No activity will be permitted anywhere except on the 5th floor.

Being new to our group, you won't want to miss the dinner at 6:00 pm in the hotel restaurant or the meet and greet from 7:00-8:00 pm at the bar. Make sure to make your reservations for both. We know you'll find our members friendly and welcoming.

Again, we are looking forward to meeting you this weekend. Come expecting a good time.

Sam
Carolina Couples and More

. . . .

"Wow, we're in," Connie thought out loud. She realized she was actually excited to be going to the swingers club. Was she really excited about getting into a swingers club or excited that their goal of infiltrating the Carolina Couples, and eventually solving the murder, was a step closer to becoming a reality? She assumed it was the latter, but there was a part of her that was glad that, in her fifties, when most women are tending to their grandkids, she could still get into a group whose sole purpose was sex; wild, crazy sex.

She resisted the urge to call Carter, not wanting to sound overly excited. She knew Tony would give him hell if he was still at the station when she called. She thought about her outfit and how she was going to look in it. While she knew she wouldn't be having sex with anyone, besides maybe Carter, she sure hoped that someone was turned on by her in that sexy outfit. There was a part of her that was going to be really disappointed if no one gave her a second look.

Connie poured the last cup of coffee and sat in her favorite chair in the family room. For the first time, her mind was now consumed with tomorrow's event. Could she actually go through with this scheme? Could she even think about backing out now? This was, after all, her idea. Many of her and Carter's adventures were her idea. But this time, had she gone too far? She knew some guy, probably more than one, was going to try to get her to screw him. Would he go too far? Would she get caught up in the moment and go too far? Would some woman have Carter in a corner and he not be there to protect her? 'No, he's always there for me,' she thought. 'He always protects me, no matter what stupid thing I get us into. But what if he couldn't be there?' Even she could tell there were some high powered men, and women, in the Carolina Couples. They weren't used to taking "no" for an answer, regardless of what the Carolina Couples rules stated. And she was going to tell them all "no"? For the first time since they started planning to attend this event, she was scared. No not scared, but nervous. Nervous was a better word. Maybe it was because she now realized they were really going through with it. The talk was over. She had her nervous moments before their nudist trip, but this wasn't nudism. It wasn't running around naked, playing putt-putt. This was swinging. Raw unbridled sex. And she wasn't going to be herself; she was going to be Debbie Calloway. That was another thing to think about. She was going to have to pull off an undercover operation. She wasn't a cop. She had never done anything like this before. And don't forget, one of these people could very well be a cold blooded killer. She knew if this person had killed one of their own, they wouldn't think twice about taking out her and Carter.

151

Her thoughts went on for what seemed like hours. Finally, she heard the soft growl of the TC as it pulled into the drive. Hey, if nothing else, they were going to get to lose their middle class persona and for one weekend be wealthy, she told herself. She always felt wealthy when riding in the TC. It was probably the Maserati name on it. She had gotten so angry at Carter when he bought that car back in 1989. They were still just getting started in their careers and really didn't have the money for it. But Carter, a MOPAR guy since he was a kid, just had to have it. He was convinced it was going to be a collector's car some day. He even sold his treasured 'Cuda he'd had since college to get the down payment. The five years it took to pay those six hundred dollar per month payments in early '90s dollars seemed endless, especially for a car they hardly ever used. But she never once rode in the TC and didn't feel different. At first she thought it was the convertible, but even with the hardtop on, riding in this car felt different. People asked about it; What kind of car it?, Was, it really a Maserati?, Would it hit one eighty five?. The TC even seemed to fit them better as they got older. While it had never become the classic Carter thought it would, it was becoming a sleeper classic, and in a way, as they entered their fifties, they were becoming sleeper classics themselves. While it seemed odd to see a couple of thirty somethings in the TC, it fit a couple of fifty somethings just fine.

"Got our Virginia tags for this weekend," Carter announced as he came in the door.

"The TC running ok?" she asked.

"Like a champ. I think she knows she's going to style and profile this weekend."

"It probably does," Connie said. "You treat that car like it has a personality."

"She does have a personality. She just can't talk and tell us. But I can tell by the hum of her engine that she loves us. She needs to know that we love her back."

"Oh my God! Carter Sykes, you've gone off the deep end."

"Maybe, but she's ready for this weekend. Ready for whatever the weekend brings."

"Hey, we got our confirmation back, we're in."

"Great. I guess we better start packing up."

"Yeah, I need to get a few things together."

"You sure you're ok with all this?" Carter asked like this whole thing was his idea and she was just going along with it. His tone became more serious.

"Sure, sweetie. It was MY idea after all. Remember those oysters and fried squash?"

"Now that was a supper!" He smiled at her. "But it's one thing to talk about and plan something like this, and another thing to do something like this. I've been on undercover missions before. They can be tough. One wrong word, one person being where you don't expect, and your cover's blown. That could be serious. As Doug Westlake found out, these people mean business."

"I'm ok, honey, really. Just a little nervous about it, that's all. I guess I'm a little excited, too. Our first undercover mission together." Connie smiled.

"Hey, we don't have to do this. We'll find another way to catch this killer." Carter had to give her a way out.

"But this is our best shot to find out what we need to know about the Carolina Couples. We're this close. If this leads to putting a killer in jail, it will be worth it."

"It very well might. We just have to be careful."

"I'm going to be careful. And don't you leave me tomorrow."

"Trust me, babe, it's not me who's going to be the center of attention. Those guys ain't met anything until they've met Connie Sykes." Carter paused. "Oops, I mean Debbie Calloway."

Carter and Connie spent the rest of the day going over their new personas. They could no longer call each other Carter or Connie. They had to become Marty and Debbie Calloway in a hurry. They went over their birthdays, their occupations, their kids, their cars, and their address; everything that was in the identities Tony had provided them. Their stories had to always match. They knew people would talk about them, and they had to make damn sure everyone had the same story, no matter which one of them they heard it from.

That evening, Carter also did something he had always done since the first time he went on an undercover mission. He called his mother. He told her he was going undercover and not to be worried about where he might be found or what he might be doing. He reminded her it was all part of his job. This time he made sure to tell her Connie loved her too, and that the two of them were in this thing together. He wanted her to know everything was great between them. Just in case.

Carter also insisted Connie call her parents. She didn't hesitate.

****

As the Sykes' rose on Saturday, both the excitement and apprehension of the day were evident in their house. They sat at the breakfast table, neither of them really saying anything, but both thinking about the evening's event. Carter would later compare it to a boxer, sitting in his dressing room, waiting to be called for the walk to the ring. After breakfast and coffee, Connie packed their clothes for the night, as well as a casual set for the ride home Sunday morning. At least she hoped for a casual ride home. Carter washed the TC, not because it needed it, but because he needed to busy himself until it was time to leave.

They had decided to leave about 11:00 am, no use waiting around Kingsport until the last minute and then having the added pressure of having to rush. They had decided to take Interstate 26 through Asheville and Spartanburg, all the way to Interstate 85, simply to keep the trip as easy as possible. Carter didn't feel it would make much difference in their drive time, and he wouldn't be frayed from the drive. He had picked up a prepaid debit card for one thousand dollars for Marty and Debbie, so they wouldn't look odd with a wad of cash. They had used some of the card for their cover charge, but still had plenty on it to cover their expenses, at least he hoped so.. He kept all his receipts, hoping that somehow Tedder would find the money to reimburse him once the case was solved. Being able to afford Christine depended on it.

Since the TC still had its original radio and no SirrusXM, Carter had gone to the trouble of mapping out the classic rock radio stations available along the route. It may sound strange, but Carter knew some hard, driving, classic rock tunes; ranging from Motley Crue, The Rolling Stones, Lynyrd Skynyrd, and Guns N Roses would help keep them calm and relaxed. When they hit Interstate 26 AC/DC's *Highway to Hell* was coming across the speakers. Carter hoped this wasn't an omen of things to come.

FOURTEEN

The ride to Charlotte went well in the TC. Carter and Connie stopped for lunch at The Rock Ridge Café, a local restaurant in Asheville they heard about on the local radio station. Both Carter and Connie loved to sample local cuisine while traveling. They found it a nice break from the national chains they often frequented for convenience.

During the first half of the trip, they once again went over their new identities. To their surprise, they actually knew their partner's information as well as they knew their own. Carter knew it wasn't the same as thirty years together, but he felt comfortable with their progress learning their identities.

But the tone change after lunch. Both of them knew what was at stake. The reality of what failure could mean settled into the TC's cabin. It was time for each of them to reflect, focus, and become their new persona. They wouldn't be Carter and Connie again until leaving the Uptown Suites Sunday morning.

They reached Charlotte just after 3:00, and once they exited the interstate Marty pulled the TC over and dropped the top, just as they had planned. Marty and Debbie then rolled into the Uptown Suites Hotel parking deck and one of his nightmares came true. A young, early twenty something man walked up to the TC.

"Awh, shit," Marty said under his breath.

"Nice ride. I'll park her for you, sir"

"We've got to get our bags first," Marty said, uncomfortable with this man sitting in the driver's seat of the TC.

"I'll help you with that, sir," said an older, African-American gentleman coming down the walkway.

Within a minute their luggage was out of the TC and Marty was forced to turn the keys over to the kid. "Just remember, this is my pride and joy."

"I understand, sir," the young man said politely. "I'll take care of her. I see she's a Maserati."

Marty cringed. 'It's a Chrysler, not a Maserati,' he thought, but decided this wasn't the time nor place to have that debate. "Be careful with her, I don't want to bring some of my mine bosses down here, son."

"Yes, sir."

They walked inside the Uptown Suites Hotel and checked into room 524. Debbie thought she noticed the clerk give them a funny look when she gave them their room number, but hey, what did she know. She probably only wished she could have a bunch of men wanting to screw her tonight. Besides, they were on a mission here, a mission that included more than a good time.

The bellhop brought their luggage to their room and Marty gave him a ten for his service. They had over two hours until dinner, so decided they would take a few moments and roam up and down the halls of the fifth floor, trying to get the lay of the land for later tonight. They saw that two king size beds were being set up in the lobby area; apparently this would be used for some special purpose later. It appeared most of the rooms were occupied, but there was still a couple of vacancies. Marty had hoped the place would be packed, as they were hoping for a full crowd of suspects and a better chance to get to meet as many people as possible. He knew the more people there, the easier it would be to blend in. On their return trip down the hall their bellhop was escorting another couple into room 526, just one door down from theirs. Marty saw a six foot tall, stocky man in his mid forties coming down the hall and stuck out his hand to greet him.

"Hello friend, Marty here," Marty said to the man as he approached.

"Bill Suth...uh Bill. How you do?"

"Great. Who's that angel behind you?" Marty asked as he noticed the average looking lady walking behind Bill.

"That's my wife, Jessica," the man responded.

"Hello, Jess. I'm looking forward to getting to know you better tonight."

The lady blushed. "I guess so."

"Hey, is this y'all's first time here, Bill?

"Yeah, first time."

"Well, y'all are in for a treat. Best I can tell, they'll be plenty of action here tonight, especially with the 4th celebration going on. Just join in and have some fun. And Jess, I'm looking forward to seeing you, later."

"Yeah, thanks, uh…"

"Marty. Just like Mardi Gras," Marty laughed.

"Thanks Marty," Bill said as he went in his room.

"What the hell was all that about?" Debbie asked as she and Marty went in their room.

"That's about fitting in, dear. If that guy hadn't been a newbie, then I had to come across bold. Otherwise it put me in a position of weakness. I can't afford that now, can I?"

"I guess not, sweetie. But that wasn't you."

"You can't be weak either, babe. You've got to be strong and assertive, like this is your element. You're Debbie Calloway and this is your territory. Be full of yourself, everyone else here will be."

"I'll try, but I'm not going to act like a jerk."

"Point taken, babe. Just be yourself. Don't be shy. Laugh and joke, especially about sex. You'll be fine. If you act like you belong here, you'll fit right in. I'm the one who has to put on a front. We both know I'm the shy one. I've got to figure out where Marty Calloway fits in."

"Just hang close until I get comfortable, ok, sweetie."

"I'm right here, babe. I ain't going nowhere."

****

The afternoon provided less time for Marty and Debbie than they anticipated. Not long after getting settled into their room, they began the process of getting ready for the evening: laying out their clothes, taking a shower, doing hair, paining fingernails, and so forth. Debbie dressed in the bathroom and wouldn't let Marty see her until she was ready, having to threaten him a couple of times to keep him from trying to peek through the cracked door. Marty took his time getting ready. He turned the TV on, for the noise more than anything, and waited for Debbie to come out.

"Voila," she said as she opened the bathroom door, fully dressed for the evening. She stood in the room with her shoulderless red top, her black miniskirt, and black fishnet stockings. Her auburn hair was simple, straight, and fell below her shoulders. Her earrings were the diamond ones he had given her on their tenth anniversary and added a touch of class to her provocative outfit. The black boots added at least three inches to the length of her legs and the pushup bra did its job as intended.

"Wow!" was the only word Marty could muster. His eyes were glued on his wife.

"What do you really think, sweetie?" Debbie slowly spun around, giving him a three hundred sixty degree view of her and her outfit.

"Wow!" he said again. "You are stunning, babe. Simply breathtaking."

"You're not so bad yourself, you know," she said as she walked up to him and unbuttoned the top two buttons of his light blue shirt. "That's better. You even smell pretty good, too."

"Found some Sex Appeal cologne. I just have to ask, why do you make my job so difficult?"

"Sex Appeal? I could have gotten you something not quite so...well, cheap, and '70s. What do you mean 'make your job hard?' I thought this was the look we were looking for."

"It's exactly the look we're looking for. It may be too right. You know I'm supposed to keep all these horny men from having their way with you and you come out looking like this? It's all I can do to control myself right now. These men ain't got no idea what's about to hit them, but they sure are going to want to find out when they see you. Wow!"

"That's the plan, right?" she giggled. "And what about the women after my rich, well groomed, stylin' and profilin' man? How am I going to keep the vultures off of you?"

"They won't have to worry about me; I'll be too busy worrying about you. Wow!" Marty said as he took another look at Debbie.

There was a short lull in the conversation. Then Marty said, "You ready, babe? It's about time to get this party started."

"As ready as I'll ever be."

"Well, it's chowtime." Marty opened the door to their room and Debbie walked into the hallway with Marty pulling the door shut behind them. He looked over at his wife, "You sure do look great babe." He reached out and grabbed her hand.

"I know," she smiled, squeezing his hand.

****

Marty and Debbie took the elevator down to the first floor and made their way to Shane's, the hotel's restaurant. Outside the restaurant's entrance, there were several couples, dressed in very sexy attire, standing around talking with each other. Watching them, it was easy to see a few of the couples had already been partaking heartedly in adult beverages. Marty and Debbie casually walked up and joined the group. A tall, slender, fifty something man with a close cut, salt and pepper beard, wearing a white shirt and slender black tie, turned toward Marty.

"Good evening. I don't think I've seen you here before. I'm Stan and that gorgeous girl in red, white, and blue is my wife, Tina."

Marty and Debbie turned to their left to see a stunning, five foot seven woman. She was in her early thirties and was poured into a 4th of July themed dress that covered her ass cheeks by only inches. The cleavage of her rather large, probably fake, breasts was on display for everyone's view. It seemed as if a couple of men were already trying to get an even closer look.

"Hello, I'm Marty and this is my darling wife, Debbie."

"Good evening, Stan," Debbie said.

"I haven't seen y'all around before. Is this your first time with the Carolina Couples?"

Marty knew he'd have to come clean now and admit to it being their first time. He knew if he didn't, it would draw unwanted attention to them. "First time at any event like this, actually." said Debbie, also realizing making up some story of their swinging experience was not wise. She also knew she needed to get into the flow of things, and this conversation provided the perfect opportunity. "But I think we'll be just fine." A big smile crossed her face.

"Aww, we've got a couple of newbies here. Hey Tina, come over here, I've got somebody I want you to meet."

It took Tina just a moment to break away from the entourage surrounding her and make her way to her husband. "Honey, this is Marty and Debbie. This is their first time at a lifestyle party."

"Alright!" Tina exclaimed, her deep southern draw evident in her first word. "We're going to have some fun tonight. I'll make a special effort to find you, baby, I especially love helping newbies get acclimated," she said as she kissed Marty on the cheek while rubbing his chest hair where Debbie had unbuttoned his shirt. "And damn, girl, look at you. I know the men, hell, half the women, too, will love trying to make you feel right at home," she said as she looked Debbie over. "Hear that? They're playing *Any Way You Want It*. That's how we're going to have it tonight, any way we want it! Alright!"

Debbie blushed. "Thanks, I think. Looks like everyone's already pretty comfortable," she said as she nodded toward a couple of men who were rubbing the ass of a late twenties woman in a long, low-cut, black dress.

"Most all of us have known each other in the biblical sense for a long time now," said Stan. "That's why it's so special to get newbies like y'all. It's always nice to get something new." A smile crossed his face.

"I bet it is," Marty chimed in. "I'm sure we'll be seeing a lot of you guys a little later, but we're going to mingle and see what this is all about."

"Sounds great, honey. Just remember, I gave you your first kiss tonight," said Tina.

"I won't let him forget it, honey," smiled Debbie with that tone that told Marty he would never hear the end of this. They turned to the right and walked on into the crowd.

"And you were worried about ME," Debbie whispered in Marty's ear.

"Well, at least only half the women want you," Marty laughed. "We need to focus and keep a look out for Collins. I'm betting he's here tonight. Tell me the minute you see him. We need to talk with him as much as possible."

"Roger," said Debbie.

Marty and Debbie continued scoping out the crowd and meeting some of the people. Most were getting into familiar groups; groups Marty figured had been together many times before. Finally, a fairly conservatively dressed woman, in a knee length light purple dress came up to Marty. The woman was a bit on the heavy side, in her mid-forties, with shoulder length wavy black hair and a pretty face that made Marty figure twenty years ago she was probably a very hot chick.

"You look a bit lost here," she said.

"Just a little. It's our first time at an event," Marty admitted.

"I'm Angie. Over there, in the burgundy shirt, is my boyfriend, Mike."

Marty turned slightly to his right to see a man in a burgundy shirt talking to another couple. The man looked to be in his late twenties, with black, shoulder length black hair and a small moustache. Both of them looked a bit out of place here. For the most part, the men were over forty and the women were either close to the same age as their man or much younger. Furthermore, most of the women were very attractive, and the men appeared very successful. Marty introduced Angie to Debbie who, when seeing Mike, instantly thought, 'she's a cougar'.

Mike came over and Angie introduced him. The first thing Marty and Debbie both noticed was his East Tennessee accent. He was nice enough, but really seemed out of place with all the older, more sophisticated men. Still, they both knew he wasn't here for conversation. After a moment of small talk, Mike said, "Hey, y'all are the ones I saw pull up this afternoon in that Chrysler TC, ain't ya'?"

Marty smiled, glad to see he was right. The TC was a hit, at least with one guy. "That would be us." Marty was glad to be in his element talking about cars.

"Aw shit, man, that's a classic. Not many of those babies made."

"Only five hundred like this one. It has the Maserati 2.2 turbo and the Getrag tranny."

Debbie rolled her eyes and looked at Angie. "They're gone," she said. "It'll be awhile before we get their attention again."

"Yeah, if there's one thing that can take Mike's mind off sex, it's something with wheels and an engine."

"Marty's, too," Debbie caught herself just before blurting out 'Carter'. She knew when he talked about the TC he wasn't Marty anymore, he was Carter.

"Guys, we're going in to find a seat," Debbie said to the men. "Y'all coming or not? We'll need some nourishment to get us through the night."

"Yeah, come on, man. We'll talk cars over dinner. Ain't going to be anybody fuckin' during dinner anyway."

Marty looked back at Tina, who was standing with a man who had his hand up her short dress. "You sure about that, man?" Marty gave a nod in their direction.

Mike laughed, "I've seen stranger things, I guess." The guys followed Angie and Debbie to find a dinner table.

The guys continued their car talk. Mike was a big fan of the new Japanese-built turbos, with Marty standing up for the classic American muscle cars. The girls, however, had a different conversation going on.

"What brings y'all here tonight?" Angie asked.

"I guess we're just trying to figure out how to expand our sex life. After thirty years of marriage, things can get a little, well, old, you know. I thought this might give us some excitement."

"Tell me about it. I got married at eighteen to a guy who was thirty, big age difference at those ages. It was great at first, but I started putting on a few pounds and after about eight years, he started looking for another eighteen year old. The one he found this time was his niece. Got the bitch pregnant. To be honest, I wanted out of the marriage anyway, and this gave me the chance. I got the divorce, but he got just about everything, the house, car, everything I thought was valuable. The judge gave me about thirty-five thousand dollars worth of this stupid sounding little stock the son of a bitch had acquired in this dumb ass little computer company called Apple. That was before the techs took off. A few years ago, I was living in a rented trailer and waiting tables second shift at a diner in Lenoir. A friend of mine from high

164

school found me on Facebook. When we were catching up, I told her about the divorce and how all I got was that dumb ass Apple stock. She told me Apple was now worth a fortune. I checked, and that thirty-five grand worth of stock was worth 3.5 million dollars. Three point five million. I found a great financial planner and cashed in all but about one million of it. Bought a house on Lake Norman, a new Mercedes, and been living the dream ever since. And fuckin' every dick I can get my pussy around, and a few I've struggled with," she giggled.

"All I can say is good for you, honey. And Mike?"

"Mike's alright, ain't nothing serious between us. He's here because I can get him in here. Sometimes it's nice for a girl like me to have a good looking young guy with her. With Mike, I know I'm in control. No man will ever control me again. I'll kill anyone who tries. Course poor Mike might not get any tonight if your husband keeps talking with him about cars."

"But you will?"

"Of course. Just because I'm a little heavier than most of these women here doesn't mean I can't fuck. I know how to please a man, honey. Start with a great blowjob and they're all yours. All the men here know I give the best blowjobs in the place. I'm sure I'll get the chance to prove it again tonight."

The waitress came over and asked them for their order from the three choices the event organizers had chosen. "Get the vegetables, honey; you don't want to eat meat before the activities begin. It'll slow you down later. They'll be plenty of meat to eat later on tonight." They both laughed like schoolgirls. Debbie thought that she and Angie could be friends in a different setting.

Their giggles got the guys attention. "What, or who, are you two giggling about?" Marty asked

"Not cars," replied Debbie.

"I'm giving your wife some cocksuckin' tips," said Angie. "Somebody will appreciate that tonight."

"I'll vouch for her, she's the best in the place," said a man who had walked up behind Angie and wrapped his arms around her chest. "I'm betting you two are Marty and Debbie."

Marty didn't need an introduction. He had seen the man's picture on the internet. The man who had his arms wrapped around Angie was Sam Collins.

FIFTEEN

"I'm Sam. Welcome to Carolina Couples and More. I hope y'all are enjoying yourselves so far."

"So far," replied Debbie. "Learning a lot from Angie, here," She smiled. "Are you the same Sam who answered my emails?"

"The one and only, sweetheart. Glad you guys decided to make it." Sam's eyes were focused on Debbie's face.

Debbie cringed at the thought that a man who could be a cold-blooded killer just called her sweetheart. "It took me a while to convince him, but I finally got the job done," Debbie said, nodding toward Marty.

"Can you blame me for my reluctance to turn her loose on the world?" Marty asked as Debbie stood up and spun around in her sexy outfit, modeling it for Sam.

"I'm glad you finally did," replied Sam. "She's going to have a lot of fun tonight."

"I'm counting on it," said Debbie.

"I've got a few more guests to greet. I'll see y'all at the meet and greet after dinner?"

"Of course, that's what we're here for," Debbie replied, and refocused her attention on Angie. "I was wondering if we were going to get to meet 'Sam'." The guys were listening now. Marty knew his wife, and she was phishing, trying to see what information she could get on Sam Collins.

"Yep, that's the famous Sam," replied Angie. Not the best lover in the place, but sure keeps the group together. He got the Greenville crew to start coming up here after Doug and Maggie went down to run that nudist colony."

"How long ago was that?" Debbie asked as if she didn't know.

"Four or five years ago." Too damn bad about what happened to Doug. That's seven inches of dick that my ass is really going to miss."

167

"You say Doug liked the backdoor?" Marty couldn't help but ask. He had been trying to get Debbie to let him try that for years. This was his chance to push the issue a little bit, and Debbie could tell what he was doing right away.

"Don't all men? The second key to getting men here, after great blowjobs, is to let them fuck your ass. They all want to try it," Angie explained.

Debbie nodded her head in agreement. "Why are you going to miss Doug?" she tried to get the conversation back on track.

"He was murdered last week. Found dead at the nudist colony. Heard some dog found his body. Don't reckon they found the killer yet. Doug was a pretty good fuck. Enjoyed him just a couple of weeks ago. Nice guy, too."

"That's terrible," Debbie said, proud of her acting skills.

"Yeah, and we were so close to having that place for our new event center. Sam says it'll still happen, it's just a matter of time."

"What do you mean?" asked Marty.

"Apparently, when the economy collapsed, Doug's real estate company took a big hit. Doug and Sam got together and decided that since the real estate market was so bad, they'd work on getting us a place where we could have our events without having to use local hotels or member's houses. Doug found this nudist camp that was about to go under and came up with a plan for us to acquire it. Best of all, we could all buy a place there and party whenever we wanted. We knew it'd take a little while, but Doug and Sam assured us it would be worth the wait. The folks from Charleston loved it there. Doug had to have them quit going until he could secure it for all of us. Last time I talked with him, he said the plan was almost complete. He and Sam had already started taking deposits on lots where we could build our houses in a swingers community. Talk about 'Desperate Housewives'," she laughed. "I left a thousand dollar deposit on one myself. Mike and I could run down on Friday afternoon and screw our hearts out until Sunday afternoon. Paradise."

'Or Utopia,' thought Marty. "How much did one of these places cost?"

"The lots were three quarters of an acre and cost ten thousand dollars each. Doug and Sam had already acquired the land for the lots; they just needed to wait a little while to finalize the transaction on the common areas. The houses would cost at least another two hundred and fifty to build. For most of us here that's not a major problem, at least not when we'd basically have Fuck City to go to every weekend."

"And plenty of work for me," Mike spoke up. "I'm ready to start construction on three of those houses as soon as we get the go ahead. Already got my contractor's license from South Carolina."

"When was this development supposed to begin?" Marty pried for more info.

"First of October. By that time, Doug and Sam expected to have acquired the nudist colony itself and we could start working on the houses."

The waitress interrupted with their food and the four of them began to eat their meal. Marty was not only digesting his meal, but all the information he had just learned. 'If he had picked up this much info in less than an hour, what else would tonight bring?' he thought. He was anxious to find out.

****

As folks finished dinner, many of them moved to the bar for the meet and greet. Angie and Mike had plans to go to the fifth floor and catch some of the early activity there. "Sometimes the tone for the evening is set before everyone gets back to the playground," Angie told them.

The meet and greet was held in the Uptown Suites Hotel bar, The Royal Watering Hole, so named since Charlotte is the Queen city. Here, Marty and Debbie met some other newbies joining the Carolina Couples this weekend. Mark and Sue from Columbia, South Carolina and Dennis and Joan from High Point, North Carolina were both first timers. They met a few of the long time couples who were acting as ambassadors for the club. These couples made sure to once again inform them of the rules of engagement, especially that 'no' means 'no'. They were told that none of the newbies were required to do anything, but the club hoped they would participate fully in the evening's events, as that's what made the evening fun. The newbies talked about their

169

fantasies, their inhibitions, their fear of jealousy, etc. Dennis wanted to see Joan with another man, while Sue was here to try to fulfill Mark's fantasy of being with two women at once.

Marty looked around the bar but was disappointed he couldn't find Sam Collins. After what he had just learned, he wanted to talk to him about the land at Utopia more than ever. He formulated a plan where he would make the case that he and Debbie wanted in on the ground floor of this project, knowing the financial risk was high but realizing the potential reward could be a big one. Marty knew Sam had seen their background check and knew they had the means to invest. Maybe not being able to find him was good, it could give him time to better formulate the plan and let Debbie in on it. For the time being, he and Debbie concentrated on fitting in as much as possible. They talked to several couples, Marty making sure to inform them all that he was a coal mine operator, wanting word to get out that he should be more that capable of investing in anything he chose. There wasn't a lot of serious sex talk at the meet and greet, it was more of a feeling out process. It reminded Marty of the first round of a heavyweight fight. Some of the guys did kiss Debbie on the cheek, and one couple copped a feel of her ass, but Marty kept his jealousy and anger in check, knowing that no serious harm had been done, yet.

By 7:45 all the meeting and greeting that could be done had been done. Everyone was moving to the fifth floor for the main event. Perhaps Dennis said it best, "It's time to get down to business. It's time to fuck somebody." Marty and Debbie hoped it was time to find a killer.

****

Marty and Debbie left the bar and took the elevator up to the fifth floor. Once the elevator door opened, they saw what they had witnessed thus far had been as tame as a spoiled housecat. When they stepped off the elevator they saw one of the three king sized beds that had been set up in the lobby was being put to good use. Two women were lying on the bed, and each of them had a man standing between her legs having sex with her. One of the women had a man sucking her left boob; the other had a woman sucking on her right one while a man went at her doggie style. Suddenly one of the men called out "Switch" and the two men having sex with the women swapped places; and women. Marty and Debbie watched the scene before them in amazement. It took them a couple of minutes before they were able to tear their eyes from the action and continue on down the hall.

As they walked toward their room, they noticed almost every door was wide open. Every room had some form of sexual activity going on in it. Marty and Debbie couldn't help but stop and watch as two women engaged in a sixty-nine. Soon, a naked man moved in behind one of the women and started screwing her. The other woman began alternating between licking her female partner's pussy and the man's cock as he pulled it out. It was easy to see that no holds were barred on the fifth floor.

A couple of doors down they saw why Angie had wanted to get back to the fifth floor early. She had two men in front of her, alternating sucking on their cocks, while a third was behind her, pounding away on her. They watched as one of the men she was giving a blowjob scream in ecstasy as he shot his load and she didn't miss a beat, giving the other man her full attention.

After slowly making their way down the hall, they arrived back at room 524, located near the end of the hall. Marty used the credit card style key to open the door and they went inside.

"What the hell are we going to do?" asked Debbie, saying the first words either of them had said since stepping off the elevator. "This is even wilder than I dreamed."

"Hell if I know," said Marty. Even he was not quite prepared for what he had just witnessed. "This sure as hell ain't no nudist park."

That's for sure," replied Debbie. "I guess we better see what else is going on," she half said, half questioned.

"Are we taking off our clothes?" asked Marty. "If so, I'm in trouble," he said motioning down to the bulge in his pants.

"Given the situation here, I wouldn't call that trouble, I'd call it about average," Debbie laughed. Marty was glad to see she still had her sense of humor. It seemed to lighten the moment a little.

"Let's take another look around before we take off our clothes," Marty suggested.

"I'm not going to argue against it," Debbie agreed.

They walked back down the hall, again taking in the various sex acts going on around them. They witnessed almost anything they could imagine. They were surprised to even find two men in a sixty-nine with each other, each with a woman between their legs, sucking on their balls. They watched some of the sexual acts in awe, totally unprepared for what they were seeing. They saw people they had witnessed minutes early with one partner now with another. After an hour that seemed like an entire evening, Debbie realized they were the only ones on the floor still fully dressed. Whether it was her imagination or not, she felt like being clothed was drawing attention to them, attention neither of them wanted.

"Sweetie, we've got to try to fit in," she said. "People are beginning to talk about us. Let's at least get out of these clothes so we don't look so awkward. We've been naked in front of others before."

Marty knew she was right. He reluctantly agreed with her suggestion. He didn't want either him or his wife to be naked with all this sexual activity going on around them. Their clothes felt like their last barrier to it all. But he knew it was either take them off, or leave without everything they came for. They were too close to finding out too much to leave now. He had learned so much so far. He knew he needed a real conversation with Sam Collins. Marty decided he was willing to take the chance of removing his clothes to get it. "I'm going to kiss you as I remove your top," he whispered to his wife.

Debbie didn't hesitate. She pulled Marty to her and they kissed, standing in the hall, while he removed her top. The kiss continued as he removed her bra as well. Next, she went to work on the buttons of his shirt and slipped it off his shoulders, allowing it to fall to the floor. She didn't hesitate; she continued by unbuckling his belt, unbuttoning his pants, and unzipping his fly. She dropped to her knees as she pulled his pants to the floor. Marty stepped out of them. For some reason Marty remembered he had the designer underwear on and was glad Debbie had insisted he make that purchase . Debbie then reached up and pulled his underwear over his erect cock, giving it a kiss on the head as she pulled the underwear to the floor. She gave it another kiss as she stood back up in front of him.

172

Now it was Marty's turn to finish undressing his wife. He sucked her right nipple into his mouth as he bent over to unbutton her mini skirt. As he reached behind her and unzipped it she wiggled her ass and it fell to the floor. Marty then noticed the red thong she was wearing. "Nice touch, babe," he said as he slipped his thumbs under the waistband and slowly pulled it over her exposed cheeks. His mouth released its grip on her nipple as he lowered the thong to the floor, taking a moment to kiss her cunt as his mouth passed by it. While Marty looked a bit odd in his shoes and dress socks, Debbie looked perfect standing there in her three inch heel boots and thigh high fishnet stockings. Marty grabbed the clothes on the floor and stood up. He hugged his wife and whispered in her ear, "Nice show darling."

"Who's putting on a show?" she asked. "Let's dump these clothes in the room." Without speaking another word, they walked with an arm around each other back to their room.

After dropping off their clothes and Debbie securing the room key in her boots, they headed back down the hall, this time with the lobby as their destination. As they walked naked down the hall, Debbie felt a couple of hands touch her ass and one man reached out to grab her boob before she could dodge his move. Marty had one woman going the opposite direction grab his cock, give it a couple of strokes, and say, "Nice, I'll be back for that in a few minutes," in a sultry voice. before he was able to spin away.

As they reached the far end of the hall where the lobby was, Debbie saw that only two of the king sized beds had activity on them, the third was free. "We've got to try to fit in, sweetie. Get your naked ass up on that bed," Debbie whispered in her husband's ear.

"What are you doing?" Marty asked.

"Just follow my lead, it'll be ok."

Debbie sat Marty on the foot of the empty bed and pushed him down on his back. She took his erect cock in her hands and began to slowly rub it between them. After a moment, she started to slowly stroke him, making Marty moan in pleasure. After a few strokes, she put her shoulders under his legs and pulled him to the edge of the bed, positioned herself between his legs. She then put one of her breasts on each side of his cock and placed it in the valley between them. She used her hands to press them around it, and began moving up and down on him.

Debbie could sense people were beginning to take notice of the newbies and realized she was going to have to put on a good show. After a couple of minutes, she took Marty's cock into her mouth and began to work her magic on him. Blowjobs were not her favorite thing to do, but she knew from Angie's comments earlier that it would make a pretty good show for the crowd assembling around them. She also knew being bent over in her stockings and boots wouldn't hurt her image either.

Marty was doing his best to stay aware of his surroundings, but he was quickly becoming lost in the pleasure his wife was providing him. More eyes began to settle on them as Marty moans became louder. It was now Marty and Debbie's turn to take center stage. The newbies were now in the middle of their first swinging sex act. As the crowd began to grow behind her, Debbie felt the unmistakable touch of a man's hands embrace her on each side of her waist. She stiffened as she felt the erect cock that belonged to those hands rub against her ass cheek.

'Think Connie, think,' Debbie had forgotten her fake identity. As she raised up from Marty's cock, she looked over her shoulder and saw a fifty year old man with a goatee, wearing a tan cowboy hat, with brown hair flowing out from it down to his shoulders. The crowd around them had gotten even larger and louder as they awaited Debbie taking her first strange cock in thirty years. She knew she had to act quickly. With all her might, she pushed Marty's ass farther up on the bed, giving room for her knees on each side of him. In one motion, she hopped onto the bed, straddling his cock. Debbie made a scene of allowing her pussy to hover above Marty's cock, then slowly sliding her pussy down on it. They both moaned and she leaned over him, her breast touching his chest as they slowly began to make love to each other while the crowd watched. Debbie began to pick up the pace and the crowd around them began to chant, "Faster, faster, faster."

As Debbie kept the pace up, Marty began to buck, slowly at first, like a mechanical bull on low speed. Slowly his pace increased. Debbie again leaned over Marty and whispered in his ear, "If we're going this far, sweetie, we might as well give them one hell of a show." She rose back up and began riding her bucking bronco for all he was worth. She looked back at the frustrated cowboy and commanded, "Give me your hat."

The man stood there with a dumbfounded look on his face. "What?"

The short, young, pretty woman who stood beside him screamed up at him, obviously caught up in the excitement, "Give her your hat dude."

The man tossed Debbie his cowboy hat and Debbie raised it in the air in her right hand. Then she literally began to ride Marty's cock as he bucked below her. He moved his hands from her hips to her breasts to give her more support, but no one in their audience believed she needed it now. Despite the fact that they were at the club on a mission for information about a murder, Debbie and Marty were now in the throes of passion.

For Debbie and Marty, it seemed like an hour, but in reality it was probably only a minute or two. Finally, Marty let out a series of primal moans as he erupted inside his wife. Debbie almost instinctively let loose with a wild "Yee-Haw" as her climax overtook her. Both of them spent, Debbie fell over on his chest, and Marty took his arms and wrapped them around her naked body, partly to simply hold her and, as his senses began returning to him, partly in an attempt to shield his wife from all those who looked on.

The crowd erupted in cheers and applause as the newbies completed their first public sexual act. While it may have been with each other, a newbie first is always special, and Debbie had definitely put on one hell of a show. It was definitely worth the ovation. Deep inside, she felt a strange sense of pride in herself for having pulled this thing off, and now took comfort in knowing Marty was still there, holding her, protecting her.

As she put her hands on the bed and raised up to take some of her weight off Marty, Debbie saw another sex act going on in the first room down from the lobby. In this room, a beautiful woman, in her early twenties, was on a low bed on her hands and knees. One older, rather plump man, stood in from of her getting a blowjob while another slender man with salt and pepper hair was fucking her from behind. The woman released the cock in her mouth, and turned her head toward the door. Her eyes met Debbie's.

Quickly, Debbie fell back down on her husband and frantically whispered in his ear, "Look over here," and nodded her head toward the sex act she was witnessing. Marty struggled to roll enough to see the action in the other room. When he got to where he could see, he knew why there was alarm in Connie's voice.

The woman was Emily Westlake.

SIXTEEN

Marty pulled his wife close to him. "Did she see you?"

"Yes, we made eye contact. I'm sure she recognized me."

"Aw, shit." Marty reacted. "Just act natural. Let's get up from here, you take your congratulations, and we'll walk back down to our room."

"Congratulations for what?" Debbie asked.

"That Oscar winning performance you just put on, my dear."

Debbie blushed. "I guess we were pretty good for a couple of old farts."

"All I did was supply the dick, babe. You were the star."

They rose off the bed and the crowd had largely faded away. Only about five couples remained gathered around the bed, the rest already looking for more action elsewhere. Debbie did get a couple of "great show" comments, and then looked over to see Sam Collins, wearing only a "Nudestock" tank top, heading their way.

"Well, I see you two are getting acclimated pretty well. I liked the cowboy hat."

"Oh, shit, I don't even know the man I got it from."

"I do. Don't worry about it. If I know Clint, he'll be glad to know that you have it as a memento of tonight. I'd bet he's found someone to fuck by now and won't miss it for a while."

"You're the boss, Sam," Debbie replied.

"How'd y'all find out about us?" Sam inquired. "We need to know where newbies, the good ones, and the bad ones, are finding us so we can try harder to recruit people like you guys and avoid the bad ones. We had a preacher and his wife come to our Labor Day event last year and start laying hands and praying for people to get saved while they were having sex. Talk about spoiling the moment."

"O...K....," replied Marty. "Takes all kinds, I guess. We actually heard about y'all from Doug Westlake when we visited Utopia a couple of months ago. He and Maggie seemed like such

177

great people. They told us about the Carolina Couples. He said he was hoping to have something like this set up down there in the next little bit and told us we could try it out and see if we'd be interested."

"Doug was a great guy, great business partner, and a great friend. It's so sad what happened to him."

"What happened?" Debbie asked, playing along with Marty's game.

"Haven't you heard? He was murdered last week."

"Murdered? Oh my God!" exclaimed Debbie in a hushed voice.

"Yeah, it was a shock to all of us. We had hoped to have Utopia up and running in about three months. Now it may delay our plans until the end of the year. But we'll get there soon. It was Doug's dream."

"What kind of dreams did Doug have for Utopia?" Marty asked.

"Doug planned for a lifestyle development and club. As you can see, most of our members are very well off financially, and many live within three hours or so of Utopia. Its rural location makes it a great place for a swingers community. There's only a couple like it in the county. Let's see, y'all are from Abingdon, Virginia, that's probably a bit far away for you to spend a couple hundred grand on a weekend home."

"You got a heliport there?" asked Marty.

"Heliport? Hadn't planned one yet, but who knows?"

"A heliport would allow you to expand your geographic area and bring in people you won't get otherwise. Put in a heliport and we'll fly down most Friday afternoons. It's less than an hour's flight from Abingdon. I can leave a car down there to use after we arrive."

"You've got a helicopter?" asked Collins, intrigued.

"Hell, son, I own something like two dozen coal mines. How the hell do you think I get between them? I sure as hell don't take highway 80 from Haysi to Grundy. We ain't got interstate highways in the coalfields like y'all do here in Charlotte. A 'copter is the only way to go," Marty says, exaggerating his hillbilly accent.

Sam laughs. "Well, maybe we can look at a heliport then. Do you want me to send you some information about our plans for Utopia?"

"Hell, yeah," Marty thought fast, not really having an email address that didn't give away that he was a cop. "You've got Deb's email address, just send it to her. I ain't got nothing on me to write mine down on," Marty said with a laugh.

"Me neither," said Sam. "Hey, again, great show, Debbie."

"Thanks. Maybe next time I can convince a couple of new performers to join in," she smiled, thinking of Jenny. She smiled, proud of herself for continuing to play the part of a swinger after what she and Marty had just done."

"After tonight, I'm sure you won't have a problem with that. See y'all soon".

"See you later Sam," they said in unison and laughed.

As they walked back to their room, Marty whispered, "If you get an email from him Monday morning about the Utopia plans, we're ok. If not, Emily recognized us and ran straight to him."

"What if I don't get an email?"

"We could be in deep shit.

"What are we going to do, Marty?" Debbie wanted to know as soon as they were safely in the confines of room 524. "I'm sure Emily recognized me."

"Right now, we're going to keep playing cool and not let anyone know that we know anything. Perhaps Emily doesn't know anything that's going on. No use assuming she does until she proves it. In that case, there's nothing to worry about. If she does run to Collins we'll know soon enough. There's nothing we can do about it now but watch for the signs over the next couple of days. At least we know that now we can't come back. And I don't think we need to."

"What do you mean?"

"We got some great info tonight. I want to go back home and sit down with the financials on Utopia, Westlake, and Dawson and see what I can make put together with the new information we

179

have. What we learned tonight should give Tedder enough to get the financials on Collins and his business. I know he can get at least limited access. Once I look at those, with what we've found out tonight, I'll know even more. But we know right now there's a conspiracy in place by Westlake and Collins to take over Utopia and turn it into a swingers club, no, a whole damn swingers city. And if I'm not mistaken, there's a scheme for the two of them to get rich doing it. Of course, Westlake won't get rich now. Gives Collins one hell of a motive."

"So does that point the finger at him?" asked Debbie.

"Don't know for sure yet, babe. But I'd definitely label him a person of interest. I'll know more once I compare what we found out tonight to the financials."

Debbie decided she had enough for the night, and wanted to take a shower, to both physically and symbolically clean herself. Marty decided to join her. While in the shower, he stood behind her, wrapped his arms around her, and hugged her tight. He was glad he and his wife had survived their first, and hopefully last, swingers experience with their marriage intact. They were in bed by midnight, but could still hear the sounds of the party on the fifth floor.

****

Both Marty and Debbie slept until 9:00 the next morning. Marty had dreams of sex, trying to avoid demons who would steal Connie from them. After dressing in their casual travel clothes, they made their way to the continental breakfast provided by the hotel. After eating, they went back to their room, packed their things, and went down to get the TC. Marty gave it a good going over, including checking the mileage, before they left the parking lot.

"I hope you tipped him good," Debbie reminded him.

"Getting behind the wheel of my car should be plenty tip enough," Marty said with a tone to his voice. "Yes, I tipped him."

"I'm glad."

"I'm glad they didn't hurt the TC."

Marty hit the button and dropped the top. No need to worry about their hair on the way home, it would be a top down trip. They sped off from Uptown Charlotte, making their way to Interstate 85.

"How'd we do?" Connie asked after they were safely away from the Uptown Suites Hotel.

"Quite honestly, I think we did great," Carter answered. "Getting out alive is a big plus. You, my dear, were wonderful. In more ways than one." Carter was alluding to both her performance in helping get the information they needed as well as to their lovemaking in front of the audience.

"I'm keeping the cowboy hat," she said. "It will always remind me of this adventure. You know, life ain't so bad after fifty."

"Especially when you're with the right person. I wonder if we could use this experience to make an AARP commercial?" Carter laughed, grabbing third gear as they hit the onramp for the interstate. They made their way toward Kingsport, Tennessee with Def Lepard's *Bringing on the Heartbreak* coming out of the TC's Infinity speakers, sounding as good as ever.

Part Three

Small Things Matter Most

SEVENTEEN

It was mid afternoon when Carter and Connie Sykes returned to Kingsport. The first order of business was an early supper, since they had elected not to stop and eat on the way home, wanting to put as much distance as possible between themselves and Charlotte. Then they stopped by Jenny's to pick up Thor. Of course Jenny was full of questions about their weekend, and Connie answered them carefully, not wanting to give any indication of what had really happened in Charlotte.

Thor loved riding in the TC, standing up in the back, letting the wind blow in his face. Carter, on the other hand, didn't especially like having Thor in the car. Not that he minded vacuuming up the dog hair, that wasn't such a big issue. But Thor always captured more attention than the TC. Now Carter loved Thor dearly, there was no doubt. But he reasoned there were millions of dogs in Tennessee and only a handful of Chrysler TC's still on the road in the Volunteer state. Why should one of the dogs get more attention than this rare automobile? Then again, it was Thor, and he definitely was not 'just a dog'.

Arriving home, Carter and Connie watched an old movie on one of the over-the-air broadcast subchannels, Connie with Thor in her lap. Carter considered going to his desk to study financials and try to put the numbers together with what they had learned the night before, but he needed a break from the case, even if for a couple of hours. He and Connie had been immersed in this case for the past two days. Even the ride home was not without suspense, as Carter kept one eye in the rearview mirror, looking to see if anyone was following them. He needed the downtime to clear his head of the case. He could get a fresh look at the facts and numbers tomorrow. He was also hoping Connie would receive an email from Sam Collins first thing tomorrow, providing more information into what Collins and Westlake had been up to at Utopia.

During a commercial, Carter began laughing when he saw an ad for an upcoming episode of Columbo, thinking of all the people at Utopia who referred to him as the famous sleuth.

"What's so funny?" Connie asked.

"Just Columbo. That's all I heard the last few days at Utopia. You'd think they were still getting first runs of it down there."

"I wonder how they do it." Connie asked, almost rhetorically, her mind a million miles from Columbo.

"I guess they get their TV either by satellite or over-the-air."

"No, no, I mean screw other people. I mean, here we are, back at home, and I still feel a little weird about last night and I didn't touch anyone but you. But you saw how those people were going at it. What are they thinking now, now that the alcohol, drugs and excitement has worn off and they're back at home? How do they dealing with it all the next day?"

"I have no idea, babe. I couldn't do it. Wouldn't want to. But you know, there's one thing about it. At least they were in it with their partner, not running around behind their back cheating on each other. They were honest with each other. I have a much harder time with people who cheat on their spouse than these swingers. The cheater is living a lie; a lie to their spouse and a lie to themselves. You know there's men and women right here in Kingsport, sitting on the couch with their spouse, watching TV, who last night were secretly screwing someone else. I think it's that lying, cheating, deception, and sneaking around that I really don't understand. At least the swingers don't lie and cheat, they just do a lot of weird, crazy sexual stuff right in front of their spouse."

"I guess. I just keep getting the image of Emily Westlake in my head. We know her parents are, or in Doug's case were, swingers. We know they had parties right in their house, with all the stuff we saw last night going on right in their living room. I wonder how long she's been a part of this lifestyle. Seeing her doing what she was doing last night with those old men makes me wonder if she will ever get out of the lifestyle and be able to have a normal life with a husband, kids, and so on."

"Might give a whole new prospective on the librarian," Carter laughed. "Somehow I just don't see her standing on the porch of the house with the white picket fence and the Golden Retriever."

"I'm serious, sweetie. It's a bit sad."

"Some people, whether swingers or not, will just never know what we have together. Some people are simply not monogamous. I guess if I had my druthers, I'd rather see them swinging than running around behind their spouse's back."

"I know, but don't you think there's a lot of jealousy?"

"I'm sure there is. I'm sure some of the guys get insecure when their wives are screwing a man with a big goober, and some women get tired of hearing their husbands talk about huge boobs. That may be why there was so much plastic surgery evident last night."

"All I know is I just couldn't do it."

"Neither could I, babe. I want adventures, but I want them all to be with you."

"We seem to be having our fair share of adventure lately."

"That's for sure. This retired life ain't been so boring after all."

****

It was nearly 10:00 am before Cater cranked the TC, deciding to take a final ride in it before he washed it and put it back in the garage to await the next special event. He was glad they took it to Charlotte and given it a good workout. After the fifteen minute drive to the police station, he checked his old parking spot; only to find it had been assigned to Ambrose. It felt odd parking the TC in a visitor's spot, he hadn't done that in nearly three decades. Carter could almost feel the TC trying to turn into his old parking spot. After he parked, he walked inside to return Marty and Debbie's ids, tags, registration, and other items to Tony.

"Marty, you're back, alive I see. I don't guess any of those wild women screwed you to death," joked Tony.

Carter thought of his and Connie's show at the event, and as much as he wanted to make a comment about Connie screwing his

187

brains out, he decided to give it a rest. "Back to being Carter now. It feels pretty good."

"Well, how'd things go?" Tony waited anxiously for the complete details of Carter and Connie's trip to Charlotte.

"I got a lot of good information on the swingers club and its connection to Utopia."

"That ain't really what I'm talking about, man," Tony's shit eating grin told Carter he was more concerned about the Carolina Couples adventure than about what they learned about the case.

"What happened in Charlotte stays in Charlotte," Carter said in a tone that let Tony know he wasn't going into specifics. He told him what they learned about the plan for the Carolina Couples to transform Utopia into a swingers city. "I'll know more after I've sat down with the financials and learned how the money fits into this thing. And hopefully, after Connie gets the email from Collins."

"Cons ok?"

"Yeah, she's fine. It was a big shock for her, but she's handling it fine. Hell, things were a bit shocking for me. I've seen a lot of shit in thirty years of law enforcement, but I've never seen anything quite like that." Carter stopped, there was no way he was telling Tony Ward about their performance in the lobby of the 5th floor of the Uptown Suites Hotel.

"Well, I'm glad y'all didn't have any problems. I was worried, man."

"We're not out of the woods yet. We'll know if we have any problems in the next couple of days. If we get that email, everything's ok."

"Uh oh. What email? What happened, man?"

"Con's is pretty sure we were recognized."

"Who the hell would have recognized y'all at a swingers club in Charlotte?"

"The twenty-two year old daughter of the man who was killed."

"Aw shit, you've got to be kidding me. What the hell was she doing at the swingers club."

"Best I could tell she was sucking one man's dick and fucking another. I sure as hell didn't expect it," said Carter. "But there she was, with two old geezers going at her. Anyway, we should know by the end of the day how involved she is in this whole thing. Westlake's partner, Sam Collins, is supposed to email Cons today with information on the plans for Utopia; Marty and Debbie are interested investors, you know. If she gets an email with information, we'll figure everything is cool. If not, we'll assume we're in deep shit."

"Have you got a gun, man?"

"Yeah, I've got my 9mm."

"If you don't get an email, or if it looks suspicious, like he's hiding something, put it in your truck. Hell, put it in your truck anyway, he may be smoother than we give him credit for. It appears he's smooth enough to take over an entire nudist colony."

The image of Ravishing Rick Rude coming to the ring to his theme song *Smooth Operator* popped into Carter's mind. He shook his head to clear it. "Good idea. No use being stupid."

"Call me on my personal number if you get into trouble. I can get you help quicker than going through those clowns in dispatch."

"Thanks, Tony, but I'm sure everything will be ok. I'm counting on it."

"Just be prepared. Be ready for anything. You're dealing with crazy sex and millions of dollars."

"You know I was a boy scout," Carter said as he was walking out of Tony's office. "Talk to you soon, man".

"Be careful, Carter. "

****

Before washing the TC, Carter went in to check with Connie, hoping she had received an email from Sam Collins. So far, nothing. To say he was disappointed was an understatement. He was hoping all the connections between Utopia and the Dawson Corporation would be evident in that email. Without the email, he'd have to go to work on the financials, which was not his specialty. And without the email, he knew he and Connie still had to worry.

189

Carter remembered Tony's advice about putting his 9mm in the Ram. He went to the master bedroom, got the gun, and made sure it was loaded. Every time he did this, he thought about Barney Fife and the bullet in his pocket. Yep, the fifteen round clip was full. He checked the safety, walked to the Ram, and put the gun in the top of the center console, where it would be easy to reach if he needed it. Carter never was an expert marksman. He always laughed at all the cop shows that had their stars shooting the heart out of a target on the range. Most cops were adequate, but few were truly skilled marksmen. Carter was adequate at best. Hell, being a detective didn't exactly leave a lot of spare time to practice at the range. He honestly couldn't remember the last time he had fired a gun in the line of duty, and he was glad of it.

Most police officers were not great drivers either. He had never met one who could rival Jeff Gordon. They were better than the average driver, simply because they had the opportunity every now and then to spend a Saturday at the state's northeast Tennessee driving grounds and make a car do things you couldn't do on the street. But if you wanted a professional driver, go find a quality race driver, not some cop behind the wheel of a Crown Vic. Carter was a better driver than most officers on the force, but even he was limited in his skills. That's why police cars came equipped with radios. Bad guys might outshoot or outrun the cops, but they couldn't outrun the radio. And Carter was an expert at the radio.

"What are you doing, sweetie?" Connie called out to him.

"Just putting something in the truck. I guess my mind got distracted," he replied, not wanting to worry her by telling her he was packing his gun.

She walked out to the Ram. "Don't you think you ought to be working on the case?"

"Babe, I'm a detective, I think I know how to work a case." Carter had an edge in his voice.

"Don't get a tone with me, Carter Sykes. I just asked if you were going to work on a case."

"When I get to it. Right now I'm going to wash the TC and put it away."

"I should have known, that damn car. You know, I'm invested in the case too. I had a hundred people watch me screw you trying to catch this killer. Then you put washing this damn car ahead of OUR case."

"Don't start on me, Connie. Don't start. I know what I'm doing. I've done this a long time, you know."

"Whatever." Connie shakes her head in frustration, turns and walks back into the house. She knows Carter is mumbling under his breath, but she really don't care what he's saying.

Carter finished washing the TC, put the hardtop back on, parked it in the garage, and covered it with a cover he had specially made for it. He decided the Ram could use a quick bath as well, so he went to work on it. About half way through the truck's bath, He saw Connie and Thor come out of the house and walk toward the Avenger. She opened the driver's side back door and Thor jumped into the backseat. She sat behind the wheel, looked at Carter with a look that could kill, and off they went. Carter was glad to see her get out. It didn't happen often, but when she got in moods like this, she could be unbearable. Maybe the stress of going undercover and the weekend's events were getting to her. He also knew the next order of business would have been to wash the Avenger. As much of a car man as he was, that car wasn't his baby. As he finished the Ram, he remembered he needed to contact Tedder and once again request financials on Collins based on the info they had obtained at the swingers event. He went inside and sat down at his desk, intending to email him. He changed his mind and decided to just call him instead, figuring sometimes low tech was the quickest way to get things done. He never could understand why everybody wanted to email or text when a phone call was so much quicker and easier.

"Sheriff Tedder, please," Carter said to the voice on the other end that identified himself as "Mitchell".

"One moment please." Carter waited through the silence. He always preferred the silence to elevator music, but really wished companies and agencies would play something a little more contemporary when putting him on hold. Hell, he'd even take George Jones over elevator music.

"Tedder," the voice finally came from the other end.

"Sheriff, Carter Sykes. How's things in the big city?"

"You know, it's been a busy day. Had two cats in trees this morning. I'm surprised Mitchell had the strength to answer the phone," he chuckled. "Got a visit from Maggie Westlake this morning. Not a call, a visit. She wanted an update on her husband's murder case. Actually, she demanded one. And asked about you, wanted to know what you were doing on the case."

"Aw, shit," Carter said as he clicked off his Pandora station playing Foreigner's *Double Vision* so he could focus his full attention on this call. He instantly knew Maggie's visit to Tedder was not a good thing. "What did you tell her?"

"Just followed normal procedure. Told her we were trying to obtain and process all the evidence available. Told her we had some leads we were following up on and when we had more, I'd be in touch with her. She then asked specifically if I had heard anything from you. I thought that was odd, so I nipped her in the bud pretty quickly. How'd things go this weekend?" Tedder asked, interested in both any information Carter picked up concerning the case and curious about details on their experience at the swinger's event.

"Sounds like Emily's been talking to her mother," Carter said, then told him about seeing her in Charlotte, leaving out the details. "And I'll bet if she's talking to Maggie, she's talking to Collins as well."

"I'll bet you're right," replied Tedder. "I was afraid Maggie was on a phishing expedition this morning. I'm hoping we have enough ammo to get that warrant for Collins' financial records."

"I think we do. People will do anything to cover up a murder. From what I've found so far, we also have a huge financial project in the works too. I haven't figured out the specifics yet, but I do know Westlake and Collins were working to take over Utopia and turn it into a swingers paradise for a very upscale crowd. Looks like there was a lot of money involved, well in the millions of dollars. Not to mention the sexual aspect of this whole thing. Lots of money and wild sex, not a bad scheme in a bad economy. I'm expecting an email from Collins with a few more details, but so far it hasn't arrived. I'm afraid Emily tipped Collins off as to who I really am and I won't get it."

"Let me use this new info to try to get you as much of Collins' financials as the judge will turn loose. I've got to convince him that we're not phishing here, that we have solid evidence to back up our request for Collins' records. I think with all the new information you picked up this weekend, we've got enough to convince him. As I told you, with Collins being a CPA, the judge wants to make damn sure we don't go into his client's information.

"Ask him specifically for any financial transactions relating to The Dawson Corporation, Doug and Maggie Westlake, Emily Westlake, Chad Collins, and the Utopia Sun Club. That ought to about cover it and should limit our scope enough to satisfy his concerns. Email it to me as soon as you get it. I'll probably spend the rest of the night going through those records."

"Sure thing, Columbo. I think if we limit our search to these specifics, the judge will go along with it. Let me get to work."

"Yeah, and I'll have a lot fewer numbers to look through," mumbled Carter.

"Hey, Columbo, be careful. Money, sex and murder are a dangerous combination. If Collins is involved in Westlake's death and this Utopia scheme, he may come after you."

"You don't have to tell me about it. I've put the 9mm in the truck just to be safe." Carter was well aware of the seriousness of the situation he and Connie now found themselves in.

****

Carter hung up the phone and went into the kitchen to make himself a roast beef sandwich for a late lunch. The fact that Maggie had visited Tedder asking specifically about his and Connie's activities weighed on his mind. He couldn't kid himself, he knew if Maggie was asking about him, then both she and Collins knew it was he and Connie at the Carolina Couples event. Could it be that Collins and Maggie had become lovers beyond their Carolina Couples romps? Could it be they needed Westlake out of the way in order to share both each other and all the money from the Utopia venture? Carter thought it odd that Emily would be helping her mother if she had any idea she had a part of her father's death, but he had seen much stranger things happen.

193

Whatever was going, on, whether Maggie was involved or not, all roads seemed to lead to this planned takeover of Utopia by Collins.

After he finished his sandwich, Carter noted that Connie and Thor had been gone a long time. 'I really should have stopped her,' he thought to himself. 'Especially after what I learned from Tedder.' His mind paused for a second. 'Maybe they got caught up talking to someone.' Carter knew that often happened when out with Thor. He's such a personable dog and everyone loved to pet him. And Thor loved it too. Carter had to quit taking him to car shows because everyone wanted to talk about his dog and he couldn't look at cars and parts. 'That's probably it, she's just raving over her boy,' he thought.

But after not receiving an email from Collins and after learning about Maggie's visit to Tedder, today was no ordinary day. Too much had gone on over the weekend. He, and Connie, now knew too much, about too much. While Collins and the Westlake women didn't know how much they had actually discovered, they had probably already figured it was too much for comfort.

"Where did she go?" Carter mumbled aloud, walking through the house, looking for a clue to her whereabouts. At the front door, he spotted her canvas sneakers she usually wore during the summer. "Hmm," she said. He went to her closet, not to look for what was there, but to see what was missing. He noticed an open spot in her line of shoes. After checking to see which shoes were still there, he determined she had worn her light trail shoes. She always wore them when she and Thor went for a walk on the trail at Robinson Park.

After a half hour of trying unsuccessfully to focus on financial reports, Carter decided to go to the park where Connie often took Thor for walks. He was glad to see her Avenger when he pulled into the parking lot, and pulled the Ram beside it. He followed the park's walking trail a couple of laps, but there was no sign of them anywhere. Carter, beginning to get worried, got Connie's picture out of his wallet and began asking some of the park's patrons if they had seen this woman with a big black lab. The first ten people he asked hadn't seen her, but when he got to the basketball court, he asked a teenage boy waiting with his pick-up team to play the winners in the next game.

"Yeah, dude, I saw that dog," he said, even before taking a look at the picture. "I think that was the lady too."

"When did you see them?"

"About two hour ago, I guess."

"Where'd they go?"

"Got into a silver van with some guy. The van took off. That's all I saw."

Carter's heart stopped beating. He knew what had happened. A man with a silver van? Connie would never voluntarily get into something like that. Someone had kidnapped Connie and Thor. Thoughts rushed through his mind. He'd bet a million dollars it was Collins, or at least someone Collins had sent to do his dirty work. "Don't go anywhere,", he commanded the kid. "This is important. I'm a cop, I'm going to need your help." Carter realized he had lied about the cop part but at this point, he really didn't give a damn. He found his phone and steady as he could, he pulled up Tony Ward's personal number from his contact list.

"Ward," Tony answered the phone.

"They've got Connie."

"Carter? What the hell's going on, man? Where are you?"

They've got Connie," he said again, his voice wavering. "And Thor. A kid here at the park said he saw them getting into a silver van about two hours ago. Shit, they're supposed to come after me, not her."

Tony could tell Carter was losing it. "Calm down, man, calm down. I need you to focus now. I need you to focus so we can find her. Remember, they're using her to get to you. You know how they work. They want you, so they need her. She'll be ok as long as we can focus on that."

"Alright, alright, I'm trying," Carter said, still frantic, but understanding Tony was right. He knew Connie needed him to focus on finding her.

"Where are you at, man?"

"Robinson Park."

"I'll get a uniform there immediately. Keep that kid there, I'll see if we can get a sketch artist to help us ID the man who….," Tony paused to choose his words carefully, "she got in the van with." Tony was glad he caught himself before he said something that would make an already frantic Carter Sykes worse.

"He's here with me. Hurry, man, hurry."

"I'm on it, man. The whole damn force is on it." The phone hung up.

In less than five minutes, Clancey, an uniformed cop, arrived at the park and recognized the Ram. Carter knew Clancey and told him that Connie had been kidnapped. He introduced him to the kid at the basketball court . The officer explained to the kid he needed him to talk with a sketch artist as soon as possible. The kid protested at first, saying he needed to get home for supper or his mother would be worried. Clancey calmly explained to him he would call his mother and explain the whole thing to her. He told the kid he would take him home when they were done, that the kid wasn't in any kind of trouble. In fact, it was just the opposite. The kid could be a hero if the information he provided the police helped to save the life of a cop's wife. The kid agreed and the two of them took off, while another uniform who had just arrived, stayed with Carter and began looking around the area for any obvious evidence.

About the time Clancey and the kid were pulling out of the park, Connie's ringtone came over Carter's phone.

"Cons?" You ok, babe?"

The voice on the other end sounded strangely familiar, but Carter couldn't place it. But it definitely wasn't Connie's. "We've got the bitch."

"You son-of-a-bitch," Carter shouted into his phone. The cop looked up and ran back toward Carter.

"Watch it, big guy. We've got her. We're in control now. You'll do what we say or the bitch dies...After I show her what a real man can do for her, that is."

"What the hell do you want?" Carter tried to remain as calm as possible, knowing Connie's life depended on it.

"I want you, Marty, or should I call you Carter? What the hell kind of name is Carter, anyway?"

"The name of the man's who's going to bury your ass if you hurt my wife."

"Yeah, yeah. Remember, bud, I'm in control here. Or didn't they teach you that in rookie cop school?" Unfortunately, Carter knew he was right. Right now, the kidnapper held all the cards. Carter had to outplay him at his game.

"How do I know you have her?" Let me speak to her."

"I knew you'd eventually ask. Say, 'please' and I might let you."

Carter didn't argue back. "Please let me speak to my wife."

"That's better. Keep it short and sweet, bitch, or I'll pull the fuckin' trigger."

"Carter?"

"Connie, you ok?" Carter asked as calmly as he could.

"Carter, they killed Thor." Connie's soft voice rang in his ears.

EIGHTEEN

"Satisfied?" The man was back on the line.

"I'm going to find you, you sorry piece of shit."

"I know you are. And I'm going to let you watch me fuck your sweet little wife before I kill you. Bye now." The phone went dead.

Carter stood there shaking with both anger and fear. How could he have been so stupid and let Connie go to the park by herself today? How could he have gotten her involved in this case? Case hell, it wasn't even a case. He wasn't even a cop anymore. 'She is a nurse, for God's sake, not a cop,' he thought. He knew the son of a bitch on the phone was trying to rattle him, he'd seen the bad guys play this game many times over the years. Usually they came across as amateurish, almost comical. But this guy knew what he was doing. He seemed to mean business. He knew too much, even alluded to the events in Charlotte. Carter felt the man's threats toward Connie working on him, stirring him to do things he knew he shouldn't do. He knew he needed to gain control of his emotions, for Connie's sake. But how? He stood helpless in the park as he and the uniformed officer saw Tony's Crown Vic, lights flashing, enter the park and pull in beside the Ram.

Tony moved toward his partner as quickly as he could without running. He knew he had to stay calm, professional. He couldn't show Carter the urgency he felt. He knew his actions, as well as his words, had to give Carter the impression that things were under control. "Hey, man, they're in our jurisdiction now. Now we can get these sons of bitches. We can do something to solve this. The whole damn department is being mobilized."

"They killed Thor, They've got Connie and they've killed Thor. Connie said they killed Thor." Carter was at the point of tears as the consequences of her words finally hit him.

'Aw, shit,' Tony thought, without saying anything. These emotions would make it even harder to focus Carter for the job at hand. He was going to be way too emotional to be a lot of help. "Hey, man, right now I need you to focus. All the help you can give me, I need. We're going to find her. Connie's still alive, man. She just needs you to focus with me on saving her, ok?"

"I'm trying. I'm doing my best."

Tony could see the tears in his partners eyes. "Good, because Connie is alive and she needs us right now. The sketch artist will be with the kid soon. That was great work on your part to find him. It might save her life, man. Great job." Tony was trying to focus Carter's attention on the positives, things that were going right for them. He knew that even in his current state of shock, Carter could help in ways normal victims couldn't. "Did she give you any hints as to where she was?"

"No." He shook his head. "He didn't give her time. He knew what he was doing."

"Ok, What did he say? Did he say anything that might help us?"

The look on Carter's face made Tony regret asking the question. Carter couldn't repeat the words about what he threatened to do to Connie. But he did remember the man said he was after him, not her. Suddenly he remembered that in his macho threats was the promise that Connie would be alive when he found her. "Yeah, he said he was after me. He implied that she'd be alive when I found him." That was as much as Carter was going to, or was able to, reveal right now. It was really all Tony needed to hear.

"Was there anything else we can use?" Tony was glad his bad question had turned out well.

"Connie said THEY killed Thor. There's more than one of them." Carter was sure his wife was trying to warn him so he and the cops didn't go in and get blindsided only expecting one perp. "She's still thinking, she's warning us."

"Great job Carter. I knew I could count on you, man. You and Connie both are thinking like cops. We're going to get these mother fuckers. You know we are. We are the best damn detective team in Tennessee." Tony sounded like a football coach trying to build on the momentum. The uniform, finishing his sweep of the grounds, walked back to them.

"Find anything?" Tony asked.

"Nothing, sir." The reply was short, calm, and to the point.

"Didn't think you would," Carter said. "The kid said he saw her get into the van, not that a man in a van abducted her. To him, it must have looked normal. No one else in the park even noticed. My guess is he had a gun in her side and she felt like she had no choice but to do as he said."

"Or she recognized him," Tony added.

"Or both," Carter thought aloud. From the man's threats, Carter was sure the man must have been at the Carolina Couples event.

"Anything else, Carter?" Tony was glad his friend was beginning to focus on the job of catching the kidnappers.

"Yeah, I know that voice. I don't know who it is, but I've heard it before, recently. He made reference to things that happened in Charlotte over the weekend. It had to be someone who was at the swingers club," Carter began opening up, knowing Tony's insight would help find Connie.

"Almost guarantee it, man. You ok to drive?"

"Yeah, I can drive."

"Come on over to my house, Suzie will have some supper ready. They'll call from the station when the sketch artist is finished with the kid." Tony didn't wait for an answer. He gently grabbed Carter's arm and led him toward the driver's door of the Ram.

****

Tony followed Carter the five miles back to his home. He called Suzie to fill her in on the situation, trying not to get too detailed He explained only that Connie had been kidnapped and that he needed her help in keeping Carter calm. She said she had already fixed some homemade soup and corn bread for supper and should have plenty when they arrived.

Carter and Tony sat at the kitchen table and Suzie brought them each a bowl of soup and a piece of cornbread. They discussed the call from the kidnappers as they ate, Tony asking about background noises, anything that might hint to the location. The work on finding Connie occupied Carter's mind and helped him eat, almost absentmindedly. This was Tony's plan, he knew Carter would need his strength.

Since Carter said the voice was familiar and the kidnapper made references that led Carter to believe he had been at the swingers event, Tony went ahead and called the judge, requesting a warrant for the list of attendees who rented rooms on the fifth floor of the Uptown Suites Hotel, hoping to match a name if Carter recognized the face in the sketch. He knew getting the information across state lines would take longer than if the hotel was in Tennessee. He hoped they would have some answers before they even received the list and wanted to make sure they had it as quick as possible. All he could do was hope the kidnappers had signed in under their real names. After all, Carter and Connie hadn't.

Both Carter and Tony knew they were in the most grueling time of the ordeal. It was the waiting that was the hardest. First, there was the wait for evidence; the guest list, the sketch artist, and so forth. Then there was the wait for the kidnappers to contact Carter again with their instructions. They both knew in this case the ransom was Carter himself. Carter had his phone on top of the table where he could reach it quickly, but it didn't ring. In his mind, he envisioned the horror Connie was going through. She had just been kidnapped, seen her dog killed, and knew the kidnappers wanted to kill her husband. He knew there was the distinct possibility she had been raped as well. Carter only hoped the son of a bitch wasn't going through with his threat before he got there to save her. He thought about Thor and how Thor must have died trying to protect Connie from these SOBs. He was proud of Thor for making the ultimate sacrifice.

After they ate, Carter asked Tony if he could be alone for a few minutes. Tony led him to the spare bedroom. There Carter laid face down across the bed and a myriad of thoughts rushed through his head, too many for him to comprehend. In a few moments, his mind went blank, nothing, no thoughts at all. Carter wasn't a religious man. He and Connie had attended church for a couple of years after they got married, but he never could understand why what he believed made any difference in the grand scheme of the universe. His beliefs couldn't change the truth, whatever truth really was. He hadn't prayed in many years, but now he began praying, cautiously at first, then more fervently. Something inside him knew if he didn't pray, if he didn't ask for divine intervention, and the unspeakable happened to Connie, he couldn't live with himself. Or with God.

"Dear Lord," Carter began. "I don't know why I want to tell you what's going on, I'm sure you already know. Connie is in trouble. Lord, I know I've not prayed in a long time, and I can't really promise I'll pray again for a long time. But God, Connie and I need your help. Please protect Connie right now. Give her the strength she needs to make it through this. And Lord, give me the strength and the wisdom to find her, to bring her back home safely. Lord, a long time ago, when we got married, the preacher said you gave her to me. Please don't take her away from me now. Not like this. I love her God. Help me get her back home. She has so much good to give to the world, please don't take her away now."

Carter realized his prayer was beginning to ramble, but he really didn't care. He wasn't about to stop. God knew what he meant, regardless of what he said, or how he said it. He continued praying, but now he had no idea what he was saying, or if he was really saying anything at all. He just prayed, whatever come from his mouth he just prayed it. For a moment, he wondered if this was what it was like to pray in tongues, like the people back home used to talk about. It was as if someone, or something, else was praying on his behalf and the words were simply coming from his mouth. This wasn't like praying in church, or before supper, or before a football game. Carter was praying with all his might. It was physically exhausting. He didn't know if five minutes or five hours had passed, the concept of time seemed to have vanished. Carter had lost control, something bigger than he had taken charge of this prayer, of him. He was startled and literally jumped off the bed when he heard Tony Ward's voice and the knock on the bedroom door.

NINETEEN

"Carter, we've got a sketch." Carter quickly got up and rushed out of the room.

"You alright, man?" Tony looked at Carter. It was as if he had been somewhere else, in another universe, another dimension. Tony couldn't place it, but knew something was different about his friend.

"No. Why?"

"You just look different, that's all. I can't explain it, but something looks different about you. Wash your face and let's get to the department. We've got a sketch of the kidnapper."

Carter didn't bother washing his face. He and Tony got in the Crown Vic and, with lights flashing, drove to the police department. They had just finished with the kid and were taking him home as Carter and Tony walked in.

"Hey, dude, I hope they find your wife," the kid told Carter.

Carter stopped and looked at the kid. "Thank you, dude. When we find her, you're going to be a hero, you know." The kid smiled.

Within minutes Carter and Tony were with the sketch artist. He explained it wasn't his best work, but the kid remembered the dog better than the man. Carter understood that; he was used to Thor stealing all the attention. Then he showed Carter the picture he had drawn from the boy's description.

Between the face in the drawing and the voice on the phone, Carter knew exactly who he was looking at.

"That's Mike, the young guy I had discussed cars with over dinner Saturday night," Carter said, calmer than he or Tony expected.

"You sure, man?"

"Yeah, I'm sure. Seeing the face made me recognize the voice. His girlfriend is Angie. She has a place on Lake Norman. He has a 370Z."

"You've always had a hell of a knack for details, man."

"I'm a detective," Carter said. "Let's get that guest list from the hotel so we can match names and get an address."

"I'm already on it," Tony replied.

Within an hour, Tony had the Saturday night guest list from the fifth floor of the Uptown Suites Hotel. There were two women registered as Angela, but only one was registered with a Michael. A check of the address showed she lived on Lake Norman. The Mecklenburg County Sheriff's Department did a physical check of the address and found Angie at home alone. She said Mike Ratliff didn't live with her, but she provided them his address and cell phone number, which they texted to Tony. She said she hadn't seen him since he left her place late Sunday afternoon.

The Mecklenburg Sheriff's Office checked the address Angie gave for Mike's apartment and no one was there. A check of DMV records for Mike Ratliff at his address showed a Nissan 370Z was registered to him, but the car was not found in the apartment complex's parking lot. While all this evidence was circumstantial, it was more than enough to confirm to Carter and Tony that they were after the right man.

Maybe it was strength from a higher power, maybe it was he had a suspect in his sights, but Carter was now more focused on finding his wife than ever before. For Carter, the game was on the line and he wanted the ball in his hands. He'd have it no other way. What else was he going to do? He had been a cop his entire adult life. There was no way in hell he was going to sit back and let someone else, not even Tony, try to solve the most important case he'd ever worked. No way! Connie's life depended on him, no one else.

Once they got his name and address, Tony and Carter ran the rap sheet on Mike Ratliff. A couple of misdemeanor drug charges, a couple of domestic abuse charges from a previous marriage, and oddly, a federal income tax charge. Tennessee, Virginia, and North Carolina all issued APBs for both Ratliff and the white 370Z. They knew the silver van was involved as well, but so far had no leads on it. The kid could only tell them it was a silver full size van and that Connie and Thor had gotten in the back.

"Collins is involved," said Carter slowly and methodically. "He and Ratliff are tied together in the swingers club. Ratliff does remodeling work for Collins and I'll bet they're tied together in Ratliff's tax case. Maybe killing us is a payback for a favor."

"I know," said Tony. "Just don't have anything solid enough to go after him yet. Asking South Carolina to send a cop to question him at this point would only alert him that we're on to him. Then he'd probably alert Ratliff. Best to wait until we have a concrete connection." Carter knew Tony was right.

Darkness had settled on Kingsport. Carter suddenly realized he hadn't heard anything from the kidnappers. Carter knew from his short phone conversation with Ratliff that he was the target. Connie would simply be collateral damage. He needed her as bait to lure him in. He also knew Ratliff was trying to make him emotional, irrational, so he would do something stupid and thus be an easy target. Ratliff probably figured making him wait was the best way to accomplish this goal. And Carter knew he was right.

"How else could they get 'hold of you?" Tony asked.

"Phone or email I guess," answered Carter. Quickly they moved to Tony's computer and Carter checked all his email accounts, including his KPD account that tech hadn't yet closed. Nothing. Then Carter said, "Collins never had my email address. Collins had Connie's from her inquiry about the Carolina Couples. He was supposed to send her information on the Utopia project I need to check her email."

"Go ahead," Tony nodded at this computer monitor.

"I don't know her password."

"Can you get it?"

Carter thought for a moment. No, he knew of no way to get the password. He thought a second more before he got an idea.

"I bet she has her Yahoo! account set to automatically log her in on her computer at home. We'll have to go home to check it."

"To the batmobile," Tony dared to make the first joke of the evening. The detectives headed out the door, running for the

207

Crown Vic. They left the station with lights flashing. A few minutes later, they pulled into Carter's driveway.

Carter started to run into the house but Tony yelled at him to stop. "Those sons of bitches are after you, man, they could be hiding in there by now. Let's do this right."

Carter stopped dead in his tracks, realizing his emotions had affected his judgment and could have nearly gotten him killed. "Thanks man."

Backs together, guns drawn, the pair entered the house as one. There was no sign of anyone as they opened the front door. They moved room by room through the house until they were sure it was clear. Carter ran to Connie's computer. It was still on; she had quit turning it off after she retired. He opened Mozilla Firefox and on the screen appeared Connie's Yahoo! home page. Carter clicked on the mail tab and saw four messages in the inbox. One was from Jenny, the other three were sent by "Joe Blow Me" and had no subject. Carter opened the first email:

....

Reply to this email when you get it. I'll be in touch afterwards.

....

Seeing nothing that would help, Carter then clicked on the second email.

....

Man you're slow. I'm still waiting on your sorry ass. Reply to this email or the bitch will pay.

....

Again, nothing to help. Carter closed the email and checked the time stamp on all three emails. The first was sent at 6:15, not long after he got the call from Ratliff. The second at 7:32. The third at 9:05. Carter looked at his watch. That was 45 minutes ago. Carter clicked on the third email.

....

Some god damn detective you are. I'm still waiting on your sorry ass. Reply to this fucking email whenever you're smart enough to find it, dumb ass.

....

"This son of a bitch is really getting on my nerves," said Tony.

Carter hit the reply button. The email address that appeared was a generic one and it would be nearly impossible to quickly trace, probably requiring resources from the TBI. Carter typed into the box on the screen.

....

Where are you Ratliff?   I'm coming for you, you sorry piece of shit.

....

Carter started to hit the enter key. "No, no, man. Way to personal. Let's not get all Dirty Harry here. Ask about Connie. Make him understand that you finding her is the only reason you're coming for him."

Carter backspaced over the words on the screen. Then he bgan to type.

....

Where is she? Where's my wife? No more email, call me if you want me. I don't move until I hear her voice. 423-555-0461.

....

"Good, now send it," Tony instructed.

Carter hit the send button. He noted the time was 10:04.

"I'd guess at this hour you won't hear from them until in the morning. They appear to like daylight. After all, they were bold enough to take her from the park in broad daylight. Make sure your phone is charged. We're going back to my place. I don't

209

want to risk being trapped in here if they come expecting to find you. Besides, we don't want them to find us, we want to find Connie."

Carter didn't want to leave his house, but Tony insisted, and Carter knew he was right. If Ratliff was smart enough to use the email to determine when Carter had come home, they could attack in the next few minutes. Reluctantly, he rode back to Tony's house in the Crown Vic. Tony called the IT guys in the KPD to go to Carter's house and see if they could get the computer and trace the IP address, but figured it was probably from Ratliff's smartphone.

After hanging up with IT, Tony called Suzie to inform her they had a guest coming home and to ask her to make sure Carter would be comfortable in the spare room.

****

Carter tossed and turned most of the night and was up with the first peek of the sun. Suzie made coffee but Carter opted for a Diet Coke. About half way through his glass of soda, his phone began playing Ambrosia's *You're the Only Woman*. It was Connie's ringtone.

"Sykes."

"What the hell took you so long to check her email? I should have had you dead last night. Hell, I was looking forward to fucking the bitch before I went to bed. If you hadn't been such a dumbassed detective, I would have. Oh well, a little afternoon delight will be just fine."

Carter knew Ratliff was trying to rattle him and this time he was ready. He wasn't going to let it work. "Ratliff, let me talk with my wife."

"Well, at least you'll know who'll be fucking her before I kill you."

"Let me talk to her. You won't get me until I know she's alive." he paused slightly. "And well."

Carter had similar conversations with suspects in the past, but the emotions were very different when Connie's life was involved. He was trying to go by the book, follow the first rule of negotiation, and get something for anything he gave. He was willing, as he knew all the friends and families of those involved in his cases were, to give up anything the kidnapper wanted to get her back. But he also knew it never worked that way. He had to try to make sure Ratliff focused on his end game, on him. As long as Connie was bait, she was probably safe.

"Oh, she's alive. I hate putting these damn things on speakerphone. Hey, bitch, yell something to your soon to be dead husband."

"Carter, I love you."

"I love you too, babe. I'm coming to bring you home." Carter heard the speakerphone click off.

"How touching that was. Now here's what we're going to do. Come over 421 and meet me at the courthouse in Mountain City. Be there at ten o'clock, not early, not late. I'll bring you here from there so you can get an up close and personal view of me screwing your wife. If there's any trouble, if I get a hint of a cop, my partner here will kill her on the spot. I hope you don't make me kill her, I'm so looking forward to seeing your face as you watch me make her scream."

Carter didn't respond. He knew if he did, he'd say the wrong thing. He just hung up the phone.

"He doesn't want to meet you in Mountain City, he wants you on 421. That's one of the most crooked roads in the United States," Tony, who had been able to hear the conversation over the phone's earspeaker, said. "He's going to try to kill you on 421."

"Yeah, and he's going to get a piece of me on that crooked ass road, too. I know that road like the back of my hand." Carter smiled for the first time since the kidnapping. "The son of a bitch is in my backyard now."

"You still got your ham radio GPS thing on your truck?" Tony asked, remembering something Carter had shown him a few times over the past couple of years.

"APRS, great idea. Yeah, I'll set up the site on your phone so you can track me. Just make sure you stay far enough back so you're not noticed. I don't want to give the piece of shit any reason to hurt Cons. I can handle him on the road."

211

"Don't worry, I've got your ass covered, man. I've done this before."

"I know, you always do."

Carter glanced at the clock as Suzie brought sausage and egg biscuits to the table. After eating, Carter and Tony went to retrieve the Ram, where Carter activated his APRS and made sure Tony was showing his location on the smartphone. Everything set, they headed toward highway 421.

****

Carter sped through Shady Valley, Tennessee and began climbing Iron Mountain on US 421. Suddenly, the road went from being a typical rural back road to one of the most winding roads in America, all while gaining nearly two thousand feet in elevation. Curve after curve, the Ram climbed the mountain. Carter kept checking his rearview mirrors, expecting to see Ratliff at any moment. He didn't have to wait long. A white Nissan 370Z pulled out of a side road and quickly closed in. The sports car was much more agile than the three quarter ton, four wheel drive Ram on the mountain road, and it quickly pulled behind him. A curve later, Carter heard the gunshot. The bullet hit the rear bumper, just to the right of the left corner of the truck. "The son of a bitch is trying to shoot my tire out," Carter thought aloud. He hit the brakes hard before entering the next curve, causing Ratliff to send another shot flying through the air as the Nissan skidded to a stop. Carter hit the gas, but the Z was lighter and quicker. In a couple hundred yards, it was back on his rear bumper. Carter realized Earnhardt himself would not be able to get the Ram to out handle the Nissan on this winding mountain road. As they hit a short straight stretch, Ratliff pulled the Z along the left side of the Ram and tried to force the truck off the road. Even in the intensity of the moment, Carter nearly laughed at this move, there was no way in hell that little Nissan was going to push the Ram off the road. Carter turned the Ram left into the Z, slamming hard into the Nissan's side, forcing the Z to back off and fall in behind him. Again a shot came from the Nissan, going through the tailgate of the Ram.

Quickly, Carter thought of his options. His best bet was to find a way to use the Ram's size to his advantage, but that was nearly impossible unless Ratliff made another boneheaded move like the one he just tried. His next best advantage was the Ram's off-road capabilities, but he figured at that point Ratliff would quit following him and head back to where he was keeping Connie. This move, he reasoned, might very well save his life, but would risk Connie's, something he couldn't, he wouldn't do. He had to have a more subtle advantage somewhere. As they neared the top of the mountain, Carter saw a sign on the left indicating utility work ahead. He remembered reading that there was a new, upscale, mountaintop development being built near the top of the ridge with underground utilities that wouldn't obstruct the resident's views. He and Connie had driven through it a month earlier, Carter thinking it might be a great place to retire and build a mountaintop ham shack. When they checked it out, the first part of the road had been paved, but turned to dirt a quarter mile later, so the utility lines could be buried. Suddenly, Carter had an idea. It was risky, the road conditions he needed might not be in place yet. But he knew it provided his best chance to make the most of the Ram's advantages. He couldn't stay on 421; once they topped the mountain he would have even more difficulty controlling the Ram on the downhill side. He slammed the brake pedal to the floor, turned the wheel hard left, and the truck skidded sideways as it made the turn onto the single lane paved road. Carter smiled when Ratliff followed, making the turn with much less difficulty than the Ram. He looked in his rearview mirror and could see the smile on Ratliff's face. He knew Ratliff was recalling their conversation in Charlotte about the advantages turbo imports had over American muscle. Carter pushed the gas to the floor and just as he remembered, the road turned to a smooth dirt surface. Dust rose behind the Ram as Carter checked his mirror again and sure enough, Ratliff was in hot pursuit. They followed the dirt road for a couple of miles with Ratliff staying on his tail. Then he saw just what he had hoped for. A utility truck was laying buried electric lines into the development and had cut a ditch across the dirt road. Carter slammed on his brakes to slow down and the Z skidded sideways to avoid hitting him. With the touch of a button, the Ram was in four wheel drive. He made his way across the ditch as quickly as possible, while Ratliff tried to recover from his skid. By the time he found his gun and was ready to shoot, the Ram was already rounding the curve ahead. That bullet too hit the Ram's tailgate, piercing Carter's airbrushed badge.

Carter knew the road formed a loop through the development that led back to the short, paved entrance a quarter mile from 421. He knew there was only one way in and one way out of the development, and it was down that entrance. Carter came upon the ditch a little sooner than he had hoped, just past the halfway point of the circle. He knew he had to hurry to get on through the rest of the development and back to the entrance/exit before Ratliff made it back by retracing his tracks. Carter hoped a frustrated Ratliff, having lost his prey, would take his time, giving him more time to execute his plan. Not bothering to take the Ram out of four wheel drive, he stomped the gas pedal. Being tossed around in the rugged Ram, Carter rushed back to the spot where the circle completed itself. He saw no dust to indicate Ratliff had escaped his trap. Carter slid the Ram to a stop sideways across the road, blocking any way out for Ratliff. He slid across the seat, grabbing his gun, his billystick, and jumped out the passenger side door. Running to the front of the truck to keep the Ram's Hemi engine between him and one of Ratliff's bullets, he extended both his arms across the hood with his 9mm in his hands and waited. Soon he heard the Z approach, not in any hurry now. Carter figured Ratliff thought he had simply traveled up the road and escaped, not realizing it was a loop. When Ratliff rounded the curve and saw the Ram sitting across the road, he stopped dead in his tracks, knowing he was caught between the Ram and the ditch. Carter could see Ratliff dialing his phone as he yelled, "Get out of the car ,motherfucker, with your hands up."

Ratliff put down the phone, raised his hands so Carter could see them, and opened the door of the Z. He slid out, hands in the air. Carter looked him dead in the eye, gun trained on him, and said, "I told you, motherfucker, I'd find your sorry ass." Then he fired his 9mm.

****

Ratliff lay on the ground as Tony rounded the curve in his Crown Vic. Carter walked over to Ratliff's side, raised his billystick with his right hand, and landed a blow across his ribcage. "That one's for Thor," Carter said as Ratliff screamed in pain. He raised the stick again.

"Carter, no. Don't do it, man," Tony yelled, now running toward his partner.

Carter stood there with the billystick raised over his head, ready to strike again. He took a step back as Tony arrived. "Calm down, man. Great job, you've got this motherfucker. Now let's find Connie."

Carter remembered seeing Ratliff trying to dial his cell phone before he got out of the car. He looked in the Z and found an iphone on the passenger seat. He opened the door, picked up the phone, and looked at the screen. 'The last number called,' he thought, 'that has to be his partner.' Not familiar with an iphone, Carter started dialing the last number, only to find it two digits short of a full phone number.

"What the hell is the number?" Carter yelled towards Ratliff.

Ratliff only moaned.

Carter quickly memorized the last five of the number he had and began looking for a similar number in the recent calls list. A moment later, he found the number he was looking for. It took a second to figure out the iphone, but Carter dialed the number.

"Did you get him, bro?"

"Yeah, I got him, bro, and now I'm coming after your ass, motherfucker."

There was silence on the other end.

Tony did a quick assessment of Ratliff's condition and made sure he didn't have a weapon on him. He ran up beside Carter. "Let me have the phone, let me find out where Connie is." Carter handed the phone to Tony and hung his head, knowing he was in no mental state to negotiate with his wife's other kidnapper.

"We've got Ratliff," Tony said into the phone. "This doesn't have to get any worse. Tell us where you're at, we'll come get the lady. Then this whole thing will be over."

"Is he alive? Is my brother still alive?"

Tony covered the phone with his hand. "Call in and see if Ratliff has any brothers, hurry. I need a name." Carter grabbed his phone from the Ram and made the call to the Kingsport PD, the number still in his speed dial.

"Yeah, he's still alive. All we want is the lady. Where are you, we'll come get her."

"No, man, I'm not going to go to jail for this shit. Not for ten grand," the man on the phone was in between panic and tears.

"If you help us…"

Tony looked at Carter, who whispers, "Tom, Tom Ratliff"

"If you help us, Tom, things can be a lot easier for you."

There was silence on the phone.

"We're going to eventually find you, Tom. If we have to hunt you down, all bets are off. If you turn yourself in and no one gets hurt, I can help you out."

Carter whispered to Tony, "He's got a '02 Ford Econoline with Tennessee plates. A Shady Valley address."

"Are you at home, Tom?" Tony resumed his phone conversation. A sheriff's car pulled up and a fat deputy walked to the scene. Carter quickly explained that Tony had one of the kidnappers on the phone and believed he was in Shady Valley. Tony and Carter ran to the Crown Vic while the deputy began to take care of Ratliff. Tony turned the Crown Vic around and drove back down the dirt road as Carter gave him the address and put it into the car's GPS.

"It's only five miles from here," said Carter, looking at the GPS.

Tony nodded, still on the phone. "Come on, man, help me out here. I'm trying to give you a break….." Tony heard a gunshot on the other end, then nothing. "Tom, Tom. A couple of seconds passed with nothing but dead air on the other end. "Oh shit. Holy fuck."

"What's going on?" Carter frantically asked.

Tony threw the phone in the console, put both hands on the wheel, and stomped his right foot to the floor.

"What the hell is going on, Tony?" Carter asked again.

"Carter, I heard a gunshot," Tony said as he slammed on the brakes to slow the Crown Vic as it slid into the next curve.

"Oh, shit. What else."

"That's it, just one gunshot, then silence."

"Come on, make this son of a bitch go," Cater yelled desperately.

Tony didn't respond. He had both hands on the steering wheel, his feet working alternately between the gas pedal and the brake as he drove down the mountain road, tires squalling. The Crown Vic tossed the men from side to side, but neither said a word, their silence screaming their fears.

The five minutes of winding down US 421 into Shady Valley was the longest five minutes of Carter's life. His mind raced with questions. Was Connie dead? Could he and Tony get there in time? What would be their first move when they pulled in? The men heard the female voice on the GPS tell them to turn left in five hundred yards.

Tony slammed on the brakes and turned the Crown Vic hard to the left as the car slid onto the road leading to Tom Ratliff's house. Tony again stomped the gas pedal and the sedan roared down the dirt road, a cloud of dust rising behind it.

"There's the silver van," Carter yelled.

Tony slid the car to a stop. Both men opened their doors, guns drawn, looking first toward the old, white, run-down frame house, then around its perimeter for any signs of Tom Ratliff. They saw nothing.

"Ratliff," Tony yelled at the top of his lungs. "Kingsport police. Come out with your hands up."

Nothing.

"Ratliff," yelled Carter this time.

Still no response.

Both men knew from training and experience the thirty yards leading to the house's front porch were a dead man's zone. Taking the quickest path and running straight in was suicide. Without speaking, Tony nodded to his left, indicating he would proceed on that flank. In return, Carter looked to his right, surveying the yard in that direction. Both men looked back at each other, nodded their acknowledgement of the unspoken plan of attack, and in unison ran across opposite sides of the yard, The yard provided each of them shields every few feet: a tree, the van, an old freezer, which they used for cover before proceeding to the next. Both men were surprised as they reached the porch without a shot being fired.

"Ratliff, we're coming in. On the ground, NOW!" yelled Tony.

No response.

Tony nodded at Carter and opened the screen door. Their backs together, they entered the old house. Suddenly, Carter rushed for the couch in the living room as Tony turned to cover his ill-advised move. Carter threw his arms around Connie, who was sitting; leaning forward with her face in her hands. A .38 was on the floor in front of her.

Tony spotted Tom Ratliff's body, face down, on the floor, on the other side of the room, motionless. An iphone was on the floor beside him. The back of his head was shattered by a gunshot. He moved slowly toward the fallen kidnapper, his gun focused on him just in case. When Ratliff didn't move, Tony turned the body over.

"He's dead," Tony said, softly.

Carter didn't hear him. He was holding Connie in his arms, her head on his shoulder.

"You ok, babe? God I love you. You ok?"

"Is he dead?" Connie weakly asked her husband.

"He's dead, Connie. You did good, girl. You did real good," Tony told her, walking their way.

Connie began crying into Carter's shoulder as sirens and blue lights entered the front yard.

TWENTY

With the deputies arriving at the scene, Tony went to the front porch and gave them the 'all clear' signal. They turned off their blue lights and sirens and walked to the porch to meet Tony for a quick briefing on the situation. Tony provided the basic details of what had happened; the kidnapping, the car chase, the dead bodies of Tom Ratliff and Thor inside. The deputies began securing the area in yellow police tape. They waited as long as possible before approaching Carter and Connie and assisting them from the scene.

With Carter and Connie in the back seat, Tony drove the Crown Vic slowly back up the mountain to retrieve the Ram. When they arrived, the volunteer rescue squad was loading Mike Ratliff into the ambulance. He had one gunshot wound in his left thigh, multiple broken ribs, and what appeared to be a day old bite wound on his left forearm. He'd lost a lot of blood, and was in quite a bit of pain, but the paramedics felt he'd survive.

"Where are you taking him?" Tony asked.

"Bristol Regional," the paramedic gave the name of the hospital.

"Any way you can take him to Holston Valley? I'd like to have him in my jurisdiction. He kidnapped the wife of one of our retired officers."

"I think that can be arranged. In fact, I think I heard the patient request that, didn't you, Donnie?"

"Sounded like it to me," the second paramedic agreed.

Tony walked over to where Carter was helping Connie into the Ram. "How is she?"

"Shook up pretty bad. I don't see anything major wrong with her physically. Some bruising on the face and arms. Looks like he hit her pretty hard a couple of times. I'm taking her to the hospital for examination anyway."

"Was she...." Tony couldn't find the words to finish his thought. He didn't have to.

"I don't think so. She hasn't said anything and I'm not going to push her. They'll let me know after they examine her."

"How are you, man?"

"If she's ok, then I'll be fine."

"I can get the Ram home if y'all want to ride with me."

"Thanks, Tony, but I'll be ok. Hell, I'd just worry about the Ram. I think Connie will be more comfortable riding in it, it's familiar to her. I'll take it slow, there's no need to rush now." Carter paused. "Thank you, man, thank you for everything," he said, as he threw his arms around Tony, letting off a flood of emotion in the process.

"Hey, man, that's what we do for each other," Tony said, as he threw his arms around Carter. "We won, man. We beat those sons of bitches. We got her back safely. We got the bad guys."

"Yeah, but I don't ever want one that close again."

"Neither do I, man, neither do I."

The men broke their hug and both looked at the Ram. It had three bullet holes in the rear, and the driver's side showed significant damage from the impact with the Z. Carter instinctively checked the left side tires but it was obvious there was plenty of clearance on the three quarter ton, four wheel drive. He stepped on the running board, lifted himself into the driver's seat, turned the ignition key, and turned the truck around. He and Connie headed down the one lane road, back to US Hwy 421. Their next stop was Holston Valley Hospital.

Tony, the deputy, and the paramedics finished their work at the scene and headed out. On the crooked mountain road, Tony easily caught the ambulance and was glad to see it take highway 394 towards Kingsport. Tony followed it until he turned to go to his office. Once there, he requested all the information available on the Ratliff brothers, figuring he might need it for his report. He also knew Carter was going to need it to tie them to the murder of Doug Westlake.

****

After three hours at the hospital, and a stop at Pizza Hut to pick up a large supreme pan pizza, Carter and Connie made it home. Other than some cuts, bruising, and mental trauma, she had checked out ok. Carter was relieved that she hadn't been raped, especially considering Mike Ratliff's threats. He had, after all, watched their performance for the Carolina Couples. 'The Carolina Couples,' Carter thought. Up until now, the Westlake case hadn't entered his mind, all his concern being for Connie's safety. Now that she was safe at home, the case again began to dominate his thoughts. He wasn't working on it tonight, though. Tonight was for holding his wife and taking care of anything she needed.

However much he tried to comfort Connie and be there for her, he could feel something was missing for both of them. That something was Thor. He should have been right there, in Connie's lap, welcoming her back home. He hadn't yet asked her about him, or what happened during her abduction. He wanted to, but he knew he needed to give her time to absorb and deal with everything herself. Only then, in her own time, would she share with him what had happened to the dog they both had raised from a puppy, the dog they both loved dearly. Carter made a note to call the Johnson County Sheriff's Department in the morning and arrange to get Thor's body bought home for a decent burial.

****

Carter slept better than he expected, considering the day he had just been through. He figured he was simply worn out. When he woke up around eight, he was anxious to get on with the work that lay ahead. He knew he needed to call Tedder and inform him of the progress they had made in the Westlake case, but figured that could wait until he and Tony had a chance to interrogate Ratliff at the hospital. Carter figured there was a good chance the Westlake case would be solved during that interrogation. Then he would call Tedder with the good news.

He attempted to make coffee, and poured a cup for Connie, who was just beginning to stir. He sat at the kitchen table with his morning glass of diet Dr. Pepper and a notepad, and, as he always did before an interrogation, prepared the questions he wanted to ask Ratliff. He wasn't sure exactly how much Ratliff knew about Collins' and Westlake's Utopia scheme, but doubted he knew much, if anything, about the details of the planned takeover. He figured Ratliff was more like Collins' gofer, doing the dirty work while Collins kept his hands clean. Carter figured Ratliff was the man Collins sent to kill Westlake. He wanted Ratliff put away for a long time for what he had done to Connie, but he also needed his help to tie Collins, the mastermind, to the kidnapping. That, in turn, would further tie him to both the Utopia scheme and the Westlake murder. He was hoping the ballistics on the .38 Connie had killed Tim Ratliff with would match the Westlake murder weapon. It would sure make wrapping up the Westlake case easier.

By ten o'clock, Carter and Connie had finished their breakfast of Muffin Tops cereal and Connie had convinced him that she was ok to stay at home by herself for a couple of hours. He called Tony and drove the battered Ram to the police station. From there, the plan was to compare notes, then ride to the hospital to interrogate Ratliff. For Tony, it should be a simple matter of getting Ratliff's statement, plus any info he wanted to spill. He already had enough evidence to put him away for kidnapping Connie and attempted murder on Carter. But Tony knew Carter needed more. More for himself and Connie, and more info for the Westlake case.

Carter's plan was first, to stay calm. He knew keeping his emotions in check would be harder than he imagined. His strike to Ratliff's ribcage with the billystick was evidence of the anger he felt. If he could keep himself under control, he would first tie Collins to the kidnapping, then attempt to find out how much Ratliff was involved in the plot to take over Utopia and in the Westlake murder. 'If I can control myself, this investigation might be over with sooner, rather than later,' he thought.

When they walked out of the police station, Tony caught a glance of the driver's side of the Ram. "Aw, man, I'm sorry about the Ram."

Carter hadn't really thought much about the truck before Tony's comment. "Yeah, that'll kill the Carfax on it. I guess I'll have to run it until the wheels fall off now, I won't get anything out of it on trade."

"I've got a buddy who runs a body shop. I'm sure he can fix it cheap."

"That's what I've got insurance for, so I can get it fixed RIGHT."

"Hey, man, if you don't want my help…"

"I love you, Tony, but I've seen your truck." Both men laughed. Tony's '99 Ford Ranger was a rolling piece of shit. Nearly two hundred thousand miles, many dents, and lots of rust had been part of its fourteen year life.

"Point taken, man."

****

At the hospital, Tony and Carter were directed to room 521 where Ratliff was being treated. The nurse informed them the gunshot wound to the thigh had caused him to lose quite a bit of blood and the broken ribs were causing him a lot of pain. "Poor guy," Carter said sarcastically. She noted Ratliff was under some pretty strong painkillers, but should be able to handle an interrogation, as long as it didn't get too heated.

"Take him off the fucking painkillers," Carter muttered under his breath.

"Got a couple of visitors for you," the nurse announced to Ratliff as they entered the room. He looked surprised at first, then he stiffened as if at attention when he saw his interrogators.

"Mike Ratliff, I'm detective Tony Ward with the Kingsport Police Department," Tony formally introduced himself. "I think you already know former detective, and my partner, Carter Sykes."

"Fuck y'all," Ratliff weakly uttered.

"Don't think you'll be doing that today," Tony said calmly. "But I'm sure there will be some boys who will be taking you up on that when you're in the state pen. Question is, how long do you want to stay there enjoying their services?"

"You ain't got shit on me."

"Why do they all say that?" Tony's eyes glanced toward the ceiling. "Dude, there's no need for you to say a thing, I've got enough on you right now so you'll have your midlife crisis with

Tyrone. The cop's wife you kidnapped will ID you. The cop you tried to kill can ID you. Let's just get this over with. You're going to jail for a long time, no matter what you say. The question is, how much can you tell us so that the DA and the judge will go easier on you? You might want to see the outside world again before you're eating baby food."

Ratliff said nothing.

"For the record, did you kidnap Connie Sykes?"

Ratliff laid silently on his bed.

"For the record, did you try to kill Carter Sykes?"

"Hell, I was just racing the son of a bitch. Trying to prove that a turbo could kick a V8's ass."

"How'd that work out for you, Ratliff?" Carter asked.

"Anything else you want to say in a statement?" Tony asked.

A few moments past. The wheels turning in Ratliff's head were obvious, but he said nothing.

"Carter, he doesn't want to talk to me. What do you have for Tyrone's girl here?"

"Tell me how you know Sam Collins," Carter began his questioning.

"Ratliff's eyes showed his reaction to the question, but he said nothing.

"Do you want to tell me why he sent you to kill me? "

Again, Ratliff said nothing.

"Have it your way. I'll be questioning Collins tomorrow. Do you think he's going to help you out? Hell, he'll make the bed for you and Tyrone, probably even turn down the sheets. He'd apply the KY, but Tyrone won't use any. Collins is going to throw your ass under the bus to try to save his. But you know what? I know better. I've got the evidence to connect you to Collins. And I've got evidence to connect the two of you to a lot bigger stuff, including the murder of Doug Westlake. You do know that South Carolina has the death penalty for murder, don't you? So, you can make my job easier and tell me what I want to know, and maybe, just maybe, earn some brownie points with the DA. Or, I can turn you over to the mercy of Sam Collins' testimony. How do you think that will go for you?"

"I didn't kill nobody, man. Nobody."

"Then answer my questions. Do you know Sam Collins?"

"Yeah, I know Collins."

"How do you know him?"

"When I moved to North Carolina, he gave me a couple of jobs. Small things at first, small repairs on properties him and Westlake were involved in. Then he gave me bigger ones, ones that paid pretty damn good."

"Did he introduce you to Angie?" Carter asked, more out of curiosity than needing to really know.

"Yeah, said she needed an escort to the club. Man, that bitch ain't a lot to look at, but she gives the best blowjobs ever." A smile appeared on his face.

Carter wanted to come back with a smart ass comment about the blowjobs he'd get, and give, in prison, but resisted the temptation. He had Ratliff talking now, and didn't want to rock the boat. "What did he give you to come after me?"

Ratliff said nothing.

"Do I need to get a warrant for your bank account? That'll take about ten minutes. An hour later, I'll have the money trail linking you two together. I'm just trying to give you the chance to cooperate, here, to earn yourself some points with the judge."

"Twenty grand," Ratliff said.

Carter raised his eyes, upset with the amount. He had expected something along the lines of fifty grand to kill a cop. "Why did you kidnap Connie?"

"Collins said I should use her to get to you. He said you two were really in love, said he could tell it at the club. He said y'all didn't fuck, y'all made love, even in front of a crowd. He said you'd do anything to try to save her, including making yourself an easy target. He told me telling you how I was going to fuck her would make you crazy, make you an easy target. So we took her."

Carter realized just how close Collins was to being right. "By 'we' you mean you and Tom?"

"Yeah," Ratliff looked down. "He didn't really want to do it, you know. I offered him five grand to help me. With him still living in Shady Valley, he had the perfect location."

"What were you going to do with Connie after I was dead?" Carter asked, more for his knowledge than for the case.

"I knew we'd have to kill her. I really didn't want to, but I knew we'd have to."

Anger filled Carter. He wanted to beat the living hell out of Ratliff right then and there. But he knew he had a job to do. He had him talking, he had to go for more information. "What do you know about Collins' business dealings?"

"Nothing, man, nothing at all. I just worked for him when he called me for a job. That's all, I swear."

It was obvious to both detectives that Ratliff's attitude had changed. Carter was hoping to close this case right now. "How much did he give you to kill Doug Westlake?" Carter used the assumptive close technique, giving Ratliff an easy way to admit the murder.

"Man, I didn't kill Doug Westlake. I didn't even know the man that well. Just seen him at the club a few times."

"You did know him though?"

"Yeah, I knew him. Fucked his wife once. Always wanted to fuck that daughter of his, but she was always with the money men. I was doing ok, but it took more than construction pay to get that girl. Seen her with some of the biggest names in the Charlotte area."

"So you're telling me Collins didn't send you to kill Doug Westlake?"

"Man, if Collins killed Westlake I don't know anything about it. I told you, I ain't killed nobody, nobody."

"Except the best dog on the planet. I'm done with this piece of shit, Tony. I've got all I need. I don't think we'll need this guy again before the trial."

"I'm telling you, man, I didn't kill nobody," Ratliff said, as Carter and Tony turned and walked out of the hospital room.

"I guess it's a trip to Rock Hill, South Carolina next?" asked Tony.

"Yeah, but let me talk to Tedder and look at Collins' financials first. I'd like to have all my ducks in a row before our visit with him. A surprise visit tomorrow morning should work just fine."

"Yeah, I agree. We are bringing him back to Tennessee, right?"

"Get the extradition warrant. But I bet he'll be going back to South Carolina for the murder of Doug Westlake," Carter said.

TWENTY-ONE

After he got home, Carter called Sheriff Ralph Tedder to give him an update on the case. He told him about the kidnapping, the car chase on highway 421, the attempt on his own life, and the capture of Mike Ratliff. He explained how Westlake and Collins were planning to take over Utopia and turn it into a swingers paradise, and make a ton of money in the process. Carter probably didn't need to go into detail with Tedder as deeply as he did, but it helped him to organize the case in his mind.

"Sounds like one hell of a plan," Tedder said in his southern draw, referring to the plan to acquire Utopia. "But why kill Westlake? He was basically the point man, keeping any attention off of Collins. Besides, he was in position to run the new swingers resort. Sounds like Collins made a bad mistake if he killed Westlake."

"A few million reasons by the time everything was said and done," replied Carter. "Instead of being a partner in the venture, he'd own the whole thing. Maggie or Emily would have a hard time coming after something that was illegally gained to start with. And I'm not so sure Maggie isn't involved with Collins. I'm sure they knew each other in the biblical sense. She sure tried hard to keep us off the track of the Carolina Couples"

"I guess so. But I wouldn't have done it that way. I would have left Westlake in place to take the heat and run the show. And I would have kept getting his wife at the swingers parties. Of course a million dollars can make people do strange things."

"Seen it happen many times before. I'll probably know more after I've had a chance to go through Collins' financials this evening. Maybe I'll find something there that will clear this up."

"I glanced through those things myself," Tedder said proudly. "Looks to me like the guy had a hell of a CPA business going on in Rock Hill. He sure as hell couldn't have done that here in Herbsville."

"I guess between a million dollars and lots of crazy sex his judgment was clouded. I'll take a look at the financials tonight, and tomorrow we're heading to Rock Hill to arrest him and bring him back to Tennessee for hiring Ratliff to kill us. All the details are being worked out with the South Carolina authorities as we speak."

"It will be good to get the case closed. Hell son, solving this murder case will virtually mean my re-election. I may have to hire you as a deputy."

Carter laughed, "I may have to take you up on that Tedder. Connie might make me get out and find a paying gig. But don't let Sam go, cause I ain't climbing no trees. Hopefully, in a couple of days this whole thing will be behind us."

"Yeah, hopefully. Thanks for your work, Columbo."

"I owed it to somebody," Carter said. "Take care, I'll fill you in after we get Collins."

"Be careful," Tedder said, as he hung up the phone.

****

That afternoon, Carter sat down at his computer and began to pour over Collins' financials. Tedder was right about one thing, Collins was doing well for himself as a CPA. He had some of the biggest clients in the Charlotte area, some Carter was sure he had seen at the Carolina Couples event. While it appeared Collins had seen some impact from the Great Recession, his business was still strong, netting him nearly a million per year in pretax income. At least Carter knew Collins had the means to spend twenty grand or so to hire a hillbilly like Ratliff to kill him, or Westlake.

For nearly two hours, Carter looked for some kind of red flag, but found nothing. Sam Collins was squeaky clean, too clean for Carter. But the man was a CPA and apparently a pretty damn good one. He would know how to avoid red flags. Carter wasn't an accountant, he was a small city detective trying to find something a big city cop would turn over to their accounting squad. His head was starting to swim in all the numbers, so it was a relief when Connie called him for supper.

The Sykes' sat down for a quiet supper of meatloaf, mashed potatoes, and green peas. It was one of Carter's favorite dishes.

He called it 'a dish' although it was really three dishes, because he always mixed them together and ate them as one. Their talk over supper was simple. Carter still didn't want to push Connie about her ordeal. At this point, there was no reason to make her relive it.

Carter could tell her heart really wasn't into the case the way it had been before the kidnapping. She asked for superficial information on Ratliff's interrogation, but she was glad he didn't go into details. Carter could tell the passion with which she once talked about the case was no longer there. She had been through a lot, and she would have to come to grips with all she had been through in her own time.

Enjoying a tequila and diet Sunkist, Carter got back to business on the financials. After another hour of digging, he finally found the financial link to Ratliff, a ten thousand dollar transfer the day Connie was kidnapped. He did not need to dig further at this point; he knew what it was for. A 'half now, half upon completion' arrangement was common in criminal circles. Carter often wondered if this was conjured up in the movies and bad guys just followed it, or if the movie writers got it from real life. Carter resisted the urge to relive the chicken and egg debate. It really didn't matter, the ten grand was half the amount Collins was to pay Ratliff to kill him. That was enough to verify Ratliff's story and tie the two of them together.

Carter sat back at his desk, proud that he had found the link between Collins and Ratliff. He knew before the trial a good financial attorney would do a better job than he had, but he had plenty for Tony to make an arrest. As he sipped on his second drink, one thing bothered him. He couldn't find a similar transaction for the Westlake murder. He went back to early June and again looked through the transactions. He found nothing linking Collins to Westlake's murder. There was the Carolina Couples connection and their involvement in the Utopia transaction. But these ties were only circumstantial to the murder. They would not stand up in court. Frustrated with not finding the financial smoking gun, he knew he would need more to arrest Collins for Westlake's murder. He walked away from his desk to spend a little time with Connie. He needed to rest. He had all he needed to bring Collins back to Tennessee. Tomorrow was the three-hour plus ride to Rock Hill and the arrest of Sam Collins.

"I see you're finally pulling yourself away from that computer," Connie said when Carter walked into the living room. "I was beginning to think you'd gone back on the force again."

"I guess in a way I have, with the way this case has turned," Carter said. "Only difference is I ain't getting paid for it."

"That stinks. I'm sure there's something I could use the money for," Connie laughed.

"Yeah, me too," said Carter. He began to tell her about what he had found in Collins' financials. Connie half listened, wanting to hear about the case, but not really wanting to understand all the details of it right now.

"He didn't have time to be careful," Connie told him after Carter described his concerns about finding the transaction to Ratliff but not for Westlake's murder.

"What?" Carter asked, shocked that Connie had finally said something after he had been talking for ten minutes.

Realizing she had hit on something seemed to reignite her enthusiasm. "He didn't have time to make any other arrangements. With Westlake, he had probably planned his moves, may have actually saved the cash back and paid the hit man that way. With us, he had to act quickly, we were on his tail. Once he knew who we really were, he knew we had connected him to Westlake and their dirty dealings. It's like you're always telling me about football, a quarterback needs time to stand in the pocket. If he doesn't have time, he makes a mistake and throws an interception. Same thing here. We had Collins under pressure. He didn't have time. He had to act quickly. He made a bad throw and you picked him off, sweetie."

Carter noted this was the first time she had called him "sweetie" since the kidnapping. "Damn, girl, who taught you so much about football? I didn't think you listened to me when I went on about it."

"I do listen from time to time, sweetie. Besides, after hearing it for thirty years, it was bound to sink in sooner or later."

Carter gave his wife a kiss. "I love you, babe."

"I know."

****

Tony picked Carter up in the Crown Vic at 6:00 am and they headed off to Rock Hill to visit Sam Collins at his office. Carter went over his findings in Collins' financials and Tony agreed with them. He also agreed with Connie's deduction that Collins' error had most likely been a result of being under pressure to take action. The better than three hour drive passed quickly as the two friends talked: about the case, about their lives and families, about retirement, and about the department.

"What the hell possessed you to go to a nudist colony in the first place?" Tony finally asked as they crossed Lake Norman on I 77.

"Actually, Connie did," Carter admitted. "One of her coworkers went to one last year and came back telling Connie how great it was. She came home telling me that we just had to go. This was nearly a year ago. I figured, 'this too will pass', but it didn't. She kept talking about it, researching it on the internet, and so on. She even found a group of ham radio operators in Texas that were nudists and operated from a nudist park down there. Finally, I gave in. I told her I'd go after I retired, knowing I wouldn't have you guys asking me every day where I'd gone. That worked out, well, didn't it?"

"And everybody was nekkid?"

"Yep. Men, women, children, everybody. Some were young, some old, some skinny, some fat. But everyone was bare ass nekkid."

"Did you see anything….you know, hot?"

"Yeah, some of the women were pretty hot. And there were plenty of not so hot women too. Most people were there as couples. Even the gay guys," Carter added, just to get Tony's reaction.

"Gay guys? Awh, man. Don't tell me that a bunch of naked queers were running around down there. Awh"

"There were a few. But the nice thing was, except for not having any clothes on, it was just like any other campground in America. No one tried to hit on us. There was the occasional off-color joke, but no one was out of line."

233

"I just don't think I could handle being around a bunch of naked women."

"After about fifteen minutes you hardly notice it at all. Except on the putt-putt course."

"What happened on the putt-putt course?" Tony asked, with wonder in his voice.

"Connie and her distractions, that's what happened," Carter used his fingers to put quotation marks around distractions. "You know, the funny thing was, the only woman that I wanted while I was there was Connie. And everything she did turned me on that much more. She kicked my ass at putt-putt because all I could think about was, well, her ass. The other women didn't bother me at all, just her. But I did get my revenge at tennis."

"Sounds like y'all are even then."

"Yeah, we were supposed to play cornhole for the Sykes family naked athletic championship, but then all this murder shit came up. I guess now we'll always be even."

The traffic had picked up substantially as they entered Charlotte, so Tony paid more attention to the road. Carter began mentally reviewing his plan of attack on Sam Collins. He wanted to make sure he got all the information he could about both Collins' attempt on his and Connie's life, as well as the murder of Doug Westlake, before they put the cuffs on him.

****

Tony parked the Crown Vic in downtown Rock Hill, and they made their way to Collins' office. The office was busy, and they were unnoticed as they approached the receptionist.

"We're here to see Sam Collins," Tony announced to the attractive, late twenties receptionist. Tony couldn't help but wonder if she was part of the Carolina Couples as well.

"Do you have an appointment?" the lady asked.

"I don't think we need one ma'am," said Tony, showing her his badge. "We're with the Kingsport, Tennessee Police Department. We're here on official business."

The lady looked stunned. "Wait a moment, please." She reached for the phone and spoke to someone they assumed was Collins. After a short conversation, she hung up. "Right this way, gentlemen," she said, as she stood up and led them down a hallway to Collins' corner office. "Mr. Collins, these gentlemen with the police are here to see you."

"Show them in, Polly," Collins said, as he stood up and walked from behind his mahogany desk. Holding out his right hand to Tony, he introduced himself. "I'm Sam Collins."

"Tony Ward, detective, Kingsport PD. I think you already know my partner, Carter Sykes?".

"Well, I know him as Marty. Good morning."

Carter nodded.

"Polly, call Paul Trotman and ask him to come over here immediately."

"Yes sir," she said, as she turned and walked out the door.

"Gentleman, have a seat." Collins pointed to two big leather chairs in front of his desk. The detectives walked over and sat in the chairs as Collins walked behind his desk, sat down, and leaned back. "What brings y'all to Rock Hill?"

"A kidnapping and attempted murder," Tony spoke up.

"Oh no. Who were the victims?" Collins asked. Carter noted he referred to 'the victims' in plural, despite the fact Tony had not indicated there was more than one.

"That would me my wife and I," Carter responded. "Lucky for us, the murder attempt wasn't successful."

"I would say so. But why are you here?"

"Because we have one of your contractors, Mike Ratliff, in custody for the crimes. Since Mr. Ratliff works for you, we wanted to ask you a few questions."

"Yes, I know Mike. Nice guy. Bit of a hillbilly, but he sure knows how to renovate a property ."

"It's a shame he's not quite as good at finishing off a murder, isn't it?"

"I guess that depends on which side of the murder you're on," Collins replied with a sly smile.

235

Tony took over. "Mr. Ratliff tells us that you hired him to kill Mr. and Mrs. Sykes."

"Now why would he say something like that? I've been nothing but good to the boy. I found plenty of work for him, good paying jobs for a man in his field. Even introduced him to the nice lady he dates. I've been under the impression we were friends."

"I asked myself the same question," Tony continued. "The only reason I could think of was that it was true. So we came down here to talk to you, to see if you could shed some light on the situation."

"Why in the world would I hire anyone to kill Mr. and Mrs. Sykes?" I just met them last weekend and, quite frankly, enjoyed the show they put on." Collins looked at Carter and winked.

"Because you found out who he really was. You realized he was on to your plans for the Utopia Sun Club." Tony stopped, not yet wanting to mention the murder of Doug Westlake, wanting to see where Collins would take the conversation.

"Utopia what?" Collins replied.

About that time the receptionist's voice came over Collins' speakerphone. "Mr. Collins, Mr. Trotman is here."

"Thank you, Polly, send him in." The men turned their heads toward the door and waited on Trotman to enter the room. In a few moments the door swung open. Carter immediately recognized the man. It was the same man he and Connie had seen standing in front of Emily Westlake at the Carolina Couples event.

"Gentleman, this is my attorney, Paul Trotman. Paul, these two men are with the Kingsport, Tennessee Police Department. Apparently, one of the guys I recommend to clients has said I hired him to kill Mr. Sykes." Collins looked at Carter.

"Well, that's nonsense," said Trotman. "If a man of Mr. Collins' stature were going to have a man killed, he'd do it right. The fact that you are standing here, Mr. Sykes, says that the killer didn't do it right. Therefore, I don't think my client could be guilty." Trotman stood up straight, proud of his logical argument.

"Oh, but there's plenty more, Mr. Trotman. We have the confession of Mr. Ratliff. We have motive, Mr. Collins' connection to the Utopia Sun Club. And we have the money trail. We found the payment he made to Ratliff for the murder. We have all we need to arrest Mr. Collins' for kidnapping and attempted murder."

"You've been through my client's financials?" Trotman wasn't standing so straight now.

"We're not rookies, Mr. Trotman. Of course we went through his financials," Tony responded.

"Why are you still here then?" asked Trotman. "Why haven't you arrested my client if you've already decided he's guilty? I'll answer that. You know he's not guilty. You're looking for something here."

"We know, way beyond a reasonable doubt, he's guilty. We haven't arrested him yet because we'd like to hear from him concerning the murder of Doug Westlake."

"What does Westlake's murder have to do with this?" Collins' blurted out.

"You tell us," said Carter.

"Doug and I were close, real close. We had several business dealings together over the years. Most of them through his real estate business. I invested in, and assisted with, many of his projects here in the Charlotte area. And yes, we were both members of the Carolina Couples, there's no crime in that. But I don't know a damn thing about his murder. Doug's death is a huge loss to me. He was a trusted friend. I assure you, I had absolutely nothing to do with his death. Hell, his death will cost me a lot of money. And I don't like losing money."

"I think we both know you had him killed, Collins," Carter said. "The biggest question I have is whether Maggie Westlake was in on it with you."

"Hell, no I wasn't involved with Maggie, except for a few flings at Carolina Couples events, a couple of which Doug himself was a part of. And why in the hell would I have killed Doug? I told you, he was my friend. A man in my position doesn't have many friends, you know. He was a business partner. We were members of Carolina Couples together. I didn't need to kill anyone to get with Maggie, I could fuck her every month at an event. Give me one good motive I have to kill Doug Westlake and I'll give you a hundred why I wouldn't do it."

"You were going to have to split a small fortune with him when the Utopia project came to fruition," Carter said calmly.

Trotman began putting together where Carter's line of questioning was going. "Sam, I think you've said enough here."

"But I didn't kill Doug. I needed Doug. He was the key to Utopia."

"How was Westlake the key to the Utopia project?" Carter probed.

"Sam," Trotman tried to stop Collins, but realized he was going to give up the Utopia project in order to put a quick end to the murder accusations.

"The plan was almost complete. There was no way I would have rocked the boat at this point. Not even for Doug's half of the project. The whole thing had been Doug's idea anyway. Why the hell would I kill him now? His death is only delaying things. Acquiring the nudist camp's land was only part of the story. We stood to reap many times that amount in building houses, running the club, and so forth. I needed Doug for that. His death is going to cost me both money and aggravation."

"Sam, shut the fuck up!" yelled Trotman. "Gentlemen, if you're going to arrest my client, then do so. If not, this meeting is finished."

"What was the plan after the takeover"" Carter pressed on.

"Someone has to run the damn club. Membership fees to an upper end swingers club in the middle of nowhere, where people can carry out their wildest fantasies; screw by the pool, in the woods, even on the putt-putt course, will be extremely profitable. We have it all lined up. The cream of society in four states will be coming to the club. These people can, and will, afford the type of experience we are going to provide for them. And it's not dependent on the damn economy. The residual income potential from this project is ridiculous. But I need Doug Westlake to pull it off. I had the least motive of anyone to kill my friend."

"Gentlemen, I insist. This meeting is over. Arrest my client or get out," Trotman insisted.

"Sam Collins, you're under arrest for conspiracy to kidnapping and conspiracy to attempt murder." Tony read Collins his Miranda rights. "I'm sure that before this is all said and done, there will be plenty of other charges surrounding the Utopia scheme and the murder of Doug Westlake. But these charges alone should put you away for quite a while."

"I'll get bail taken care of and have you back here tomorrow afternoon," Trotman told Collins, as Tony cuffed him and led him down the hall, out the door, and to the Kingsport PD squad car with the uniform waiting to transport Collins to Tennessee.

Carter looked over at Trotman, who had followed them out and watched Collins being assisted into the squad car. "I could tell by your reaction that he had you investing in his Utopia scam. Had you just paid a deposit, or were you one of the ones who paid the entire ten grand up front?"

"Up front," Trotman weakly replied, hanging his head. "What man my age wouldn't pay up front for the opportunity to fuck a girl like Emily Westlake?"

As they were getting into the Crown Vic, Carter put both hands on the roof of the car as if to stop himself. He looked across the roof at Tony, who was opening his door. "You know, I think we need to go talk to Emily Westlake. She keeps popping up in a lot of strange places for a girl studying library science."

"When?"

"Right now, it's not even out of our way home if we go back through Spartanburg."

"You know Trotman will have Collins out on bail tomorrow by noon. We'll lose time to work on him."

"I know. But we'll still have plenty of time with him. By the time they get him booked and settled in, we'll probably be back in Kingsport. And quite honestly, after hearing him, I'm not convinced he killed Westlake. His story makes sense. He needed Westlake. As long as there was more money to be made, Collins had incentive to keep Westlake alive and share in the profits. And, if the type of people I saw in Charlotte was any indication, there were plenty of profit to go around."

"Ok then, where to?"

"Let's stop at Wofford College in Spartanburg, I'll get the address to the library with my smartphone and put it in your GPS. I'm sure someone there will know Emily Westlake."

"She sounds hard to forget."

"Once you see her, you'll know why."

TWENTY-TWO

The one-hour trip to Spartanburg went by quickly for Tony and Carter. Tony knew there was more to Emily's involvement in both the Utopia scheme and her dad's murder than he understood. Carter wasn't sure he understood her role, but reasoned it was now time to find out. The ride to Spartanburg gave Carter just enough time to lay out his case for wanting to talk to her immediately.

"She just keeps popping up in too many places at the right, or wrong, time, depending on how you look at it," Carter explains to Tony why he wants to talk with Emily. "First, she leaves her mother the day after her father is buried. Then she shows up in the Dawson financials Next we find her screwing Trotman, among others, at the Carolina Couples event. Now she pops up again, this time in Trotman's comments as we arrest Collins. There's nothing incriminating by itself, but we've got to know more, we've got to know why she keeps popping up every time we find something new in this case. This girl ain't no ordinary twenty-two year old library science major. We've got to find out what she knows. If we're lucky, she'll lie about something we already know, which will point us in the right direction. Either way, I know we have a lot to gain by even a casual conversation with her."

"Ok, man, I'm convinced. But how are you going to start the conversation? 'Emily, every time I turn around I find you fucking somebody involved in your daddy's murder?'"

"Not a bad way to put it. Sometimes the direct approach scares them into talking."

"Or scares them to silence."

"Let me ask some general questions first and we'll see how things go from there. I don't like to do it, but I'm kind of playing this one by ear, hoping she'll give us what we need, or at least point us in the right direction."

"Alright, man, this one's in your court."

For the final few minutes of the trip, Carter pondered how he would begin the interview with Emily. Part of him liked the direct

241

approach, thinking the shock value of showing up and asking blunt questions might just unravel the young woman. Then again, she wasn't your normal college girl. She was living in a high flying swingers world, one with lots of money, and lots of power. Carter was sure she was the one to tipped Collins off as to who he and Connie really were. He knew she would be more poised than most women her age. He just needed to find a way to get her to talk.

Upon arriving at Wofford, Carter and Tony checked in with campus police, who they had contacted and informed of their impending arrival. The campus cop escorted them by electric golf cart to the library. As they walked in the front door, Tony noticed a beautiful young woman behind the front desk. He nudged Carter on the arm. "That has to be Emily Westlake."

Carter saw Emily, who was working with a library patron, and nodded. As they walked closer, Emily looked up and saw them coming toward her. She dumped the library patron and bolted to the back room. Carter and Tony knew immediately she was making her way out of the library through a back exit.

"Aww, shit, she's going to run," Carter said. "I'm too damn old to chase down young girls."

"Not one that looks like that," Tony couldn't resist the comment.

"She'll head to the loading dock," said the campus policeman. "Come on this way. It'll be quicker." The cop turned and ran toward the door they had just entered. The detectives followed.

The three of them headed back out the front door and around the side of the library. As they ran, the campus policeman called for backup on his handheld radio. They rounded the back of the building and saw Emily jumping over the loading dock's railing and running down the sidewalk. The campus cop stopped running, out of breath.

"Come on, we can't let her go," Carter yelled.

"She ain't going far. She's heading right for my partner, Gary. Come on, we'll follow her and catch her when she turns around." The campus cop began a slow jog toward the alley Emily just ran down. Carter and Tony began to jog, following him. They slowed to a walk as the reached its entrance.

Sure enough, in about a minute, here came Emily running back down the same alley she had just run up, trapped between the other campus cop on the far end and the three of them on Carter's end. Emily saw she was caught between a rock and a hard place. She stopped, bent over with her hands on her knees to catch her breath, then raised her arms over her head. The four men continued walking toward her, Gary getting there first.

"What are you running for, Emily?" Carter asked as he approached.

"What are you doing here?" she asked.

"I think you know why I'm here or you wouldn't be running from me. I've come to have a chat with you."

"A chat about what?" she said with an attitude in her voice.

"Your father's murder for starters. And your involvement with the Carolina Couples. I think you know some things we need to know to solve your dad's case."

The campus policeman led Emily and the detectives to the golf cart, then drove them back to the campus police station. The station was a couple of offices in the corner of an administrative building with an outside entrance. He escorted the trio to what looked like a small conference room, with a folding table and six chairs.

"I guess campus police isn't a high budget item at Wofford," Tony laughed.

"We're lucky to have this, with all the budget cuts and everything" the campus cop said, taking a look around the station. "It's not like they'd cut a dime from the football program and pass it our way, you know."

"It'll work just fine," Carter said.

Carter followed Tony and Emily into the room and shut the door behind them. "Go ahead, sit down, Emily," Carter instructed her, walking around and pulling a chair out on the far side of the table. He was careful to make sure he and Tony were between her and the door. "I don't think you'll be able to run out of a police station, even if it is the campus police."

Emily sat down in the chair, not saying a word.

"Why'd you run from us, Emily?" Carter began his questioning.

Emily said nothing.

"Is it because you have a pretty good idea why we're here?" he asked.

Again, silence was her answer.

"Emily, how do you know Sam Collins?"

Emily didn't say anything at first. Like in a cartoon, the detectives could almost see the cogs turning in her head as she considered how or if she should reply to the question. Finally the young woman spoke, "He and my fatter were business associates."

Carter was glad the conversation was finally moving forward. "But how do YOU know Sam Collins. What is YOUR relationship with him?"

Again, Emily thought for a long moment, carefully selecting her words before answering. Carter waited on her, knowing this time she would answer. Experience taught him once someone starts talking, they rarely stop. "Like I said, I know him through my father. I've seen him around."

Carter sensed the carefulness in her answers. He knew he was going to have to up the ante a bit.

"Do you know him through Carolina Couples?"

"Carolina Couples?"

"The swingers group. Don't be so innocent, Emily, you know Connie and I saw you there." Carter's tone was now soft and almost fatherly.

Once more, she thought for a moment, measuring her words before answering. "Yeah, I know him through Carolina Couples, So what?"

"Why did you tell him that you saw us there?" Carter decided to use an assumptive approach, letting her think he knew for fact what he assumed. He felt this would be the quickest way to move the conversation forward. He wanted her to admit she told Collins, so leading her in the right direction wouldn't hurt.

At this point, something inside Emily broke. She started talking. Perhaps it was she realized Carter knew too much and would see through her facade. Perhaps Carter's soft, fatherly tone comforted her. Perhaps, with her father's death and all she had been through, she had just had enough. Carter wasn't expecting her to open up, at least not this quickly, but was glad to see her do so. He would play Freud and try to understand what happened inside her mind later. Right now, he was just glad to have the dialogue. "Yeah, I told him I saw you at the club. I couldn't understand why a cop and his wife would be having sex at our club. By the way, your wife puts on a pretty good show."

"I'll relay your complements," Carter said calmly, fighting to keep a smile from crossing his face. "It looked like you were putting on a pretty good show yourself."

"I don't get any complaints."

"You mean Trotman wasn't cross examining you while you were servicing him?"

"Not unless 'Oh my God!' is cross examination."

"Did you know who Trotman was?"

"Yeah, I know Paul. I know he's Sam's lawyer. His firm also represented my dad in a few real estate transactions in Rock Hill. So what?"

"Do you usually blow your dad's business associates?"

"A lot of them," Emily said, now in a rather matter of fact manner. "I was always well compensated, though."

In spite of everything, Carter was a bit stunned at her response. "How long have you been doing this? Having sex with your father's business associates." Carter asked, more out of curiosity than needing to know for the case.

"About six years or so, I guess. Ever since my parents let me attend my first Carolina Couples party at the house. It was my sixteenth birthday present from them. Mom thought just having me there would be a big turn on for those old men. When they saw me walking around in one of her sexy dresses, I was more than just a turn on, I was an instant hit. I felt like the princess of the party. I was there finding my prince charming. And these men were nice, considerate, even romantic. Not like the high school boys I'd been with. These men knew how to treat a princess. Dad made sure I was taken care of, too. I think the first blowjob was worth about five hundred. Hell, I'd been giving it away for free to those high

245

school boys.   Not anymore. I liked the money and I liked the attention. I liked being the princess."

Carter wasn't sure he believed what he was hearing, but he didn't hesitate to press for more information. "Who set up the sessions?"

"Dad usually set them up with people he knew. I assumed they were business associates. At first, I didn't care, they were paying me, not him. Then I realized that if they had money to pay me for sex then they had money and influence to make my life a lot easier. I figured it was a pretty good gig. I thought it was weird my dad was pimping me out, but hey, we both were benefitting. In more ways than one, if you know what I mean."

"Did he pimp you out with Sam Collins?"

"Yeah, at first. He set up my first time with Sam. But I liked Sam. When I came back up here for college, Sam took care of me. He started introducing me to his friends and getting me set up with the Charlotte group. That's how I first ended up with Trotman."

"Is that why you came back here to school?"

"Part of it. I had been saving some money, so I took a year off and toured Europe. Cool place, a lot less uptight than South Carolina. When I came back, I realized there was nothing for me in Herbsville. That little town wasn't for a girl like me. No big money men looking for a girl to make them feel powerful. Dad had asked all the swingers down there to leave for awhile, until he could complete the Utopia project. I thought it was an odd plan, to run them all off, only to get them all to come back again, but dad was playing it masterfully until someone killed him."

"Who killed your father, Emily?" Carter asked with anticipation of her answer.

"I don't know."

"Was it Collins?"

"Hell no, it wasn't Sam. Sam needed dad and dad needed Sam. They were partners in this whole Utopia thing. Dad and Sam had already acquired the community land where everyone was going to live or have their weekend home. From what I hear, he was real close to getting the club itself. Once that was done, Utopia was going to become the playground of the Carolina Couples. Just the fees they could charge these rich and powerful people for the opportunity at wild, deviant sex would make dad and Sam rich. Not to mention the land sales in the community."

"Was that what Dawson was for?

"I think so. Dad and Sam said Dawson was for Chad and me. The plan was for Dawson to own Utopia and charge the club rent for the grounds, pretty big rent from what I understand. Chad and I would be set, Dawson bringing in money every month for something dad and Sam stole for us. I think they had it planned that we'd get married and then their grandkids would be set for life as well."

"Did you want to marry Chad?" Carter tried lessening the pressure a bit. He really did want to know, though.

"I don't know. Chad was Sam's son. I liked him ok, but it would have been weird being married to him. I had screwed his dad and he had screwed my mother. Sam and dad always wanted us to get married, though. It was funny, they wouldn't even let us screw each other, as if they were saving that for our wedding night. Here I was, screwing lawyers, politicians, judges, and businessmen, but I couldn't even touch Chad. It was pretty strange."

"How was Dawson going to acquire Utopia?" Carter was trying to get back on topic.

"Had something to do with the tax money, I'm not quite sure. Sam's the accountant, not me. I just know what I overheard them talking about."

"Why the name Dawson?," Carter asked more out of curiosity than anything.

"Dad named it after my dog. I got him when I was five and named him Dawson. He was the cutest little thing, a pound puppy. After he died, I heard dad and Sam talking about what to name this corporation to keep it off the radar and I suggested Dawson, in his memory. It stuck."

"I understand," said Carter, thinking of Thor. "Listen, Emily, I need you to really think. Do you have any idea who could have killed your dad?"

"No, everybody loved him. He had Utopia eating out of the palm of his hand. As far as they knew, he had saved the nudist park. I don't think anyone knew about the plan. I can't imagine anyone wanting to kill him." Then she stopped for a moment, a thought entering her head. "Unless someone at Utopia found out about the plan. When I was down for the funeral, mom said she didn't think anyone knew anything. But who knows. If dad had hid the plan for nearly five years maybe someone is hiding their knowledge of it."

"Ok, Emily, I'm glad we had this chance to talk," Carter said, now feeling more empathy for the girl than anything. "I'm going to find who killed your dad, I promise you. I've got one more question though. Why library science?"

"I thought it would be so cool. You see, the librarian is always so nerdy. The old lady no one thinks ever screws anybody. Here I am, screwing everybody, and I'm the librarian. See the irony?"

"Yeah, I get it. Kind of like 'Looking for Mr. Goodbar.'"

"Yeah, that's it, except I'm the librarian, not a teacher."

"Thanks for talking to us," Carter said, as he and Tony got up to leave the room. They were half way out the door when Carter stopped and turned around. "I'm going to tell the officer out here to let you go. I can't think of any reason to hold you. Hope this librarian thing works out for you. Maybe Connie and I will see you at Utopia again someday."

"That would be nice. Hey, if you go back to Utopia, tell that son of a bitch Randy he still owes me. I haven't forgotten about it.

TWENTY-THREE

Carter stopped dead in his tracts. "Randy who?"

"You know, Randy who comes to Utopia. Has the wife named Jill."

"What does he owe you for?"

"Sex, of course."

Carter and Tony both came back into the room. "Sex? With you?"

"Yeah. I told you, I quit giving it away after that first night blowing that old guy. Randy still owes me for a couple of times. I knew better than to let him pay me later, but he'd always paid before, so I let it ride."

"How did this start? He and Jill seemed happily married when we were at Utopia."

"They're all happily married," she said sarcastically. " Not long after we got down to Utopia, dad sent me over to Randy's house. Jill was working a part-time job at the time, and dad told me to give Randy a good blowjob and get out before she got home. I did. I didn't even charge him for that first one, figured Dad had plans. It wasn't long before dad sent me back again. I began charging him about five hundred dollars. He could afford to pay. He had just sold his trucking company. He was always bragging about how much that big corporation that bought him out paid him for it. Anyway, after a few times, he started wanting more, so I started screwing him. This went on a couple times a week for a month or so. Then he started saying he didn't have the money to pay me. He said Jill was getting suspicious. I let him slide on the first one, but after the second time, I told dad. He told me not to go back there anymore, so I didn't. But the son of a bitch still owes me a thousand dollars. A college girl can use that money."

"Why did your dad send you down there to Randy in the first place?" Carter asked.

"I really don't know. I was just seventeen. I hadn't been with anyone since we left Greenville, and kind of missed the action and attention as well as the money. I didn't really ask dad, I just assumed he had his reasons."

249

"Did Jill ever find out?"

"I don't think so. It only happened when she was gone to work. I don't think she knew. They kept coming to Utopia like nothing had ever happened and nothing was ever said. Randy was real cool about it, he never let on that we were screwing. He never even said anything out of the way."

"Did he ever find out your dad had sent you down there the first time?"

"I don't think so. Dad told me to make sure he thought it was all my idea. I told him I needed some action, a real man. I told him I was lonely with no one my age at the park every day, and not being able to bring the few friends I had at school home. Later, I told him I needed the money for college. I think he bought it all."

"How did he take it ending?"

"He never said a thing. I guess he was fine with getting a thousand dollars worth of my ass for nothing. I thought about threatening to tell his wife if he didn't pay up. I could have used the cash back then. But I went to Europe, then came here to school, so I figured it was water under the bridge."

"Well, I probably can't get the thousand dollars, but maybe I can do a little better than that, Emily. Maybe I can get your father's killer. Thank you for talking to us."

"It actually feels good to tell the truth to someone for a change. Leading two lives is tough."

"Yeah, I know," said Carter, remembering his brief time undercover with the Carolina Couples.

Again, thank you so much, Emily. I think what you have told us will help us solve your dad's case. I'll ask the campus police to release you as soon as they finish their paperwork. Good luck with your senior year. I know you'll be a great librarian." Then Carter and Tony left the room. The men resisted the urge to high five each other. They not only had arrested Sam Collins, but Emily Westlake had put them on the track of her father's killer. Carter asked the college police officer to let Emily go, telling him she had been very cooperative and given them what they needed. "She's been through a tough time, cut her a break if you can," he offered in her defense. Within minutes they were in the Crown Vic and heading toward I-26 and back to the Tri-Cities.

****

"Well, that changes our suspect list," Carter said once they were back in the Crown Vic.

"Our list?" Tony questioned. The murder of Westlake is your case. I've got my guys, man, Ratliff and Collins. Saving your ass was my case." Tony was careful not to mention Connie's kidnapping, not wanting to upset Carter.

"Now, Tony, you know we're in this together. We always have been, ever since I sent you that first request for information from Utopia via Winlink."

"No, no, no, man. You're solving Westlake's murder. I've solved my part of this, thing. The part you got yourself into. You've got that Sheriff to help you on the murder."

"Oh, shit, Tedder. He can get me more on Randy. Maybe he can even find the money trail."

"Didn't you meet this guy Randy at the nudist colony?"

"Yeah?"

"Didn't you even suspect him as a killer?"

"No. He seemed down to earth. Just an old country boy who had done well in trucking. Seemed to really be happy at Utopia. Everyone seemed to like him. I could see him wanting a girl like Emily, hell, I can see most any man wanting a girl like Emily, but I just didn't picture him as a cold blooded killer."

"You must be losing your touch, man. After all, you are an old, retired cop now," Tony chided him.

"Retired? Retired? What am I doing here?"

"Well, you are barely retired then. How's that, man?"

"Barely retired, that's better. I can be completely retired only when it suits me," Carter chuckled.

As their joking died down, Carter turned his attention to his cell phone and called Sheriff Tedder.

"Tedder," the sheriff answered.

"Sheriff, Carter Sykes."

"Columbo, how the hell are you doing? Any new information on our case?"

Carter spent the next few minutes filling him in on the arrest of Sam Collins and their conversation with Emily Westlake.

"I knew that was a screwed up family. Just never could put my finger on what they were up to. What do you need to wrap this thing up?"

"Get me all you can on that Randy at Utopia, the one who's married to Jill. I don't have a last name. I know he's a retired trucker and sold his trucking business, Hartland Trucking, a few years back before moving down from Ohio. I'll especially need his financials, for at least the past five years, longer if you can get them. Anything I can find out about him would be great."

"I can't imagine it will be a problem. I'll get it to you ASAP."

"Thanks, Sheriff. I'll call you when we're ready to talk to Randy."

"Sounds good, Columbo. I'm ready to wrap this case up. It's working me to death, all this investigative work I'm having to do." the sheriff said with a smile in his voice.

"You and me both, Sheriff. You and me both," Carter laughed.

****

Even before getting back to Kingsport, Carter's attention had turned to Randy. Who was this man who had sold his trucking company in Ohio to retire at a nudist park? Why had Westlake sent his daughter to seduce him? Westlake had to have had some scheme in mind. He had obviously used Emily to get things he wanted before, and he had to have planned to use the repercussions of an affair with a teen against him. Obviously, Randy must have known it as well. But this all happened four or five years ago. Did it really lead to Randy murdering Westlake now? As the saying goes, 'time heals all wounds'. At this point, if an accusation were made against Randy, it would be highly questioned and next to impossible to prove. Both Randy and Westlake would know that. Then, Carter remembered Tony telling him, "Follow the money trail." He needed first to find out who Randy really was. Second, he needed to get that financial report on Randy and put all the numbers together. Carter knew somewhere in there was the key to the murder of Doug Westlake. It was simply a matter of finding it.

To make the best use of their time and resources, Tony and Carter decided once they arrived in Kingsport, Tony would visit Sam Collins, and Carter would excuse himself and head home. He wanted to fill Connie in on Collins' arrest and what he had learned from Emily. For all intents and purposes, they had solved her kidnapping, and Thor's murder. He hoped this resolution would give her some relief, some peace of mind.

Carter was hoping to find information and financials for Randy waiting for him as well. He expected tonight to be a long one, poring over those reports. Digging through accounting reports was not Carter's favorite exercise, but he was well aware that often money was the root of all evil. He didn't relish the thought of hours looking at number, but knew it had to be done.

After a couple hours of filling Connie in on the day's events, Carter went to his computer to check his email. He was disappointed to have no emails from Sheriff Tedder. He knew that in Herbsville things moved slower than normal, but he had hoped the information he needed would be waiting on him when he got home. Just before dark, as the temperature cooled, Carter and Connie decided to go for a short walk, hoping to shake off some of the stress and clear both their minds of the past few days. Carter called for Thor before remembering the dog was no longer with them. Remembering Thor's death caused him to grab his gun before heading out the door. After walking for a bit, Carter asked, "What do you think of this police work now, babe?"

"Well, not too many dull moments," she said, with a bit of a smile. "But I'm not sure it's as exciting as a Saturday night during a full moon in the ER."

"Honey, I didn't mean for all this to happen."

"I know, sweetie. But it's funny, the whole time I was kidnapped I knew you would come for me. I was scared to death, but I never lost hope, because I knew you were out there."

"But I've failed before, babe. There have been cases I haven't been able to solve."

"But you've never failed me. You've always been there for me. It's funny, Mike knew that too. I could see it in his eyes. He knew you'd come for me. And I think he knew you'd win. You had one intangible on your side, you love me."

"You know, all I could think about was getting you back. You were all that mattered. Tony was there too. In fact, the whole department was behind us. They all love you, Cons."

"I know," she said. "I let them borrow you for thirty years."

"Well, I'm retired now. I'm all yours."

"I think barely retired is a better way of putting it. Does a cop ever really retire?"

"Probably not. But you know, now I've got the best partner I've ever had." He squeezed her hand tightly.

"Like *McMillan and Wife*?" she asked.

"Yeah, like *McMillan and Wife*," he replied.

They walked on down the street together, not saying a lot, holding hands, just being with each other.

Carter and Connie's short walk at dusk turned into about an hour, half of it stopped for a cold soft drink at a small convenience store/grill. They both enjoyed the time spent outside with each other. After spending seven hours in the Crown Vic, Carter was especially glad to get a little exercise and fresh air. As they approached their house, Carter's mind once again turned back toward the Westlake case. Part of him hoped there would be no email from Tedder. He knew if there was, he'd be up half the night going through the information it contained. At this point, he really wanted just to get some rest. It had been a long day.

****

Arriving home after the walk, Carter settled in at his desk and checked his email on Outlook Express. This time he found Tedder had sent some of the information on Randy. Carter opened the first attachment labeled "personal info" and found what amounted to a biography Randy and Jill Hart started Hartland Trucking as wide-eyed twenty five year olds as a one truck operation in the early '70's. The fact they started Hartland during this period caused

Carter to raise an eyebrow. Starting a trucking company in the '70s was odd, it was a time when many truckers were struggling due to the economy and fuel prices. By 2000, Hartland Trucking had grown to over fifty trucks with its headquarters near Washington Court House, Ohio. He had sold Hartland for twenty million dollars in 2006, paid off all the company's debt, and still had a tidy ten million to retire on. 'Just in the nick of time,' Carter thought, remembering the rising fuel prices and economic downturn of 2008. The Harts moved to Herbsville, where Randy became the president of the Utopia Sun Club and ran the club until Westlake was hired. Randy and Jill had two children, both grown and still living in Ohio.

Next, Carter looked at the attachment labeled "Hartland Trucking", which contained the financials on the company. From what Carter could tell without digging too deep, Hartland Trucking was basically a normal trucking company. It had its share of issues with state DOTs across the country, but nothing out of the ordinary. There was a tax issue or two with the IRS and the state of Ohio, but again, nothing that any other company its size wouldn't have. One thing Carter noticed was whenever Hartland hit a financial bump, there always appeared to be an income spike to get them out of it. "Hmmm, how lucky can one man get?" Carter wondered aloud.

The one question that kept creeping into Carter's mind was Randy's unwillingness to continue paying Emily Westlake for her services. He had told her he couldn't pay, but obviously he had the financial means to do so. Carter was sure he enjoyed the sex. Why, then, not just pay her and keep a good thing going? Carter knew there was something he was missing here, there always was when things just didn't make sense. Carter was sure if he could find this missing piece, find out why Randy quit paying, the rest of the case would fall into place. Then he'd have the motive for Westlake's murder.

After a couple of hours of staring at his computer screen, Carter decided midnight was late enough. It was time to give it a rest for the night. He walked into the kitchen, put a little ice in his glass, and poured his last drink of Diet Dr. Pepper for the day. As he was walking toward his office, he saw Connie had the light on in their bedroom. He walked to the door to find her in the bed, reading nothing less than a James Patterson's *Now You See Her*. He chuckled in his mind at her book choice, a suspense/thriller of all things.

"Can't get enough suspense, huh?" Carter laughed.

Connie looked up with a puzzled look on her face. "What are you talking about?"

Carter pointed at the book.

"Oh, a Patterson novel," she chuckled. "I guess that is kind of funny. Of course, I understand it much better now. I can really feel the emotions of the characters. What are you finding out about our real-life murder mystery?"

Carter explained to his wife what he had learned about Randy and Hartland Trucking. Even at the late hour, Connie listened intently, wanting to help put the pieces together.

"You know, I just can't figure out why Randy gave Emily up so easily."

"What I can't figure out is why he nearly let Utopia go under. Wasn't it under his watch that all its tax problems occurred? How was he such a bad manager? And why, once he stepped down, did he not simply pay the taxes himself and let Doug start running the club without all that stuff to deal with? He could easily have afforded it."

Carter sat on the edge of the bed, his tired mind trying to synthesize what Connie had just said. Indeed, why hadn't he paid the taxes incurred under his tenure as president? Why hadn't he paid Emily Westlake? Carter sure hoped the answer was in Randy's personal financials.

"Babe, I think you've hit on something. Why didn't Randy pay? I hope the answer is in there somewhere."

"I guess I know where you're headed?"

"Yep. I'll never sleep until I find something."

"I know, sweetie, I know. I'm going to sleep. Good night." Connie put the bookmark in her book and set it on the nightstand.

Carter leaned over and kissed his wife. "Good night, babe. Thanks for the great idea. I think you're on to something here."

"I always have great ideas when you listen to them."

Despite the hour, Carter sat back down at his computer. He opened the third attachment labeled "Randy Hart Financials." Here Carter began to look through the numbers, hoping to see something that would tie Randy to the Utopia tax situation in 2008 and 2009. Going back to 2008, he looked through the transactions, looking for large numbers or anything to Utopia, Collins or Westlake. After an hour of looking at the screen, Carter was ready to give up for the night. He was tired. His day had started before six this morning. He put his hands behind his head, stretched, reached down, and put his hands on the arms of his chair to assist himself in standing. Then his eyes fell back to the screen. "What the hell is that?"

On the screen was a transaction for ten thousand dollars. Carter straightened up in his seat and began to look closely at it. Here was a transaction for ten grand to none other than the Dawson Corporation. "Holy shit, Batman," he said. "Now what the hell was Randy doing sending ten grand to Dawson?" He opened up the email that contained the Dawson financials. Sure enough, there it was, the dates checked. And what was this? Two days later, Dawson paid the IRS ten grand, apparently cleaning up Utopia's tax problems. Carter knew he had just found the missing ten thousand dollars of Utopia's tax bill, and a motive for murder. Randy had paid ten grand to save Utopia. He must have learned of Westlake's scheme to take over the nudist camp and realized he had been played for a sucker. He had to talk to Randy Hart and find out exactly what he knew.

After closing the open windows on his screen, Carter sent a quick email to Tedder. It was short and sweet. It was the one Carter had been hoping to send since he started working on the case back at the Utopia Sun Club.

....

Tedder, I think I've found our killer.

Carter

....

TWENTY-FOUR

Carter Sykes' phone rang at 7:15 the next morning to find him at Great American Ballpark in Cincinnati, Ohio. He was standing on the mound for his beloved Reds, trying to close out the National League Championship Series. There were two outs, and he was facing the Cardinal's Carlos Beltran in the top of the ninth, with the Reds leading 2-1. "Damn it," he muttered. "Now I'll never know if I led the Reds to the World Series."

"Carter Sykes," he sleepily spoke into the phone.

"So, Columbo, you've got our killer?" Tedder asked with anticipation in his voice.

"Tedder?" Carter asked, still not quite sure whether his was in Cincinnati or Kingsport.

"Yeah, it's me. Now tell me, who's the killer?"

"I'll let the killer incriminate himself. Can you get an interview with Randy Hart lined up?"

"When do you want it?"

"I can be there tomorrow afternoon." Carter knew he could get there sooner if he had to, but at this point there was no reason for he and Connie to push themselves. He wanted time to formulate a plan of interrogation, figuring Randy wouldn't cave to a murder charge very easily.

"I'll try to set it up for 2:00 pm tomorrow."

"Great. You got any motels in that one horse town?"

"The Cotton Inn is the best one we've got. Of course, it's the only one we've got," Tedder laughed.

"I'll make a reservation then. See you tomorrow morning and will get you up to speed on the case."

"Well, who's the killer? Is it Randy Hart?"

"Like I said, I'll let the murderer incriminate himself. You just get Randy Hart in your office tomorrow afternoon. We'll see what happens from there."

"Alright, then. Anything else?"

"Yeah, one more thing.", Carter paused. "Do you have room on your force for two more deputies?"

"Why do I need two more deputies? You ain't expecting any trouble are you?"

"No, no trouble. In order to solve this case and make the arrest, you'll need two more deputies. I'll explain tomorrow morning. Just be ready to deputize two people tomorrow."

"Who?"

"I'll tell you tomorrow, just have badges."

"Alright, Columbo. But I want to know what's going on first thing tomorrow morning."

"No problem, Sheriff, I'll see you tomorrow." Carter closed his phone. He looked over at Connie, still sound asleep. 'I'll wake her in a little bit,' he thought, as he walked to the kitchen for his morning glass of Diet Dr. Pepper.

****

Over a breakfast of sausage, eggs, and biscuits, Carter and Connie discussed his discovery in Randy Hart's financials. After deciding they would ride to Herbsville this afternoon, Carter used his smartphone to look up The Cotton Inn. He found the phone number. He called and reserved a room for two nights. After finishing breakfast, they each packed a bag, and Carter called Tony to inform him of their new plans. Carter jumped in the Ram and Connie got behind the wheel of the Avenger. They drove to the Chrysler dealership, where Carter left the Ram at the body shop for repairs from the chase on highway 421. Connie moved to the Avenger's passenger seat as Carter slid behind the wheel. Connie would have been happy to drive, but was content to let Carter have the honors. She liked having the freedom to look around and enjoy the surroundings as they traveled. Before noon, they were driving east on I-26, on their way to Herbsville.

Once on the road, Carter explained the details of the financial path that led to Randy Hart now being their top suspect. Connie listened and asked questions when something wasn't clear to her. This practice had become common for the two of them over the past few years. Connie was often able to find weak areas in Carter's theories. By Connie exposing the weakness before the opposing defense attorney did, he was able to clean up his case and do a more thorough job interviewing the suspect. Carter figured Connie had saved the DA many sleepless nights over the years.

"So, do you think Doug was blackmailing Randy into silence?" Connie asked.

Carter didn't hesitate in answering. "I'd almost bet on it."

"I bet he found out about Utopia's new tax situation."

"Probably. And Westlake threatened to expose his affair with Emily if he told anyone. Left Randy in between a rock and a hard place; lose the nudist club that he moved to Herbsville for, or be exposed as a sexual pervert."

"Or kill Doug Westlake," Connie added.

"Looks like he chose the latter."

Despite all the evidence, Connie kept asking, "Are you sure Randy committed murder?" It's one thing to cheat on your wife with a beautiful, young, willing girl, it's another thing to kill a man."

"We'll know for sure tomorrow afternoon," Carter promised. "If he did it, I think he'll either confess or give us all the missing pieces we need. Whichever way it goes, we'll leave Herbsville with our killer behind bars. And I've got a special surprise for you."

"What's what kind of surprise, sweetie?"

"If I told you it wouldn't be a surprise. You'll know it when it happens, though."

****

When the Avenger arrived in Herbsville, Carter and Connie checked into The Cotton Inn. Carter gave specific instructions to the clerk not to let anyone, no one, know they were here. He pulled up to their room and backed the Avenger into its parking place in order to hide the Tennessee tag. He and Connie grabbed their bags and the microwaveable meatloaf, mashed potatoes and broccoli they had picked up for dinner. Carter knew once they got in their room they needed to stay there' they couldn't risk word getting back to Randy that they were in town.

The Sykes' topic of discussion for the evening was the interrogation of Randy Hart. Carter went over his plan, and Connie made suggestions. By the time they called it a night, Carter was satisfied that he would get a confession out of Randy Hart tomorrow afternoon.

Carter turned the TV to Leno, and laid with his head propped up on the headboard of the king size bed. Connie walked out of the bathroom, took off her clothes, and brushed her hair. Carter's mind drifted from Leno to watching his wife. Finally, she finished with her hair and walked over to the bed.

"You're beautiful, babe," he told her.

"Thank you, sweetie," she whispered back.

"I don't mean just your looks, but you're beautiful inside and out. Your mind, your heart, all of you. You are one beautiful woman, Connie Sykes."

"You're not so bad yourself, Carter Sykes. I wouldn't be me without you." She reached over and kissed him.

Carter reached under her arms and gently pulled her into the bed, close to him, giving her a kiss. "How was I so lucky to have found you?" He kissed her again.

"I don't know, but I'd suggest you take full advantage of fate," she said, as she crawled into his arms. Their kissing became more passionate, and finally they made tender love. It was the first time they had made love since the kidnapping, and the sensation they felt seemed new. As they came back to their senses, the Tonight Show Band was leading the way into a commercial break.

"I guess you missed the monologue," Connie kidded, cuddled against her husband.

"Jay'll get over it," Carter laughed, as he softly kissed Connie's forehead. Carter reached for the remote, turned off the TV, and they drifted off to sleep.

****

The next morning, Carter and Connie received their wakeup call at 8:00 AM and after showering, tossed the frozen bacon egg and cheese biscuits into the microwave for breakfast. Connie was glad the motel had a coffee maker and individual packs of coffee; she knew she couldn't take Diet Dr. Pepper for breakfast. After they finished eating, Carter grabbed his notes and they drove down to the Herbsville Sheriff's Department. Carter thought about walking, but decided the chances of someone seeing and recognizing them walking were greater than if they drove in the Avenger, He parked around back, out of view of the street, and they walked into the sheriff's office.

"Good to see you, Columbo," Tedder enthusiastically announced when they entered the office. "I didn't know we would have the honor of your daughter joining us."

"Must be election time again, huh, sheriff? You know we can't vote down here. Connie, you know Sheriff Tedder."

"It's a pleasure, Sheriff," Connie said. "And thanks for the compliment."

"Well, tell me what's going on," Tedder demanded. "Who's the murderer? It's driving me crazy."

"In due time, Sheriff, in due time. Have you got the badges?" Carter asked.

"Yeah I got 'em. Now, what's all this about?"

"Well, before we go any farther, I want you to deputize us both."

"Carter?" Connie half said, half asked.

"That's right, babe. For all your assistance and all you've been through in this case, you deserve to be a law enforcement officer."

She threw her arms around Carter. "I can't believe this, sweetie. This must be the surprise."

"Part of it, there's more later. Sheriff, deputize the lady."

"How much do I have to pay her?"

"Uh," Carter thought for a second. "One dollar. She won't really be a cop if she doesn't get paid. I don't want anyone calling her a rent a cop, ya' know."

"Connie Sykes, I, Sheriff Ralph Tedder, do hereby make you a deputy of the Herbsville Sheriff's Department." He handed her the badge."

"Thank you, Sheriff," she said as Carter helped her put the badge on the belt loop of her shorts.

Now, what about this other badge?" Tedder asks

"That one's for me. I can't be out here solving cases for you and not be a cop, can I? You do want the Department to get the credit, right?"

"Ok. I guess you want a dollar, too?"

"You bet your ass. I'm on a fixed income these days."

Tedder handed Carter the other badge and Connie helped him pin it on his chest. "Ok, now tell me about this case and how Randy Hart fits in."

For the next two hours, Carter laid out his case against Randy Hart from start to finish. He told Tedder about their trip to the Carolina Couples event, leaving out Connie's performance, of course. He went over Connie's kidnapping, leaving out the part about Thor being killed. He described the car chase up Iron Mountain on US 421. He described his and Tony's encounters with Collins and Emily Westlake. Finally, he explained the money and sex trails that led them to Randy Hart. By the time high noon arrived, Tedder was in agreement that Randy Hart was their man.

"Why don't we just go arrest him?" asked Tedder. "Why go through this show, this interrogation?"

"It's really more for the DA's benefit. The case is much easier to prosecute if we can get a confession," Carter explained. "I don't want Randy getting off on some technicality. If he confesses or gives us a vital piece of information, we can lock him up and throw away the key."

"What now? Hart won't be here for two hours."

"Well, it's time for lunch and time to make sure everyone in town knows we're here to arrest a murderer. Right now, although he might be a little concerned, Randy's not sure why you want to see him. I'm sure he's worried but probably not convinced you've got anything on him. Once he sees us here, he'll know. I want him to have a few minutes to concoct a little plan, but not enough time to think it through." Carter paused for a moment. "Where's the best food and highest visibility in town?"

"Most people will be at the Herbsville Diner. It's usually packed for lunch."

"Oh well, I was hoping for a better name, maybe "The Happy Gizzard" or the "Ptomaine Palace." It would sound better when this case is made into a made-for-TV movie. I guess the Herbsville Diner is where we're heading for lunch."

****

At lunch, the sheriff and his two deputies took a prominent spot in the Herbsville Diner, hoping someone would inform Randy Hart that Carter and Connie were in town. Sure enough, a half hour later, Connie noticed Jill Hart walking into the diner. Jill saw the three of them, made eye contact with Connie, stopped, turned and walked back out the front door. Connie watched her walk quickly down the street.

"I'm glad you recognized her, babe. I'm not sure I would have with her clothes on," Carter laughed.

"Oh yeah, what does she look like without her clothes?" Tedder teased.

"Not bad, not bad at all for a lady her age. If I were ten years older..." Carter took a punch in the arm from Connie.

"Not as good as you, babe," Carter tried to recover.

"Too late, sweetie. I'll be keeping an eye on you."

Tedder laughed and shook his head. "You two are something else."

After lunch, the three of them went back to the sheriff's office with almost an hour to spare before Randy was to arrive. Carter didn't think Randy would run. He had seen it happen before, but usually a man with Randy's money who had built a business from scratch felt he could work his way out of any situation. Carter knew Randy obviously had plenty of experience dealing with governmental agencies. Just in case, Tedder had Sam Mitchell watching him, with orders to stop him and bring him in if he started heading out of town.

About 1:45, Randy and Jill Hart arrived at the sheriff's office. Both the sheriff and Carter were surprised to see Jill come with him.

"Hello, Mr., Ms. Hart," the sheriff welcomed them in. "I must admit, I'm a bit surprised to see Mrs. Hart. I only asked for you to be here, Mr. Hart."

"I insisted," said Jill. "Anything that involves my husband involves me as well. After all, I spent the best part of my life helping him build Hartland Trucking."

"Come on in then, Ms. Hart," said Tedder. "I believe y'all know Carter and Connie."

"We know them from Utopia," Jill said. "What's all this about, sheriff? Why are they here?" She looked at Carter and Connie.

"We need to ask Randy some questions," Carter said. "We'll take him into this room over here and talk to him. You can wait here if you want, but this might take a little while."

"I ain't going nowhere," Jill said, defiantly. "I'll stay here with my husband."

"That's fine, then," Carter said. "Connie will stay out here with you and keep you company while Randy, the sheriff and I go in here and talk."

"I'm going in there, too," Jill demanded. "Anything you've got to say to him, you can say to me."

"No ma'am, you're not," Carter told her, with a harshness in his voice that told her not to push him on the issue. "You can sit out here quietly or I'll ask deputy Connie Sykes to escort you out of the building. Or there's always a jail cell over there." Carter nodded his head toward the single jail cell. Connie smiled at the authority being a police officer gave her, even if for a day.

Jill didn't protest. "Randy, I'll be here if you need me."

Randy said nothing. He followed Tedder and Carter into the makeshift interrogation room and Tedder shut the door behind them.

"What's all this about?" Randy asked.

"We've got some questions we need to ask you, Randy," Carter said.

"I don't have to answer anything you ask," Randy said. "Best I remember you're a retired cop."

"I've brought Mr. Sykes out of retirement," Tedder said, pointing to the badge on Carter's chest. "He's my deputy right now."

"Tell us about Doug Westlake," Carter began.

"Good man. Saved Utopia from our tax problems. If we hadn't hired him, Utopia wouldn't be here today."

"Tell me about his daughter, Emily Westlake."

"Beautiful girl. I think she'll be a great librarian."

"How are her blowjobs?"

"What?" Randy sat up straight. Tedder even seemed a bit shocked at the bluntness of the question.

"I bet it felt pretty good to screw that seventeen year old beauty," Carter continued without hesitation. "A girl like that can do a lot for a man your age, Randy, even if it does cost you a little to get it. After all, you worked like hell your whole life to earn that money. You might as well…well, blow it. And what a better way to do so than with a beautiful teenage girl."

Randy sat there without saying a word. Carter and Tedder just stared at him. Carter knew this was the crucial moment. He knew Randy had to speak next. He had asked him a question, he had to make Randy say something. If it took an hour of silence, they had to let Randy Hart speak next. This time, two long minutes passed while Randy gathered his thoughts.

"Yeah, I screwed her. Who wouldn't? My age or twenty years old, she was a hot bitch, offering me a fine piece of ass. I figured 'what the hell'. Even if Jill left me she'll only get half of everything and I'll still be set for life. Odds were she wouldn't leave, better to be part of it all than have all of half, right? So I took my chances. Would have worked fine, too."

"Why didn't it work out fine, Randy?"

"Turns out the bitch's dad, Westlake, sent her down to seduce me. Pretty damn low, pimping out your own daughter. I never saw that one coming. He said he needed ten grand to keep Utopia running, to cover the tax debt. Said if I'd pay it, then he'd forget about me and Emily. I paid the son of a bitch and like he promised, that was the end of it. One thing about Doug Westlake, he held up his end of that bargain."

"Why did you kill him then?"

"Kill him? Wait a minute, here. Hell, no, I didn't kill him or anybody else. That was five years ago. It was settled and done with. I sure as hell wouldn't have killed him over it, especially not now."

"Maybe he needed more money?" Carter had hoped to keep the conversation moving forward, but now knew he was going to have to work for the murder confession. "Perhaps he threatened to tell Jill if you didn't cough up more."

"Tell Jill?" I don't think so. Jill knew about it. She figured out that's where all my spending money was going. She is a stickler for every dollar, always has been. Hell, I couldn't even pay Emily for the last time we screwed because she was questioning me about the money."

Carter sat there, thinking about what Randy was saying. He was telling him things he already knew were true, without being asked about them first. That was a clear sign that he was telling the truth. But Carter still knew all the evidence led to Randy being the murderer. He pressed on.

"So you're going to sit here and tell me that in spite of him sending his daughter to entrap you and taking ten thousand dollars of your money, you hadn't had enough and just killed the sorry son of a bitch? I could understand a man doing that."

"I told you, I didn't kill anybody. I'm a truck driver, not a killer. I've done a lot of things in my life; cheated the IRS, run drugs in my trucks, even had some whores while sleeping at truck stops; but I ain't never killed a man."

Carter was starting to believe him. He was admitting to things he didn't have to. He could just be giving them something, hoping to avoid giving what Carter really wanted. But it didn't make sense anymore. Carter's thoughts were interrupted by a knock on the door. Tedder got up and answered it. It was Connie.

"Honey, we're in the middle of an interview right now," Carter looked at her and said with both frustration and impatience in his voice.

"But there's something you need to know."

"It's not a good time, babe."

"Deputy Sykes, I need to talk with you NOW," Connie demanded this time.

Carter understood the tone in her voice. "Sheriff, give me just a couple of minutes here." Carter and Connie left the room and went to the other office. Carter shut the door behind them.

"What's going on, babe?"

"I've been talking to Jill. She knows too much, Carter. Way too much. She knows about Utopia's current tax troubles. I think you need to talk to her."

"How does she know about Utopia's tax situation? Randy doesn't seem to have a clue."

"I don't know, but she alluded to them in our conversation. From our talk, I'm guessing she is the one who ran the trucking company. I'll bet she knew about Randy and Emily, too. But there was no way she was only taking half of what SHE built. And there's one more thing I remember."

"What's that?" Carter asked, amazed at what Connie had learned in her informal conversation with Jill.

"After the murder, we were at the pool and she mentioned that the Westlakes had a .38. Why would she mention that? I didn't know Doug was killed with a .38 at that point. How would she have known it?"

"Perhaps Tedder told her."

"Let's ask him and see."

Carter and Connie walked back into the room where Tedder and Randy sat. "Tedder, did anyone know what kind of gun Westlake was killed with?"

"You, me, the state guys, I don't think anyone else knew."

"Could you have slipped and told someone, someone you were interviewing?"

"Columbo, I don't have a lot of formal training, but even I know better than to make information like that public knowledge."

"Hell, I didn't even know what kind of gun Doug was killed with," Randy spoke up, hoping to somehow prove his position.

Carter looked over at Connie. "You might have a point, babe. Let's switch suspects here and see what Miss Jill really does know. Keep Randy company while we talk to her."

"Yes, sir, deputy Sykes," she said.

Carter went back into the interview room. Tedder led Randy out while Connie brought Jill in. "Jill, come on in for a few minutes. Have a seat, we've got a few questions we need to ask you."

"About what?" she asked, not sitting down.

"A few things. First, when did you find out about your husband and Emily Westlake?"

This time it was Jill's turn to think about where this line of questioning was going. "I had suspicions for a couple of weeks before I found out. Randy wasn't that good at covering his tracks."

"Bet that made you mad. Your husband screwing that pretty young thing."

"Well hell yeah it made me mad. Wouldn't it you? I'd spent my life building our life together and here he was, throwing it all away on a seventeen year old piece of pussy."

"Why didn't you divorce him?"

"Believe me, I thought about it. Even talked to a lawyer. But I just couldn't give him half of everything I'd built. He'd blow it, just like he blew the club's finances when he became president. I couldn't let him blow half of what I'd built. No way."

"You built? Wasn't Hartland Randy's company?"

"Officially, yes. Randy was a great truck driver. But he was an idiot when it came to finances. And he couldn't deal with the authorities. So I started taking care of the books. As the business grew, I ended up making the decisions. By the way things ended up, I didn't do half bad."

"Not bad at all, Jill. Looked like you avoided a lot of potential problems over the years."

"Yeah, there were tough times. But I always did what was necessary to deal with them."

"Like what?"

Jill stopped. Carter could see that she was pondering her response. This wasn't what Carter wanted, he didn't want her thinking, he wanted her talking.

"What did you do when times got tough, Jill?"

Jill was careful with her words. "I made the calls I needed to get the freight we needed to haul."

"In other words, you ran drugs?" Carter asked, already knowing the answer.

"I did what I had to do."

"How high up did your contacts go?" Carter asked, trying to gain a better understand of what she was capable of.

"To some of the highest levels of the Mexican government. You'd be surprised. Like I said, I didn't always like it, but I did what I had to do." She continued to choose her words carefully.

"I'm really not here about you running drugs, Jill. I'm here to solve the murder of Doug Westlake."

"Well, good. Someone needs to find out who killed him. It's put Utopia in an uproar. I don't know if we'll ever get our club straightened out."

"But you'll do what you have to do, right? You know Doug sent Emily to seduce your husband?"

"I don't doubt it. Doug was a lot like me. He'd do what it took to get what he wanted."

"Did you know about the ten grand Randy paid Doug to keep him quiet about the affair?"

"Randy gave him? Randy ain't wrote a ten grand check in his life. I stroked that check. I just wanted the whole damn thing to go away. Doug swore that was the last money needed to clear Utopia's tax bill. The way I figured it, Randy was the one who screwed up Utopia's finances. In a way, it was my fault, I let him run the thing. I should have watched over him. But he wanted to do it. So I let him. Learned my lesson, but it only cost me ten grand."

"Tell me about Utopia's tax problems."

"Pretty bad. But somehow, Doug got them cleared up. Pretty masterful job, if you ask me."

"I'm not talking about the old problems. I'm talking about the ones that are about to hit the fan very soon."

"What current ones?" Jill asked innocently.

Carter took a chance with a bit of a stretch of the truth. "Jill, I know you know about Utopia's current tax situation." He reached over on the table and grabbed the Utopia financial report he had printed. "I don't want to have to go through this report line by line and drag it out of you. But like you and Doug, I'll do what I have to do."

Jill sat down, not sure what to say. As she thought, it gave Carter time to reconcile these new findings to what he already knew. He didn't know for sure that Jill knew about the tax problems, but it was a good educated guess. Pushing it as a fact was a gamble he felt comfortable taking at this point. But Jill was on guard now, as opposed to when she was casually talking to Connie. He had to make her think he knew more that he did. The way this case had gone, he wouldn't rule out anything, but if he were betting, he would bet Jill had learned about the tax problems through Grace. She was the only one besides Doug who had access to Utopia's mail, she laid it on Doug's desk on his days off. She must have opened a tax letter or form out of curiosity. If he were betting; hell, Carter was betting the house on this one right now.

"Which form from the government did Grace show you that first tipped you off to Utopia's current problems?"

Again Jill sat there, not saying a word. Carter knew she was sorting out her next move. But her silence said volumes. Her lack of a denial told him he was on the right track. "You know I'll have Grace in here next. There's no reason for her not to tell me everything I want to know. It may take me a couple of hours, but I'll get the answers, Jill. How long we spend here today is up to you."

Jill sat there a few minutes longer, her face now seemingly glazed over. It wasn't the same confident look he had seen from her moments ago when she was bragging about building Hartland. Now she had the look of a defeated woman, a woman whose dreams were caving in on her. Then suddenly she spoke in the voice of a woman proudly making her last stand.

"That son of a bitch prostituted his own daughter to take my marriage, then he took ten thousand dollars from me. There was no way he was going to take Utopia from me, no fucking way. When I confronted him with what I had learned of his plan, he just laughed and admitted it all to me. He walked away, went into the woods, probably to make sure no one heard our conversation. I followed him into the woods. 'What are you going to do about it?' he asked me when we got down there. 'You gonna tell on me, Jill? You know I'll let the whole fuckin' club know about your husband and how he screwed poor little innocent Emily and how you bought our silence with ten grand for her college fund. You'll be the laughing stock of the whole damn club, a fucking disgrace. Everyone will think you're a really stupid bitch. But it won't really matter. In a few weeks, this whole fuckin' place will be mine, and you'll be gone forever. Unless you want to come back to one of our swinging parties and let me fuck your brains out. You know, I'd probably enjoy that immensely.' That was it, I had enough. I reached into my fanny pack and got the .38 I had brought with me and shot that son of a bitch. It felt good. He wasn't taking anything else from me. I shot him again for good measure. I rolled him behind a tree and onto his belly and covered him up with old leaves, dirt, and twigs. I left him there, hoping it would be a long time until anyone found his dead ass. And it would have been, if you and that damn dog of yours hadn't showed up."

Carter sat back in his chair. This was the confession he had come for, but not from the person he expected to get it from. It took him a few seconds to gather his thoughts. He saw Tedder walking toward Jill, reaching for his handcuffs.

"Wait a second, Tedder," Carter said. "I've got to do this the right way." He then opened the door and called Connie into the room. "Deputy Sykes, I need you to arrest Jill Hart for the murder of Doug Westlake."

Connie looked at Carter with disbelief. "The surprise," she moved her lips, then gathered herself back in. "Yes, sir, detective," she said, as she moved toward Jill, taking the handcuffs from Tedder. "Jill Hart, you're under arrest for the murder of Doug Westlake. You have the right to remain silent. Anything you say may be used against you in a court of law. You have the right to an attorney......." Connie finished reading Jill her rights, and turns her over to Sheriff Tedder.

"Nice job, deputy. I'll take it from here." Tedder led Jill Hart out of the room and placed her in the jail cell.

Carter walked toward Connie. "Nice job, babe. You solved this one for us. You're a pretty good detective in your own right." He kissed her on the cheek. "I'm proud to have you as a partner."

"Do you really think you should be kissing a sworn officer of the law?" she asked him with a smile.

"Well, you have been for thirty years, babe."

"I guess we ended up like McMillan and Wife in the end, didn't we?"

"Yeah we did, babe. I'll bet if I'd had you as my partner, my crime solving record would have been almost perfect."

"Well, with Naked Woman on your side, you are one for one."

"Who's Naked Woman?" Tedder asked, as he entered the room. "There's a lot of paperwork to do, and I have two very capable deputies to delegate that too."

"Sheriff, I've heard about that paperwork for thirty years. I think I'll resign my position. But I still want my dollar. And I'm keeping this badge. It'll go good with my cowboy hat."

Barely Retired

Part 4

The Return

TWENTY-FIVE

The first frost of the year descended on Upper East Tennessee, but that didn't seem to bother Carter and Connie Sykes. They were in Herbsville, South Carolina, on their first visit to the Utopia Sun Club since solving the murder of Doug Westlake. Connie and Mary Ann became regular email pals. They friended each other on Facebook, and they talked on the phone several times over the past few months. Mary Ann tried to talk Carter and Connie into coming back to the nudist park for a visit, even offering them a free week in honor of them solving the murder and, in essence, saving the club. Despite their barely retired life, local commitments kept getting in the way. Connie was volunteering at the hospital a couple of days per week. Carter was helping with a local Pee-Wee football team. However, when Mary Ann called with the news that Gil had proposed to her and they were going to have a nude wedding at Utopia on October 24, Carter and Connie could not pass up the celebration of the love and marriage of their friends.

As the Ram and Coachmen pulled into Utopia, Connie quickly undressed as soon as they were safely inside the gate; she had actually removed her pants a couple of miles earlier. "Nobody can see my naked butt in this big truck," she told Carter as he scolded her. When they got to the office, Carter took off his clothes before he and Connie walked into the office. In the back room was a naked Mary Ann, her head buried in what looked like an endless mound of paperwork.

"Uhm, we'd like a place to stay tonight," Carter said. "Is this a decent campground?"

"It's a great campground if you want to be naked," Mary Ann said, as she looked up from her paperwork, seeing Carter and Connie on the other side of the counter. "Ahhh, Connie, Carter!" she yelled as she ran to them with her arms open wide. She hugged Connie first, then Carter. "It's so great to see you guys."

"We wouldn't miss your wedding for the world," said Connie. "You're looking great. Look at your tan, girl."

"You're looking great too, girl, except for your tan, or should I say lack of one. You're all white again."

"I've actually started building a fence in the backyard, but I don't have it finished yet," Carter said. "Maybe by spring we'll have a place at home to lay out au natural."

"Besides, it's already cold in Tennessee. They're calling for frost tonight," Connie said. "So, what finally prompted Gil to ask….and you to accept?"

"I really don't know. One day we were sitting at the camper drinking a beer, and he just said, 'Let's get married'. I looked at him kind of dumbfounded and he said, 'Well, say SOMETHING'. I looked deep into his eyes and said, 'What the hell, why not? I do love you, you know.' Next thing I know, we're planning this nude wedding. I know it's not the most romantic story in the world, but that's the way it happened."

"I'm so happy for you." Connie squealed like a schoolgirl as they hugged again.

"It's going to be interesting, though. My family's not nudists and they're coming to my wedding. They'll be wearing clothes, as will a few other people. But we decided our wedding would be a nude wedding. We told them about it and most of them are ok with it, as long as they can wear clothes. I think some of them just want a chance to see me naked," she laughed. "I don't know who's more nervous, mom, or me."

"Your dad, probably," Carter chimed in. "I remember how nervous I was our first time; not so much about being naked myself, but about having other men seeing Cons naked. Your dad will be sitting there while everyone will be looking at his naked little girl. It'll be tough for him until he realizes it's just the way things are down here."

"I hadn't really thought about dad. Yeah, he's probably scared to death, but he'd never admit it. Hey, we've got a special surprise for you guys tomorrow, I hope y'all don't mind."

"What is it?" Connie asked.

"If I told you it wouldn't be a surprise, now would it?"

"Why do I always keep hearing that?" Connie asked rhetorically.

"Well, I've got y'all back in lot E. You know where it is. Go on around and get set up. Gil and I will see y'all in a little bit."

"Do you need our driver's licenses or anything?" Carter asked.

"It's not like y'all are strangers or anything. All that stuff is in the file. Set up your camper and we'll talk over supper. I've got a few things to finish up here." Mary Ann glanced back at her stack of paperwork.

"How much do we owe you?" Carter asked.

"I told Connie in the email, this is on us. All you did, finding Doug's killer and saving the club in the process, is more than enough payment for a week here. Heck, a free membership wouldn't come close to paying for what you guys did."

"This will help make up for that hundred and fifty dollar haircut I had to pay for," Carter mumbled.

"Thanks Mary Ann, we'll talk to you a little bit." Connie said, ignoring her husband's complaint as she grabbed Carter's arm and led him out the door.

****

As the sun began to set on Utopia, Carter and Connie walked over to Gil and Mary Ann's camper for dinner. Gil was grilling steaks and Mary Ann had made a salad and baked potatoes. The late fall air was not uncomfortable in eastern South Carolina, but after the sun went down, it was a bit too cool to be naked. All four sat on the porch clothed for the first time.

"You look pretty good in clothes, Mary Ann," Carter couldn't resist.

"Well thank you, Carter," Mary Ann said, as she stood up, twirled around, and showed off her College of Charleston sweat suit.

"It's great to have y'all back down here. We've missed you a lot. So much has happened since you were here," Gil said, then took a sip from his beer.

"As I walked in, I noticed one change immediately," Carter said. "Mary Ann was in the office."

"After y'all arrested Jill and exposed Randy's actions, the club hired Mary Ann to fill in as the General Manager. At first, it was on an interim basis, but as she began to actually get some of the issues straightened out, they decided to hire her on a permanent basis. It's been a challenge, but I think she's enjoyed it. And it gives me a reason to be here more often. I've been helping Jim with a few projects around the park."

"We saw the new golf cart parking lot at the pool, pretty cool," Connie said.

"And best of all, I get to go to work naked," Mary Ann jumped in. "Once everything is settled with the land over there, we'll have a lot of work to do on it as well, We're still a ways away, but the lawyer tells us we should have everything settled by spring. Then the long process of starting the nudist community begins. We're not going to let this thing sit like it did before."

"That's great. So the nudist community is once again a dream here?" Carter asked.

"In some form or fashion, yes," Mary Ann answered. "We may decide to use part of the land to hold nationwide nudist events. Someone suggested we build a softball field and hold the World Series of Nude Softball. We could have co-ed teams come in from all over the country, maybe all over the world, and play in a nude softball tournament. They do it with volleyball in Florida and get real college volleyball teams to bare it all, so who knows. Maybe we can get normally clothed softball teams to come in and give nudism a try."

"That's too cool," said Connie. "It's good to see the club looking past all the problems and looking toward the future."

"For the most part, we have a great group of people here. Most just want a place where they can come, relax, and have a good time without having to deal with clothes. What happened here; the murder, the tax problems, and the scheme to take over the club for a swingers paradise, was very disturbing. But most people have banded together, determined to make Utopia an even better place. Our lawyer has helped us to get these tax issues behind us. The IRS and South Carolina Department of Revenue were very good to work with us once they found out about Doug's scheme. The local government has not been so great, but there has been one voice of reason there for us."

"Oh yeah? Who's that?" Carter instinctively asked.

"Sheriff Ralph Tedder, of all people," said Gil. "It's like he's had a change of heart about us. Hell, about once a day he does a cruise through, just to make sure everything's ok."

"And to take a look at the ladies," Mary Ann interjected. "Let's not get too idealistic here. I know, he stops in and says 'hello' to me everyday day."

"Can you blame him?" Carter laughed.

"Well, I guess not."

"He's even helped us get cell phone service and internet out here. In the spring we plan to have wifi run throughout the park," Mary Ann added.

"There's you a project to help with, sweetie. One thing Carter knows is radio. You can come down and help install the wireless network for the club," Connie giggled. "And I'll work on my tan."

"Yeah, and I'm sure we could do a work for rent trade off with you, Carter," Mary Ann offered.

"We may have to take you up on that one. When does it warm up down here?" Carter asked.

"By early March, most days are pretty good. By the end of March it's generally nude during the daytime warm all the time," Mary Ann said, sounding like a Chamber of Commerce advertisement.

"After a cold, hard winter, we could probably use a nice, warm break, sweetie," Connie coaxed her husband. "And you'll need the work; we wouldn't want you to go feeling retired or anything like that."

"We'll see," was the only promise Carter would make.

The conversation turned to other matters as the four of them ate their dinner, drank a few drinks, and enjoyed their reunion. Mary Ann asked about their swingers club experience, which Carter and Connie shared with them, the first time that had told anyone all that had happened. They talked about how the revelations about Randy and Jill had affected the club, discussed the upcoming wedding, and a host of other topics. A couple of golf carts rode by and people yelled out greetings, to which the four of them responded with yells of their own. Before long, 11:00 pm rolled around, and Carter and Connie decided to call it a night.

"Thanks so much for having us over," Connie said

"It was our pleasure," Gil said, as he gave Connie a hug.

"We'll see y'all tomorrow," Mary Ann gave Carter a hug and a small kiss on the cheek. "And don't forget we have a surprise for y'all tomorrow."

"Surprises always worry me," Carter complained under his breath.

"See you tomorrow," said Connie, as she grabbed Carter's hand and led him to the dirt road and back to the Coachmen.

"I'm glad everything's ok here," she said. "I like this place. I like coming here."

"Me too. I guess it will always hold a special place in our hearts."

"I'm sure it will, sweetie," she said, as she kissed her husband and led him by the hand into their camper.

TWENTY-SIX

After breakfast, Carter and Connie packed a cooler and walked to the pool. By 10:00 am, the temperature was in the low seventies, with bright sunshine. For Carter and Connie, this was a nice relief from the mid-fifties that had become the norm in the Tri-Cities. Connie was glad to be getting some sun on her body again, even though she knew any tan she got would be short-lived, quickly disappearing after they returned to the colder weather in Upper East Tennessee.

Since it was Friday morning, there were only about fifteen people around the pool, but Carter and Connie had plenty of people to talk with. Even though they had not been to Utopia for four months, solving the Westlake murder had made them celebrities of sorts at the park. It seemed everyone wanted to take a few minutes and talk to the couple who saved Utopia from becoming a swingers paradise.

By noon, the crowd at the pool had doubled in size. A couple of people were taking advantage of the warm weather to get one last dip in the pool for the year. Mary Ann, Gil, Jim, and Grace came out of the office, and a group of about twenty-five naked people joined them around Carter and Connie. "It's time to unveil our surprise," Mary Ann announced. "Y'all come with us and we'll show you what we have for you."

Carter and Connie looked at each other and rose from their chairs. They each reached down and picked up a towel. "You won't need a towel," Jim said. "Just come with us." They dropped their towels and walked with the group.

They walked to the back of Utopia's property and into the woods to the place where Thor had found Doug Westlake's body four months earlier. Once they reached that spot, they saw something covered with a cloth. It was nearly three feet tall and four feet long. Everyone gathered in a semicircle around it, with Carter and Connie facing it. Gil, a Vietnam War veteran, moved up beside the object, in front of the gathered crowd.

"Carter and Connie, it was with great sadness that the members of the Utopia Sun Club heard about your loss as you fought to find the killer of Doug Westlake and in effect save our club. Had it not been for Thor finding Doug's body, this club probably would no longer be in existence today. We know he made the ultimate sacrifice in an attempt to save you, Connie, when you were in trouble. Because of what he means to this club and the sacrifice he made, we want to dedicate this memorial to him."

Jim walked forward to assist Gil, and the two of them raised the cloth from the object. Unveiled is a life-sized statue of a dog, a lab-mix that looked remarkably like Thor. In front of the dog was a plaque

In Memory of
Thor
Who Made The Ultimate Sacrifice
For The Utopia Sun Club And His
Owners. Thor, Your Deeds Will
Not Be Forgotten And Our Love
For You Will Last Forever.

Jim continued, "Many thanks to our friends, Carter and Connie, who shared Thor with us for a short time. Carter, Connie, please know that what Thor did to save our club, and to save you, will remain with us forever." With that, Gil and Jim stepped aside.

Carter and Connie stood in front of the memorial to Thor with tears in their eyes. Their lives had often seemed to be missing something since Thor had been killed. They knew what was missing, but neither of them had really commented on it. Now they were confronted with both their loss and with the fact their loss had meant so much, to so many. No one said a word as they took in the meaning of the memorial and what Thor and his discovery meant to the park. After a couple of minutes, Connie stepped forward, turned around, and face the crowd.

"Thank you so much," Connie began with a broken voice and tears in her eyes. "Thor found Doug Westlake's body in this spot and his life forever became intertwined with this place, and the case that evolved from it. A couple of weeks after finding the body, Thor and I were approached by two men, one of them we had met while undercover at the Carolina Couples swingers club. Thor cut a shine, but I told him to calm down. The men then pulled a gun on us and ordered us into their van. Thor and I had no choice, so we did as they ordered. When they got us back at their lair, I asked the man from the swinger's club what all this was about. At that point, he said 'shut up bitch', reached up, and slapped me across the face. I guess that was more than Thor could take. He attacked the man, latching on to his arm. The man hit Thor on the head several times, and when he got loose, he grabbed his gun and shot Thor twice. He died instantly, not so much as a yelp from him."

By now, there wasn't a dry eye in the woods. Connie was telling the story of what had happened to her and Thor during their kidnapping for the first time. Carter listened intently, as he had not even broached the subject with her before, waiting for her to discuss it in her own time.

"I screamed, and sank down on the couch. Now I knew that these men could do whatever they wanted, and there was nothing I could do about it. A few minutes later, they called Carter, using my phone. I knew he would find me. They let me talk to him, and before I thought, I blurted out what had just happened to Thor. I was afraid for him to come after me, but I knew he would. And I knew he was my only hope of getting home again.

"We didn't hear back from Carter for several hours, which caused the men a lot of distress. Sitting there on that couch, about dusk, something inside me began to pray. I'm not religious, but I began to pray like I have never prayed before. Not your usual 'Oh God help me' prayer, but a prayer that came from the deepest part of my soul, a part I didn't even know existed. I don't even know what I said, or if I was even saying it, but I prayed for what seemed like the longest time. It was something I had never experienced before. Don't ask me how, but I'm convinced those prayers made a difference in us being here today."

Carter sat there, recalling his own prayers. Her account sounded eerily similar to what he remembered experiencing. Could Connie, in fact, have been praying at the same time he had been? Could their prayers have combined to produce a supernatural, spiritual force protecting them? Goose bumps covered Carter's body. He wasn't sure, but he certainly wasn't going to discount it, at least not now.

"That night was the longest night of my life. No sleep, no rest. I didn't ask for food or water, and the men never offered any. I think we all knew this ordeal would end, one way or the other, in the morning. I sat on the couch, thinking of Thor, thinking of Carter. I tried to pray again, but I couldn't pray anymore. All I could do was sit on that couch and stare into the darkness.

"As morning arrived, I could tell by the phone conversations I overheard that Carter was coming. I also heard the threats of rape and murder made by my captor. I was scared, but had a strange peace that Carter would prevail. As the time for their encounter came closer, I think the kidnappers felt it too. Their tone changed. They were determined to carry out their evil plans, but they almost resigned themselves to the fact that they were going to fail. Finally, the man I knew from the swingers club left in his sports car without saying a word. No more threats of rape, torture, or murder. He just drove away. His brother paced nervously, but no conversation. After what seemed like hours, the phone rang. I could tell the man was shocked by the call, but couldn't make out the details. In his distraught state of mind, he laid his gun on a table along his pacing path, not far from me. I saw it and knew this was my best chance of getting out of this thing alive. As he stepped around the corner, phone to his ear, I rushed to the gun and grabbed it, then just as quickly got back on the couch. I raised the gun the way Carter had shown me those times he took me to the shooting range. As the man came back into the room, I aimed and pulled the trigger. I could only force myself to shoot once, but apparently it was enough, the man fell to the floor without a sound."

No one in the crowd made a sound. Connie began to cry again as she finished telling the story of her kidnapping for the first time. Carter walked up to join her, and put his arms around her, and she buried her face in his shoulder. They stood there for a few moments, only the sounds of sobs breaking the noise of the woods. Then someone in the group yelled, "Here's to Thor." The crowd erupted in a chant, "Thor, Thor, Thor, Thor." Then silence again. Each person in the group came up to Carter and Connie, gave their

286

condolences over Thor's passing, and gave them a hug. One couple at a time, they went back to the main part of the club.

After Gil and Mary Ann hugged them, Carter and Connie stood alone in front of the memorial, with tears in their eyes, thinking of their boy. They held each other a few minutes longer, neither of them wanting to let go of Thor's memory. With tears in their eyes, hand in hand they left the memorial, and walked back to the pool.

TWENTY-SEVEN

Connie spent the rest of the day with the ladies of the Utopia Sun Club, helping Mary Ann get ready for the wedding. While there would be no wedding dress, there would be plenty of flowers. And yes, the bride would be wearing a veil. That afternoon, Mary Ann learned her youngest brother decided not to bring his eight year old daughter to the wedding. He had originally given his permission for her to be the flower girl, and Mary Ann had bought a special dress for her. But the more he considered the nudity, the more apprehensive he became about exposing her to it. Mary Ann tried to explain there would be other children from the club there, but that seemed to make things worse. "We're not a bunch of sexual predators," she told him, but it made no difference. He was bound and determined not to expose his daughter to all the nudity, and even more so to the public nudity of kids her age. Mary Ann had heard all the excuses before, and soon realized her flower girl was a lost cause. She finally told him, 'That's fine, you do what you think is best for Miranda." After the call was over, she looked at Connie.

"Connie, would you like to be my flower girl?"

"Mary Ann, I'd be honored, but I'm a little old for that."

"It doesn't really matter how old you are, honey. Hell, I'm a little old to be a bride, too. It's about how we feel about each other. And I'd love to have you in my wedding. I don't think we'll even have to alter the dress," she laughed.

"Well, honey, I'd love to be in your wedding. Of course I'll be your flower girl. And I'll do my best to look and act eight years old." All the ladies laughed.

****

Carter joined the men at the pool, where they were hanging out. It seemed strange seeing no women at the pool. As usually happened on Friday afternoon, couples arrived at Utopia, but today, the ladies went to Gil and Mary Ann's camper while the men gathered at the pool. "Hey Gil, where's the bachelor's party?" a man entering the pool area yelled out.

"Right here, I guess," Gil replied. "I hear that in a few minutes, a really hot chick is going to come in and put all her clothes on for us." The men erupted a chorus of laughter.

"But this looks weird, all these naked men around the pool," one man commented.

"Yeah, but we have plenty of beer up here," Gil answered, holding up his can.

"Sounds good enough to me, I'll be there in a second," came a voice from outside the pool's fence.

By 6:00 pm the club was nearly full. Several RVs had been pulled into the camping area, a few tents had been set up, and most of the permanent campers had a car parked beside them. That night, several couples organized a potluck dinner in honor of Gil and Mary Ann. They gave them the place of honor in the clubhouse. They roasted the soon to be newlyweds; some stories were serious, some funny. When the dinner ended, the women escorted Gil to one of the club's rental campers that had been reserved for him. The men escorted Mary Ann back to her and Gil's camper. From this point until the wedding, the two would not be allowed to see each other.

The next morning, Connie went to Mary Ann's camper to join the bridal party and prepare for the wedding. Connie felt a little self-conscious of her nudity, since Mary Ann's sister, Ginger, was part of the bridal party, but refused to be nude. Mary Ann had agreed to allow her to wear a yellow dress, which matched the flowers and accessories of the other ladies in the bridal procession. Mary Ann reminded her she would be the only member of the wedding wearing clothes and she would be the one to stick out like a sore thumb amongst all the nudity. As the time for the bridal procession to walk down the aisle neared, Ginger became overwhelmed by the prospect that everyone would be looking at her, since she would be the only one wearing clothes. Just a few minutes before the bridesmaids were to start their march toward the alter; the feeling finally got the best of her. With a, "What the hell, when in Rome...," she took off the dress, left it laying on the bed in Mary Ann's camper, and prepared to walk naked down the aisle in front of her sister.

The men gathered at the rental cabin that had been set aside for Gil and took turns warning him about the horrors of married life. They told him that no matter how good things were now, and how much he loved Mary Ann, things were sure to change after they were married. One man said that he'd never seen a woman not have an allergic reaction to wedding cake. All of Gil's attendant's were participating in the ceremony wearing nothing but a light blue bowtie and matching flip flops, including Gil's eighteen year old nephew, Josh. It wasn't long before it was 11:30 and the ushers left to escort guests, most nude but a smattering of dressed people, to their chairs in the middle of the field set aside for the wedding. A few at a time, the men left Gil's cabin and walked to their seats in the field. Carter had to sit alone since Connie was in the wedding, so he waited until the last minute to leave the camper. The preacher, an Unitarian minister who had been coming to the club for several years, came to the cabin at ten minutes 'til noon and asked Gil if he was ready. For the first time, Gil showed nervousness, but yes, he was ready. The last of the men, along with the preacher, the best man, and the groom walked to the field to await the bride.

When they arrived at the field, Gil, the best man, and the preacher went to the front of the assembled crowd and stood there, awaiting the arrival of the bridal party. Various love songs from the 60s and 70s played on the makeshift PA system. Finally, after The Captain and Tennille's *Love Will Keep Us Together* ended, the music changed to Foreigner's *I've Been Waiting*, the song Gil and Mary Ann chose as their wedding march. Connie came down the aisle between the chairs, wearing a headband of Carolina blue and yellow flowers. She donned a similar necklace, belt, wristbands, and anklets, tossing flowers out of her basket. She was followed by Josh, wearing his bowtie and flip-flops, carrying a pillow with the rings on top. Next came the bridesmaids and ushers, arm in arm, similarly attired to Connie and Josh. Mary Ann's family let out a small shriek when they saw Ginger walk down the aisle au natural. From her expression and stance, it was obvious she was a bit nervous about her first nudist experience. Finally, Mary Ann appeared, wearing flowers like the bridesmaids, with a yellow veil covering her face and flowing down her back. She was escorted by her seventy-five year old father, who wore a light blue tuxedo and flip-flops to match the men in the wedding party. If he felt awkward escorting his naked daughter down the aisle, it didn't show. A moment later, the wedding party was standing before the preacher and the music ended.

The preacher began, talking about why they were gathered and the sanctity of marriage, usual wedding verbiage. Gil and Mary Ann stood there, looking alternately at each other and at the preacher, listening to his words for them. After about ten minutes, the preacher got to the vows.

"Gil, do you take Mary Ann to be your lawfully wedded wife, to love and to cherish, as long as you both shall live?"

"Ya' bet I do," Gil beamed proudly, as the crowd chuckled.

"Mary Ann, do you take Gil to be your lawfully wedded husband, to love and to cherish, as long as you both shall live?"

"I do," said Mary Ann, more traditionally.

"By the power vested in me by the state of South Carolina and our father above, I now pronounce you man and wife. You may kiss the bride."

Gil raised the veil to expose Mary Ann's beaming face for the first time since the ceremony began. They kissed in a kiss a bit longer than normal, but no one seemed to care. Their friends and family cheered them on.

Once the kiss ended and the cheers subsided, the preacher turned the couple so they were facing the crowd. "I now present to you, Gillman and Mary Ann Richards."

Some in the crowd cheered, some held their breath, and some couldn't help but laugh at another reference to *Gilligan's Island*. Someone even noted that if she got tired of being on *Gilligan's Island* she was now Mary Richards from *The Mary Tyler Moore Show*. The newlyweds walked to their golf cart, which had been decorated in blue and yellow toilet paper and covered in shaving cream. The couple drove back to their camper. Slowly the rest of the crowd left the field and headed to the reception at the pool.

At the pool, a typical Utopia Saturday afternoon party had begun, with people sunning in the lounge chairs and one of the last water volleyball games of the year taking place for those daring the pool's cool water. It was odd to see several clothed people, most of them Mary Ann's family and former coworkers, sitting around the pool area. When Mary Ann and Gil made their appearance at the reception, there was a roar from the crowd. They waved to everyone then Mary Ann went over to her still naked sister sitting beside her now nude husband.

"Thanks, sis for being part of my wedding. I know it was difficult on you, and I appreciate you being here."

"You know, sis, I'm starting to understand why you like this place so much. Everybody seems to be having a good time and no one seems to care about being naked. It's funny; I was the one who felt odd with my clothes on."

"Looks like you remedied that pretty quickly," Mary Ann chuckled.

"Yeah, looks like Robert approved too." She glanced over at her husband, grinning.

"It was shocking to see her walking down that aisle naked. All that ran through my mind was 'WOW'!"

"Hey, honey," Mary Ann called to her husband. "I think we've got a couple of new converts here."

"If they're anything like you, I knew it would only take one time."

"Hey, we need two more for the next volleyball game," someone yelled from the pool.

"I'm in," Ginger jumped up and headed for the water. "How about you, Robert?"

"Dude, you can't let her out do you," one of the men sitting nearby said.

"As long as I'm not on her team," Robert said.

"Don't worry, babe. Get on over there, I'm going to kick your ass," Ginger said as she jumped into the cool water with a scream.

Carter looked at Connie. "You know, she is going to kick his ass, don't you?"

"Yep. Come to think of it, I think I still have a cornhole game to kick your ass at too," Connie said, her grin saying the rest.

"Hey, I want part of that action," Mary Ann said, elbowing Gil in the ribs.

"Dude, we're screwed," Gil looked at Carter.

"Naw, we can do this, man. Focus, brother, focus."

The four of them walked to the cornhole boards that were set up outside the pool's fence. Carter and Mary Ann stood at one board, while Gil and Connie stood at the other. "So, one game, to twenty-one, for the naked athletic championship of our two families," Connie announced. "Bags are on your end, sweetie."

Carter and Mary Ann picked up their corn bags. Carter took his position, ready to toss his bag, when Connie, standing behind the board, turned around and bent over, tying her shoe. "Oh, my shoe's just untied, don't let me bother you, sweetie."

Mary Ann laughed. "You go, girl," she yelled.

"I won't be distracted this time," Carter mumbled to himself, as he let the corn bag fly, landing two feet behind the board, causing Connie to jump out of the way.

"Great job not being distracted, partner," Gil hollered to Carter.

"Just getting warmed up," Carter replied with a laugh.

****

The folks at Utopia talked Carter and Connie into staying for the week and participating in their annual Halloween party. Carter and Connie never had kids of their own, but always decorated their house and passed out candy to all the ghosts and goblins each year. At Utopia, each camper was decorated for the holiday in hopes of being named the most haunted camper. Carter and Connie made a trip to Herbsville to pick up some orange and purple lights, a hanging ghost, and a couple of tombstones so the Coachmen would fit the theme of the park. On Friday night, about ten campers hosted stops in the club's trick or treat, with alcoholic treats replacing the traditional candy for the adults. Saturday night featured the last big party of the year, the annual Halloween party. Carter and Connie went as Dracula and Mina. Carter had full vampire face makeup, a cape, and a bloody place over his heart. Connie picked up a sexy see-through nightie, high heels, a cross necklace, made her face pale, and placed two bite marks on her neck.

Late the next morning, Carter and Connie focused on packing down the Coachmen. Neither of them looked forward to facing the colder weather that awaited them in Kingsport. Tony had told Carter it was twenty-nine degrees on Friday morning. As they finished getting ready to leave, they stepped inside and got dressed. As they stepped out to get into the Ram, Carter looked at Connie and stopped.

"You know, babe, we don't have to leave."

"No, I guess we could stay here a few more days. I'm not looking forward to temperatures below freezing."

"No, I mean we could just move here and stay. We have nothing holding us back."

"I guess we could," she said. "But we will be back. You know, there's a lot more adventures waiting for us out there. I really don't want to miss them by stopping at our first one."

Without a word, Carter walked to the driver's side of the Ram and got in. Connie did the same on the passenger's side. They both knew she was right, they needed to move forward to their next adventure. As they pulled out of the gate, Carter hit a button on the SirrusXM radio. KISS' *I Was Made For Loving You* streamed from the speakers of the big blue Ram 2500.

About The Author

Born in the small town of Clintwood, in southwestern Virginia's coalfields, Adam Lawler was the son and grandson of coal miners. Determined not to work in the mines, Adam graduated from high school at age sixteen and attended Coastal Carolina Community College in Jacksonville, North Carolina, where he not only earned an Associates degree but met his wife Karen.

Adam continued his education at Appalachian State University in Boone, North Carolina, where he earned a B.A. in history with a minor in psychology, and a M.A. in Appalachian Studies. Finding little work for professional hillbillies, Adam went to work in the retail automotive industry, holding several sales and finance management positions over a twenty-year time span. He also taught Western Civilization and Southern Culture at Wilkes Community College.

Adam is a ham radio operator, holding the callsign WK4P. He has been actively involved in the hobby for over twenty years and supports our sailors and marines by serving in the Navy-Marine Corps Military Auxiliary Radio System (MARS) program.

Adam and Karen settled in West Jefferson, North Carolina where they raised three children; Cyndi, a fourth grade teacher, Wayne, a glass artist, and Rachel, an art history student at UNC-Wilmington. They are currently empty nesters and live in West Jefferson with their Doberman Pinscher, Freyja.

Reaching Adam:

By email: cqwk4p@yahoo.com
Facebook: https://www.facebook.com/adam.lawler.3382